Praise for Amanda Hocking's
Kanin Chronicles

"Hocking is a paranormal YA favorite, and her latest does not disappoint. Readers will feel transported by this beautifully written story. There's adventure, heart, and thrills. Protagonist Bryn is filled with such power and determination, she will do whatever it takes to follow her dreams—and her heart. Hocking's latest will have no trouble keeping the rapt attention of thrill seekers and romantics alike."

—*RT Book Reviews*

"Returning to the troll world of her Trylle trilogy, Hocking explores another tribe of trolls in this first book in the Kanin Chronicles. The novel's lingering questions and the author's knack for cliff-hangers are reason enough to anticipate the next installment."

—*Publishers Weekly*

"With a thrilling climax and a haunting resolution, *Frostfire* brings us back to the world of the Trylle with a bang. Fans of Hocking's previous titles won't want to miss it. I can't wait to see where Bryn's story takes us next!"

—*The Teen Bookworm*

"Drawn in from the first page . . . this was an exciting, action-packed story with intriguing characters and an extremely enjoyable plot. If you're after a great read, be sure to pick this up."

—*Head Stuck in a Book*

"*Frostfire* had everything. . . . It just drew me in, and I didn't want to put it down! If you read the Trylle series, I recommend that you read this too. I think *Frostfire* is even more spectacular. Amanda Hocking just keeps getting better and better!"

—*Whatcha Reading*

"A must-read . . . now I have to run out and buy the Trylle trilogy as well!"

—*Jump into Books*

"For those who love a great trilogy, there's a new one on the horizon. . . . *Frostfire* is a great first installment of the Kanin Chronicles. I eagerly await the next book in the series."

—*Sukasa Reads*

Crystal Kingdom

Amanda Hocking

St. Martin's Griffin ✹ New York

CRYSTAL KINGDOM. Copyright © 2015 by Amanda Hocking. All rights reserved. Printed in the United States of America. For information, address St. Martin's Press, 175 Fifth Avenue, New York, N.Y. 10010.

www.stmartins.com

The Library of Congress Cataloging-in-Publication Data is available upon request.

ISBN 978-1-250-04988-9 (trade paperback)
ISBN 978-1-250-07535-2 (hardcover)
ISBN 978-1-4668-5088-0 (e-book)

St. Martin's Griffin books may be purchased for educational, business, or promotional use. For information on bulk purchases, please contact the Macmillan Corporate and Premium Sales Department at 1-800-221-7945, extension 5442, or write to specialmarkets@macmillan.com.

First Edition: August 2015

10 9 8 7 6 5 4 3 2 1

For Eric J. Goldman, Esq.—this book may be
the final chapter in one of our finest adventures together,
but I know there are still many more escapades
for us to enjoy.

Crystal Kingdom

friends & enemies

So, what do you say, white rabbit?" Konstantin Black asked. "Friends?"

He sat on the stool next to me, his gaze unwavering. His thick eyebrows arched hopefully above the dark silver of his eyes, and the coal-black waves of his hair fell over his face as he tilted toward me.

All I could do was gape at him, too stunned to think or move. I didn't even know if he was really there or not. It would make more sense that I had unknowingly passed out in a random diner in Missouri and I was suffering from a stress-induced nightmare or possibly a lysa.

There was no way that Konstantin could be here with me. Not after I'd spent five days on the run from Doldastam after being arrested for treason and accused of murdering the Skojare Prince Kennet Biâelse and my friend Kasper Abbott.

I'd done everything in my power to stay under the radar—I

only used cash and a burner phone, and I hadn't even built up the nerve to actually use the phone and call anyone back home yet. I moved constantly and stayed off the grid in dive motels in small towns.

There was no possible way that anyone could've found me, not even Konstantin Black.

"Bryn?" Konstantin asked, since I'd done nothing but stare at him for the past minute.

Then, because I had to be sure he was real, I reached out and touched him, pressing on the black leather jacket covering his bicep, and he looked down at my hand in bewilderment. I half expected the coat to give way and him to disappear in a puff of smoke, but instead I felt the firmness of his muscle underneath.

"Are you feeling all right?" He looked back at me with what appeared to be genuine concern in his eyes, but I wasn't sure if I could trust him. "You really look like death warmed over."

"That's how you're going to sell the idea of friendship? By telling me I look awful?" I asked dryly.

Not that he was wrong. I wasn't sleeping or eating much, so I was even paler than normal. My attempts at dyeing my hair black to help mask my identity left my normally blond waves an odd gray color, since dye never really took hold in troll hair. The swelling around my left eye had finally gone away, but the bruise had shifted to a putrid yellow color that I wasn't able to cover completely with makeup.

"I'm selling it with brutal honesty," he said with a wry smile. "I want you to know that you'll get nothing but the truth from me."

I scoffed. "There's no way in hell I'm gonna believe that."

"Come on, Bryn. Try me." He rested his forearms on the counter, almost pleading with me.

"What are you even doing here? What do you want with me?" I demanded.

"I already told you—friendship."

I rolled my eyes. "Bullshit. Everything is always bullshit with you."

"How can you say that?" Konstantin shot back, incredulous. "I've been nothing but honest with you."

"Sure, sure. You've been nothing but honest when you attempted to murder my dad or when you tried to kidnap Linnea."

He pressed his lips into a thin line. "I already apologized about what happened with your dad." I glared at him. "Not that anything I say will ever make that okay, but you know that I regret it."

"How can I know that?" I shook my head. "I don't really know anything about you."

"Why are you being so combative?" Konstantin asked, his voice getting louder. "I'm only trying to help."

"You're a traitor who's been working with someone that nearly killed me!" I yelled back, not caring how loud I was being in the small diner.

"Yeah, well, right back at you!" Konstantin shouted.

The waitress came over, interrupting our heated conversation, and set down in front of me the iced tea I'd ordered. She stood with her hand on her hip, eyeing us both with suspicion. Before, she'd looked at me with concern despite her weariness, but with my bad dye job and Konstantin's agitation, it had to be obvious we were on the run.

"Is everything okay here?" she asked, her eyes flitting back and forth between the two of us.

"Yeah, it's fine," Konstantin replied curtly without looking at her.

"Well, you better keep your voices down, before you start upsetting the customers," she said with a slight Southern drawl, and she slowly turned and walked away.

Konstantin waited until after she had gone to the other end of the diner before speaking. "And I tried to save Linnea." He sat up straighter, indignant. "I did save her, actually. Without my intervention, she'd most likely be dead."

From what Linnea had told me, that sounded true enough. Since I couldn't argue with Konstantin, I turned the stool away from him and focused on my iced tea.

He sighed, then he leaned toward me, and in a voice just above a whisper he said, "I know what you're going through. Four years ago, I was almost exactly where you are. I know how frightening and lonely it feels when the kingdom turns against you."

I took a drink from my tea and didn't say anything, so he went on. "You and I have been on opposite sides for a while, and I've made a lot of wrong choices. But I'm trying to make up for them, and . . . now I'm alone, and you're alone. So I thought we could be alone together."

He leaned back away from me. "But I won't force this. If you wanna go through this all alone, then be my guest. Take on the world by yourself. I won't fight you." He reached into his pocket and tossed a few dollars on the counter. "The drink's on me."

I heard the stool creak as he got up, but I didn't look back. Not until I heard the door chime did I turn to watch him walking out the door, into the bright spring day. In a few more seconds he'd be gone, and I'd have no way to contact him or find out what he knew.

So even though I wasn't sure exactly how this friendship thing would play out, or even if this wasn't some kind of trick, I knew what I had to do. I cursed under my breath, and then I jumped off the stool and ran out after Konstantin.

tracking

"Where are we going?" I asked. It might have been a better question to ask before I'd gotten in the black Mustang with Konstantin, but I hadn't wanted him to leave without me. And did it really matter where we were going? I had no place to be. No place to call home.

"I don't know." He glanced in the rearview mirror, watching the diner disappear behind us as he sped down the highway. "Do you have somewhere in mind?"

I shook my head. "No." Then I looked over at him. "But we should find someplace where we can really talk."

"How about a motel?" he suggested, and when I scowled at him, he laughed. "If I was going to murder you, I would've done it already, and if I was just looking to get laid, believe me when I say there are easier ways to do it than this."

"Why don't you come out with it right now? I think a talk is long overdue."

He smirked. "You sound so menacing."

I looked out the window, watching the lush greenery as we sped by it. Even with me moving all over as a tracker, it was always jarring to go from the harsh cold of Doldastam to the bright warmth of anywhere else. Home was so far away, and this felt like a whole other world.

"How did you find me?" I asked, still watching the full ash trees that lined the side of the road.

"It was actually quite simple," he said, and I looked back at him. He reached into the pocket of his leather jacket and pulled out a blond lock of hair held together with a thread.

Hesitantly, I took it from him. It was a pale golden color, with a subtle wave to it—exactly how my hair looked before I destroyed it with the bad dye job. This was my hair.

And all the pieces suddenly fell together. How Konstantin had been able to find me no matter where I was, like the hotel room in Calgary, or outside of Storvatten when I'd captured him. Even when he'd visited me in the lysa before.

Konstantin had been a Kanin tracker, from a long line of trackers, and thanks to his strong bloodline, he'd had a powerful affinity for it. Like many trackers, he had the ability to imprint onto a changeling if he had something from them— a lock of hair usually worked best.

It turned the changeling into a kind of homing beacon. Konstantin couldn't read minds, but he could sense extreme emotions in the trackee that meant they were in trouble. The recent events in Doldastam, along with my general fear and anxiety the last few days, would've turned me into a megawatt searchlight.

And Konstantin had been tracking me.

"Where did you get this?" I asked, twisting the hair between my fingers.

Like all trolls, changelings are born with a very thick head of hair, and a lock of hair is taken from them before they're placed with a host family. That way a tracker could find them later.

But I'd never been a changeling, and this hair felt much coarser than my hair had as a child. This had been taken recently.

"Why do you even have it?" I turned to look at him. "Why were you tracking me?"

He opened his mouth, then closed it and exhaled deeply through his nose. "That is a question that's best answered when we get to the motel."

"What? Why?" I sat up in the seat, putting my knee underneath me so I could face him better and defend myself if I needed to. "What's happening at this motel you keep bringing up?"

"Calm down." He held a hand out toward me, palm out. "You're already getting worked up, and I think when I start telling you things, you'll get even more worked up, and I've had enough fights in a car to know that it's better if we wait until we're someplace that isn't flying seventy miles per hour down the road to have a heated conversation."

His explanation sounded reasonable enough, so I relaxed a bit and settled back in the seat.

"For being on the run, this seems like a rather conspicuous and expensive choice of car," I commented, since that seemed like a safe topic.

"Conspicuous, maybe. Expensive, no," he said. "I kind of stole it."

"You really know how to keep a low profile," I muttered.

"Hey, I kept a low profile for four years. I know a thing or two," he insisted. "And I used persuasion, so it's not exactly like that owner is gonna report it to the police."

Persuasion was a psychokinetic ability trolls had where they could make people do what they wanted using a form of mind control. From what I knew about Konstantin, his ability wasn't strong enough to work on other trolls, but humans were much more susceptible to that kind of thing. So Konstantin probably hadn't had to try that hard to convince the human to part with his muscle car.

"So who exactly are you on the run from?" I asked. "Other than the Kanin, of course."

He hesitated, and his grip tightened on the steering wheel. "Viktor Dålig and his men."

"But I thought you were like Viktor's right-hand man or something. How'd you end up on the outs?"

"I told you back in Storvatten, when I was in the dungeon. I didn't want to get any more blood on my hands. That's why I warned Linnea. I wanted to make things right." He shifted in the seat. "And as you can imagine, that didn't exactly sit well with Viktor. I'd been on his shit list ever since I convinced him not to kill you."

"Thank you for that, by the way," I told him softly.

"You weren't supposed to get hurt." He glanced over at me, his eyes pained for a moment. "You weren't supposed to be down there."

While Linnea had still been missing in Storvatten, I had snuck down to the dungeon where Konstantin was being held to find out what he knew. I was desperate to find Linnea. But instead I'd interrupted Viktor helping Konstantin make his escape.

To prevent me from stopping them or telling anyone, Viktor had bashed my head against a wall repeatedly. Viktor had wanted me dead, but I'd suspected that Konstantin had intervened to save my life.

Still, I had a gash under my hairline to show for it. It had required six stiches, though it was nearly healed. The worst part of the injury was the vision in my right eye would get wonky sometimes, especially if I hit my head or somebody punched me.

"So why did Viktor finally kick you out?" I asked, changing the subject.

He shook his head. "Viktor didn't. Besides, he doesn't kick anyone out. Once you've served your purpose, you're dead." He shot me a sidelong glance. "You remember what happened to Bent Stum."

"You left, then?" I asked.

"Yeah. I'd finally had enough of it." He breathed deeply.

"Viktor doesn't care about anything but revenge. A lot of innocents are gonna die. And I couldn't be a part of it anymore, and I didn't know how to stop it."

I swallowed hard and sank lower in the seat. Konstantin hadn't really said anything that I didn't already know, but hearing it aloud didn't make it any easier to take.

Even if I were back in Doldastam, I wasn't sure how much I could do to help, but at least I would be able to fight alongside my friends—Ridley, Tilda, Ember—to protect the town filled with people I cared about.

Now I was trapped so far away from them. They were up against the worst thing ever to hit Doldastam, and I was powerless to help them.

THREE

ember

Bryn—   May 13, 2014

I'm not totally sure why I'm even writing this. I don't know how you'll get it, and if you do get it, I don't know if you'll even care. Hell, it might even be treason trying to talk to you. But I can't help it. It just feels strange not being able to talk to you about everything—especially with everything that's going on.

I just realized that I don't know if I'll ever see you again. I want to believe that I will, but the whole world feels like it's been turned upside down.

Kasper's funeral was yesterday. I kept expecting to turn around and see you there, coming in late, but you never did.

I don't know where to start with the funeral. Tilda has been trying so hard to hold it all together. I don't know how she's done as well as she has. It was almost creepy being around her. She was like a statue. She hardly ever cried. She'd just talk about the practical things that needed to be done.

Yesterday, she finally broke down. It was the first time she'd seen Kasper since he died. All fixed up in his Högdragen uniform, lying motionless in the coffin. The first thing she said when she saw him was, "He'd be so upset about his hair. It's not quite perfect."

And then she started sobbing uncontrollably. She basically collapsed, so her sister and I practically had to carry her back to her seat. To see Tilda like that . . .

The most heartbreaking part was probably Kasper's little sister Naima. She just cried and cried, and her mom kept trying to comfort her. But it's all so surreal and insane. There's no comfort in that.

The King and Queen came to give a eulogy, and it was all so bizarre. The King seemed so out of place. He kept sweating, and his face was all red, like he had a terrible windburn. The Queen kept doting on Tilda, almost pushing Tilda's own mother out of the way so the Queen could be the one to comfort her. When the King went up to give his speech, he mentioned a few things about Kasper—how great he was, how he died protecting his kingdom, and other generalities.

But it all seemed memorized, and he stumbled over the words a lot. Right after that, the King switched into this war propaganda speech. It was so gross and tactless. He started going on and on about how we can't let Viktor

Dålig do this to our people, and we can't trust anyone because Viktor can get to anyone.

Then he started saying that they would stop at nothing until you were captured, and that's when Tilda stood up and said that she didn't think that this was the time or place to discuss these things.

The King finally shut up after that, but I'm almost surprised he let her talk back. He's cracked down on everything since you've been gone. It reminds me of that book I had to read for an English class at a human school when I was tracking a changeling. 1984, I think. Everywhere you go, the King is watching, and he won't let you forget it.

There are even posters hanging up all around town saying just that. It's this weird black and white image of his face, but somehow his eyes are always following you, and it's super disturbing. Above it says, "THE KING IS WATCHING," and below it says, "TRAITORS OF THE KINGDOM WILL BE CAPTURED," with the Kanin symbol stamped over it.

Members of the Högdragen were going around tacking up all these posters—some of them are WANTED ones for you (you made the Kanin's Most Wanted list, that has to be kind of exciting, right?).

I wanted to tear them all down, but I didn't think now was the best time to deal with the wrath of the King. There was this freak rainstorm yesterday anyway, and most of them are all destroyed and hanging in tatters. But my mom said she saw Högdragen replacing them already today.

There are Högdragen everywhere, and they'll stop you for no reason and demand to know where you're going and what you plan to do there. The guards have even grabbed random people off the street to bring in them in for questioning.

They brought your parents in, too, but I suppose that's not random. Your father has been put on suspension from his job as the Chancellor, and your mother was fired from her job as a teacher. Your mother's job wasn't a direct order from the King, though. People in town started complaining that they couldn't trust her with their children, given what happened with you.

At least your parents are free, though, and that's more than I can say for Ridley. They brought him in for an "interrogation" the day after you left, and he hasn't come out since. I've tried to ask about him, but nobody knows what's happening.

They would tell us if they executed him . . . wouldn't they? Another tracker was talking about how they used to have public executions of traitors in the town square. I think that's what they'd do, if they decided to hang Ridley. So he must still be alive.

Östen Sundt has been promoted to working as the "acting" Överste, but they haven't given him the official title yet, so I'm hoping that's a good sign and it means that Ridley still has a chance to return to his position. To be truthful, though, I don't think anything is a good sign anymore.

I'm just keeping my head down, training and doing what they tell me. I visit Tilda most nights, because I'm afraid to leave her sitting alone in her apartment. I've tried to sneak around to see Delilah. We only just officially became an item, and both of us are getting nervous about what would happen if we got caught. At least I still get to see her training.

The King and Queen have such a stranglehold on Doldastam now. It's like they want to crush us before Viktor gets a chance to. I guess the King thinks that if he couldn't trust you, he can't trust anybody, and there is some truth to that. Except I know that he could trust you.

I know you didn't do the things they said you did, but I wish I knew what happened. What did you do? And why did you do it?

Will I ever see you again?

I know you can't answer these questions, at least not like this. But I do feel better talking to you, even if you can't hear me. And hopefully someday, you'll be able to read this.

> *Your friend (no matter what),*
> *Ember*

FOUR

impetus

I t wasn't the worst place I'd ever stayed, but that was by a very, very, very small margin. The room smelled like dirty gym clothes and cigarettes, but the motel had met the requirements of small and secluded.

Konstantin had driven about an hour before finally spotting this sketchy-looking little motel off the edge of the highway. Based on the lack of cars in the lot, it appeared that we were the only ones here.

I tossed my duffel bag onto one of the two small beds in the room, and a plume of dust came out from the worn comforter. Konstantin had gone to the window and pulled the heavy drapes shut, casting the room in darkness.

"Sorry about that," he said and turned on a bedside lamp.

"The room sucks, but I don't care, because we're here." I had my arms crossed over my chest, and then I held out my hand to him, presenting him with the lock of hair. "Now you can tell me about this."

"That was the deal, wasn't it?" Konstantin grimaced before sitting back on the bed. "The long and short of it is that the Queen gave it to me."

My heart skipped a beat. "You mean Linnea?"

"No." He shook his head. "Mina. The Kanin Queen."

The room suddenly felt as if it had pitched to the right. The whole world seemed to go out of focus for a moment as I tried to comprehend the full of implications of what Konstantin had just told me.

"Why?" I asked breathlessly. "Why would the woman I was sworn to serve and protect want to cause me harm?"

"She didn't want to cause you harm . . . at first," he corrected me. "After the whole incident where you made off with Linus Berling before I could stop you, Mina just wanted to keep tabs on you and keep you out of the way."

"But why?" I pressed on. "Why was she involved with any of this?"

"The same reason as anyone else—she wants power." He shrugged helplessly.

"*Power?*" I scoffed. "She already has the fucking crown in the most powerful kingdom in the troll world. What more does she want?"

"Mina's power is contingent on Evert. He has the final say on everything, and if something happens to him, she's shit out of luck. She's under his thumb just as much as anyone else, and she hates it. She wanted to rule in her own right."

I'd taken to pacing the room, processing everything Konstantin was telling me. "And how does she plan to do that? If Evert's out of the way, they'll just find a replacement . . ." As soon as I said that, it dawned on me. "That's why you went after Linus Berling."

"Our plan was to remove as many of the next-in-line royals as we could until it would just make the most sense for the Chancellor to leave Mina in charge," Konstantin explained. "It wasn't a guarantee, but the idea was also that if the community was in turmoil, they might be reluctant to change horses midstream. And in the meantime, Mina is doing her best to make herself seem beloved by all."

"And she thought the best way to do that was to get hooked up with Viktor Dålig?" I asked.

Konstantin lowered his eyes. "It's not that simple. Viktor promised men to help the kingdom feel threatened. Mina wanted there to be the threat of war so she could step up and show everyone how well she could rule, and she would get Evert out of the way so she could 'crush' the enemy herself and no one would depose her."

I narrowed my eyes. "Get Evert out of the way how?"

"I don't know exactly. I wasn't privy to all the details of the operation."

"If Mina's got this great plan for war on her kingdom, why'd you end up sidetracked with the Skojare?" I asked.

"To get enough men for a war, we needed money, and Mina couldn't very well take money from the Kanin. I don't know exactly how it all started, but she was at some event or another hobnobbing with other royals, and she got to talking to Kennet Biâelse, and together they cooked up this great scheme where he would get her all the sapphires she needed in exchange for getting his brother dethroned."

I sighed and sat down on the bed across from Konstantin. "So that's how Kennet got involved. How did you?"

"I was the Queen's guard. I spent night and day by her side for a year." He stared down at a stain on the carpet, then swallowed hard. "She asked me to help her, and I couldn't say no. I went after your father for Viktor. It was his revenge for your father choosing Evert for the crown, and Mina said I needed to do it to strengthen our alliance with Viktor."

He sat at the side of the bed, with his hands holding the edge, and he gripped it more tightly every time he mentioned Mina. His brows bunched up, and his jaw tensed under his dark stubble.

"That's not good enough," I said at length, and he looked up sharply at me, his eyes flashing like freshly forged steel.

"What?"

"You took an oath," I reminded him, and then began reciting the key component to him: *"In times of war, I swear to defend the kingdom and fight our enemies. In times of peace, I vow to protect the King at all costs. It is my duty to kill if necessary, but never murder. A life must only be taken in preservation of the kingdom."*

As I was speaking, Konstantin looked away and groaned loudly. "Come on, Bryn. You've seen enough to know that life is never that black-and-white."

"My father was an innocent man," I growled at him. "You tried to kill him because the Queen didn't like being married but still wanted to be rich and powerful. Tell me what shades of gray I'm missing."

"I'm sorry about your father! I made a mistake!" Konstantin shouted and stood up. "But I was trying to protect Mina." He let out a rough breath. "I was in love with her."

I waited a beat before deciding to ignore his confession about his feelings for Mina—at least for the moment. "Protect her from what?"

"Evert." It was Konstantin's turn to begin pacing the small motel room. "He was cold and cruel to her. When we were alone together, Mina would cry to me and tell me how awful the King was to her. That's how the affair started between us. I only wanted to comfort her and make her happy . . . and it turned into something more."

"Evert can be cold." I agreed with his summation. "But I've never known him to be cruel to Mina. In fact, I've never seen him treat her with anything but respect."

It hadn't even been a week ago when I'd been in the King's parlor with Evert and Mina, both of them drunk on wine. He'd been so tender and loving with her, asking her what he'd done to deserve her, and she smiled at him.

Not to mention that Mina was constantly professing her love for Evert. I knew that abuse wasn't always obvious—people tended to do everything they could to hide it. But just the same, Evert didn't seem to fit the description Konstantin had laid out.

"I'm not saying I believe her *now*," Konstantin corrected me. "I'm saying I believed her *then*. I'll be the first to admit that I was far too blinded by love."

"Why didn't you just run away with her, then? Why did you resort to murder and treason?" I asked.

"I suggested it, but where would we run to? She grew up in Iskyla—a frozen, isolated wasteland that doesn't even have proper electricity. She wasn't going back to that, and she wasn't about to give up the life she'd created for herself.

"And killing Evert was out of the question, because he was the King. Somehow she convinced me that the only way for us to live happily ever after was for me to get rid of the Chancellor and start working for Viktor."

He shook his head at his own ignorance. "I don't even know how she did it. All I can say is that there is something very powerful about the conversations you have in bed with your forbidden lover."

I scowled, trying not to let myself think too much about Konstantin in bed with Mina, his arms entwined with hers as they lay in the satin sheets of her bed.

"If you loved her so much that you were willing to give up everything you worked for, everything you believed in, how can you go against her now?" I asked. "How can I trust you?"

He thought for a minute before finally saying, "I am still in love with the idea of her, the mirage that Mina showed me that was beautiful and warm and loving. But now I've come to know her well enough to see that that was nothing but a lie. The idea I had of her never existed."

"What made you realize that?" I asked.

"I'd started to realize that she was far more cold and calculating than I'd first suspected, but it was when she asked me to kill the changelings," he replied. "Initially we were only supposed to scare them off so they'd never go back with their tracker. But after Linus Berling, she told me to start murdering these innocent children . . . and that's when I knew her lust for power was the only thing that mattered to her.

"Well, that and her damn rabbit," he corrected himself.

Like many other Kanin royals, Mina had a pet Gotland rabbit. They were a symbol of hope and prestige for our people, and Mina used to carry hers around everywhere she went, until Evert made fun of her for it at a party once. Then she started leaving the white rabbit in her room, but she still brought it with her anytime she went on a trip out of Doldastam.

"If she's as awful as you say she is and I do believe you that she is—then how did it take you so long to figure it out?" I asked.

"For starters, I couldn't see her that often, because I was a wanted traitor," Konstantin expounded. "It was very tricky for her to sneak out to nearby villages to see me, usually under the guise of visiting royalty or family members. Once I think she said she'd gone for a spa weekend in a human town, but she really spent it with me.

"So I only saw her for small glimpses, and she was always putting on a good show of being this helpless victim." He sighed. "And I—being the lovesick idiot I was—ate it up."

"Why has it been so long?" I asked, realizing that he'd been lying in wait for years. "Between your initial attack on my dad until Linus Berling, there was a four-year silence. Why didn't Mina command you to make a move sooner?"

"Viktor had been trying to gather more men, and Mina had been trying to gather more money," Konstantin explained. "But time was running out. Evert was getting more impatient about having children, and Mina refused to have kids."

I shook my head. "Why?"

"Because if something happens to Evert, then her kids will inherit all his power—not her."

"Holy crap. She really is power-hungry." Then something else occurred to me. "She's been plotting her attack for *four years?*"

Konstantin lifted his eyes to meet mine. "Honestly? I think she's been plotting her attack since the day she met Evert, and she is one determined bitch."

FIVE

exile

L ying on top of the covers, I was still fully clothed in my jeans and tank top. Konstantin promised me that he wouldn't murder me in my sleep, and even though we had struck an uneasy alliance, I still wasn't sure how much I could trust him.

In the darkness of the motel room, I lay awake for a long time, trying to process everything that Konstantin had told me. I reanalyzed every interaction I'd had with the Queen, and the more I thought about it, the more I saw that everything Konstantin had said added up.

It explained all kinds of little things about her—her insistence on wearing her crown so often, even when Evert didn't, her constant mood shifts from warm to icy, her unreasonable hatred of me.

And then everything that had happened with Kennet. She must have instructed Kennet to flirt with me in Storvatten in an attempt to keep me too distracted to figure things out. When Kasper and I had put the pieces together, we'd told her, and she'd had us arrested before we could find out her involvement.

For the first time, some of my guilt about Kasper's death had eased. There was no way that either of us could've known that Mina was involved, and she would've had us executed. Escape had been the smartest move we could have made.

I lay awake, letting my thoughts go over the scenarios again and again, because it was so much better than sleeping. When I closed my eyes, I knew that only nightmares awaited me. Horrific images of Kasper's death haunted me every night, replaying in nauseating clarity.

Other times, my dreams would start out nicer, with Ridley. We would be in the middle of nowhere, with the aurora borealis dancing above us, and he'd look down at me with that heat in his eyes that made my heart flutter.

He'd pull me close to him, and his lips would meet mine. Somehow, in the dream, I knew this would be the last time I'd ever be with him, and I kissed him desperately.

Then, without warning, he'd be ripped from my arms. An unknown force would pull him away, dragging him off into the darkness, and I would scream his name. I would run after him, but no matter how fast I ran, I never caught up to him.

Over and over, I had these nightmares of Kasper dying and Ridley being taken away. So I fought sleep as much as I could, but eventually it won out, and darkness enveloped me.

It didn't last for long tonight, though, before it was interrupted by bright blue water. It shimmered like sapphires, and it seemed to fill every corner of my vision. I could almost feel it, cool and delicious running over my skin.

I heard her shouting before I saw her—"Bryn! *Bryn!*"

"What?" I asked, and my voice sounded like a strange echo, bouncing off of everything.

Suddenly a hand gripped my ankle, yanking me underwater. I started to fight it, but I realized with some surprise that I could breathe easily in the clear water that surrounded me. Even though it should all be terrifying, I felt oddly relaxed.

Linnea floated up in front of me, and the way her platinum blond curls floated around her head made her look ethereal. Under the water, her eyes somehow managed to look even more blue than normal, but a worried expression aged her youthful face.

"Bryn," Linnea said again, and it sounded like she was speaking directly inside my head. "What's happened? Where are you?"

"I don't know where I am." I looked around, as if there would be some kind of sign telling me the exact location of my underwater dream.

"Not here. This is a lysa." Linnea took my hand, making me focus on her. "Everything is crazy in Storvatten. They say you killed Kennet."

"I didn't kill Kennet!" I shouted, then corrected myself. "I tried to save him, but I couldn't. But he was behind everything, Linnea. He's the reason Mikko was arrested."

Her eyes widened and she gasped. *"Kennet?* But he loved Mikko!"

"It's too much to explain now, but you have to believe me. Kennet was into some bad things, and you can't trust the Kanin Queen either. She was working with him."

"Who can I trust?" Linnea's lip began to quiver. "Everything is falling apart here. My grandma is trying to run things, but the board of advisers is pushing her out. They won't release Mikko, and they're trying to bring Bayle Lundeen back, but they can't find him anywhere."

"Don't let Bayle run anything!" I warned her. "If they find him, make them question him. He knows what Kennet was up to, so maybe he can help free Mikko."

The water seemed to grow colder. It had been the whole time, but I began to feel the chill running deeper in me. And it was getting harder to breathe. Each breath I took seemed to be equal parts air and water, and I was starting to choke.

"Don't trust the Kanin. Don't accept any aid from them," I told her as water filled my lungs. "Stray strong."

Her expression hardened with resolve. "I won't let anyone hurt me or Mikko anymore," Linnea promised me. "And I will clear your name, Bryn!"

That was the last thing I heard her say before the dream collapsed on me, and I woke up in bed, gasping for breath.

alliance

With one hand I tousled my damp hair with a towel, and with the other I pulled back the drapes, allowing the blinding sun to spill into the dark room. When my eyes adjusted, I half expected to see Högdragen or maybe Viktor Dålig's men outside, waiting to capture me.

But it was only an empty gravel parking lot on a relatively deserted highway. Being on the run made it awfully hard to not feel paranoid, especially when it turned out there was actually a conspiracy plotting against me.

"Anything exciting out there?" Konstantin's voice rumbled from behind me, making me jump.

I let the shades close, and I turned back to see him standing in the bathroom doorway. His dark curls were wet, and he was wearing only a pair of jeans. Seeing him shirtless, I realized that he was more muscular than I'd originally imagined.

While the smooth definition of his torso was a pleasant sight, his deep olive skin was marred by scars running all over his chest and arms. Some of them were undoubtedly from the days when he partook in the brutal sport of the King's Games, but some of them had probably been from more sinister actions with Viktor Dålig and his men.

On his chest, just above his heart, he had a black tattoo of a rabbit—the same tattoo many members of the Högdragen shared. They usually got it after they took their oath, and I was sure that Konstantin had been the same. He'd once been as young and determined as I had been, but somewhere along the line he'd taken a much darker turn.

"No, nothing." I lowered my eyes and tossed my towel on the dresser next to the small television.

"You used all the hot water," Konstantin grumbled absently as he picked his black T-shirt up off his bed. I peered over at him, watching as he pulled the shirt over his head, then quickly looked away once he'd gotten it on.

"Sorry. I guess I'm not used to sharing."

"I doubt this place had much hot water anyway." He looked over at me. "At least your hair's looking better now."

I tugged at a lock of my shoulder-length hair so I could get a better look at it. The faded gray had mostly washed out, and it was returning to its usual color again.

"So what's the plan now?" Konstantin asked.

"I don't know." I leaned back against the dresser. "What's your plan?"

"My plan was to find you, and I've found you." He

motioned in the air, making a checkmark with his hand. "Mission accomplished."

"You didn't have any idea what would happen after that?"

"Not really." He sat on the bed across from me, leaning back so he propped himself up on his arms. "I didn't know what would happen when I found you. But you've been on the run for some days now. Haven't you had time to come up with your next move?"

"No." I sighed. "I mean, I know what I want to do. I want to get back to Doldastam and avenge Kasper. I want to make sure my family and friends are safe, and I want to get the Queen out of there before she hurts anybody else, which probably means that I'd need to take on Viktor Dålig and his army along with the Kanin army.

"And then once all that is done, I want to go to Storvatten and make sure Mikko is freed and that he and Linnea are safe, and then I need to make sure they get a good, honest guard in place."

Konstantin let out a long whistle. "That's an impressive list you got there, white rabbit."

"I know. I just have no idea where to get started." I ran my hand through my hair. "And I don't know how I can possibly take on all of that by myself."

"Hey, you're not by yourself." Konstantin stood up and stepped closer to me. "I'm with you now. Remember?"

I stared up into his eyes, desperate to believe him. Not just because I was faced with an insurmountable task and I needed his help. But because there was something about him, something that still made me slightly breathless. It was almost as if nothing had changed since I was a kid.

I had trusted and believed in him then, and now I wanted nothing more than to feel that way again.

"I'm glad that you're with me, I truly am," I admitted. "But there's still only two of us, and we're enemies of the state. *No one* will believe us, and we can't defeat an army by ourselves."

Konstantin took a step back, considering this for a moment. "Maybe we don't have to."

"What do you mean?"

"I mean . . . Bent Stum."

"Bent Stum is dead," I reminded him.

He snapped his fingers. "Exactly! Bent was killed by Kennet Biâelse, who was working on orders from Mina."

I shrugged, since Konstantin hadn't told me anything I didn't already know. "So? How does that help us?"

"Bent Stum is Omte," he said, grinning.

"The Omte?" I shook my head. "They're unreasonable and grumpy and, quite frankly, they're kinda stupid."

"Trust me, I know. I spent months working with Bent." Konstantin frowned. "Bent was murdered, and that sucks, but he was awful to deal with. It was like working with the Hulk, if the Hulk was dumber and angrier."

"And you want to go to them for help?" I laughed darkly.

"Look, I get that it's not ideal. But the Omte already kinda hate the other tribes. They've always been jealous of them, because everyone else is richer, smarter, and more attractive. But the Omte are so much stronger. Their physical strength is unparalleled by any other tribe, even the Vittra."

"And you think they would help us over Bent? I thought the Omte Queen didn't care about him," I said, remembering what Ridley had said when he'd first been investigating Bent Stum after the Linus Berling incident.

"It doesn't matter." Konstantin shook his head. "The Omte are overly emotional and quick to anger. And now one of their people was killed in some kind of conspiracy between the Skojare and the Kanin? They'll be all over that."

"But I don't want the Omte to destroy the Kanin or the Skojare," I pointed out.

"I've heard the royals are smarter and more reasonable than the average Omte civilian. Maybe if we get a meeting with the Omte Queen, we can gauge how rational she seems, and we can go from there," Konstantin suggested.

I chewed the inside of my cheek, still not completely sold on Konstantin's idea. It wasn't an awful idea, but with a tribe as unpredictable as the Omte, I wasn't too keen on getting involved.

"Besides, their capital isn't even that far away," Konstantin added. "I think it's only a day's drive from here."

Unlike most of the troll tribes that preferred to make their homes in the colder temperatures of the north, the Omte had just kept moving south before eventually settling in the swamps of southern Louisiana. It was as if they'd done everything they could to distance themselves from the other tribes.

"All right." I relented finally. "What have we got to lose? Let's go see the Omte Queen."

SEVEN

commute

A s the Mustang lurched along the gravel road, I leaned over into the backseat. Konstantin hit a bump, and I bounced up, hitting my head on the ceiling.

"Hey, what are you doing?" he asked.

I'd been reaching back to grab my duffel bag, but his bag was sitting beside mine, unzipped, and a flash of metal caught my eyes. Resting right on top of the clothes were two daggers, and I reached in and picked one up.

"What do you have these for?" I narrowed my eyes at him and held up the dagger for him to see. "These are the Kanin daggers you were given when you became the Queen's guard."

It had been a large ceremony in the palace. I'd been standing as near to the front as I could get, on my tiptoes to get a glimpse of it. They were beautiful daggers, with long sharp blades and ornately carved handles of silver and ivory.

"They're for protection," he replied gruffly. "And they're the only things I still have from being a Högdragen, so I'd like it if you stopped playing with them and put them back."

"Yeah, sure. Sorry." I leaned back over the seat and put his dagger safely back in his bag, then grabbed my own duffel before sitting back down. "I was just getting my own bag anyway."

"What for?"

"I don't trust that you know where you're going, and I'm hoping there might be something in here that could help," I replied as I unzipped the bag.

"I already told you. I've been to Fulaträsk before," Konstantin said, sounding indignant. "I went with Mina on a peace-keeping mission years ago, and I never forget how to get anywhere."

"As reassuring as that is, the sun is starting to set"—I gestured out the window at the amber skies showing through the branches of the willow trees that lined the road—"and I'd like to get where we're going by nightfall."

"That's a great idea, but if you packed a buncha maps to the troll capitals, you should've let me in on that sooner," he said with sarcasm dripping from his voice.

"I didn't." I dug through my bag, pushing through the clothes I'd picked up from thrift stores and garage sales over the last few days. "I didn't even pack this bag. Ridley got everything together."

As I moved a pair of jeans, the cell phone fell out of the pocket. I stared at it for moment, once again finding myself trapped under the tantalizing possibility of calling Ridley. It was a prepaid phone, so it was virtually untraceable, and I would do almost anything to be able to call Ridley and hear his voice and find out he was okay.

But I knew I couldn't risk it. It was still too soon, and if anyone in Doldastam found out I'd contacted him, he would be in serious trouble. Assuming that he wasn't already locked up for helping me escape in the first place.

"Who's Ridley?" Konstantin asked. "Wait. Wasn't he like the Rektor or something?"

"It doesn't matter." I brushed him off, since talking about Ridley still felt far too painful, and I buried the phone back in the bag. "But this looks like a standard bag for new trackers, which means that they pack it with a few emergency essentials, including a handbook . . ."

Finally, I unzipped a pocket hidden at the bottom of the bag and found the handbook. Since this bag was going out into the human world, we tried to keep the handbook as hidden as possible, in case the bag fell into the wrong hands. But it was a nice asset for trackers out on their first few jobs because it had tips and tricks, along with important information for them to remember.

It also had rundowns on all the other tribes in case you ran into them (which wasn't completely unheard-of, especially when tracking changelings in popular destinations like New York City or Chicago).

"Aha!" I held up the book to show Konstantin, but he seemed less than impressed.

"Does that have an address in it?" he asked with an arched eyebrow.

"Let me find out." I tossed my bag into the backseat, and then I got comfortable, sinking lower so I could prop my bare feet up on the dashboard with the handbook spread open on my legs.

The first few sections were all things to help trackers do their jobs better, and I flipped through them quickly until I got to the parts about the tribes. When I saw that there were only a couple pages on each tribe, my heart sank.

It didn't help that the top quarter of one of the pages on the Omte was a detailed sketch of their emblem—a brown-bearded vulture, staring at me with small black eyes. There were a few basic facts about the Omte, and finally, at the bottom, I found a sentence that seemed remotely helpful.

"The Omte capital of Fulaträsk is located in the wetlands in the human state of Louisiana," I read aloud. *"Fulaträsk has an estimated population of six thousand, making it the second most populated capital of the five tribes. They live under the rule of their King and Queen, Thor and Bodil Elak, who reside in the palace there."*

"That must be an older printing," Konstantin commented when I'd finished reading.

I turned back to the cover, and it looked new enough to me. "What makes you say that?"

"Because Thor died, like, three years ago," he said. "Bodil is still allowed to rule, though, because she and Thor have a little kid."

"How do you know this stuff?" I asked. "I don't even know this."

"I traveled with Bent for a while, remember? And he *loved* talking about all the stupid crap the Omte would get themselves into."

"What happened to the King?"

"There's a tavern in Fulaträsk called the Ugly Vulture." He shook his head, like he thought it was a dumb name. "According to Bent, it's a real roughneck place, although, also according to him, all the bars in Fulaträsk are really rowdy places. But the Ugly Vulture is apparently the worst."

The road had become narrow, so the swamp came right up to the edges of it, and Konstantin slowed down. As the sun continued to set, everything around us seemed to glow an eerie red.

"Thor really loved the Ugly Vulture," Konstantin went on. "That is one nice thing that Bent said about the Omte—their royals have no problem getting down and dirty with the commoners."

"How progressive of them," I said dryly.

"So anyway, I guess Thor got really drunk on eldvatten—"

"Eldvatten?" I interrupted him.

"It's this really, really strong alcohol that the Omte make. It's like a cross between wine and moonshine, but I have no idea what's in it," Konstantin explained.

"So the King is totally wasted at this point, and Bent didn't know the full details of it, but another patron starts getting mouthy with Thor," he continued. "So the King starts hitting this guy, and the guy gets pissed, so he rips out Thor's throat with his bare hands."

I gaped at him. "This is who we're going to for help? Their King died in a bar fight!"

"We don't have a lot of other options," he countered. "And besides, the King was drunk. He was probably less of a dick when he was sober."

I leaned my head back against the seat. "We are so screwed."

The car started to slow down, and I looked out the window, hoping to see a palace or some sign that we were getting closer. But it was only cypress trees and dark water.

"What's happening?" I asked.

"We've run out of road." Konstantin put the car in park and turned it off. "Now we get to finish the journey on foot."

EIGHT

everglades

The heat was oppressive. It's hard to explain exactly what it felt like to come from twenty-degree temperatures and snowstorms to more than eighty degrees and humid. The air seemed to condense on my skin, and bugs buzzed wildly around me.

As we waded through the bayou, with the murky water coming up to our knees, I hoped against hope that Konstantin knew where we were going.

"Watch for alligators," Konstantin warned.

I looked around the water, which was getting harder to see in the fading light, but even in bright afternoon it would be hard to tell a log from a large reptile. "There are alligators here?"

"I have no idea." He glanced back at me, smirking. "I don't know anything about what lives down here."

"I guess we'll find out, then, won't we?" I muttered.

A mosquito buzzed loudly around my ear, and I tried to swat it away to no avail. It finally landed on the back of my neck, and I slapped it hard to be sure I got it.

"You should be careful about making loud noises, though," Konstantin said as I followed a few steps behind him.

"Why? Will it attract alligators?" I asked sarcastically.

"No, but the Omte startle easily, and we definitely don't want them startled."

Beneath the water, the thick mud threatened to rip off my boots with every step I took, making it very slow going. I told Konstantin that there had to be an easier way to get to Fulaträsk, but he reminded me that the Omte didn't want to be found. They made it as difficult as possible for anyone to stumble upon them.

It had gotten dark enough that we needed to pull out our cell phones and use them as flashlights to help guide our path. But there was still so much around us we couldn't see, and the wetlands were alive with noise—frogs, insects, and birds were loudly chirping their nighttime songs.

Somewhere high above us, I heard the flapping of wings, but I couldn't move my light fast enough to spot them. I'd also heard the high-pitched squeaks of bats, so I figured that they were zooming around to feast on the plethora of bugs.

Occasionally I felt something swim up against my leg, but since nothing had bitten me yet, I tried not to worry about it.

Lightning bugs flashed around us, their tiny bodies twinkling through the trees and reflecting on the water. In the twilight, surrounded by the music of the animals and the still waters underneath the thick canopy of branches, there was something beautiful about the marsh, something almost enchanting.

"Bryn," Konstantin hissed, pulling me from my thoughts.

I'd fallen a few steps behind him because I'd paused to look around, but now I hurried ahead. He held out his arm, blocking me, when I reached him.

"Shh!" he commanded, and then he pointed toward where his light had picked up two glowing dots on a log, just barely above the surface of the water. It was an alligator, not even a meter away from us, and it looked massive.

"What do we do?" I whispered.

"I don't know. Back away slowly, I guess."

He kept the light on the alligator, and we started to move away when I heard the sound of flapping wings again. It sounded much too large to be a bat, and it was followed by more flapping. Whatever it was, it was very close by, and there were more than one.

I turned my flashlight toward the sky, and it caught on a huge brown bird flying above us. The bird circled us for a moment before settling down on a long branch, and I finally got a good look at it.

With its large wingspan, pointed beak, and thick feathers down its long neck, it was unmistakably a bearded vulture. Bearded vultures weren't native to this area—they were something that had been brought in with trolls from the old world, like Gotland rabbits and Tralla horses.

We were in Omte territory.

The cypress and willow trees around us towered several stories into the air, and from the corner of my eye I saw a flash near the top of one. I shone my light up toward it, and with the weak power of my TracFone, I could just make out the outline of a large tree house.

It wasn't exactly a luxury tree house, but it was much more than the average one you might find in a child's backyard. The wood seemed warped and worn, with moss growing over it, and a sagging porch was attached to the front. But it was easily large enough to house a family, and it even had a second story attached to the right side that climbed up along the trunk of the tree.

A large head poked out of the window, looking down at me. It was slightly lopsided, the way Bent Stum's head had been, with one eye appearing larger than the other.

"Konstantin," I said quietly. "I think we're here."

"What?" he asked.

No sooner had the words escaped his mouth than a massive ogre jumped out of a tree and came crashing down into the water in front of us, sending muddy water splashing over us. As soon as the water settled, the ogre let out a long, low growl, and I knew we were in trouble.

"I told you that we shouldn't startle them," Konstantin said.

NINE

monstrosity

I'd heard of ogres and seen pictures of them in textbooks, but I'd never actually met one in real life. I knew that the Omte occasionally gave birth to ogres and they had several of them living in their population. But it's one thing to read about massive, hulking trolls and it's another thing entirely to have one standing directly in front of you.

The ogre stood well over eight feet tall, and he had thick arms bulging with muscles like boulders. His whole body tilted to one side, with his right shoulder rising above his left shoulder, and his right hand was even bigger than his left. His head was massive, making room for a large mouth filled with uneven yellowed teeth. It all made his eyes seem disproportionately small, and he stared down at us with either rage or hunger—I couldn't tell which.

"Why disturb my home?" the ogre demanded, his voice booming through everything.

"We mean you no harm." Konstantin held up his hands toward him.

The ogre laughed at that, a terrible rumbling sound. "You no harm me! You *can't* harm me!"

"That's true," Konstantin allowed, and I wished that we'd brought some kind of weapon with us. We were defenseless if this giant decided he wanted to grind our bones to make his bread. "We only wish to speak to your Queen."

The alligator had begun to swim closer to us, but I'd hardly noticed it, since my attention had been focused on the ogre. It wasn't until the ogre lunged, swinging his massive fist out, that I realized how close the alligator had gotten. The ogre punched it, and sent it flying backward into the swamp.

Konstantin and I both took a step back, and I started to think that coming here might have been a very bad idea.

Then the ogre turned back to us with his beady eyes narrowed. "What you know of Queen?"

"We're Kanin," Konstantin explained. "We're allies."

"Friends," I supplied when the ogre appeared confused.

"Queen no tell me friends coming." The ogre bent down so he could get a better look at us, and the stench from his breath was almost enough to make me gag. "Queen tell me when friends visit."

"Well, it's a bit of a surprise, actually." Konstantin smiled, hoping to make light of things, but the ogre wasn't having any of it.

"Queen tell me to squash visitors," the ogre said. "Me think she want me to squash you."

"The Queen wouldn't want you to squash friends, though," I said, hurrying to come up with a reason for us not to end up like the alligator.

The ogre straightened up again and glowered down at us. He seemed to consider my proposition, but before he could make a decision, we were interrupted by the sound of a fan propeller coming from behind him. A headlight bobbed on the water toward us, and within a minute, an airboat had pulled up beside the ogre.

A woman stood on it, one of her thick rubber boots resting on the front edge. She appeared to be in her late twenties, and with smooth skin, large dark eyes, and a totally symmetrical body. Her long chestnut hair was pulled back, and she wore a black tank top that revealed the thick muscles of her arms. She wasn't much taller than me, but she could easily break me over her leg if she wanted to.

"What's all the commotion about, Torun?" she asked the ogre, but her eyes were on Konstantin and me.

"Squash visitors!" Torun told her, motioning to us with his massive paw.

"We're from the Kanin tribe," Konstantin rushed to explain before she became sympathetic with the ogre's position. "We're only here to talk to your Queen. We think we may have information that she may find useful."

She narrowed her eyes at me. "You look familiar." Then she tilted her head. "Didn't the Kanin just send us WANTED posters with your face on it? You killed someone important, didn't you?"

"That's part of what we would like to speak to the Queen about," I said, trying to remain unfazed.

She thought for a moment, then nodded. "All right." She leaned down and held out her hand to me. Her grip was almost bone-crushingly strong, and she pulled me up onto the boat with ease.

"But me squash!" Torun yelled plaintively as she helped Konstantin onto the airboat.

"Not this time, Torun," she said and turned the boat on. Torun splashed the water with his fists in a rage, and she steered us away from him, turning back.

There were no seats on the boat, so I held on to Konstantin to steady myself and hoped I didn't go flying off into the swamp as she picked up speed.

"Who are you anyway?" she asked, speaking loudly to be heard over the large propeller.

"I'm Bryn Aven, and this is Konstantin Black."

"I'm Bekk Vallin, one of the Queen's guards," she explained. "The Queen won't give you amnesty, if that's what you're looking for. But I'll take you to her anyway. She might be curious about what you have to say."

"Thank you," Konstantin said. "All we really want is an opportunity to speak with her."

Bekk didn't say any more as she drove us along, weaving through the trees. It was only a few minutes before we reached their palace anyway, and it wasn't exactly what I was expecting.

It was a square fortress, made of what appeared to be mud and stone, with thick layers of moss and vines growing over it. With the rest of the Omte living in tree houses, I'd assumed this to be higher off the ground, but it was nearly flush with the swamp, sitting on a small hill above it.

Konstantin and I followed Bekk up the muddy bank toward a massive iron door. Rust left it looking dark brown, and it creaked loudly when an ogre opened it, causing a nearby bearded vulture to squawk in protest.

Inside the palace, it was just as humid as it was outside, and moss grew on the interior walls. Slugs and snails seemed to have made themselves at home in here, and a giant spider had spun a web in the corner of a doorway.

Bekk said nothing as she led us through. Iron chandeliers dimly lit the way through the smallest palace I had been to. It reminded me more of the ruins of a castle in Ireland I'd seen in textbooks than of an active palace where trolls lived and worked.

A set of stairs ran along the side of the wall, jutting out from the stone with no railing or wall to keep one from falling over the other side. Bekk went up them, so Konstantin and I followed her.

At the top of the landing there were three heavy wooden doors, and Bekk pushed one of them open. It was a small room, with a dingy-looking bed, a metal toilet and sink in one corner. There were bars on the only window to prevent an escape, though bugs and birds could come and go as they pleased.

"You will wait here until I come get you," Bekk instructed us.

"Will that be soon?" I asked.

"It will be whenever the Queen decides," Bekk replied curtly.

Since we had no other choice, Konstantin and I went into the room. As soon as we did, Bekk shut the door loudly behind us, and we heard the sound of locks sliding into place. Just to be sure, Konstantin tested the door, and it didn't budge. We were trapped inside.

"Does this make us prisoners, then?" I asked.

Konstantin sighed. "It does seem that way."

TEN

confined

There was blackness, and then strong hands were on me, closing in, crushing me. I didn't remember anything before that, but all I knew was that I had to fight if I wanted to survive. I lashed out, hitting everything I could until I registered Konstantin's voice, crying out in pain.

"Bryn!" he shouted.

And slowly, the world came into focus. Early morning sunlight streamed in through the open window of our cell. Konstantin stood with his back pressed against the wall, wedged in the constricted spot between where I knelt on the bed and the mossy stone behind him.

I blinked at Konstantin, trying to understand what was happening, and without warning he lunged at me, grabbing my wrists and pinning me back on the bed.

"What are you doing?" I growled and tried to push him back with my legs.

"What are *you* doing?" he shot back, his face hovering just above mine as he stared down at me. "You started attacking me."

"I did not," I replied instantly, but then realized that I actually did remember hitting at *something*. So I corrected myself. "If I did, I was just protecting myself. What did you do?"

"You were moaning and freaking out, twitching your legs like a dog having a bad dream," he explained, his expression softening from accusatory to concerned. "I thought something might be wrong, so I put my hand on your arm—just to check on you—and you went ballistic."

I lowered my eyes. "I'm sorry."

"It's fine." He let go of my wrists and moved over so he was sitting next to me. "Are you okay now?"

"Yeah, I'm fine." I sat up more slowly and ran my hand through my tangles of hair.

Since there was only the one bed—a narrow, lumpy double mattress on a rusted iron bed frame—Konstantin and I had decided to share it last night. I'd honestly considered the floor, but there were centipedes and bugs of all kinds crawling all over it, and while the bed probably wasn't a much safer bet, I knew I wouldn't have gotten any sleep on the floor.

I'd slept as near to the edge as possible, rigidly on my side, and I was acutely aware of every breath he took and every time he shifted. Five years ago, if someone had told me that I'd share a bed with Konstantin Black, I would've been too excited to believe it, but now I had no idea what to think about any of this.

"What was the bad dream about?" Konstantin asked.

"I don't remember," I said honestly, but most of my nightmares were variations of Kasper dying, or of Kennet dying, or of me killing Cyrano, or of Ridley being ripped from my arms. None of them were pleasant to recall.

I got up and slid between Konstantin and the wall to the larger area of the room. My hair tie was around my wrist, and I pulled back my hair into a ponytail. My stomach rumbled, reminding me that it had been nearly twenty-four hours since the last time I'd eaten, and I had no idea when I'd eat again.

So, without anything better to do, I dropped to the floor and began doing push-ups. My jeans and tank top were both splattered with mud that had dried and become stiff, but I was hoping the more I moved, the more mud I'd lose.

"What are you doing?" Konstantin asked.

"I'm not just gonna sit and wait for the Queen to summon us. Assuming she ever does summon us." I looked up at him as I worked out. "Besides, we might have to fight our way out of here."

"And you think those extra twenty push-ups will help you fight off an ogre like that Torun guy?" he asked with a smirk.

"I'm doing a hundred," I grunted but didn't argue with him.

In truth, I had no idea how we could possibly escape from here. The Omte were much too strong for us to fight hand-to-hand. If they wanted us trapped in this tower forever, then that was what would probably happen.

Konstantin got up from the bed and walked over to the

window. His arms were folded over his chest, and the rising sun cast a long shadow behind him that overtook the room. When I finished my push-ups, he was still standing like that, staring through the bars.

I stood up and wiped the sweat from my brow. "I can't believe how hot it is for how early it is. How can people live like this?"

"It is actually kind of beautiful here," Konstantin said.

I went over to see what he saw. Our room was just above the tops of the trees, and from here we had a stunning view of the trees and the water below. A few birds flew by, their wings like arcs in the bright sun, and I had to admit that he was right.

"Do you think you could fit through these bars?" he asked.

"What?" I'd been looking past the window and now I turned my attention to the three thick bars that held us in the room.

"The bars." He started pushing at the stones that lined the window. "This place isn't in the best shape, so I think I could loosen a couple stones, and"—he glanced over at my waist, then looked back at the width between one bar and the window frame—"I think you could just squeeze through."

I leaned forward, poking my head through the bars and looking at the sheer drop many stories below to the muddy banks. The image of Kennet falling to his death flashed through my mind, and I looked away, hoping to stop the replay.

"Maybe, but then what?" I asked as I stepped back from the window. "I'll die on the way down."

"You can climb. There's grooves between the stones." Konstantin peered down. "If you climbed out carefully and went slowly, I think you could do it."

"Even if I can, what would you do?" I asked. "I'd probably just barely be able to squeeze through, and you're much broader than I am. You wouldn't be able to make it."

He turned back to me and shrugged. "So?"

"So?" I scoffed. "How will you get out of here?"

"I won't," he replied simply. "I'm the one that suggested we come here and got us into this. We don't both need to rot in this tower until the end of time."

I shook my head. "We'll come up with something so we can both get out of here together. I'm not leaving without you."

His mouth hung open for a moment, like he wanted to argue with me, but there was something in his eyes—a mixture of surprise and admiration—that stopped him. He seemed stunned that I meant what I said, and in all honesty, so was I.

I'd spent years plotting my revenge against him, and now I had a chance to leave him behind to suffer, and I wouldn't do it. I *couldn't* do it. After everything that had happened, and everything we had been through, I realized that Konstantin Black had somehow become my friend, and I wasn't going to let anything bad happen to him if I could help it.

The locks on the door started to creak, and we both turned

our attention back to the door. The heavy wood slowly pushed inward, and Bekk Vallin came in, carrying black fabric in her arms.

"The Queen has agreed to meet with you for breakfast," Bekk said, and she tossed the clothes at me. "She wishes for you to get changed and ready yourself for the meal, and I will come back and get you when she's ready to receive you."

"Thank you," I said. Bekk simply nodded and left, locking the door behind her again.

I set the clothes on the bed to see what she'd brought us, and the clothes smelled musty and looked worn, with holes and threads coming loose. My outfit was a black dress with a corset waist, off-the-shoulder sleeves, and a large ball gown skirt. It looked like something someone might've worn to a Gothic wedding. And then they'd been buried in it for a few months.

Konstantin's outfit was about the same—a worn black suit with a Victorian flare to it. He changed before I did—slipping off his muddy clothes and pulling on the new ones while I had my back to him. When he'd finished, he came over to help me lace up the corset in the back of the dress.

"I feel like Dracula or something," he said, looking down at himself. "But after he's been staked." He sighed. "There's still time for you to escape instead."

"No, we're doing this," I told him firmly. "It's our only chance of making things right. We have to get the Queen on our side."

ELEVEN

carnivorous

A big black beetle scurried across the long wooden table, running directly toward the fried rabbit carcass in the center, and Helge Otäck walked over and smashed it with his fist. One might have expected him to wipe the mess off the dining table, but instead he left it and returned to his place standing behind Queen Bodil.

It felt like Konstantin and I had somehow slipped into a bizarro world, where everything was like a twisted version of troll culture, and nothing was quite right.

To start with, the dining hall was a rather small square room with no windows. It wasn't nearly as mossy or moldy as our room had been, but it was still dank. In compensation for the lack of windows, two large tapestries were hung on the wall, and they appeared to be depicting rather brutal Omte battles that I wasn't familiar with. The edges were frayed and coming loose, and I saw a huge brown spider crawling across one.

Two iron chandeliers hung from the ceiling, both of them lit with candles, and there were four torches on the wall. It seemed like overkill for such a small space, but the interior still ended up somewhat dim.

Like most meals I went to with royals, there was a massive spread of food covering the large table. Unlike every other meal I had been to, this one had lots of meat. Trolls weren't exactly vegetarian, and the Skojare especially had a fondness for fish. But we didn't eat it very often, preferring fruits, vegetables, whole grains, and some dairy, because everything else tended not to sit well with us.

But apparently the Omte felt differently. One platter was overflowing with whole crawfish, and I swear that I saw one of them still moving. Another had leathery soft-boiled alligator eggs on it, which the Queen insisted were delicious, but the thought of them made my stomach roll.

Four whole fried rabbits sat on a platter. Their heads were still on, which was especially unnerving, and I couldn't help but feel it was meant to be some kind of message for us as Kanin.

The only things that seemed edible were a bowl of figs and blackberries, but even they didn't look that good, thanks to the platters everything was served on. They were oxidized and dirty-looking, and despite my earlier appetite, I no longer wanted to eat anything here.

Queen Bodil Elak sat at the other end of the table from us, happily loading up her plate. On the back of her chair perched a large black-bearded vulture she'd introduced as Gam.

Bodil was only a little bit taller than me, making her small by Omte standards, and she was very pretty. Her long dark waves of hair were pulled up into a braided updo, and her gown looked similar to mine, although hers was in much better shape.

Her crown sat crookedly on her head, in large part because it looked like it had been bent many times, and given what I knew about the Omte, I imagined that it had been thrown against the wall on more than one occasion. It was a thick bronze, twisted around in an attempt to look ornate, but it reminded me more of an ambitious child's art project.

She wore a necklace adorned with large gemstones, along with several gaudy rings and a bracelet. All the gems appeared to be imperial topaz, an expensive amber-colored stone. And these were all very large rocks she had.

For her part, Bodil hadn't said much to us, other than insisting that the alligator eggs were delicious. It was her Viceroy, Helge Otäck, who had done most of the talking. He stood directly behind her, not eating anything, and he'd made all the introductions. He appeared much older than Bodil, probably in his fifties, but it was hard to gauge for sure because of how leathery and worn his skin looked.

Large and brutish, there was something very imposing about Helge. His scraggly light brown hair went down to his shoulders, and he wore just as much jewelry as the Queen. His eyes were the color of burnt caramel, and they were much too small for his face.

Along with the Viceroy and Queen, the young Prince Furston was here. He couldn't have been more than five, and despite the fact that a place was set for him, he hadn't sat down once. Instead he ran around the room, his dark brown curls bobbing as he laughed and squealed, and he'd grab whatever he wanted from the platters, preferring to eat on the go, apparently.

"Go ahead, eat," Bodil said in a way that sounded much more like an order than a suggestion. She stood up and reached over, roughly ripping off a leg from one of the rabbits, then sat back down. So far she'd eaten her entire meal with her hands.

"Yes, of course." Konstantin stood up first, serving himself an alligator egg and some fruit, before dishing up a similar plate for me.

"Thank you," I mumbled softly when he handed me my plate.

I took a sip of the eldvatten they'd poured for us in heavy chalices. It smelled like turpentine, but it didn't really have a flavor, unless "burning" and "fire" could be describe as tastes. I did my best to keep my expression even instead of gagging, and set the cup back on the table.

"So what brings you all here?" Helge asked, smiling in a way that reminded me of a viper.

"We've come to offer you information, and ask if you might be of some help," Konstantin said carefully.

As Bodil tore into the rabbit leg, ripping the meat off with her teeth, the vulture squawked and flapped his wings. She finished the leg quickly, then tossed the bone up to the bird, who caught it easily in his beak. Gam swallowed the bone whole, the brown feathers of his head and neck ruffling as he did.

"What information do you have?" Bodil asked, licking her fingers clean.

"Bent Stum," Konstantin said. "He was a member of your kingdom."

Furston suddenly darted over to me and grabbed a fig off my plate. Food already stained his face, and he laughed in delight before running away again.

"Bent was exiled over a year ago, and last we heard, he was dead," Helge said. "I'm not sure what information you have that could be useful to us."

"We know who killed him," I said.

"Furston, come sit with Mommy." Bodil held her hands out toward him, and the little boy ran toward her. She pulled him onto her lap, and he settled into the folds of her dress, quieting down for the first time since we'd gotten here.

"Do tell," Helge said, still smiling that reptilian smile of his.

"Viktor Dålig," I explained, lying to streamline the story. Viktor had ordered the hit on Bent, and while it hadn't been his hand on the sword, it might as well have been. "He's a sworn enemy of the Kanin, and he killed Bent to prevent anyone from finding out his plans of attack. He recruited Bent, used him up, and then killed him."

Helge inhaled through his nose. "That's unfortunate, but that's the path Bent chose when he left us."

"He didn't leave us," Bodil corrected him, giving him a hard look from the corner of her eye. "We exiled him."

Helge's smile had finally fallen away. "Bent broke the rules. He wouldn't fall in line."

"I told you when we exiled him that this could happen." Bodil ignored him and held her son closer to her. "It left him vulnerable to forces worse than he is, like this Viktor Dålig."

"My Queen, we've already discussed the matter. Bent wouldn't abide by the rules, and we must have order," Helge said. "And besides, we don't know if they're exaggerating about this Viktor Dålig. He may not have had anything to do with Bent's death. The Skojare said it was suicide."

"The Skojare were misled," Konstantin said. "I was there. I know Viktor did it." Helge glared at him, and one corner of his lip pulled up in an angry snarl.

"I believe him," Bodil decided. "Bent was my sister's son. He was strong-willed and arrogant, and he'd never have killed himself. I told you that when we heard the news. None of it made sense, and you wouldn't listen to me. Now we need to clean up the mess we've made."

As furtively as I could, I exchanged a look with Konstantin of pleasant surprise. With only limited communication between the Omte and the Kanin, I knew next to nothing of the royal family. In Ridley's conversations with the Queen after the initial incident in Chicago with Bent and Konstantin, she hadn't let on that she had a connection to him, but that was typical for the Omte. They were a very secretive people.

Now that I knew that Bent was so closely related to the Queen, it boded well for our plan to enlist the Omte to help us.

Helge bent over, lowering his voice when he spoke. "Perhaps now isn't the best time to talk about this."

"My sister will never forgive me for what happened to Bent, but maybe there's still time for me to make it right," the Queen said, turning to us. "Do you know where this Viktor Dålig is?"

"Not his exact location, but he's near Doldastam, planning an attack on the Kanin," Konstantin said.

Bodil narrowed her eyes behind her long lashes. "So that's what you wanted from us? To help you stop him from attacking?"

I nodded. "Yes. I thought we might share an enemy, and we could work together."

"As strong as you are, even sending a few of your people would do irrevocable damage to Viktor and his men," Konstantin elaborated.

"Why do you care what happens to the Kanin?" She shook her head, not understanding. "You've been banished."

"Everyone I love is still in Doldastam. I don't want them hurt or killed," I told her honestly.

For a few moments, the room was filled with a tense silence as Bodil considered what I'd said. The vulture ruffled his feathers, and a crawfish crawled free from the platter, moving slowly onto the table.

"All right," Bodil said finally. "We'll help you."

"My Queen, this Viktor Dålig has an army." Helge was nearly shouting his protests. "We don't need to get in the middle of the Kanin's fight."

"He killed Bent. No one gets away with killing one of our own," Queen Bodil said firmly. Her strong jaw was set, and her dark eyes were filled with resolve. "We must be the ones that punish him."

distrust

As Bekk led us up the long, winding staircase to our room, I lifted the length of my skirt to keep from tripping and tumbling to my death. I had to be careful because I'd smuggled a few figs in it, since I had no idea when we would eat again.

The Queen had directed us to wait in our room while she consulted with the Viceroy and other advisers to come up with a plan of attack. Helge had made it abundantly clear that he thought we'd be waiting a long while.

"How did your meeting go?" Bekk asked, looking over her shoulder at Konstantin and me.

"It went well, I believe," Konstantin said, but he didn't sound very confident.

I gave him a curious look. "It was better than I expected, actually."

"Me too." He met my gaze. "That's what makes me nervous."

"What exactly did you want from the Queen?" Bekk asked when we reached the landing. "If you don't mind me asking."

I looked over at Konstantin, who gave a noncommittal shrug. "I suppose if the Queen goes through with it, you'll find out anyway," I decided. "We asked for her help in fighting off Viktor Dålig."

The smooth skin of Bekk's brow furrowed. "I've heard that name before." She looked away, thinking. "I can't remember where, but it's definitely familiar."

"Maybe you've seen him on WANTED posters," I suggested, since she'd seen me on one. "He's been the Kanin's number one enemy for fifteen years."

"Maybe," Bekk agreed, but without much conviction. "Anyway, why do you think the Queen would help you with that?"

"Because he killed her nephew," Konstantin replied.

Bekk nodded. "And she agreed to it, then?"

"She said she would send people with us to help fight Viktor Dålig," I explained. "She's just deciding who and how many."

"For what it's worth, I'd be glad to go with you," Bekk said. "To see something outside of these walls, and to fight any enemy that's hurt our people. It would be a great privilege."

"Thank you." I smiled. "We'd be more than happy to have you."

She smiled thinly, then motioned for us to go back into our cell. When we were inside, Bekk paused before closing the door.

"We're a good people," she said. "But we're a temperamental people. We mean well, but we can't always be trusted. That's something you have to keep in mind."

I wanted to ask her what she meant by that, but I didn't think she'd really expound on it. She closed the door, leaving Konstantin and me standing in the middle of the room, and the locks clicked loudly.

Konstantin took his jacket off and tossed it on the bed. "Something doesn't feel right."

"What do you mean?" I went over to the sink and set my figs in it, since it seemed like the only clean place to store them.

"I don't know." He shook his head. "There's just something . . ." He trailed off and then lay back on the bed, letting out an exasperated sigh.

"Bodil seemed on board with everything." I went over and knelt on the bed beside him. "That Helge guy seems like a total snake, but I think she'll insist on sending at least a few men, and that will be enough for us to make a dent in Viktor's army. We might even be able to stop them before they get to Doldastam.

"Then, of course, all we have to do is get back and somehow get rid of Mina, but that's another problem for another day. We need to take all of this one step at a time," I said.

"You're right," he relented, but he still sounded defeated.

When he looked up at me, he seemed so forlorn. His gray eyes had never looked so soft and sad before.

The sleeves of my gown fell just off the shoulder, revealing the scar on my left shoulder, and he reached up and touched it. An odd shiver went through me as he traced his finger along the thin ridge.

"That's from me, isn't it?" he asked thickly.

I nodded. "Yes."

"I'm sorry, white rabbit." He ran his fingers down the scar to my collarbone, and it made my breath catch in my throat, then he dropped his hand. "I never wanted to hurt you."

"Why would you care if you hurt me?" I asked, forcing a smile. "You didn't even know me then."

The night Konstantin had attempted to kill my dad had been four long years ago. I'd only been a fifteen-year-old kid in tracker school, while he was older and a member of the elite Högdragen. We'd moved in entirely different circles, and I wasn't sure he even knew my name when he stabbed through the shoulder.

"You looked so hopeful that night. Your eyes were so wide and so blue when I talked to you." He smiled, looking both pained and wistful. "The whole world belonged to you for a moment."

It actually had been an amazing night. I'd felt drunk on happiness, and talking to Konstantin had added to that. Of course, that was before everything came crashing down.

His smile had fallen away. "And the look on your face when you saw me with your father . . . I broke your heart."

"I . . ." I started to argue, but it was then that I realized it was true. He had broken my heart. I swallowed hard and looked away.

"Why that night?" I asked. "Why did you have to do that when I was there?"

"Mina had been asking me to do it for weeks, and I had an opportunity." He hesitated before adding, "I almost didn't go through with it, and I think honestly my attempt was half-hearted. That's why your father was still alive when you walked in."

"You knew it was wrong," I said. "How could you do it at all?"

"I loved her, and I would do anything she asked." He breathed deeply. "But that can't be love, can it?"

"I'm not sure that I'm the one you should be asking. I've never been very good at love."

He sat up, moving closer to me. He used one arm to prop himself up, and his hand was resting right next to my thigh. "I know I can't get absolution. I don't deserve it. But do you think that I'll ever be able to make up for the things I've done?"

"I don't know," I admitted, meeting his gaze even though that made it hard for me breathe. "But I forgive you."

"You don't have to do that," he said softly.

"I know. But I want to."

He lowered his eyes, and abruptly, I got up. The air felt too thick, and I'd become acutely aware of the intensity of his proximity. I went over to the window, putting my back to him and breathing in the fresh air. And I wondered with mixed emotions how much longer Konstantin and I would be trapped in this room.

THIRTEEN

longing

I woke up with Konstantin's arm draped over me. I didn't know how or when he'd put it there, but there it was—strong and sure around my waist. Carefully and quietly, so I didn't wake him, I slid out from underneath it and got up.

A full moon shone brightly in the night sky, bathing our cell in white light. Konstantin slept in just his boxers with a thin sheet over him, since the heat had gotten even more oppressive. I'd only worn my tank top and panties to bed, but I'd tried to keep distance between us. It hadn't worked, apparently.

I stood next to the window, for a moment watching Konstantin sleep. His curls lying around his face, his dark lashes fluttering as he dreamt, his well-muscled bare torso—it was impossible to deny that Konstantin was a handsome man, especially when he was sleeping.

But something about this moment made me think of

Ridley, and how I'd snuck out of bed that cold night when all I'd wanted was to stay in bed with him forever. And despite whatever feelings Konstantin seemed to bring up in me, I still felt that way. I still wanted to be with Ridley more than anything.

The very thought of him made my heart ache. I missed him terribly, and I had no way of knowing if he was safe. If Mina was as insane as Konstantin made her sound, she could've locked Ridley up forever.

I knew that we needed to be here now, getting the Omte to help us put a stop to Viktor's army, but the second that was over, I needed to get back to Doldastam. I didn't care what it meant for me, but I would do whatever it took to make sure Ridley was safe.

My jeans lay on the floor in a rumpled pile, and I brushed a cockroach off them. I crouched down in the moonlight and pulled the TracFone out of my pocket. The battery was nearly dead, since it hadn't been charged while we'd been here and I'd used quite a bit of battery life on the flashlight.

It was after midnight, and according to the clock, that made it Friday, May 16. It had been over a week since I'd left Doldastam, since I'd last seen Ridley. Would it be safe enough to call? And it was in the middle of the night. Who would be monitoring his calls now?

I bit my lip, staring down at the flashing battery on the screen, and debating what I should do. All I wanted was to hear his voice, to know that he was okay.

And then without thinking, I started dialing a number I

had dialed hundreds of times before when I had been on missions. At that moment, the consequences didn't seem to matter. I just needed him.

I held the phone up to my ear, listening desperately. It seemed to take forever until I heard the sound of ringing—faint and tinny. I closed my eyes, and in my mind I was begging Ridley to pick up.

But instead of Ridley's voice I heard a despondent beep. I held the phone out, looking at it. The call had been dropped, and the message below the date warned me there was no service. I'd barely had a bar when I'd dialed in the first place, but I'd hoped that would be enough.

Now, staring at the useless phone in my hands, I wanted to scream or throw it against the wall. But I didn't want to wake up Konstantin and explain what exactly had me so upset.

So I lowered my head against my chest and wrapped my arms around my head and took deep breaths. My whole body was trembling, and my chest felt like it had been ripped out. I squeezed my arms tighter, trying to literally hold myself together.

The locks on the door started to click open, and I nearly did scream then. I jumped to my feet, and I saw that Konstantin had done the same—throwing off his covers and leaping out of bed. We were ready for whatever was coming our way.

Since Bekk had delivered us back to the room after we'd had our meeting, we'd had no visitors. I'd been right about taking the figs, or else we would've had nothing else to eat for the day.

And now someone was coming in, in the middle of the night.

I saw the orange flame of the torch before I saw the figure coming in behind it. He had to bow down to get in the door, but as soon as he straightened up, it became clear that it was Helge Otäck, the Viceroy.

"It's time for you to go," Helge said with that serpentine smile.

"What?" I glanced over at Konstantin. "Are the men the Queen is sending ready to go?"

"No, I'm afraid you won't be taking any men with you," Helge continued calmly. "The Queen spoke in haste today, and she's changed her mind about everything. So it's best for you to get out of here, since her hospitality has run dry."

"But the Queen—" I started to argue.

"The Queen wants you to go," Helge snapped. "And if you don't leave on your own, I'll get Torun and he can make you go." He smiled wider then, revealing his jagged teeth, and I had a feeling that he'd get a great deal of enjoyment from watching Torun tear Konstantin and me apart.

"Bryn," Konstantin whispered, probably sensing that I wanted to continue fighting with Helge anyway. "We need to go."

And since there wasn't anything more that we could say, Konstantin and I gathered our clothes and fled in the middle of the night, like prisoners making a break for it.

repossess

W e'd sprung for the Holiday Inn, since we both needed a place where we could feel clean after our time in Fulaträsk. After we had made our way through the wetlands, Konstantin had driven for hours before we stopped, on the off chance that the Omte decided to give chase.

"It just doesn't make sense," I said for the hundredth time as I paced the room.

"It doesn't have to make sense. They're the Omte!" Konstantin was growing exasperated at having the same conversation with me. "Bekk even said they couldn't be trusted."

"But Bodil wanted to do this!" I insisted. "I know she did. The Queen was for it. It's her stupid Viceroy that interfered."

"That's probably true," Konstantin admitted. He rummaged through his duffel bag, tossing clean clothes on the bed beside him. "Since you seem too worked up to shower, I'll go first."

"Why would Helge talk her out of it, though?" I asked. "And did he even talk her out of it? Maybe the Queen was still for it, and that's why he made us leave in the middle of the night. We should've fought him."

"And what if he'd brought Torun up?" Konstantin turned to look at me. "What then? We'll somehow bring down Viktor's army after we've been torn limb from limb?"

"I don't know!" I stopped pacing and let my shoulders sag. "Why did Helge do that?"

"Because he was right." He walked over to me with his clothes in hand. "This isn't the Omte's fight—it's the Kanin's. They have no reason to risk their people for somebody else's fight."

"But—" I started to protest.

"It's just how it is, Bryn. We'll have to come up with something else." He put a hand on my shoulder to comfort me. "We'll figure it out, though."

"How?" I asked him plaintively.

"I don't know. We will, though," he assured me. "But first, I'm showering."

He left me alone in the main room and went into the bathroom. As soon as I heard the water running, I swore loudly, and then flopped back on one of the two beds. I closed my eyes and tried to think about where we could go from here.

If we went to the Vittra or the Trylle, they would just hold us captive until the Kanin could come retrieve us for a trial.

They were close allies, and since the Kanin had the largest army, they wanted to keep the alliances.

The Skojare were out of the question. With everything so crazy there, they wouldn't be able to help us at all, even if they wanted to.

There might be other expatriate trolls we could team up with, but it wasn't like I could post an ad on craigslist saying, "Troll seeking other trolls to combat evil troll army."

I opened my eyes when something occurred to me. How had Bent Stum gotten mixed up with Konstantin and Viktor? Bodil had made Bent sound like he was rebellious, but I doubted he wanted to attack the Kanin. At least not without an incentive from somebody else.

So how did Viktor enlist him?

That would be something I'd have to have a discussion about with Konstantin when he got out of the shower, but all my plans were interrupted when his duffel bag began ringing.

At first I thought it might be my phone, and my heart skipped a beat. But then I realized it was coming from his things, so I got up to check it out. His cell was sitting right on top of his bag, and the screen said BLOCKED CALLER, but I hadn't really expected any different for someone like Konstantin.

I glanced over at the bathroom, where the shower had just turned off. It would be easy to knock on the door and hand Konstantin the phone. But we were friends now, and allies. There shouldn't be secrets between us anyway.

With that justification in mind, I answered the phone and grunted hello in as deep a voice as I could muster.

"It's done," came the gravelly reply.

Before I could say anything, the bathroom door opened, and Konstantin came out wearing only a towel around his waist. When he saw me holding his phone up to my ear, he rushed over and snatched it from me.

"Hello?" he said, casting an uneasy glare at me. "Sorry. I have bad reception here." He paused. "Okay. Thanks for letting me know."

And that was it. He hung up the phone and turned his attention to me. "What the hell were you thinking, Bryn? You could've gotten us both killed!"

"Why?" I demanded. "And who was that? What's done?" He turned away, so I grabbed his shoulder, forcing him to look at me.

"It was Viktor," Konstantin said, exhaling deeply. "Evert Strinne is dead."

notify

Bryn— May 16, 2014

The King is dead.

Even writing the words, it still feels so unreal. King Evert Strinne is dead.

They announced it yesterday. He died in the early hours, just after dawn. The Queen says he was murdered, and everyone is in a panic.

This is the first moment I've had to sit and collect my thoughts about all of this, and I just have no idea what to think.

Murmurs around town are saying poison. Linus Berling told me his father had heard the King's lips were stained black from it. They'd been slipping it in his drink for over a week, and it finally took hold.

That explains how out of sorts the King seemed at Kasper's funeral. But that just leads to a much bigger, *darker question—who exactly are "they"? The Queen says that we have a mole in our midst, but she'll root them out.*

"We must be on guard always." That's what she said when she announced his death, perched on the balcony of the clock tower in the town square. Speaking to us all between tears while we all stared up at her anxiously, wondering what the fate of our kingdom will be.

And how can we be on guard any more than we already are? The Högdragen are everywhere, but they're not making us feel any safer. In fact, with them always watching, I feel even more vulnerable.

What if I accidentally do something and they think I'm the mole now?

In training today, I heard a few rumblings of your name, that you might somehow be behind all of this. I was quick to tell them to shut the hell up. You weren't even here. It's not even possible. And I know you would never do anything like this anyway.

The whole town is running scared, though. We're all eyeing up our neighbors. Are they the enemy? Do they know who poisoned the King?

Delilah came over last night. She didn't even care if anyone saw her. She was scared, and she needed to feel safe. So she came to me.

I held her in my arms for a long time, telling her that it would all be okay, when I wasn't so sure that it would be anymore. But she looks at me with those eyes of hers. (And those eyes, Bryn—they're unlike anything I've ever seen, dark chocolate and so big, I could get lost in them for days, and I wish I could, I wish I could just hold her and look at her, but there isn't time for that.) Everything is so royally fucked right now.

I've been thinking that you might be the lucky one because you're not here. The town is on lockdown. No one can leave or come back. There's a curfew. (But that worked to my advantage last night, because Delilah couldn't go home or she'd risk getting brought in for questioning, so she spent the night with me.)

You would be going crazy if you were here. That's something that you can take comfort in, at least. You're avoiding all the madness.

Today, the Queen appointed a new Chancellor to take your father's place. She said this isn't the proper time for an election, but with everything that's happening, they need someone doing the job.

There should've been an uproar. The Queen removed the people's only voice in our political process by cutting out the election. But nobody made a peep. We've all just accepted our fate.

In slightly better news, your parents are fine—they're making do with your father's pension, which the kingdom is apparently still paying. For now. Tilda is holding up okay. Or as well as one would expect given the circumstances.

Oh! I do have good news for you!

Tilda and I were walking through the town square this

morning to get breakfast. (I try to get her out of her apartment at least once a day.) I saw Ridley on the other side of the square, walking through a crowd.

He didn't look well, I'll be honest with you, but he was free. He was walking without guards. I called his name and waved to him, but he never looked my way. I wanted to run over to him, but Tilda stopped me.

"He heard you, Ember. I don't think he wants to be noticed right now," she said.

But she promised me that she would stop by his place tonight.

I just can't wait for this all to be over.

The snow has been melting, and it's been doing this weird cold drizzle thing all day. All the posters they'd had up were getting destroyed by the elements, so the Högdragen were out replacing them. The good news is that they took down the WANTED posters of you.

The bad news is that they replaced them with a reward being offered for anyone who knows anything in connection to the King's death. With the King being dead, he can't always be watching us anymore, so they replaced those with black and white posters of Queen Mina, looking twice as severe as Evert ever did.

The only thing it says is I AM ALWAYS WATCHING YOU, but somehow I believe it more than I did the King.

Your friend (no matter what),
Ember

SIXTEEN

duplicity

For a moment, there was only the shock of hearing that the King was dead.

To someone outside of the troll community, it would be hard to explain what it felt like to learn that the King was dead. The best I can come up with is to find out that the President and your favorite pop star had been killed at the same time, along with the Pope and the Queen of England.

It's this mixture of impossibility—even though Kings die all the time, they still have this bizarre sense of immortality to them. Then there's the reverence and loyalty. Despite our differences, Evert was *my* King, and I had sworn to protect him.

The wind felt like it had been knocked out of me, and I actually had to hold on to the dresser for support.

"Bryn?" Konstantin asked, moving closer to catch me if I needed it. "Are you okay?"

And that was enough to snap me out of it. I glared up at him, and there must've been something harsh in my eyes because Konstantin took a step back.

"Why is Viktor still calling you?" I asked, my voice a low hiss. "Why did he think you'd want to know that the King was dead?"

"I told you that I'd defected, and that's true." He hesitated. "But they don't know it yet."

"You lying asshole!" I shouted at him. "How could I have been stupid enough to trust you?"

"Bryn, it's not like that."

I turned away from him to start packing my bag. "Don't try to sell me your shit anymore, Konstantin. I'm not buying it."

"I did it to protect you!" he insisted.

I looked back at him in disbelief. "Fuck you." And then I couldn't control my rage anymore, so I lunged at him.

He grabbed my wrist before I could hit, and when I tried to kick him, he grabbed my other wrist and pushed me back, slamming me into the wall harder than he needed to. He held me there like that, pinning my wrists beside my head, and his body pressed against me, still wet from the shower.

"Let go of me," I growled, too angry to think properly about how to get out of the hold. I just wanted to hit *something*, preferably his handsome face.

"No! You have to calm down and listen to me!"

"I don't have to do anything you tell me!" I shot back.

"Bryn!" Konstantin yelled in exasperation. "Just listen to me for five minutes, and I'll let you go, and then you can do whatever the hell you want."

I grimaced and fought against his grip. His legs were pressed against mine in a way that made it impossible for me to kick. So I finally relented, since I didn't have a choice.

"Viktor sent me to find you and kill you," Konstantin explained. "He thinks you know too much about what's going on, and if you find someone that might believe you, he and Mina are screwed."

"So when are you planning on killing me?" I asked.

"I already told you—if I was going to kill you, I would've done it by now," he said, meeting my gaze evenly. "I went after you to keep you safe and because I didn't want to keep doing what they were doing. I'm done with Viktor and his men, but if I tell them that, he'll send people after us both and kill us. You can't just quit Viktor's army."

I pursed my lips, hating that his reasoning sounded plausible. "Why didn't you tell me this before?"

"I didn't think you'd believe me. Was I wrong?"

I looked away from him, considering everything he'd said. "I listened. Now will you let me go?"

"Fine." He sighed, then let go of me and stepped back. He stood with his hands on his hips, watching and waiting to see what I'd do.

"Who killed the King?" I asked, rubbing my wrists.

"Viktor didn't say, but I would assume that Mina did."

"How?"

"He didn't say that either, but when they'd spoken of it before, poison had been their top choice."

"Why did Viktor think you wanted to know?"

"I've kind of been his right-hand man. He's kept me apprised of everything."

I arched an eyebrow. "So when everything big is about to go down, he sent you out on an errand?"

"It was supposed to be quick. He thought I'd be back by now."

I walked closer to him, stopping so I was nearly touching him, and I looked up at him. "What does he think you're doing now?"

"Tracking you. I told him that you've been very elusive."

"And he believes you?" I asked.

"For now." He paused. "But he won't for much longer."

"What happens then?"

"He'll send men to kill us."

"So what do we do?" I asked.

"*We?*" A soft smile touched his lips. "Does that mean you trust me?"

I sighed. "I don't have much of a choice, do I?" I moved away from him and sat back down on the bed. "So what is our plan? Where do we go from here?"

"We keep moving. We can't sit still." He motioned to the bathroom. "You should shower, and then we should get out of here."

SEVENTEEN

summoned

From the window of our room, I could see the mountains behind us. Since Konstantin had gotten the phone call, we'd been driving nearly nonstop for over twenty-four hours until we finally stopped at a bed-and-breakfast in Wyoming.

Konstantin had insisted on driving most of the way, so he crashed as soon as we'd checked in—sprawled out on top of the covers on the bed. It was a small room with a kitschy western feel, but it wasn't bad. Besides, we didn't need a credit card to check in, and the less of a paper trail we had, the better.

Between using a card at the Holiday Inn and our interlude with the Omte, Konstantin felt especially paranoid that Viktor would be able to find us if he wanted to.

On the long drive, I'd tried to talk about what to do next, but Konstantin seemed unable to think of anything beyond "get away right away."

And truthfully, I didn't know what to do or where to go from here. With Konstantin sound asleep, I decided to go outside to get some fresh air and think.

The bed-and-breakfast held eight rooms, and it was a quiet place. There was a wraparound porch with a few rocking chairs facing a magnificent view of the mountains. It was a bit chilly out—only in the fifties and breezy—so I had it all to myself, and I sat on one of the chairs, crossing my legs underneath me.

I still wasn't sure if I should trust Konstantin, but without him, I was completely alone and isolated with Viktor's men and Kanin scouts after me. With Konstantin, I wasn't much better off, but he knew a few more things than I did, and at least he was here.

One thing I did know for sure was that I couldn't stay on the run like this, not for much longer. Running wasn't accomplishing anything. Konstantin would argue that it was keeping us alive, and he was right, but to what end? What was the point of doing this if it meant constantly moving and looking over our shoulders everywhere we went?

Beyond that, I knew that with the King dead, things in Doldastam had to be descending into chaos. That was just what Mina wanted so she could be the one to save them. But only after she got rid of anyone who stood in her way. Things were only going to get worse before they got better—*if* they got better.

If Mina was willing to do all these awful things to those who loved her, like Konstantin and Evert, then what kind of monarch could she possibly be? She was vindictive, greedy, and remorseless. The kingdom could only suffer under her rule.

I rocked slowly in the chair, feeling the warmth of the sun, and wondering what my fate might be, when my pocket began to vibrate. It took me a few seconds to realize that my phone was ringing. I scrambled to get it out before it went to voice mail, and saw that it was an unknown caller.

I debated not answering it for a second, but then I realized that if Viktor Dålig or Mina had somehow gotten this number, I was already in deep crap whether I took the call or not. So I went for it.

"Hello?" I answered, feeling a little out of breath.

The caller waited a beat before saying, "Bryn?"

Relief washed over me so intensely I nearly cried, but I held it back. "Ridley."

"It is you, thank god it's you," he breathed in one hurried sentence. "When I saw the missed call on my phone, I thought it had to be you."

"How are you?" I asked. "How is everything?"

"Everything is . . . not good." He sounded pained. "Everything's falling apart, Bryn. I'm calling from a phone that Ember got me, and I don't think they can trace it. They shouldn't, since they don't know it exists. I had to talk to you. I had to know that you're okay. Are you okay? Are you somewhere safe?"

"Yeah, I'm safe. I'm okay. But what happened after I left? Are you all right?"

He hesitated for so long I was afraid that the call might've dropped. "I don't want to talk about that now."

My heart sank, and I felt like throwing up. "Ridley, I'm so sorry. I never meant to get you in trouble."

"No, don't be sorry. I did what I had to do to protect you, and I would do it again," he said. "And I'm fine now."

"Are you really? Promise me that you're okay."

"I'm okay. I am." He sighed. "I mean, I'm as okay as anyone else in Doldastam." He paused. "The King is dead."

I thought about lying to him, but I didn't want to lie to Ridley. Not now, not ever. "I know."

"You know?" The tension amped up his voice. "What do you mean, you know? How?"

"It doesn't matter." I brushed him off, because explaining Konstantin seemed like too much.

"Of course it matters!" Ridley was nearly yelling.

"Ridley, I just know, okay? Let that be enough for right now."

"Fine," he relented. "I can't talk long, and I don't want to spend this time arguing with you. I just called to tell you that you need to go to Förening and see the Trylle."

"What? Why? They're allies of the Kanin. They'll arrest me on sight."

"No, I don't think they will," Ridley said. "Ember talked to her brother, and he thinks that you might be able to sway the King and Queen into granting you amnesty."

"That's a huge risk to take. I can't end up back in the dungeons of Doldastam. They won't let me out of there alive."

"I know, but Ember seems convinced that the Trylle are your best hope. Her brother says that the Queen has granted amnesty before," he said. "And I know it's not safe for you out there, on the road alone like that. You need to get somewhere where you're protected."

"Okay," I said finally. "If it's what you think is best."

"I do." He breathed deeply. "I should get going, though."

"So soon?" I asked, hating that I could hear the desperation in my voice.

"Yeah. I can't raise any suspicions right now," he said huskily. "But it was worth it to hear your voice." He paused. "I miss you."

"I miss you too."

"Be safe, okay?" he asked, sounding pained again.

"You too, Ridley. Don't do anything dangerous."

"I won't if you won't," he said, laughing softly. "Good-bye, Bryn."

"Good-bye, Ridley."

I kept the phone to my ear long after it had gone silent, as if I'd be able to hear him after he'd ended the call. Talking to Ridley had somehow left me feeling more heartbroken and yet rejuvenated all at once. I missed him so much, and I hated it that I couldn't be there with him and that I didn't know what he was going through.

But now at least I knew that he was alive and okay, and he'd given me a direction. I had to reach the Trylle.

EIGHTEEN

parting

I can drive," I offered, not for the first time. The journey from our bed-and-breakfast in Wyoming to the Trylle capital of Förening on the bluffs of the Mississippi River was over twelve hours, and so far Konstantin had driven all of it.

"I took this car so I could drive it," Konstantin said, and pressed his foot down on the gas of the Mustang, pushing it over eighty to prove his point.

"I'm just saying. If you need me, I'm here." I sat slouched down in the seat with my bare feet on the dash and stared out the window at the world flying by.

He softened and let the speedometer fall back a bit. "I'm used to doing things on my own."

"Yeah, I've kinda figured that out."

"Are you sure that the Trylle will give you amnesty?" Konstantin asked, retreading a conversation we'd had a dozen times since I'd told him about Ridley's phone call.

"No, I'm not sure. But I trust that Ridley and Ember wouldn't send me somewhere to get hurt."

He didn't say anything right away. His lips were pressed into a thin line, and his eyes stayed fixed on the road before us. His knuckles momentarily whitened as he gripped the steering wheel tighter, then relaxed again.

"What?" I pressed, since Konstantin seemed anxious.

"Trust and love can be very dangerous things," he said finally. "I loved Mina, and I trusted her with everything, and you've seen how that worked out for me."

"Ridley and Ember are nothing like Mina." I paused as something occurred to me. "You trust me."

He glanced at me from the corner of his eye. "I do," he said, his voice low and gruff, like he hated to admit it, even to himself. "But everything's different with you."

"Yeah, I know what you mean," I agreed quietly.

I turned away to look out the window again. An odd tension settled in the car, and I felt like talking would only make it worse.

The roads became more winding, reminding me of a piece of string tangled up among the overreaching maples and evergreens. The car rolled up and down the hills along the bluffs, and between the branches I'd occasionally get a glimpse of the dark waters of the Mississippi racing along beside us.

When we reached the top of the bluffs, the road began to narrow, making it nearly impossible for more than one car to pass at a time. Fortunately, there weren't any other vehicles for us to contend with, so I didn't have to see how the Mustang would handle the sharp embankment that began right at the edge of the asphalt.

For a moment I could see the river clearly over the tops of the trees, and then the car was plunging down a steep hill, with Konstantin laying heavily on the brakes to keep us from going off the road and crashing into the trees.

The pavement leveled off a bit, and Konstantin pulled over as far to the side as it would allow and put the car in park.

"What's happening?" I looked around, searching for any sign of the Trylle palace, but it was only trees that surrounded us. "Why did you stop?"

"Förening's just up there." He motioned in front of us, but the road curved just ahead, so I couldn't see anything. "Maybe a quarter of a mile. You can walk it from here."

"I can," I agreed tentatively. "But why would I? Why aren't you driving?"

He turned to face me, a sad smile on his lips and his gray eyes hard. "I can't go with you, white rabbit."

I sighed. "I know that you don't know Ridley or Ember, and you have major trust issues, which I get, but—"

"Ridley doesn't know you're with me, does he?"

I hesitated. "No."

"And if he did, I doubt he would've suggested I go with you to Förening to ask for amnesty."

"The Queen is open to things here—" I tried again.

"Yes, but the difference between you and me is that *I* did the things I'm accused of. You didn't," he said, smiling wanly at me. "I would not fare as well there as you, and I would only hurt your case."

I pushed back my hair from my face and let out a heavy breath. For some reason, it hadn't occurred to me that Konstantin wouldn't come with me. We'd made it together this far. I thought we'd go together until the end.

"What are you gonna do?" I asked finally.

He shrugged. "I don't know. I'll figure something out. I always do."

"Will you go back to Viktor?" I asked.

"No." He shook his head with finality. "I'll do what I can to buy some time, to keep them from coming after me, but I'm not going back."

"Good."

Since there was nothing more to say, I smiled at him, and then opened the car door. Konstantin got out and walked around to the back of the car, so he could grab my duffel bag from the trunk. I went over to him, and we stood together awkwardly after he handed me my bag.

"Should we hug or something?" I asked.

Konstantin smirked. "I don't think either of us is the hugging type."

"That's true. So this is good-bye, then."

He shrugged one shoulder. "For now."

We walked back together until we reached the driver's-side door, which he'd left open. I gave him a small wave, then walked ahead down the road. The asphalt felt hot on my bare feet, but I didn't mind. Konstantin hadn't left yet, and I could feel him watching me, so I glanced back over my shoulder.

"I'll find you if you need me," he called to me, and he got into the Mustang. I made it around the curve, and then I heard his engine rev and the tires squeal as he sped off, leaving me to continue the journey on my own.

NINETEEN

compound

A massive gate blocked the road heading into the Trylle compound, not unlike the one in Doldastam. This one was shiny silver, whereas ours was made of worn iron. The guard shack appeared freshly painted sage-green, with vines growing up the side.

The guard manning the gate slid open the glass window and leaned down to get a better look at me. He wore a uniform of dark emerald, and he had eyes that nearly matched.

"This is private property," he said, not unkindly. "If you're lost, you need to head back up to the main road." Since he was Trylle, he probably wasn't used to seeing blond trolls and assumed that I was a human.

"I'm not lost," I told him. "I'm here to see Finn Holmes. He used to be a tracker, but I believe he's a guard now."

The guard pushed up the brim of his hat and narrowed his eyes at me. He scrutinized me for so long I was afraid he'd had a stroke or something, but finally, he nodded. He closed the sliding glass window, and I watched as he picked up a black phone that sat on his desk.

When he hung up, he glanced back at me, but he didn't open the window. I wasn't sure what was happening, but I knew I had no place else to be. I dropped my duffel bag on the road and I leaned against the gate, pressing my face against the cool metal so I could peer into Förening.

I spotted a few luxurious cottages, nearly hidden among the trees, all poised to take in the full view of the river below us. Knowing trolls, I was sure there were more that were camouflaged better. But still, it reminded me of an affluent gated community in northern California that I once visited while tracking a changeling. The Trylle were by far the most contemporary of the troll tribes.

My feet were sore from walking down the road, so I sat down on my duffel bag, using it like a chair, and leaned with my back resting against the bars. And I waited, and I waited some more.

Without warning, the gate groaned and started to move back. I scrambled to get to my feet before I fell over, then I turned around to see Ember's older brother Finn walking toward me. I wasn't sure what he'd been doing before I arrived, but he was dressed in black slacks, a dress shirt, and a vest. He wore variations of the same clothes every time I saw him, and I was beginning to wonder if he slept in them.

Finn walked with slow measured steps, and there was a rigidity to him that would make the Högdragen envious. His dark hair was smoothed back, and his mahogany eyes reminded me of Ember's, though hers were even darker.

"Bryn," he said, without any hint as to whether he was happy or upset to see me. He kept his expression and voice completely neutral.

"Thank you for meeting me like this," I said. "I'd heard that Ember had talked to you, and you'd agreed to help me."

"I did." He motioned for me come inside, so I grabbed my bag and walked through the gates into Förening. "How are you? Did you get here all right?"

"Yeah, I got here okay. I'm as fine as I can be."

"Good." Finn started walking ahead, so I followed alongside him. "Are you ready to see the Queen? I've told her about your arrival, and she's anxious to meet with you."

I wouldn't have minded a few minutes to gather my thoughts and get cleaned up. Especially since I was wearing jeans with holes in the knees, a tank top that showed my black bra strap, and my hair was just pulled back in a ponytail. But I also knew better than to keep royalty waiting.

"I can meet the Queen now."

"Good." Finn smiled for a moment. "She's a fair Queen, and there's no reason for you to worry."

"Thanks." I smiled back at him. "I'll try not to."

The roads inside Förening were even more winding than the ones that led to it, and it sort of felt like we were walking in circles until we finally reached the palace. Unlike many of the other troll palaces, which were designed more like castles, the Trylle palace was an opulent mansion.

Long vines grew over the three-story structure, nearly masking the bright white exterior, and the back was made entirely of windows. It sat perched on the edge of a bluff, with the back of the palace supported by beams overgrown with vines. It appeared as if it might fall off the edge and plummet into the river many feet below, but the Trylle had enough magic that I knew that would never happen.

Finn opened the grand front door, and I'd expected a footman to greet us, but the Trylle apparently had a much more help-yourself kind of operation. Inside the main hall, the floors were marble, and from the front door I could see straight through the house to the breathtaking view through the windowed back wall.

As Finn led me through the palace, I was once again reminded of the gated community in northern California and the mansions I'd seen there. The chandeliers on the ceiling, the velvet jade runner that lined the corridor, even the furnishings—it was all lavish but it was all so modern. Other than the paintings on the wall, which appeared to be of former Kings and Queens.

Finally we reached the throne room, where I'd be meeting with the Queen. Finn pushed open two massive doors with vines carved into them. I'd been here once before, when I'd visited Förening as part of a field trip in tracker school and had been given a tour of the palace. But the beauty of the throne room would never cease to impress me.

It was a circular room, with rounded walls, and the one behind the throne was made of floor-to-ceiling glass, to take in more of that stunning view. In all honesty, it felt more like an atrium with a domed skylight stretching high above. Vines grew over the ornate silver and gold designs etched on the walls, making this room feel much closer to nature than anything we had in Doldastam.

The throne sat in the center of the room, covered with lush emerald velvet, and I could've sworn that when I'd been here last, the throne had been red. It was made of platinum that swirled into latticing with bright emeralds laid into it.

Queen Wendy Staad sat in the throne, wearing a long flowing gown. The fabric was a deep evergreen, nearly black, but there was something iridescent about it, so when she moved, it would shimmer and change color.

Her dark brown curls were arranged perfectly, with one bright silver lock in the front. She appeared young, even though she was actually a few years older than me, but she had a severity about her when she smiled at me.

On either side of her there was a smaller chair fashioned in the same way as her throne. To her left was Bain Ottesen, the Trylle Chancellor I had met before in Storvatten. He was a rather slight young man with dark hair and features, so only his bright blue eyes gave away his partial Skojare heritage.

To her right was the King, Loki Staad. He sat rather casually for a King, tilting to one side and resting on his elbow, and he grinned when I entered the room. His hair was lighter than most Trylle's, and it was slightly disheveled.

"My Queen." Finn bowed slightly as he entered the room,

so I followed suit. "This is Bryn Aven of the Kanin. I told you about her."

I stepped forward and bowed again. "Thank you for taking time to meet with me."

"You've come here asking for our aid." The Queen folded her hands over her lap, and raised her chin slightly as she looked down at me. "Tell me exactly why we should do that, given that you've been charged with treason by one of our greatest allies."

correspond

Bryn—   *May 18, 2014*
I wanted to be the one to call you, but Ridley wouldn't let me. He said it's too dangerous, and even though I know it's true, I still wish I'd been able to actually talk to you.

Maybe I can soon though. If the Trylle give you amnesty. But they have to, right? Finn promised he'd help you. I know Queen Wendy has gotten stricter over the past few years. (Finn says that the battle with the Vittra changed something in her.) But you need help, and she has to see that. She has to be fair.

I say that as if anything in life is fair or right. After what happened to Ridley . . . I mean, I don't even know what happened with Ridley. Ever since he came back, he's been strange. He won't talk about anything. Tilda says I push too much and I need to just let him be but I just want to know that he's okay.

The funeral for the King was this morning. It was held inside the ballroom in the palace, and it was standing room only with people spilling out into the street. People turned out from other Kanin communities, but Queen Mina wouldn't let them in. She said that they could be spies for Viktor's army, so they had to wait outside the gates of Doldastam listening to the bells toll.

She wouldn't even invite any of the royalty from the other kingdoms, because she claims she can't trust them. She says that we can't trust anybody. During the funeral, the Queen spent most of the time swearing vengeance.

The worst part is that everyone ate it up. They were all cheering when she promised bloodshed to Evert's enemies. Not that I blame them entirely. Somebody in our midst murdered our King.

At the funeral, Ridley stood in the back by himself. When everyone started cheering, I looked back and saw him sneak out. I hope nobody else noticed because that won't look good for him.

I'm training harder with Delilah. We have to prepare for what's coming. I don't know what it is yet, but it's something dark and something big. And I can't let her get hurt.

I know this is terrible timing, but I can't help it. I'm falling head over heels for Delilah. I feel so guilty, since our whole world is falling apart, but my heart doesn't give a damn about time or place. All that matters is how we feel about each other.

But she has given me so much strength through all of this. I feel like I can do anything for her, and I will. I'll do whatever I must to keep her safe when this war finally begins.

Can I tell you an awful truth? I'm looking forward to this war. The tension and the waiting is maddening, especially when paranoia is running rampant.

I'm not sure if I should tell you this, but by the time you get this, hopefully everything will be all over, and you'll want to know about it. Even if it hurts to hear.

Astrid Eckwell tried to accuse your father of poisoning the King. It was right after the funeral, when everyone was milling about. She just stood up and pointed to him and said it was him. She was hysterical, and the guards eventually dragged her away.

Queen Mina silenced the crowd, reminding them that the Högdragen had already investigated your father. But that was all she said, so people kept giving your parents these awful glares until they finally slunk out. Well, they didn't slink exactly. You know your mother. She keeps her head held high no matter what anybody throws at her.

They should leave Doldastam, but I don't think the Queen will let them. No one can go in or out. Tilda has talked about making a break for it, but I don't know if she will. I don't blame her, though. I can't imagine having a baby here, even though she's not due for a few months.

You're so lucky that you're not here. I don't know if you're safe. I don't know if you'll ever be safe again. But I still think you're the lucky one.

Your friend (no matter what),
Ember

asylum

I t was the look in her eyes that caught me off guard. In the corridor, right before we reached the throne room, there had been a massive painting of Elora Dahl, the Trylle's most recent Queen before Wendy. Jet-black hair, flawless olive skin, dark piercing gaze—she was as beautiful as she was imposing.

But it was that look from the painting. Somehow, even in a rendering on canvas, Elora made me feel like I was two inches tall. And it was that exact look that Queen Wendy now shared with her mother.

I wanted to falter under her gaze, but I stood tall, with my shoulders back.

"I have been falsely accused," I told her coolly, and that caused King Loki to cock an eyebrow.

"That seems a bit like a convenient excuse, doesn't it?" Queen Wendy asked, unmoved.

"I was working in Storvatten, under direction of my kingdom," I explained. "The Queen there felt unsafe, and I, along with my comrade Kasper Abbott, was sent to find out the cause of her unease.

"Upon returning to Doldastam, I discovered information that tied the problems in Storvatten to the Prince, Kennet Biâelse," I went on. "When I tried to bring this to King Evert, Queen Mina blocked my attempts. Kasper and I explained the situation to her, and she accused us of treason and had us sent to the dungeon."

"What did you say that made her allege treason?" Queen Wendy tilted her head, appearing interested.

"She said that simply making any claim against an ally was treasonous," I answered.

Wendy sat up straighter and exchanged a look with her Chancellor, Bain. Then she looked back at me. "Go on."

"I was afraid that we'd be locked away in the dungeon, so Kasper and I escaped in order to clear our names," I said. "We went to Kennet's room, since he was staying in the Doldastam palace. He admitted to his involvement in the attempts on both Queen Linnea and King Mikko's lives in Storvatten."

Loki let out a surprised whistle, causing Finn to cast a harsh look at him. For their parts, Wendy and Bain appeared unfazed.

"An altercation ensued between Kennet, Kasper, and myself," I went on. "Kennet killed Kasper, and I began to fight with Kennet. During the struggle, Kennet fell out the window and died."

Bain leaned forward, resting his arms on his knees. "So you think Kennet was behind everything in Storvatten? What about when you arrested Konstantin Black and Bent Stum for the crimes against the Skojare kingdom?"

"Kennet admitted to hiring them to do his dirty work," I said, lying a little. "He wanted to be King himself, instead of his brother."

Kennet had confirmed that he'd hired someone—he just never talked to Konstantin himself. Mina had been the intermediary, but I thought if I accused Mina of anything without substantial evidence, Queen Wendy would question everything I was saying.

I didn't thinking aligning myself with Konstantin right now would help my case, and he was the only way I had been able to put all the pieces together. That meant that I had to leave out a few things and twist a few facts.

"But why wouldn't Queen Mina hear you out?" Wendy asked.

"Her reasons were never made clear to me, Your Highness," I said. "You'd have to ask her that yourself."

Wendy leaned back in her throne and exhaled. "I don't know what I should do with you." She considered for a moment. "I know the Kanin would want me to return you to them so they could devise a punishment for themselves."

"With all due respect, My Queen, if you send Bryn back

to the Kanin, they will execute her," Finn interjected. "Do you really think anything she's done deserves execution?"

"And you have granted amnesty before," Loki said with a sly smile, and Wendy cast him a look.

"Those were under vastly different circumstances," she said, almost whispering.

"I am inclined to agree with Finn," Bain said. He'd settled back in his seat and crossed his leg over his knee. "I worked with Bryn in Storvatten, and she seemed intent on serving her kingdom, not destroying it."

"Since both Finn and the Chancellor are vouching for you, and my husband seems to think it's a good idea, then we will grant you amnesty. *For now,*" Wendy said, emphasizing the fact that it could be revoked if she decided it should be. "Under one condition."

"And what's that?" I asked, feeling so relieved that I would've agreed to nearly anything at that point.

"Finn must keep an eye on you as long as you reside within the Kingdom of the Trylle." She turned her hard gaze to him. "Any trouble that Bryn gets herself into falls on you."

He nodded. "I understand."

The Queen looked back at me. "The King, the Chancellor, and I will continue discussing these matters. But for the time being, you are safe and you're free to stay here." She smiled. "Welcome to Förening, Bryn."

TWENTY-TWO

domestic

As soon as Finn opened the door to his squat cottage tucked away inside the bluffs, children dove at him—two squealing balls of delight with mops of curly hair. Both of them had mud smeared on their clothes, probably from a day spent out in the yard on the warm spring day.

Finn scooped up both of the kids with ease, holding one in each arm. I'd met them before, at Ember's house, since Finn tried to visit his family whenever he had a chance. Hanna, the little girl, was about five years old, and she was babbling excitedly about the adventures she'd had that day with her mom and her brother.

The younger boy, on the other hand, was much more observant than his older sister. Liam couldn't have been more than two, with chubby cheeks and dark brown eyes the size of saucers. He stared back at me over his dad's shoulder, studying me intently.

Finn's wife Mia came out from a back bedroom, shaking her head and making her ponytail bob. The long sundress she wore fell over the rapidly growing belly. It had only been a little over a month since I'd last seen her at Ember's birthday party, but by the way she looked now, it seemed like the baby must be due soon.

"Sorry about the kids," Mia said, offering me an embarrassed smile as she walked over to Finn and the kids.

"No, it's fine," Finn assured her, and gave her a quick peck on the lips.

"Since Bryn is here, I take it that the meeting went well?" Mia asked.

Finn nodded. "She'll be staying with us for a while, but that's what we'd planned anyway."

"I hope it's not too much trouble having me here," I said.

"It's no trouble at all." Mia smiled. "I'll take the kids to Liam's room to play, and let you get settled in." Liam allowed his mom to pick him up, but he turned his head, unwilling to take his eyes off me for a second.

And then suddenly it hit me, watching Mia and Finn with their children like that—this would've been Tilda's life. This should've been her and Kasper, and their unborn child, but now it never would be.

Because I had failed to act fast enough, Kasper had been killed, and this whole life was ripped away from Tilda and their baby. And now I couldn't even be with her. I couldn't even apologize for what had happened.

It all fell on me so hard, I was afraid my knees would give

way for a moment. I wanted nothing more than to collapse on the cool dirt floor and let the sadness overtake me, but I couldn't do that. I couldn't let it.

"Bryn?" Mia's eyes widened with concern. "Are you okay?" Then she turned to her husband, sounding panicked. "Finn, I think she's gonna pass out."

Finn dropped Hanna quickly but safely on the floor, then hurried over to me. "Bryn?"

"I'm fine," I said but my words sounded hollow. He put his hand on my arm to steady me, and I wanted to push it away, but I didn't have the strength.

"Have her sit down and get her a glass of water," Mia said, taking Hanna's hand.

Finn took my duffel bag from me, and I didn't even try to fight it. He led me over to the kitchen table and pulled out a chair for me. I sat with my head in my hands and let him fuss over me until the weakness finally began to subside.

When I looked up, Finn was standing over me with a worried crease in his brow, and Mia was sitting at the table beside me. I hadn't even heard her come back out.

"Sorry," I mumbled. "I don't know what that was about."

"No need to be sorry." Mia reached out, touching my forehead gently. "You're cool and clammy. Are you feeling sick at all?"

I shook my head. "No. I've just had a very long week."

Mia leaned on the table, studying me the same way her son had before. "When was the last time you've eaten?"

It wasn't until she mentioned it that I realized I hadn't in a very long time. While I'd been on the road, I'd hardly been able to find anything that sat with my sensitive troll stomach, and when I'd been with the Omte, they hadn't been much on feeding us.

"It's been a while," I admitted sheepishly.

"I'll make you something." Mia pushed back the chair to get up.

"No, you shouldn't be waiting on me," I said, glancing over at her belly.

She smiled and waved me off as she stood. "Nonsense. I've still got another month left with this one, and I can't just spend it sitting around." She rubbed her stomach. "I've got things to do."

"Do you need any help?" Finn asked.

"No, you sit down and talk to Bryn," Mia said as she began bustling about the kitchen.

Finn sat across from me. When I'd had my head down, either he or Mia had poured a cup of tea for me. He leaned across the table and nudged it closer to me.

"You should drink something."

"Thank you." I took a long sip, and the warmth of the drink felt amazing.

Finn's home, like many troll homes, was built sort of like a rabbit burrow—with most of it underground in the bluffs. This kept it warmer in the winter and cooler in the summer, which was nice on days like today when outside temperatures had risen into the seventies.

In a lot of ways, Finn's house was similar to Ridley's house back in Doldastam, except since it was a bit warmer here, they got to have more earthy features, like dirt floors and bushes growing around the doorway.

Remembering Ridley, and the times I'd spent in his house with him usually sitting beside a crackling fire talking about work, only made me feel worse. My stomach clenched and my heart throbbed painfully in my chest. I missed him terribly, and I wanted only to wrap my arms around him.

"You look like you have the weight of the world on your shoulders," Finn commented.

"I kind of feel that way," I said honestly. "I've made too many mistakes, and too many people are paying for them."

"I've had to learn a hard lesson, and I think you might need to, too." Finn leaned back in his chair. "Everything can't be your fault. You're not that powerful. The whole world isn't in your control."

I swallowed hard and stared down at my tea. "I know that."

"But it still feels like you should be able to prevent every disaster and protect everyone you care about from any pain?" Finn asked, and I nodded. "But you can't, so sometimes you need to trust that people can take care of themselves."

I thought of Kasper, and how he'd died trying to take care of himself. And Ridley, and how I didn't know what the Queen had done to him after I left. And Tilda, and how she was dealing with so much now. And Linnea, and how she was alone in Storvatten, trying to fight for her life and her husband's. And Konstantin, and how if Viktor or his men found him, things would end very badly for him.

I shook my head. "I can't turn my back on them, Finn. If I can help them, I have to."

"I'm not saying you should stand by and watch people suffer," Finn clarified. "But you can't save everyone. You can only do as much as you can, and then you need to move on."

"But . . ." It was hard to speak around the lump in my throat. "Kasper died."

"Did you kill him?" Finn asked me directly.

"No."

"Then it's not your fault."

"But I could've done more." I looked up at him. "I *should've* done more."

Finn leaned forward, resting his arms on the table. "Bryn, if you could have done more, you would have. That means you did everything you could."

I couldn't argue that, so I lowered my eyes again.

"From what I gather by what Ember's told me, and what you told the Queen, you've been trying to fight a massive enemy on your own," Finn said. "You've been taking on far too much for one person, and I think you should get some rest for a while."

"I can't," I insisted. "Not when people I care about might be in danger."

"You're no help to anyone if you're falling apart."

"That's the worst thing about Finn," Mia said, smiling at me as she set a heaping bowl of vegetable soup in front of me. "He's usually right."

"Thank you," I told her, and I used all my restraint to

keep from wolfing down the soup. I didn't think anything had ever smelled as wonderful or tasted as delicious in my life.

"You can stay here as long as you need to," Mia told me, as I devoured the soup. "Our door is always open to you."

I wanted to thank her for that, and tell her that I didn't think I'd be staying here that long. I couldn't just rest on my laurels, no matter if my body needed it or not. But I was far too famished to do anything besides eat.

reevaluate

Before this had become Finn and Mia's home, it had been the house that both Finn and Ember had grown up in. Ember's old room had become Hanna's, but she would stay in Liam's room tonight, so I could use her room. I'd tried to insist that they didn't need to go to any trouble for me, but Mia just did it anyway.

Despite my exhaustion, I lay awake in Hanna's slightly-too-small bed, my feet hanging over the end. A lighted mobile hung above the bed, casting shapes of the moon and stars over the ceiling.

The walls were a pale blue with clouds on them, and Finn had told me that Ember had been the one to paint the room this way when she'd been ten. I remembered her telling me about her childhood, when she would lay awake at night plotting her escape from this small boring house and her boring life. Ember had been determined to escape and have an adventure.

Now I couldn't help but feel a certain kinship to her, lying awake the way she had, wishing for an escape. Of course, I would happily trade all the troubles that were stretched out before me for a boring life with my friends and family again.

As soon as I thought it, I wondered if that was entirely true. Obviously, I would gladly get rid of Mina and Viktor and all the dangers that went along with them. But would I ever be content to just settle down and lead a normal life the way Finn and Mia had?

Before everything had completely gone to hell, Ridley and I had made plans to be together when this was all over. Of course, now it seemed impossible. I wasn't even sure if I'd ever be able to see him again.

But for a brief moment I allowed myself to fantasize about the life we might have led together. It wouldn't be exactly like Finn and Mia's life, since I wasn't sold on the idea of having kids myself. Staying at home and raising a family was great for people who wanted it, the way Mia so obviously did, but I wanted something different.

I could work as a tracker for a few more years, traveling and seeing the world. When I came home, Ridley would be there waiting for me, pulling me into his arms. Sipping wine by the fireplace in the winter, and riding the horses out to the bay in the summer. Arguing about the politics in Doldastam, or what movie to watch. And falling asleep at night in each other's arms.

We could have a life together.

Or at least we could've, before I'd been accused of treason.

But still, when I drifted off to sleep, I couldn't help but imagine the life that Ridley and I had almost had together. How we'd so nearly made it.

In the morning, I awoke to a little boy standing next to the bed, staring right at me. When I opened my eyes, there he was, and I almost screamed. Funny that after everything I'd seen lately, it was a two-year-old boy that nearly gave me a heart attack.

I wasn't sure how Liam would react to me picking him up, but I decided to give it a go anyway. When he didn't scream, I took that as a good sign, and proceeded to carry him out to the kitchen, where Mia was making breakfast.

She immediately apologized for him waking me, but I brushed it off. Besides, I honestly felt better than I had in a while. Getting a decent meal and a good night's sleep did wonders for the body.

I didn't even mind that since I'd picked Liam up, he refused to let go of me. Eventually, when he began tugging on my hair with his pudgy hands and poking me in the eyes, I realized where all his fascination came from—he hadn't seen many people who looked like me in his life.

After breakfast, I finally managed to detangle myself from Liam and headed outside to work out. I'd been trying to work out every chance I'd gotten, but since Konstantin and I had been on the move, and I'd been starving, exhausted, and anxious the whole time, I hadn't gotten as much done as I'd have liked.

Finn and Mia's house sat on a plateau, with a small field of grassy flat land extending out over the bluff. A split-rail wooden fence wrapped around it, preventing any animals or small children from tumbling over the edge.

Finn and Ember's mom used to use the land to raise angora goats, but since their parents moved, taking the goats with them, Finn hadn't picked up the tradition. The only animal he and Mia had was a solitary pony that Finn had apparently gotten as a birthday gift for Hanna.

The pony, rather inexplicably named Calvin, came over to investigate what I was up to. It was dark gray, with a long mane and fur around his hooves, so in many ways he appeared to be a miniature version of my Tralla horse Bloom, admittedly a much stouter version. He only came up to my shoulder, and he appeared bemused behind his thick bangs as he watched me stretch.

When I started running laps along the fence, Calvin trotted along with me, his short legs hurrying to keep up. But he quickly grew bored of that and went back to nibbling at the grass and flowers.

Eventually, I'd moved on to doing burpees—which was dropping down to a squat, getting in a push-up position, and then immediately jumping back to the squatting position and standing up again. I'd done about a million of them when I'd been in tracker school, but the last few weeks had taken their toll on me, and I was going way too slow.

Whenever I'd drop to the ground, Calvin would sniff my hair, as if it to make sure I was okay. I was on about my twentieth burpee when I heard the gate to Finn's property swing open. I stopped what I was doing long enough to look over and see the Chancellor, Bain Ottesen, standing just inside the gate.

"Finn's inside the house," I told him, wiping the sweat off my brow with the back of my arm.

"Actually," Bain said with a sheepish expression, "I'm here to see you."

hunted

With my heart pounding in my chest, I walked across the field to meet Bain. There weren't guards with him, so it felt safe to assume that the Queen hadn't decided to recant her amnesty and arrest me. But that didn't mean that she hadn't decided that it might be better for her kingdom if she sent me away.

Bain stepped carefully toward me, avoiding particularly muddy spots in the yard since he was barefoot. Because they had nicer weather in Förening than we did in Doldastam, the Trylle got to spend a lot more time free from footwear.

He was dressed nicely in black slacks and a dress shirt with a tie, and his brown hair was styled off his forehead. With his earnest expression and clean-cut appearance, Bain reminded me of those guys who went door-to-door dropping off religious pamphlets.

"What'd you want to see me about?" I asked when I reached him.

He pursed his lips for a moment. "I have some strange questions to ask you, and I don't know if you'll be able to answer them. But it would be helpful to us if you did."

"I'll do the best I can," I replied carefully.

Calvin had followed me over, and he began sniffing Bain. When Bain spoke, he began absently petting the pony.

"What do you know about what's happening in your kingdom?" Bain asked.

My stomach clenched, and I shook my head. "Not much. I haven't really been in contact with anyone there since I left. I briefly talked to the Överste, Ridley Dresden, but he wouldn't say much beyond the fact that everything is falling apart there."

"Did he tell you that King Evert was dead?" Bain asked, watching for my reaction.

"Yes, he did."

"And I am assuming that you had nothing to do with Evert's death?" he asked, and it did sound more like a formality than a serious inquisition.

"No, of course not!" I said, probably too forcefully. "I was in—" I stopped myself before I accidently let it slip that I'd been locked up in the Omte palace when Evert had died. "I was long gone by then."

"I thought as much." Bain looked away from me, staring out at the river below, and a warm breeze blew past us. "The Kanin Queen has begun acting very . . . strangely."

I tensed up. "How so?"

"About a week and a half ago, your kingdom sent out a blast of WANTED posters." He glanced back over at me. "Of you, obviously. But along with them was a letter stating that Doldastam would no longer be allowing visitors of any kind."

"That's insane. Did the letter say why?" I asked.

"Just that they were running an investigation. But that's not the really strange part," Bain went on. "It was signed by Queen Mina. And with the Kanin, every official letter or decree I've ever seen from them has been signed by the King. Sometimes the Queen cosigns, but she's never alone."

I shook my head. "The Queen is never allowed to make pronouncements like that, not on her own."

"When King Evert died, our Queen Wendy called to offer her condolences," Bain said. "Mina talked to her briefly, but she also informed her that, unlike every other royal funeral I've heard of, no other royalty was allowed to attend. Only those already living in Doldastam could go.

"Mina cited safety being her priority, but it all felt off to Wendy," he concluded.

"Holy shit." I exhaled shakily. "She has them completely isolated and totally dependent on her. Everyone in Doldastam is trapped."

"Which brings us to this morning and the strangest part about all of this." He reached into his back pocket, where he'd tucked a rolled-up tube of paper out of sight. "We received these, along with a lengthy letter."

He handed a tube to me, and I unrolled it to reveal two sheets of paper. The top one was a black-and-white poster of myself. The photo was the official tracker picture taken every three months. In it, I stared grimly ahead, my eyes gray and blank.

LARGE REWARD IF FOUND

WANTED: BRYN DEL AVEN

AGE: 19

HEIGHT: 5'5"

HAIR/EYES: BLOND, BLUE

COMMITTED CRIMES AGAINST THE KANIN AND SKOJARE

INCLUDING CONSPIRING TO KILL THE KANIN KING

AND SKOJARE PRINCE

SUSPECTED OF WORKING WITH KONSTANTIN BLACK

The beginning wasn't much of a surprise, but it was the last line that made my heart stop cold.

Mina knew that we'd been together. She knew that he'd helped me.

My hands were trembling slightly when I moved my WANTED poster to see the one behind it. And as soon as I saw Konstantin's face staring up at me in harsh black-and-white, my stomach lurched.

KANIN'S #1 MOST WANTED

HUGE REWARD FOR ANY INFORMATION

KONSTANTIN ELIS BLACK

And I didn't need to read anything beyond that.

They'd turned on him. They'd figured out that Konstantin had defected, and now they were sending everyone after him. It wouldn't just be Dålig and his men—it would be the entire troll community.

"But this doesn't make any sense," I said, trying to stop my hands from shaking. "Viktor Dålig is supposed to be the most wanted man. He already tried to kill the King."

"Not according to the letter Mina sent this morning," Bain said, and my eyes shot up. "She claims it's all a massive frame job perpetrated by Konstantin Black and you."

"What?" I shook my head. "No, that's not true at all. I mean, Konstantin—" I didn't know what to say about him, so I skipped over it. "I've only been trying to protect the kingdom! I would never do anything to hurt it!"

Bain held up his hand toward me. "Calm down. I didn't say that I believed Queen Mina. I just told you what she's saying."

I rolled the posters back up, since I hated looking at them. "I'm sorry. It's just . . . it's not true."

"Mina also said that she called off the war against Viktor Dålig," Bain said. I could only gape at him, so he went on. "She says that it's all smoke and mirrors put on by you and Konstantin, and that too many people have died. So she's just keeping Doldastam on lockdown until you and Konstantin are brought to justice."

"But . . ." I shook my head, not comprehending. "That doesn't make sense."

Konstantin and I had thought the plan was for Viktor Dålig and his army to attack Doldastam, and then Mina would come in and save the day, thus becoming an indispensable savior, so she wouldn't be dethroned.

But if she was eliminating the threat of Viktor, then how would she become a necessary hero? And what was even the point of building up the Viktor threat in the first place? And why was she so insistent on keeping the town locked down?

"The behavior of the Kanin royalty is increasingly erratic," Bain said. "So Wendy doesn't plan to tell them that you're here, and she's agreed to grant you amnesty as long as you need it."

That should have been a relief, but I barely even registered what Bain had said. My mind was racing to figure out what Mina was plotting, and what that would mean for everyone in Doldastam, along with myself and Konstantin.

"It's not the royalty—it's Mina," I said, and I looked up at Bain, imploring him to understand and believe me. "Mina is behind all these crazy things. She killed King Evert."

Bain took a step back. "We may not entirely trust the Kanin Queen right now, but that's a harsh accusation. You can't just go throwing that around."

"I'm not trying to stir up trouble," I persisted. "I'm saying that the people of Doldastam are trapped under the rule of an unfit and tyrannical ruler. They need help. *You* can help them. The Trylle have a great army."

"Slow down, Bryn." Bain shook his head. "Wendy granted

you amnesty. That doesn't mean she's going to go to war based on your word."

"It's not just my word! You've seen what Mina is doing!"

"We've seen Mina acting in a paranoid fashion, but she's also under a great deal of stress," Bain allowed. "And even if she is acting in ways that you or I or even Queen Wendy would think were wrong, Mina is still the acting monarch of the largest kingdom, with the largest army, and the largest wealth behind it. She is well within her rights. Not only are we outmatched, but action is unwarranted."

"What if I could prove it?" I asked, almost desperately. "If I could prove that Mina killed Evert, then she's not the rightful ruler. Which means that Wendy—as a Queen and an upholder of the troll kingdom at large—would not only be within her rights to deal with Mina, she would be obligated to."

Bain raised an eyebrow. "Can you prove it?"

"Not yet," I admitted. "But I'll figure out how."

strategy

How well do you know Queen Wendy?" I asked Finn directly.

He'd been doing the dishes when I came into the house, but he leaned back against the counter, arms folded over his chest, to talk with me for a minute. Mia had been putting down the kids for a nap in the master bedroom, and she walked out just as I asked the question.

He shifted his weight from one foot to the other and glanced over at his wife. "I know Wendy fairly well," he said finally.

"What will it take to get her to declare war on the Kanin?" I asked.

Finn leaned away from me, his eyes wide with surprise. "What? I thought you were trying to help your kingdom, not destroy it."

"I am trying," I insisted. "The Kanin Queen, Mina, is the

one who wants to destroy it, and I'm trying to figure out a way to get her out of power so she can't do any more damage."

Finn rubbed his temple. "You're trying to overthrow your Queen. I can see why she charged with you treason."

"I know how it sounds, but you have to believe me." I looked from him to Mia, but she just stood with one hand pressed against her lower back, looking nervous about the entire conversation.

"It's not that I don't believe you—I've been at the briefings with the Queen and the Chancellor. I know there's something sketchy going on in Doldastam," he explained. "It's just that I don't really know what the Trylle can do about it."

"You guys are so powerful! You can bring the hammer down on Mina!" I slammed my fist against my palm to demonstrate, and Mia held her finger up to her lips and motioned to the kids' rooms behind her. "Sorry."

"The Kanin have a huge army, and with Mina commanding them, they'd be fighting against *us*," Finn pointed out. "That means lots of innocent people—including my sister—would be hurt or killed."

"I don't want a civil war," I corrected him. "I want Mina deposed. Your kingdom has an army that's powerful and skilled enough that we'd only need a small number to pull off a covert mission. Maybe ten, twenty of your people could sneak into Doldastam and arrest her."

"And you think Mina would just acquiesce to the Trylle's authority?" Finn asked with a raised eyebrow. "That she wouldn't fight back and summon her guards to slaughter the twenty troops that had come in to capture her?"

"Then they could assassinate her," I replied simply, and Mia actually gasped at the mere mention of killing the Kanin Queen.

Finn exhaled heavily, looking rather grim. "Now you've stepped it up to murder?"

"It's not murder," I insisted. "Not when it's done in protection of the kingdom. If it's the only way to get Mina out of power, then so be it."

"I understand your anger and frustration, but that seems rather drastic and dangerous," Finn said.

"Your family is trapped in Doldastam, under Mina's cruel reign. Do you really want them to stay like that?" I asked.

"Of course I don't," he snapped. "But I'm also not going to suggest that the Trylle start a Kanin civil war when we have no grounds for it."

"What would be grounds enough?" I asked. "What do I need to find to sway Wendy into thinking that this is a good idea?"

"Short of the Kanin declaring war on the Trylle?" Finn shrugged. "I don't know."

"What do you have on the Kanin Queen?" Mia asked. "Do you have any evidence to tie her to any of the shady things that have been going on?"

"Not really," I said sadly. "There's stuff that Wendy already knows—like how Mina is acting strange and paranoid. But that's not enough in and of itself. I think she killed the King, but I can't go back to Doldastam to find out anything more."

"What about confidants or cohorts?" Mia asked. "The Queen can't be causing all this trouble entirely on her own. She has to have people working for her or at least a friend that she's telling all her secrets to."

Kennet Biâelse knew what was going on, but he was dead. Viktor Dålig would be far too dangerous for me to confront on my own, and I didn't have any idea about who might be working for him.

There was always Konstantin Black, but he wasn't a source that anybody would believe. He'd need evidence to corroborate what he was saying, and I knew he had none.

I shook my head. "Not anybody credible."

Then something occurred to me. Konstantin and I had been talking once, and I'd been surprised to realize that Mina had been planning all of this for four years. Konstantin had replied that he thought she'd been plotting to take the crown since the day she met Evert.

But that couldn't have just occurred to her. As power-hungry and greedy as Mina seemed, this wasn't a new thing. I bet she'd been trying to figure out a way to get the crown since she was a kid.

"I can't go back to Doldastam to dig up dirt on her, so I'll go back further," I said, looking up at Finn and Mia. "I need to go to Iskyla."

"Iskyla?" Finn asked.

"It's this tiny, isolated Kanin town way up in Nunavut. It's where Mina's from. And if she's been working on this for a long time—and I'm inclined to believe she has—she probably started out working with someone up there."

Now that I finally had a plan, I didn't want to waste another second, so I turned and hurried into Hanna's room. Finn followed a few steps behind me, telling me to wait a minute.

"Bryn, I don't know if this is a good idea," he said as I hurried to pack up my duffel bag. "You have all the tribes looking for you. If you go to a Kanin town, they'll arrest you on sight."

"Iskyla's off the grid," I told him. "I doubt they'll notice me."

"Have you looked in a mirror?" Finn asked dryly.

I'd finished my packing, so I turned back to face him. He stood in the doorway looking down at me, his dark eyes grave.

"Your parents and your sister are in Doldastam," I said. "Along with my parents and my friends and a whole lot of other innocent people. I can't just hide and wait for this to blow over. Unless *I* do something—unless people like you and me do something—this isn't going to blow over."

He breathed in deeply. "You're gonna need to travel fast. The kingdom has a few motorcycles in the garage that nobody ever uses. I'll get you one."

frozen

The plane dropped in the air, making my stomach flip, and I gripped the armrest tighter.

"We're just hitting a little turbulence as we come into town," the pilot said, attempting to comfort me. He'd turned back to offer the words of encouragement, but I'd have felt much better if he'd kept his eyes locked on the controls in front of him.

While I didn't ordinarily mind flying, this was easily the smallest plane I'd ever been on, and it seemed to tilt and lurch with every change of the breeze. The flight had been a very, very bumpy one, and it had turned into the longest three and a half hours of my life.

In Förening, Finn had gotten me a motorcycle, a few troll maps, and given me what money he could. I'd tried to decline the offer of money, but the truth was that I was running low on the cash Ridley had gotten me, and I needed the funds.

As a condition of my amnesty, Finn was supposed to keep an eye on me as long as I was in Förening. Once I went through the gate, I was on my own again.

Finn warned me that there was a chance Wendy wouldn't let me back in again. Since I'd already cast her pardon aside once, she might not grant it again.

But it was a risk I had to take. Stopping Mina trumped everything else, even my freedom.

After thanking Finn and Mia repeatedly for everything they'd done for me, I hopped on the motorcycle and spent the rest of the day riding up to Winnipeg. It was scary being back in Canada, closer to the Kanin and Viktor Dålig, but I hid in a motel for the night, with the curtains drawn.

It reminded me of the time I'd spent with Konstantin, and I wondered what he was doing and if he was okay. He'd left me without any means to contact him, saying only that he'd find me if I needed him. But I had no way of even knowing if **he** needed **me**.

Seeing him on the WANTED poster had been strangely jarring. I had seen his face on dozens of them before, but this one was different. Not only because Konstantin and I had become friends, but because this was a clear message from Mina—his behavior would not be tolerated.

But Konstantin had been on the run for a long time, and he was capable and smart. He could handle himself. I had to believe that, because if I didn't, I would have to face the harsh truth that he was a dead man walking, and there wasn't a thing I could do to help him.

That night, I slept fitfully—with my usual dreams of Kasper and Ridley mixed in with new ones of Viktor Dålig torturing Konstantin while Mina watched and laughed.

In the morning, I chartered the cheapest plane I could find, which I was now beginning to realize may have been a bad idea. When we landed safely, I was just as surprised as I was relieved.

In Nunavut, there were no roads connecting any of the towns. The Arctic weather made maintaining and traversing roads an impossibility. Planes were the best way to get from one place to another, but Iskyla was so isolated that it didn't even have a landing strip, and I'd flown to the nearest human settlement.

When I got off the plane, it was blustery and snowy, which reminded me of home, the way the cold always did. Spring was descending on the north, so it wasn't as bad as it could be. After the warmth I'd felt these past few weeks, I pulled my hat down more securely on my head to keep out the cold.

Fortunately, not too far from the airstrip, I found a place where I could rent a snowmobile. In my pocket I had a map to Iskyla, and I checked it three times before I headed out onto the icy tundra. The last thing I wanted to do was get lost up here in the middle of nowhere.

From what I could tell from my map, Iskyla was supposed to be roughly a hundred miles away from the town. I figured I'd be able to make it there in less than two hours. So when I still hadn't found the town, and I was rapidly approaching the two-and-a-half-hour mark, I started to get nervous.

I circled back around, trying to recalibrate. There were no major rivers or mountains nearby—nothing in the landscape to give any indication that I was close or way off. It was just a platitude of white.

Just when I was about to give up and go back, I caught sight of something in the distance. I pushed the snowmobile to full speed and raced toward it. Icy wind stung my face and threatened to blow back the fur hood that was keeping the snow at bay.

I was getting closer, and the town was starting to take shape. A few gray houses clustered together, and a couple more buildings. Beside one of the houses, a few huskies barked at me as I approached.

In towns of Nunavut, there were a few roads connecting houses to each other or to the local market and shops. This was no different, with the road coming to a dead end just at the edge of the town. A large, faded sign sat at the end of it, and I pulled my snowmobile up to it.

In big white letters it said: WELCOME TO ISKYLA. Below it: ᑐᖖᒐᓯᓯᑯ. Living in northern Canada, I'd had to learn some Inuktitut—the language of the native Canadian Inuit people. These symbols roughly meant, "Welcome to Ice," since *Iskyla* loosely translated to "iciness" from Swedish.

I looked at the small barren collection of houses before me, and I let out a resigned breath. I had made it to Iskyla. Now I just had to find somebody who would talk to me about Mina.

TWENTY-SEVEN

iskyla

I needed a place to warm up and a way to start asking around, so my best option appeared to be an inn just off the main stretch of road, aptly named the Frozen Inn, according to the warped sign that hung above the door.

Icicles hung precariously from the roof of the large square building, and the white paint chipped off the sides to reveal the gray wood beneath. The door creaked painfully loud as I opened it, and a gust of cold wind came up behind me and helped push me in.

Inside was a rather small waiting room, with worn mismatched furniture poised toward an old fireplace that was barely going. The carpet was a faded red, and the wallpaper looked like it hadn't been changed in a century.

A staircase with a dilapidated railing ran along the far wall, looking more like it belonged in an old farmhouse than a place of business. In fact, if it wasn't for the bar that wrapped along the east wall with a bell on it and a bulletin board behind it, I would've worried I'd walked into someone's home.

The door behind the bar swung open, and a girl of about fifteen came out. Her full lips and amber eyes were set in a surly scowl.

Five or six necklaces hung around her neck, all of them appearing handmade with leather straps and wood or ivory pendants. The thick straps of leather and hemp she wore around her wrists matched.

"Unnusakkut," she said, which sounded like *oo-new-saw-koot*. It was Inuktitut for "Good afternoon," but with more boredom and annoyance than I'd heard it pronounced before.

"Afternoon," I replied, since my Inuktitut was never that good.

In school, we had to learn English and French because most of our changelings were in Canada or the U.S., and we also learned Swedish because it was the language of our ancestors. We had some interaction with the Inuit people who lived around Doldastam, so we were taught basic Inuktitut, but I'd rarely used it, so my fluency had gone way down.

"Oh." She looked up at me in surprise as I unwound the scarf from my face. "Most of the people that stop in here are Inuit."

I pulled off my hat and brushed my hand through my hair. "I'm from Doldastam, actually."

She narrowed her eyes at me, and I realized that her left eye was slightly larger than the other, almost imperceptibly. Her nose was petite and turned up at the end, and her skin appeared fair and rather pale. Unruly dark blond hair landed just above her shoulders.

"You don't look like you're from Doldastam," she said, but I'd already come to the conclusion that she didn't exactly look Kanin either.

"Well, I am."

That's when I noticed the WANTED poster tacked up on the bulletin board behind her. The one that Bain had shown me. Right next to Konstantin Black, I saw a black-and-white photo of my face staring right back at me, and I realized that I might have made a mistake coming in here.

"Are you a half-breed like me?" she asked. Her eyes brightened and she stopped slouching.

I nodded. "I'm Kanin and Skojare."

She smiled crookedly and pointed to herself. "Omte and Skojare."

I smiled back, hoping to earn some goodwill. "It's so rare to meet people that share a heritage like that."

"Maybe where you come from, but not so much around here. Iskyla is where they drop all the trolls they'd rather forget about—unwanted babies, outlaw changelings that can't hack it, half-breeds that don't fit in anywhere." She shook her head. "That's how I ended up stuck here."

"What do you mean?" I asked.

"My parents were unmarried royals that didn't want to lose their inheritance because of a bastard child, but apparently my mother loved me too much to just let me die out in the cold." She rolled her eyes. "So they dropped me here when I was a week old, and the innkeeper has been putting me to work for my keep ever since."

Truth be told, I didn't know much about Iskyla. It was very secluded, so we rarely had reason to talk about it. But since it was one of the most isolated towns in the entire troll community, it made sense that it had become a collective dumping ground.

"I'm sorry to hear that," I said, and I meant it. It had been hard enough for me growing up as a half-breed with parents who wanted me and loved me. I couldn't imagine what it must've been like for her growing up in a place like this without anyone.

She shrugged. "It could be worse." Then her forehead scrunched up and she tilted her head like something had occurred to her. "Hey, didn't the King die or something?"

I was taken aback by the casual way she broached the subject. Living in the Kanin capital and working for the kingdom, I'd gotten so used to the royalty being talked about with great reverence. But she seemed only vaguely aware that we even had a King.

Here in Iskyla, things were obviously very different. It was so disconnected from the rest of the kingdom—geographically and socially. It was like its own private little island.

"He did," I said somberly.

"I heard that nobody in Iskyla was allowed to go to the funeral," she said, then looked down and muttered, "Not that any of us would've gone anyway."

"Ulla!" a voice barked from the back room. "Stop wasting the guest's time and show her to her room."

The girl rolled her eyes again, this time even more dramatically than before. "Sorry. I'll get your room key."

She turned back around and went into the back room, where she and the innkeeper immediately began sniping at each other. As fast as I could, I leapt up onto the bar and leaned forward. I snatched the WANTED poster of myself off the bulletin board, crumpled it up, and shoved it into my pocket.

I'd just dropped back to my feet when the door swung open again. The teenage girl came out carrying a large metal key attached to a big carved chunk of wood.

"Come on." She motioned for me to follow her as she went up the stairs, each one of them creaking under her feet.

As I followed her up, I realized how tattered her layers of clothing appeared. The long tunic sweater was frayed at the edges, the fur on the hooded vest was coming out in patches, her heavy leggings were thin in the knees, and even her leg warmers had seen better days. Despite the cold, her feet were bare, and she had on pale blue toenail polish and a toe ring.

At the top of the stairs, she opened a door that had the number 3 painted on it, and she held it open for me. I slid past her into a narrow room with hardly enough space for the queen bed and a rocking chair. Several quilts were piled up on the bed, and a dusty arctic hare had been mounted on the wall.

I tossed my duffel bag on the bed and turned back toward her. "Sorry. I didn't catch your name."

"Ulla Tulin." She hung on to the door handle and half leaned on the door, so I didn't attempt to shake her hand.

"Bryn." I declined to give a last name, since that seemed less likely to trigger a connection to the WANTED poster. But either way, Ulla didn't give any sign of recognition.

"It was nice meeting you, and let me know if you need anything. We don't have any other guests, and I'm hardly ever doing anything, so I might as well be helping you."

"Actually, I did need your help."

She perked up and took a step in the room. "Yeah?"

"I was wondering if you know anything about a Mina Arvinge?" I asked, using Queen Mina's maiden name.

Ulla cocked her head. "That name sounds familiar, but I don't think any Arvinges live here now." She thought for a moment, staring off into space, then looked back at me. "Isn't the Queen named Mina? I'd heard someone say she was from here once, but I just thought they were lying. People come here to disappear." Then, sadly, she added, "Nobody ever actually makes it out."

"I'm sure some people do," I said, attempting vainly to cheer her up. I neglected to address her connection about Mina and the Queen. The less she knew about what I was looking for, the better.

Ulla gave a one-shoulder shrug, like she didn't care one way or another. "There's only eight hundred and seventy-eight people that live here, so you'd think everybody'd know everything about everyone. But truth is, most people keep to themselves. We like our secrets here."

"Do you know of anybody named Mina?" I pressed on. "She probably moved away around five years ago."

"Five years ago?" Ulla repeated, thinking. "Kate Kissipsi had a couple sisters that left. I'm not sure when, but you could talk to her. She might know something."

"Do you know where she lives?" I asked.

"On the north side of town." Ulla gestured behind her. "I could take you there if you want."

"Could you? That'd be really great."

"Yeah." She smiled broadly, probably excited about the idea of getting out of the inn. "I have to make supper first, and you can have some. It's nothing exciting. Just boiled potatoes and ukaliq."

"Ukaliq?" I echoed, doing my best to make the *ew-ka-lick* sound she made.

"Sorry, arctic hare." Her expression changed to one of exaggerated weariness. "We eat so much hare." Then she shook her head, clearing it of the thought, and her smile returned. "I'll meet you downstairs in twenty minutes for supper, and then I'll take you out to see Kate."

visitors

W e have to walk," Ulla told me as she pulled on heavy kamik boots made of sealskin and lined with fur. "It's only about a mile north, so it's not that bad."

"Why do we have to walk?" I asked, bundling up the same way she was in the lobby of the inn.

"Because Kate doesn't like visitors, so it's better if she doesn't hear us coming." With that, she turned and headed toward the front door. "Let's go. We have to be back before dark."

Dark was still several hours away, but I didn't argue with her. I just followed her out into the cold. We went down the front steps, and then walked half a block. The streets were deserted, and if I didn't know any better, I would've thought this was a ghost town. But Ulla assured me that people actually lived here.

At the end of the block, we took a right turn onto a poorly

kept path. It had obviously been shoveled at some point in the winter, since it had less snow than the areas around it, but it was covered in snow.

"Why doesn't Kate like visitors?" I asked as we walked out of town.

"Nobody likes visitors here." Ulla spoke loudly so her voice would carry through the thick scarf she'd wrapped around her face.

"It seems like a lonely place," I said.

Ulla looked at me with a snowflake stuck to her eyelash. "You have no idea."

We'd walked for quite a while before Ulla pointed at what appeared to be a heap of snow on the ground, claiming that it was Kate's place. As we got closer, it finally began to take shape. It was so low to the ground that it had to be built like Ridley's house, with most of it below the surface. Snow covered it, probably both to camouflage it and to help insulate it during the harsh winters.

Dirty snow appeared to move near the front of the house, but when two gray and white drifts began charging toward us, I quickly realized it wasn't snow. Two massive wolves had been lying outside, but now they were running toward Ulla and me, snarling and barking.

"I forgot she had wolves," Ulla said.

I started backing away, since the wolves were rapidly approaching us. "We should get out of here."

"No, don't run!" Ulla snapped. "That'll only make them chase you."

"Well, I'm not exactly an expert in fighting wolves in hand-to-hand combat, so what do you suggest we do?"

The front door of the hut was thrown open, and a dark figure stepped out wielding a large shotgun.

"Magni! Modi," she shouted, and the wolves halted mere feet from pouncing on us. "Get back here!"

The wolf closest to me hesitated, growling at me once more, before turning back and running with the other one toward the hut. The home owner was still holding a gun, but she'd called the dogs off, so I took that as a good sign. I slowly stepped closer to the hut, and a second later, Ulla followed me.

"Who are you? What do you want?" the woman barked at us.

"I just wanted to talk to you for a minute. If that'd be okay."

She was cloaked in thick fur, and a hood hung low over her face, so I could only see her mouth, scowling at me. As she considered my proposal, it seemed to take forever, with the two wolves standing by her side.

Finally, she said, "You've walked all this way. I might as well let you in." Without waiting for us, she went back into the hut, and the wolves trailed behind her.

Since I wasn't actually sure how safe any of this would be, I turned to Ulla. "You can head back to town if you want. I can handle this from here."

"No way. This is better than anything that happens in town."

I didn't want to stand out here and argue with her, especially not when someone with a shotgun and wolves was waiting on me. So I nodded and went on.

Inside the hut, the walls were made of gray exposed wood, and there was a wood-burning stove, small kitchen table, and bed all in the same room.

It was surprisingly warm inside, and the woman had already taken off her fur and tossed it on the bed. Her long dark hair was pulled back in a frizzy braid that went to her knees. She wore a loose fitting black dress with wool leggings, and, much like Ulla, she wore many pieces of wood and ivory jewelry.

When Ulla and I came in, she was busying herself filling up two metal dishes with chunks of meat from an ice chest. I took off my hat and scarf while I waited for her to finish. The wolves whimpered excitedly until she set the bowls down before them, and then she turned her attention to us.

Her eyes were dark gray, with thick lashes framing them, and without all the fur she appeared rather petite. She looked to be in her early twenties, but with her arms crossed over her chest, she gazed at me with the severity of someone much older and much more hardened by life.

"What do you want?" she demanded.

"Are you Kate Kissipsi?" I asked.

"That's what they call me," she replied noncommittally.

"I was just looking for someone, and Ulla Tulin"—I motioned to Ulla beside me, and she gave Kate a small wave—"thought you might know something."

"I live alone with nothing but Magni and Modi." Kate

looked over to where the wolves were chomping down on the semi-frozen red meat. "I don't think I can help you."

"Do you know anything about a Mina Arvinge?" I asked, almost desperately. "Anything at all?"

Her eyes widened for a moment, but her expression remained hard. Finally, she let out a heavy breath. "Ayuh. You mean my sister?"

My jaw dropped. "She's your sister?"

"I suppose I should make us some tea, then." She turned her back to us and went over to the stove. "Come in and sit down. You'll probably have a lot you want to talk about."

TWENTY-NINE

relation

"S orry about the gun," Kate said, glancing over to where the shotgun rested by the door.

"It's no problem," I told her hurriedly, eager to get on with the conversation.

Ulla and I had taken off our jackets and sat down at the table while Kate prepared the tea. The metal teapot had begun to whistle, so she came over and poured hot water over the tea bags into chipped ceramic mugs.

"We've had problems with nanuqs this year, coming too close to the house and getting more aggressive than normal. The long winter's been hard on them," Kate explained as she sat down across from us.

Nanuq was one of the few Inuktitut words I remembered—it meant "polar bear." We had plenty of polar bears that lived around Doldastam, but they were almost never hostile. Still,

I didn't want to start my interactions with Kate by doubting her claims.

"They call me Kate Kissipsi, but that's not really my name," she began, staring down at the mug. The larger of the two wolves lay close to the wood-burning stove, while the other lay on her feet. "We came here when I was seven, and nobody here wanted to take in orphaned children."

She looked up at Ulla then, who nodded solemnly.

"Too many babies and kids are dropped off here," Ulla said. "There aren't a lot of open hearts or open doors anymore."

"None of the Kanin would have us here, but we were eventually taken in by an Inuit family that lived nearby," Kate said. "That's when I adopted the name Kissipsi—it means 'alone' in Inuktitut, and that seems like the best word to describe my life.

"Arvinge isn't really Mina's last name either," she added.

As soon as she said it, it clicked with me. The Kanin had taken to using many Swedish words for official titles and names, even adopting them as surnames. It was so common, I hadn't thought anything of Mina's alleged maiden name until now.

"*Arvinge* means 'heir' in Swedish," I said, thinking aloud. And then everything began falling into place "And you came here when you were seven? It was in 1999, wasn't it?"

Kate nodded, but she hadn't even needed to confirm it. It all made sense.

I leaned back in my chair. "Holy shit. You're Viktor Dålig's daughters."

" 'Mina' was my dad's pet name for Karmin," Kate said. "She was the *only* one he gave a pet name to, but she was the oldest and his favorite." She let out an embittered sigh. "As soon as we got here, she started going by Mina Arvinge, trying to separate herself from the bad reputation our real name had garnered."

After Viktor had attempted to kill the King fifteen years ago, he'd been sentenced to death, but many felt that the harshest punishment had been saved for his three girls. Since the whole attack had been based on the fact that he felt that his oldest daughter, Karmin aka Mina, was the rightful heir to the throne, King Evert believed that his kids should be punished severely, even though they were only children.

All three of Viktor's daughters were stripped of the titles, their inheritance, and banished from the kingdom. Karmin was oldest, and she was only ten at the time. With their mother dead and their father on the run from the law, she had been left in charge of her younger sisters.

"After we were exiled, we had nowhere to go," Kate said. "We'd never been changelings. We'd lived our whole lives in Doldastam, and unlike trackers, who are trained in the human world, we knew nothing about it.

"Before we were sent away, the Chancellor brought us a bag of clothes and some money," she went on. "He told us to go to Iskyla. He said its people hardly ever followed the rules of the kingdom and no one here would even know who we were. And he was right."

The Chancellor at the time had fallen ill, which meant that my dad was working in his place. My dad had been the one to help the girls and send them somewhere safe. Years later, even knowing that he'd tried to help them, Mina would still send Konstantin to kill him in revenge for not crowning her Queen.

"Our father stayed away for a long time, and honestly, that's just as well," Kate said. "I wished he'd never come back."

Ulla leaned forward, resting her arms on the table. "Why? I would love it if my father visited, even once."

"Your father probably isn't completely obsessed with revenge," Kate countered. "To be fair, Mina was already preoccupied with it before he showed up. But once he came here around six or seven years ago, her preoccupation turned into her solitary drive. They talked only about how they would make everyone pay."

"How were they planning to make everyone pay?" I asked.

"I don't know." Kate shook her head. "I tried not to pay attention. My sister Krista and I never cared that much for it. Dad tried to get us to join, but Krista eventually fell in love and moved to Edmonton with her boyfriend. I stayed here, but I spent as much time outside and away from them as I could.

"The only plan I ever really knew about was when Mina

came to me and said she was going to a ball where she would make the King fall in love with her. It seemed ludicrous. I thought for sure Evert would recognize her, but she insisted that she'd only been ten the last time he saw her and now she was a woman of twenty.

"Not to mention that fact that Evert is our second cousin." She wrinkled her nose. "I know royals do that all the time to keep the bloodlines pure, but it's still always seemed so gross to me."

"But Evert didn't recognize her, and he did fall in love with her," I said.

Kate snorted. "Much to my surprise. She came back once after the engagement, and she tried to promise me riches and glory. I told her that I didn't want any of it, and I asked her to let it go. Vengeance never brings people happiness or peace. I said, 'What kind of life is it to be married to your nemesis?'

"Mina looked at me, with her eyes cold and hard, and she said, 'It will be my finest achievement, and I pity you that you'll never understand that.'" Kate grimaced. "And that was the last thing she's ever said to me."

"Did you know Evert was murdered last week?" I asked.

Kate lowered her eyes. "No. I'm surprised it took this long, but I guess Mina's plans are finally under way."

"Do you have any idea what she might do next?" I asked.

"Not anything specific," she said, looking at me with stormy gray eyes. "But honestly, I don't think she'll be happy until everything is suksraungiksuk."

I shook my head and didn't even attempt to repeat the word she'd used. "What's that mean?"

"There's not a literal translation in English," Ulla explained. "But it means 'destroyed' or 'finished.'"

"More like obliterated," Kate said.

THIRTY

nanuq

I awoke just after the sun started to rise, which meant that it was only four in the morning. After sleeping fitfully all night with my usual nightmares, I was happy for the reprieve that being awake provided.

We'd left Kate's hut not long after she'd confessed that Mina was her sister. Before we'd gone, I'd asked her why she'd been so open in telling us everything, and Kate had simply shrugged and said, "Why wouldn't I? Mina's never been much of a sister to me, and I have no reason to keep her secrets."

Ulla had been very excited about everything we'd found out, even though she didn't understand the implications of much of it. Growing up so isolated, she now fancied herself embroiled in plots of treason and espionage.

It had taken quite a bit of convincing for me to get her out of my room last night, telling her that I needed to get to bed early. But really, I just needed a chance to process it all for myself.

Once I did, everything Konstantin and Kate had said fit together perfectly, creating this portrait of a diabolical, unstoppable madwoman. Both Mina and Viktor had been incredibly patient, waiting *years* for their plan to come to fruition.

And now that it had, I was certain that Mina would do everything in her power to make sure that nothing got in her way. You don't plan something for a decade and let it all fall apart at the end.

I needed to get back to Förening. I thought I finally would have evidence to convince Queen Wendy that the Trylle needed to depose Mina. Assuming, of course, that Wendy believed me, since Kate wasn't about to leave Iskyla to testify.

I packed my bag and opened my room door to find Ulla on the landing just outside my room. She'd changed clothes from last night, and she was asleep, using her own bag as a pillow and her coat as a blanket.

When she heard the door open, she sat up with a start. "Finally. You're up."

"*Finally?*" I asked. "What are you doing?"

"I was waiting for you." She stood up and stretched. "I'm coming with."

"You can't come with. You heard what I told you last night. It's too dangerous."

"I know, but I can help," Ulla insisted. "And besides that, nobody wants me here. I have no reason to say."

"You may not have a reason, but I do. I can't afford to take you back with me. I have barely enough money to charter a plane and get back home myself," I explained.

"I've got money. I've saved up every dime and nickel I've ever made." Ulla reached into her jacket pocket and pulled out a surprisingly thick wad of cash. "I can pay my own way, and help you out."

I sighed. "How old are you?"

"Fourteen and a half." She stood up straighter, as if that would make her seem older. She was already taller than me, with slightly broader shoulders, probably thanks to her Omte genes. "I'm mature and strong for my age, though. I can help you."

I was about to tell her no, but the desperate, heartbroken look on her face finally made me cave. With everything that Ulla and Kate had told me about what it was like to grow up here, I didn't think it would be good for anybody.

"Fine, but if you slow me down, I'm leaving you behind," I said, which was more of an empty threat than I wanted to admit.

Ulla almost squealed with delight, but I silenced her and then walked past her and headed down the stairs. Taking her with didn't seem that bad, since I was just headed back to the Trylle. Ulla should be safe with the Trylle, and they could help her find a place in this world.

It wasn't until we'd taken the snowmobile to the nearest town that I realized that Ulla had never been outside of Iskyla before. She was amazed and entranced by every little thing, and I had to constantly remind her that we were traveling incognito and that she needed to stop making a scene.

Surprisingly, she handled the plane better than I did. Somehow the ride managed to be even more turbulent than it had been last time, and the pilot told me it was thanks to an incoming freak blizzard.

Our landing was twice as rough this time, but at least we made it alive. The pilot was right about the storm, though. A brutal wind was coming from the north, bringing with it heavy snow. Ulla suggested we get a hotel for the night and head out in the morning, but I suspected that she just wanted a chance to see more of the city.

I, on the other hand, didn't want to waste any time. I had information that I needed to get to the Trylle as soon as possible. Everyone in Doldastam was depending on it, whether they knew it or not.

So, despite travel advisories telling me not to, I rented an SUV and headed south. For her part, Ulla actually didn't seem to mind the storm or the slow going. I think she would've been thrilled by just about anything I did, though.

The first hour or so into the drive went okay. I barely went above thirty, but we were moving. And then we weren't. We hit a snowdrift so large, the SUV just couldn't get through it. We were stuck.

"Don't worry. I got it," Ulla said. She'd taken off her kamiks while I was driving, but now she slipped them back on, along with her heavy gloves.

"What do you mean, you got it?" I asked, but she was

already opening the car door and hopping out into the snow. "Ulla!"

I wasn't about to let her disappear into the snowstorm, so I jumped out after her. She'd gone around to the back of the SUV, and she'd put on what reminded me of old flight goggles. They were strapped on underneath the earflaps of her hat, and while they were comical-looking, they probably worked well at keeping the snow from stinging her eyes.

"What are you doing?" she asked me, like I was the one who had leapt out of the vehicle without explanation. "Is the SUV in neutral?"

"No. It's in park. Why? What are *you* doing?"

"I'm gonna get us unstuck." She flexed her arms.

It sounded ridiculous, but she did have Omte blood. She may not have been the size of the ogre Torun I'd seen in Fuläträsk, but she should have some of his strength.

"Be careful," I told her, but I left her to it.

I got back in the vehicle and put it in neutral. I adjusted the rearview mirror so I could watch. Her head bent down as she pushed on the back, and the SUV jerked forward a bit.

Then nothing happened at all for a few seconds, and suddenly it lurched forward, going straight through the snowdrift. Snow flew up around the vehicle, and it skidded to a stop on a clearer stretch of highway on the other side of the drift.

As soon as the SUV stopped, I put it in park and jumped out to make sure Ulla hadn't been hurt. After all, that had been an awfully big push.

"Ulla!" I shouted when I didn't see her right away, and I charged through the drift.

She was standing in the middle of the road, staring off to the right of her, but she didn't appear injured.

"Ulla," I repeated. "That was amazing."

"We should probably get out of here," she said flatly.

"What? Why?" I asked, and I looked to see where she was staring.

There, a few feet off the road and almost invisible in the snow, were two small polar bear cubs. The bigger, fluffier one hung back, but for some reason the smaller one thought it would be a good idea to trot toward us—its big eyes wide and excited.

Growing up near the polar bear capital of the world in Doldastam, there was one important lesson I had learned—wherever there was a cub, nearby was an angry mama bear.

"Let's go," I commanded.

Ulla started hurrying toward the SUV past me. I turned to join her, but it was already too late. The mama bear had come out of nowhere. The giant white beast growled and stomped between me and the vehicle. I had nowhere to run, but that didn't matter, because she wasn't about to let me run anywhere.

Before I could dodge out of the way, she swung at me with her giant paw, and that was the last thing I saw.

anguish

Searing pain. That's what kept waking me. I didn't remember sleeping or being awake. It was all one blur of pain.

My right side felt like fire, like I had been ripped open and filled with hot coals, and my head throbbed above my right eye. I remembered jostling. My body moving around without my control, bouncing and swaying.

At some point, I became alert enough to realize I was lying in the back of the SUV. From the driver's seat, Ulla kept looking back and telling me that everything would be all right.

I tried to tell her that I was okay and that she shouldn't worry, but all I could muster was a strange gurgling groan. In the back of my mind, I realized that I might actually be dying, but then the pain flared up, blotting out any rational thought.

Some time after that—I'm not sure how long, it could've

been five minutes or five hours—the SUV jolted to a stop, and I rolled forward, which caused enough agony that I screamed out.

Ulla apologized and asked if I was okay, but before I could respond (not that I would've been able to anyway), the driver's-side door opened and a male voice was yelling at her.

"Who the hell are you?" he demanded.

"Who the hell are you?" Ulla shot back.

"Where's Bryn?" he asked, and that's when I faded out again.

I wanted to stay conscious and find out what exactly was going on, but the pain was too much. It overwhelmed everything, and I blacked out.

Then I felt a hand on my face, strong and cold against my skin. I struggled to open my eyes, but my right eye wouldn't open. The vision in my left eye slowly focused, and I saw a face right above mine.

Dark gray eyes filled with worry, black curls falling forward—it took me a moment to realize it was Konstantin.

"Oh, white rabbit. What have you done?" he whispered.

"Am I dying?" I barely managed to get out, in a voice that sounded far too weak to be my own.

"No. I won't let you die," Konstantin promised me. Then to Ulla he shouted, "Drive faster! We need to get there *now*."

Gingerly, he lifted my head and rested it on his lap. It still hurt, but I tried to hide my wincing as best I could. He took my hand in his, and it felt sticky from blood.

"If it hurts too bad, just squeeze my hand," he said.

I wanted to tell him that it always hurt too bad. That the pain was so intense, I felt like I was suffocating, drowning in flames. But I didn't. I just squeezed his hand and waited for darkness to come over me again.

THIRTY-TWO

convalesce

Before I even opened my eyes, I felt the difference. My body still ached, especially on the right side, but it was no longer an excruciating fire burning me up from the inside out.

When I did open my eyes, they both opened with ease, which helped quell my fears that I had lost my right eye. They were both there, working properly, as I stared up at the mobile above me.

Sunlight spilled in through the open doorway, but the mobile still managed to cast a few dimly lit shapes of the moon and stars around me. My feet hung off the end of Hanna's small bed. I was back in Förening, at Finn's house.

I looked around, still getting my bearings, when I saw the dark silhouette of Konstantin leaning against the doorframe, backlit by the sun coming in from the front windows.

"What are you doing here?" I asked. I vaguely remembered him being in the SUV with me, but it all felt like a strange, terrible dream.

"I brought you here because you needed medical attention," he said, his voice low.

"But before you said that you couldn't come here because the Trylle would arrest you," I reminded him.

"That Ulla girl didn't know anything about where to go or what to do. I couldn't just leave you with her." He gave a half shrug. "Not if I wanted you to live, anyway. When we got to the gates, I talked to Finn, and he managed to convince the Queen to give me temporary amnesty since I was aiding an injured troll."

"Temporary?" I asked. "How long will that last?"

"I hope it lasts just long enough for me to get out of here without ending up in a dungeon," he replied glibly. His face was hidden in shadows, so I couldn't tell how concerned he really was about being locked up.

"How did you find me?" I asked.

"I'm tracking you, remember? I felt your panic, and I found you as fast as I could. I stopped your car just south of Winnipeg. Ulla didn't want to let me in at first, but I managed to convince her."

"You'll have to stop tracking me eventually," I told him.

"We'll see."

"I should probably thank you for helping me." I started pushing myself up into a sitting position, but as soon as I moved, my side screamed painfully.

"Easy, there." Konstantin rushed over. He put his hand

on my arm, helping me until I was sitting, and then he sat down on the bed beside me. "Finn got a healer to come in and help heal you, but she didn't do it completely. A couple medics fixed you up the best they could after the healer had finished."

Konstantin didn't say it, but I knew why she hadn't healed me all the way—she didn't want to waste her energy on a lowly half-breed tracker outlaw. To be honest, I was surprised she'd bothered helping at all.

"You would've died without it," he said, supplying a reason. A healer could be moved to help even the lowest of the low if they would die without intervention.

I lifted up my tank top to better inspect my wounds, but they were all bound tightly with bandages stretching from my waist to just below my breasts. Some blood seeped through, and I gently touched my ribs, which sent a searing pain through me.

"You've got quite a few stitches under there," Konstantin assured me as I lowered my shirt. "But at least she saved your eye."

I reached up and touched my eye, and unlike my side, it felt perfectly normal and pain-free. There wasn't any sign of injury that I could feel.

"The bear swiped you good across the face, but to save your eye, the healer had to fix it all completely," he explained. "Where the bear tore you open on your side, she mostly just closed up the internal organs. You lost a lot of blood."

"I'll have to thank her for that if I ever see her," I said, and I meant it. She hadn't needed to help me, especially since I wasn't even Trylle, and I was grateful that she'd gone out of her class to save my life.

Then I turned my attention to Konstantin. "How could you not tell me that Mina is Viktor's daughter?"

He inhaled sharply through his teeth. "I didn't know for sure."

"How could you not know?" I asked, incredulous. "You've been sleeping with her for years, and working with her dad? But somehow you never put that together?"

"They're not like a normal father-daughter." He shook his head. "At first I thought they might be former lovers, but I quickly realized that wasn't the case because of how cold they were with each other. They were more like colleagues. Mina never called him 'Dad.' They never talked about family. The only thing they ever mentioned was revenge and how they were going to exact it."

"And you never asked?" I pressed.

"Of course I did! But Mina just told me not to concern myself with things like that."

"And that was good enough for you?"

"No!" Konstantin leaned forward and put his hands to his face in frustration. "Nothing was ever good enough for me with Mina, but she wouldn't ever give more. You don't understand what it was like with her. Everything was on her terms. *Everything.*"

"Fine. I can accept that you couldn't push Mina, but why wouldn't you have told me?" I asked. "You obviously had suspicions."

"Really?" He looked at me with an arched eyebrow. "What would've happened if I told you that Mina was Viktor's daughter, and it turned out *not* to be the case? Not only would that have destroyed any trust you had in me, it would've destroyed any credibility you had with whoever you'd gone to with that information."

I realized that he was right. If it had turned out that his hunch was wrong, it would've undone any progress we'd made.

By not revealing unsubstantiated ideas to me, he'd protected everything we were trying to accomplish.

"And does it even matter?" Konstantin asked. "Mina is an evil bitch regardless of who her father is."

"Well, now it matters, because the information might be enough to get the Trylle involved and help the Kanin," I said. "This is proof that Mina got the crown under false pretenses, murdered the King, and she should be dethroned."

"By dethroned, you mean executed." He looked down at the floor, his arms resting on his knees.

For the first time it occurred to me what this might mean to him. He'd once loved Mina, very deeply by his accounts, and even though he realized how awful she truly was, that didn't necessarily mean he'd want to see her dead.

"Yes. Mina will be executed. Are you okay with that?"

He breathed in deeply, then nodded. "I will be."

"You can tell me how you're feeling," I said, then added, "If you want this whole friendship thing to work and want me to trust you, you can't keep things from me."

"I think you know all my secrets now," he replied wearily.

"Thank you for coming back for me."

He smiled crookedly at me. "I'll always come back for you."

tisane

Finn led Konstantin and me down a narrow gravel trail. Hedges grew up around it, blocking out the world and reminding me of Alice playing croquet in Wonderland. The path curved around the palace, and I glanced back at Konstantin to make sure he was still following.

The Queen had invited us to join her for lunch, and Konstantin seemed convinced it was some kind of trick, so I kept expecting him to run off at any moment. But he'd agreed to come and even dressed up for it.

Finn had procured a black dress shirt and vest for him from someone in town. All Finn's clothes were slightly too small, since Konstantin was taller and broader-shouldered. Before we'd left the Holmeses' house, I'd told him that he cleaned up nicely.

He'd looked down at me, his eyes going over my body in a way that made my skin flush, and then he'd gruffly said, "You too, white rabbit," before quickly averting his gaze and walking away.

Mia had given me something—a lovely white dress with an empire waist and a subtle train in the back. It was slightly too small for me, squeezing a bit on my ribs, but fortunately, my wounds were healing up nicely. It had only been a little over a day since I'd arrived in Förening and begun recuperating, but the psychokinetic healing had lingering effects, causing accelerated healing long after the healer had stopped.

The trail opened up into a lush garden on the bluffs. The balcony from the palace hung over, leaving some of the garden in shadows, but the warm spring sun bathed the rest of it.

Brick walls surrounded the garden, covered in flowering vines, with large fragrant blooms of pink and purple. Fruit trees of all kinds populated the garden—with pear, plum, and fig being just a few that I spotted right away.

The gravel trail had given way to a soft, mossy covering that felt wonderful on my bare feet, and Finn led us deeper into the garden. Konstantin had to hold back a few branches to keep them from hitting him in the head.

In the center of a small clearing, surrounded by flowering trees of white and blue, was an elegant wooden table with high-backed chairs. Wendy sat at one end of the table, while her husband Loki sat directly across from her, leaving two chairs open on either side.

A spread of tea and fruits was laid on the table. As Konstantin took a seat next to me, I was again reminded of Alice in Wonderland.

"Thank you for joining us for lunch today," Wendy said, smiling at us.

I returned her smile warmly. "We're more than happy to."

"It seems like you're recuperating all right, then?" Loki asked as he leaned over and took a crumpet from a plate.

"I'm doing much better. Thank you," I said, alternating between looking at the King and the Queen. "I wanted to come see you yesterday, but Finn insisted I rest."

Finn was pouring himself a cup of tea and looked over at me. "You're better off taking your time and making sure everything is healing okay."

"Finn has always been the cautious one." Wendy laughed lightly, then turned her eyes onto me.

While she still held herself with the same authority I'd seen in the throne room, she seemed relaxed today. Her gown had been traded in for a peridot sundress, and the sunshine played well on her bronze skin. She'd done her hair more casually today, so the soft curls were ruffled by the breeze that went through the garden.

"We invited you to lunch to see how you are all doing and what your intentions are," Wendy said directly, looking from Konstantin to me.

Loki laughed. "You make it all sound so formal." With a softer gaze, he turned to us. "We're just curious to know how long you planned on staying."

"Since you granted me temporary amnesty, I hadn't intended to outstay my welcome," Konstantin said, speaking in the low, formal way a Högdragen would speak to authority. "I only wanted to make sure Bryn was stable, and now that she is, I am prepared to head out on my own again. If that's all right."

I shot him a look, unable to hide my surprise. He'd spent most of the past twenty-four hours with me, trying to get me to rest by reading to me, preventing Liam from climbing all over me, telling Ulla and me old Kanin stories, and just generally keeping me company. And he'd never once mentioned leaving.

I knew that he couldn't stay here forever, and I hadn't planned on it myself either. But I hadn't expected him to leave so soon, and the thought sent an unwelcome pang straight to my chest that had nothing to do with my injuries.

"If you want to go, we won't stop you. You're not a captive here." She'd leaned back in her chair, appraising him with the calculated gaze of a ruler twice her age. "But we're also not throwing you out."

Konstantin had taken a sip of his tea, and he dabbed at his mouth with an embroidered napkin before replying. "Thank you, but I think it's best if I take my leave sooner rather than later."

"What about you, Bryn?" Wendy asked. "Finn told me you absconded to find out what was happening with the Kanin. Did you find what you were looking for, or are you planning to leave again?"

"Thank you for extending your amnesty to me again, My Queen," I said as gratefully as I could, clearing my mind of thoughts about Konstantin's departure.

"You can thank my husband for that." Wendy turned her loving gaze to Loki. "He pointed out that if I want the Trylle to be a more welcoming, accepting kingdom, then it must begin with myself."

"What better way to do that than housing those that no longer have a home?" Loki asked.

"I cannot thank you enough for your hospitality," I said, and turned to face Wendy. "But there is something that I wanted to talk to you about. You know that there is a great deal of unrest in Doldastam right now."

The lightness fell away from Wendy, and she pursed her lips. "The loss of your King has had a tragic effect on the kingdom, and my sympathies go out to you."

"I appreciate that, but I was hoping that perhaps you'd be willing to go beyond sympathies," I said carefully, knowing that I may already be pushing my luck.

"I thought that Chancellor Bain already spoke to you and explained that while I am empathetic to the plight of your people, we are in no place to get involved with a possible civil war." Wendy spoke with the air of a Queen giving a proclamation, but that was sort of what she was doing, so it made sense.

"I'm not advocating civil war," I clarified. "The Kanin people are innocent bystanders. It's only Mina Strinne that needs to be dealt with, and I have found new evidence that I thought you might find more compelling."

Wendy exchanged a look with her husband, her expression

unreadable. He shrugged one shoulder, then turned his attention to me.

"Go on," Loki urged me.

"Do you know who Viktor Dålig is?" I asked.

"The Kanin have apprised us on him previously," Wendy said. "We know of his attempts on the King Evert's life in the past."

"For years, he's been considered the greatest threat to the Kanin kingdom," I said, expanding on what she'd said. "I've just learned that Mina—Queen Mina of the Kanin— is actually Karmin Dålig, Viktor's daughter."

Wendy didn't say anything for a moment. She simply stared off at the garden while I waited with bated breath for her response. Still staring off in the distance, Wendy asked, "Can you prove that?"

"Her sister lives in Iskyla and confirmed it," I said. "If you were to send someone to do some digging, it would be easy to prove."

"I believe you, and that is very disturbing." Wendy finally faced me again. "But it does not change my stance."

"But Mina has no right to the crown," I insisted, barely able to keep my voice even. "She's not the rightful monarch of the Kanin. That's an offense to the entire troll kingdom."

"That may be so, but how would you propose we get the crown from her?" Wendy asked me. "We can't simply phone someone in Doldastam and ask her to surrender."

"We send in a reconnaissance mission," I said. "Konstantin and I are familiar with the palace and Doldastam at large. With as few as ten men, I think we could get in and kill Mina."

Konstantin made a soft, guttural sound next to me, but I kept my eyes on Wendy, so I didn't see his reaction.

"And if we are discovered?" Wendy pressed. "Either before or after the mission is completed, the results would be the same. The Kanin would declare war on us, rightfully so, since we'd just assassinated their Queen.

"And the war would not be with Mina, but with the actual Kanin people she's commanding," she went on. "The innocent people you want to protect." She shook her head. "I'm sorry, but we cannot do that."

Dark clouds began to roll in overhead, blocking out the earlier sunshine and warmth. A breeze came up, stronger and cooler than before, as the garden fell into shadows.

Loki offered me an apologetic smile. "We've had four years of peace after a war that cost us many innocent lives—both of the Trylle and the Vittra. So as you can imagine, we're reluctant to jump into another conflict so soon after that one, while our people and our kingdom are still recovering and rebuilding."

"What about the people of Kanin? She's trapping them and exploiting them. What will become of them?" I asked in desperation.

"If she's as cruel as you say she is, they will have to form an uprising themselves," Wendy said. "That's their only hope of regaining their independence."

return

T his is not what the Queen meant," Konstantin groaned. He stood beside me, the top few buttons of his dress shirt undone, glowering down at me with his arms crossed over his chest.

Unlike him, I'd changed out of my borrowed clothes the second we'd returned from lunch and put back on my ripped jeans and tank top. After I'd given Mia her dress and thanked her, I'd gone to Hanna's room to start packing.

"I don't understand." Ulla sat on the bed next to my bag, with her knees folded underneath her, and looked from Konstantin to me. "What exactly did the Queen say?"

"She said that the people of Doldastam need to rise up against Mina, and I'm going to go back and get them started." I stopped what I was doing to look around the room, which had gotten rather messy over the last day or so. "Just as soon as I find my passport."

"You don't need your passport because you're not going back," Konstantin said. "They will kill you on sight, Bryn!"

Liam toddled into the room, unfazed by the apparent tension, and crawled up onto the bed beside Ulla. He'd become just as fascinated by her unorthodox looks as he had been with mine, and when she pulled him onto her lap, he immediately began tugging on her dirty blond tangles of hair.

While Konstantin had been busy entertaining me, Ulla had been helping Mia around the house. She'd been sleeping in Liam's room and helping take care of him and Hanna, which seemed to make both Mia's and Finn's lives a bit easier.

"Who will kill Bryn?" Ulla asked, trying to follow along with the conversation as I went around the room, tossing aside toys and books in search of my passport.

"The guards. The Kanin. Maybe the Queen herself." Konstantin shrugged. "It doesn't matter *who*. But somebody will kill her. Mina can't let her live."

"I'll sneak in," I said absently.

"You are being ridiculous, Bryn, and you know it." Konstantin sounded exasperated.

"I'll go with you, and I can help," Ulla chimed in.

I shook my head. "No, you can't come. I told you I won't let you go anywhere dangerous."

"Why not?" Ulla whined. "I saved your life. If it hadn't been for me, that polar bear would've killed you."

"I know, and thank you." I paused long enough in my search to look at her sincerely. "But this is different. I'm not going to let you risk your life like that. You haven't had any training, and you're too young."

"I could say the same thing to you," Konstantin countered, giving me a hard look.

"What would you have me do?" I asked, nearly shouting at him. "Twiddle my thumbs and hope Mina isn't killing and torturing everyone I care about? No one will help me, Konstantin! The Omte said no. The Trylle said no. The Skojare don't have anybody left. If I don't do something, who will?"

"It's still early in the fight," Finn interjected, and I turned back to see him standing in the doorway. "There's still time for Wendy to change her mind."

"And what do we do until then?" I asked. "Wait for Mina to start killing innocent citizens off?"

"You're not the only one that has people there," Finn reminded me darkly. "You think I'm not worried about my parents and my sister? Of course I am. But I know that getting myself killed won't save them."

"He's right, Bryn," Konstantin said. "There has to be a better way."

Liam began to babble happily about something—I'm not sure what—and Ulla started to say that she could help me come up with a plan, while Konstantin and Finn were both staring me down, and suddenly it all felt like too much.

"Enough!" I held up my hands. "I just need everyone to go and let me think for a minute. Okay? I just need some space."

Ulla mumbled some kind of apology as she scooped up

Liam and headed out. Finn followed behind her, but Konstantin lingered a moment longer.

"Take all the time you need to sort this out," he said softly, then he left and closed the door behind him.

I sat back on the bed and ran my fingers through my hair. I wanted to scream in frustration, but that would only frighten Liam and Hanna, not to mention Ulla and everyone else. Finn and Konstantin were right, returning to Doldastam would be a suicide mission, but I didn't see any other option.

I couldn't just sit here and hope that something would change for the better. It had been over two weeks since I'd left Doldastam, but it felt like a lifetime. Two grueling weeks where I had no idea if my parents or my friends were okay, and from what I'd heard, things only seemed to be getting worse for them.

How could I just stand by and let it happen?

Someone knocked gently on the door, and based on the meekness of it, I assumed it was Hanna or maybe Liam. I still wasn't ready to talk to anyone, especially a child who probably wanted to play, but I didn't want to yell at them.

"Just go away for a little bit," I said as kindly as I could. "I'll be out soon."

The door creaked open anyway, and I was about to snap this time so they'd get the message, but then I saw who it was, poking her head around the door. Long chestnut hair, dark gray eyes, bronze skin, and her full lips in a timid smile.

It was my oldest friend, Tilda.

compatriot

At first I could only gape at her, in part because I wasn't even sure if she was real. But also because there was so much I had to say to her, so much that had happened since the last time I'd seen her that I hadn't been able to apologize for. Not that I'd ever be able to make up for it.

And top of all that, here she was, alive and safe. I'd spent so much time worrying about her, and now here she was at my bedroom door.

"Can I come in?" she asked quietly and opened the door a bit farther.

I meant to say, sure, or hello, or anything normal, but what tumbled out of my mouth was one big hurried, desperate apology, "Ohmygod, Tilda, I'm so sorry."

As soon as the words escaped my mouth, she began crying. In all our years of being friends, I'd only really seen her cry a handful of times, and never like this. These were big, heavy tears streaming down her cheeks, and she looked completely shattered in a way that I'd never imagined Tilda could be.

I wasn't sure if she hated me or not—I wouldn't blame her if she did. But at that moment, I didn't care. I rushed over and threw my arms around her. She leaned against me, letting me hug her, and sobbed into my shoulder. The fullness of her pregnant belly pressed rather painfully against the wounds from the bear attack, but I didn't care.

For a long time, we didn't say anything. We just stood that way—me holding her as she sobbed. Eventually, she began to collect herself and pulled away from me, wiping at her eyes.

"I'm so sorry," I said again.

She shook her head, sniffling a little. "You don't need to be sorry. I know that you never would've hurt Kasper or let anything happen to him. Not if you could help it."

"I never meant for things to happen the way they did," I said.

"What did happen?" Tilda asked, looking down at me with moist eyes. "I don't believe anything the Queen says, and nobody else was there. Nobody knows what really happened but you."

I motioned to the bed, and Tilda and I sat down. Then I began telling her the story of how her husband had been killed. How we'd gone to tell the Queen about how Kennet Biâelse and the Skojare head guard Bayle Lundeen had been working together to hurt the Skojare royalty. And how Kasper and I had escaped from the dungeon and went to confront

Kennet, and he'd gotten the best of us and killed Kasper, and how I'd fought with Kennet and he'd fallen to his death.

She didn't say anything as I spoke. She only stared at me, listening intently as I wove together the whole story. I even added in the pieces I'd learned from Konstantin, and how I'd found out that Mina was Viktor Dålig's daughter.

When I'd finally finished, she nodded once. "It's good that Kennet is dead. I'm in no shape to hunt him down and kill him, but that's what I would've had to have done. Thank you for getting rid of him for me."

"You're welcome," I said, instead of explaining that I hadn't meant to kill Kennet. I'd been hoping to get him to tell me who he was working for, but since Konstantin had filled me in later, it didn't seem to matter now.

And then I realized something. "What are you doing here? I heard Doldastam was on lockdown."

"It is." Tilda grimaced. "Everything has completely gone to hell since you left, and I couldn't stay any longer. There was no way I could have a baby there, so I had to get out when I could." She'd absently rubbed her stomach as she spoke.

"How far along are you now?" I asked.

"Almost five months." She smiled. "It's so weird because I'm already starting to feel more like a mom."

Hearing her say the word made me think of my own parents and how I hadn't heard anything from them since I'd been gone.

"Do you know how my parents are doing?" I asked.

Her smile fell away. "I've seen them around. I won't lie to

you—things are hard for them right now. They've both lost their jobs, and people don't trust them. But they're safe, and they're still together. They're as free as anyone else in Doldastam."

I let that sink in for a moment. My parents were safe, and they were together.

"How did you get out of Doldastam?" I asked.

"Pretty much the same way you did," Tilda said. "I snuck out with Ridley."

My heart skipped a beat at the mention of his name. "What do you mean, Ridley?"

"He can explain it to you better. He convinced Mina to send him out on an errand."

"He can explain it?" I asked, and my mouth suddenly felt dry. "What do you mean? Where is he?"

"He's here." Tilda motioned toward the door. "I think he's outside talking with Finn. But you can go see him." She slowly got to her feet. "Mia offered me tea when we got here, and I think I'm going to take her up on the offer."

I stood up, feeling dazed. "Tilda. I am glad you got out, and I'm really glad that you're safe."

She smiled. "Me too. And you have no idea how happy it makes me, knowing that you're safe."

We hugged again, this time quicker than before, and then she left me so I could find Ridley.

THIRTY-SIX

reserve

The clouds that had moved in earlier, darkening the lunch with Queen Wendy and King Loki, had brought rain along with them. It was a heavy garden shower, with thunder rumbling in the distance.

I stepped out into it, not minding the cold drops that fell on my bare shoulders, and looked around for Finn and Ridley. They weren't far from the house, standing underneath the awning that stretched past a barn that had once housed goats.

Ridley had his back to me as I approached, but the lines of his body were unmistakable to me. His strong shoulders, the narrowing of his waist beneath his loose olive jacket, the dark curls of his hair that could never be completely tamed.

When I reached them, Finn excused himself, and nodded at me as he walked toward the house. It seemed to take ages for Ridley to turn around to face me, but in reality, it was probably only a few seconds.

And then he was looking at me—the strong line of his jaw darkened by a few days' stubble, the richness of his olive skin, his lips barely parted as he breathed, and the dark mahogany of his eyes burning with an intensity that made everything inside me melt.

Ridley was really here. *My* Ridley.

It wasn't until then that I realized I'd been holding my breath, and I breathed in deeply. He lowered his eyes, hiding his gaze behind his heavy lashes.

"What are you doing here?" I asked finally.

"I came to find you," he said, his voice low and thick, and it sounded strangely far away. Like he was holding something back.

Calvin, Hanna's small pony, was out in the yard, running around and splashing in the puddles. Ridley turned, preferring to look out at the pony than at me.

The thatched roof of the awning had seen better days, and rain dripped in around us. It soaked the bales of straw stacked up beside us, and beneath my bare feet the ground was cold and muddy. Other than Calvin, we were alone. And Ridley wouldn't look at me.

A shiver ran through me, but it wasn't because I was cold.

"You're soaking wet," he commented, glancing at me out of the corner of his eye. "You want my jacket?"

I shook my head, but he'd already started slipping it off. He walked over to me and draped his jacket over my shoulders. His hand brushed against my bare skin, and he smelled cold and crisp, the way he always did. As he adjusted the jacket, he looked down at me. For a moment we were looking into each other's eyes, and all I could think about was the night we'd spent together.

Then he looked away and stepped back from me. I slipped my arms into the sleeves, which were still warm from his body heat. I wondered dourly if this was as close as he would get to touching me.

The distance between us felt immeasurable. The last time I'd seen him, he'd held me in his arms and kissed me deeply. He'd wanted to run away with me, but it had been dangerous, and I needed him to stay behind and make sure my parents and Tilda and Ember were okay.

Every night since, I'd had nightmares about him being ripped away from me. And as we stood here, with so much tension filling the gulf between us, I feared that all my nightmares had come true.

"Why did you come find me?" I asked. "You knew where I was. You sent me here."

"I had to get out of Doldastam," he said simply. "Queen Mina wants you captured and convicted, and I managed to convince her that I wanted that too. That you'd betrayed me so badly that I would go out and bring you back for her."

I swallowed hard. "Do you think I betrayed you?"

"No, of course not." He dismissed the idea immediately. "I just had to tell Mina that so I could get out of there."

"What's your plan now that you're here?" I asked.

He let his eyes rest on me. "Honestly, I don't have one."

"It's hard to know what to do when everything is falling apart."

Ridley rubbed the back of his neck, then turned away, again watching Calvin prance through puddles. Without looking at me, he asked, "You're working with Konstantin Black now? When did that start?"

"After I left," I said, realizing how much I had to explain to Ridley. How much had happened while we'd been apart. "He found me. He defected from Viktor, and he thought we might help each other."

"Have you been?"

"I think so," I said.

"He hasn't . . . hurt you or anything?" Ridley looked at me, and there was no jealousy in his eyes—only genuine concern.

I shook my head quickly. "No. No, nothing like that."

"Good. It's just . . ." He sighed. "For weeks, I didn't know what was happening with you. I was worrying about all the terrible things that might be going on."

"I had a run-in with a bear, but otherwise, I'm okay." I tried to force a smile, to ease some of the tension, but it didn't work.

"Finn told me about that," was all Ridley said.

"I worried about you too," I said, deciding that speaking from the heart might work better. "I thought of you every day, and I was so afraid of what might be happening to you." His jaw clenched, and he stared down at a small stone that he kicked at absently. "What happened after I left?"

"It's over now," he said, almost growling. "That's what matters."

"What does that mean?"

"It's getting cold out here. I think I'm gonna head back inside." Rather abruptly, he started to walk past me.

"Ridley," I said, but he just kept going.

I pulled his jacket more tightly around me and tried to make sense of what had just happened. This was not at all how I'd pictured my reunion with Ridley. There had been much more kissing.

I was so relieved to see him, to know that he was okay, but after that exchange, I had no idea how to feel.

From the corner of my eye, I saw movement. I quickly turned my head, but I couldn't see anything. Then it moved again, and in the shadows between the doorway to the barn and stacks of straw, I realized that I could see a black shirt, floating disembodied thanks to the chameleonlike skin of the Kanin.

Someone was there, spying on me.

THIRTY-SEVEN

derailed

I rushed over, preparing to get the jump on whoever it was, as my mind raced with thoughts of a Kanin spy stowing away with Ridley. Someone working for Mina coming to gather information and trap us.

But just before I punched at the black shirt, I heard Konstantin's voice. "Easy, white rabbit! It's just me!"

He appeared to materialize out of thin air—the brown brick of the wall and the dirty yellow of the straw quickly shifting to his normal skin tone. Konstantin had his hands up defensively, but since he had been eavesdropping on me, I punched him in the arm anyway. Not very hard, but enough to let him know that I was annoyed.

He scowled at me as he rubbed his shoulder. "That was uncalled-for."

"Why were you stalking me like that?" I demanded.

"I wasn't. I just came out to talk to you, and then you were in the middle of something, and I didn't want to interrupt the moment, so I just thought I'd hide out and wait for it to be over," Konstantin said. "And it's over now."

I narrowed my eyes at him. "That's creepy. Don't be creepy."

"What was going on with that guy anyway?" he asked. "Is he your boyfriend?"

I ran my hand through my wet hair and turned away from Konstantin. "Never mind."

"That's just as well. I didn't come out here to talk about him anyway."

"What did you come out for?"

"Mia got a call from the palace." He motioned vaguely behind me, in the direction of where the palace sat hidden among the trees a mile down the road. "Those friends of yours came in through the gate, so the Queen got word of it. She wants to meet with you and Ridley in the morning to discuss what's happening."

"Discuss what?" I asked.

"Probably why there's like half a dozen people hiding out in Finn's house, and how long everyone plans on staying here," he said.

I nodded. "That makes sense."

"I overheard Mia say that Ridley is the Överste now?" Konstantin asked.

"He was before I left. I'm not sure if he still is. I'm not sure about anything anymore . . ." I trailed off.

"Ridley's younger than me, and he wasn't on the

Högdragen, so I didn't really know him," Konstantin explained. "But you know how small the tracker school was, so I knew of him. He always seemed like a punk kid with a chip on his shoulder. I didn't know he had it in him to be the Överste."

"That was a long time ago," I reminded Konstantin. "He's grown up since then. We all have."

"Time does have a way of doing that to you."

He was right, and I realized how much the last few months had changed us—me, Ridley, Tilda, and even Konstantin. It was strange to look back and realize how much simpler things had been before I caught sight of Konstantin following Linus Berling.

"That one moment changed everything and put it all in motion," I said, thinking aloud.

Konstantin's thick brows rose in surprise, and then, as if reading my mind, he said, "When you got into my car in Chicago. It changed the course of my life entirely."

"Good. Your life needed a change of course."

He smirked. "That it did."

I turned away, staring out at the pouring rain around us. "Now where do we go from here?"

"I don't know. But I can't see anything good for you in Doldastam." He shook his head. "Only death and destruction."

gathering

An awkward night spent in Finn and Mia's increasingly cramped house did nothing to ease the tension between Ridley and me. I wanted to talk to him, to find out what was going on, but it was impossible to get a moment alone. There was always someone—usually Liam—in the way.

I'd taken the floor in Hanna's room, so Tilda could have the bed, and Ulla had gone back to Liam's room again. Ridley slept on the couch, while Konstantin strangely took the stables, insisting he'd gotten used to sleeping anywhere.

In the morning, I awoke with an awful crick in my neck. The bandages on my side were a bit bloodier than normal, probably from pressing too hard on the floor, but it was nothing that I couldn't survive.

First thing after breakfast, Ridley and I walked down to the palace for the meeting with Queen Wendy. We spoke very little on the way there, mostly commenting on the weather or the way the gravel stung my feet. Even though we were together for the first time in ages, the distance between us stretched further than ever before.

We'd been shown into the palace and left to wait outside the Queen's office. Presumably, she had some business to attend to before she'd let us in. There was no waiting area, so we stood in the hall just outside the office.

Ridley leaned back against the wall, staring down the corridor with a look of boredom and annoyance. The top few buttons of his shirt had been left undone, the way they usually were, but I noticed that his rabbit amulet was absent. It had been his gift from the kingdom upon becoming Rektor three years ago, and I'd never seen him without it before.

I wanted to ask him where it was or why he wasn't wearing it, but I doubted I'd get any kind of answer from him. Everything he'd said to me since he'd been here had been little more than a word or a grunt. It was like he couldn't even bring himself to speak to me.

I did my best to keep my head up and my expression neutral, like this wasn't breaking my heart all over again.

"One thing's for sure," Ridley said at length. "We can't all keep staying at Finn's house."

"I plan on leaving soon anyway," I told him honestly.

He jerked his head to look at me. "Why? Where are you going?"

"Doldastam."

His eyes darkened. "You can't go back there. Mina will have you killed."

"I didn't realize you even cared," I replied wearily.

"What are you talking about? Of course I care," Ridley said in an angry whisper.

I studied him, standing across from me. His hands were clenched on the chair rail that ran along the wall behind him, and his expression had softened. For one of the first times since he'd arrived in Förening, I could actually see the guy I'd fallen in love with.

"Do you?" I asked softly.

He stepped away from the wall and moved toward me. With only inches between us, he stopped, and looked down at me in the way that made my heart beat erratically. He had this wonderful, dizzying way of making the whole world disappear for a few moments, so it was only me and him, and all the rest of my fears and worries fell away.

Ridley opened his mouth like he meant to say something, but I'll never know exactly what it was, because the Queen's office door opened, interrupting us, and Ridley quickly stepped back from me.

Chancellor Bain leaned out into the hallway, hanging onto the door as he did, and offered us an apologetic smile. "Sorry to keep you waiting. But the Queen is ready to see you now."

"Thank you," Ridley said. He glanced at me from the corner of his eye and straightened his shirt, then followed Bain into the office.

I took a second longer to collect myself. Thanks in part to my much fairer skin flushing so noticeably, it was a bit harder for me to return to normal after moments like that with Ridley.

The Queen's office was smaller than I'd expected. The entire exterior wall consisted of floor-to-ceiling windows, which helped it feel a bit larger than it actually was. Two of the three interior walls were all shelves filled to the brim with books.

A large oak desk sat in the center of the room. Along the edges, vines had been carved into it, but that was a reoccurring theme throughout the room, with vines carved into crown molding and the frames around the window.

On the wall across from the desk were two large paintings—one of the previous Queen Elora, Wendy's mother, and the other was of Wendy, her husband, and an adorable boy of about three years old, presumably their son, Prince Oliver.

When I came into the room, Bain sat cross-legged in one of the leather chairs in front of the desk, while Ridley preferred to stand, leaving the other chair empty. Wendy was standing with her hands on the desk, leaning forward to look down at the papers spread over it.

"Can you close the door behind you?" she asked absently, still staring down at the papers before her.

I did as I was told, and when I came back to stand beside Ridley, I got a better look at what held her attention so raptly. It was a scroll, with a quartz paperweight placed at either end to keep it from rolling up. Still, a portion had flipped just enough for me to see the wax seal at the top—a rabbit pressed in white wax. The symbol of the Kanin.

Trolls weren't completely prehistoric—they would call or send e-mail, even text. It was so much faster than airmail, even though that scroll had probably been overnighted to a local town by FedEx and retrieved by a Trylle messenger. But we used scrolls for formal business, like invitations, gratitude, proclamations, and declarations of war.

I waited, holding my breath, to find out which one of those it was, although with Mina, I feared I already knew the answer.

THIRTY-NINE.

proclamation

T hat Queen of yours has gone totally mad," Wendy said
finally.

"She's no Queen of mine," I replied without thinking, and
Bain smiled in approval, causing his blue eyes to light up.

Wendy straightened, but kept her eyes fixed on the scroll.
"This just arrived, so it isn't what I'd invited you here to talk
about. I only meant to ask you about your plans in Förening.
But I know about your past relationship with the Skojare, so
I'm sure you'd want to know."

"Know what?" I asked, instantly fearing that something
had happened to Linnea Biâelse, or perhaps her husband
Mikko or grandmother Lisbet.

The Queen finally looked at us, her dark tawny eyes sad.
"The Kanin have declared war on the Skojare."

"What?" Ridley asked, sounding as shocked as I felt.

"Why would Mina do that?" I asked in disbelief. "She'd aligned herself with them to get their . . ."

And that's when it hit me. Mina had not been working with the Skojare as a whole—she'd been working with specific people, like the now-dead Kennet Biâelse and the now-exiled head guard Bayle Lundeen.

She had no one to get her the sapphires anymore, so she would have to take them by force.

"It's all here." Wendy motioned to the scroll. "Assuming you can make sense of her nonsense."

Ridley went over to read it for himself, but I sat back in the chair, feeling rather light-headed. Besides, it didn't really matter what reasoning Mina gave. I knew the truth.

"She's blaming Evert's death on Kennet, even though Kennet died before Evert did," Ridley said, surmising what he'd read. "She says Kennet had 'empoisoned' the wine he gifted them before he died, which is said to have killed Evert."

"Since she's accused me of killing Kennet, am I exonerated now?" I asked, not that I believed that that would actually happen. Mina would never let me go free.

"No, because you apparently killed Kennet in some sort of lover's spat, and you've been corrupted by the 'aberrations and unfettered debauchery' of Storvatten." Ridley stood up. "She keeps using all these abnormal words like that. I mean, they are words, but not ones that we actually use."

"Her language is odd, even for a proclamation like this," Wendy agreed.

"At the end, it says, when the Kanin are through, 'the ground will be *sanguinolent.*'" Ridley shook his head. "I don't even know what that means."

"It means 'tinged with blood,'" Bain supplied. "I looked it up."

"It's her British accent all over again." I rested my elbow on the armrest and propped my head up. "She's trying so hard to sound smart and important, because she's really just a spoiled, uneducated princess that got dropped in the middle of nowhere when she was too young to know any better, and nobody taught her how to act or grow up. Everything she pretends to be is just copied from Disney and Julie Andrews."

"Does that mean that she won't actually go through with all of this?" Wendy asked hopefully. "That this is all just part of her act?"

"Oh, no, she's definitely going to attack the Skojare. She's a monster," Ridley said, and that hardness had returned to his face, the same hardness that kept me at bay.

"She's going to slaughter them," I realized sadly, and looked over at Bain. "You worked in Storvatten. You know. They have no means of protecting themselves."

He nodded grimly. "Their guard is an absolute joke. The Kanin going after the Skojare will be like shooting fish in a barrel, pardon the pun."

Wendy's dark hair was up in a loose bun, but the silver lock fell over her forehead, and she brushed it back, causing her emerald bracelets to jangle. She walked around the desk, so she was closer to Bain, Ridley, and me, and leaned back against it.

"We want to help the Skojare, but we're in an awful position," Wendy began. "We're allies of both the Kanin and the Skojare, which means that technically we shouldn't get involved. But at the same time, I'm not about to stand by and let an entire tribe be destroyed.

"Mina sent that scroll asking us to rally behind the Kanin's unwarranted attack, which is so ludicrous." Wendy rolled her eyes. "I honestly don't know what she's thinking. But her overzealousness, I think, may be her downfall.

"However, that doesn't mean I can just jump into the fray," she went on. "I need to consult with advisers and talk to the board, and come up with the best possible solution I can."

I stood up. "I appreciate your position, and I know that you will do all that you can. Until then, *I'm* going to do all that I can."

"Meaning?" Wendy asked.

"I'm going to Storvatten, and I'm going to help prepare them for war."

tavvaujutit

W ait!" Ulla shouted, practically tripping over herself
as she ran up the muddy embankment toward me.
"*Wait!*"

I looked back up at the top of the hill, where Ridley, Konstantin, and Tilda were all standing at the SUV, making me feel like I was on the *Titanic* and they were escaping on the last life raft.

Instead of rushing up to join them the way I wanted to, I sighed and turned back to face Ulla. When she reached me, she was panting, and tears sparkled in her amber eyes.

"Ulla," I said as gently as I could. "We already discussed this. It's dangerous for you to come with us. Besides, you're a huge help to Mia and Finn. They need you here."

"I know, I know." She tried to shrug it off like it was no big deal, but the hurt was etched into her face. "I just . . ." Abruptly, she held her arm out, with a leather strap hanging from her fist. "I made you this, and I didn't want you to leave without it."

I held out my hand, and she unceremoniously dropped the necklace into my hand. Tied onto the strap was a piece of ivory. It had been crudely carved into a rabbit, but it was still unmistakable that that's what it was.

"Because Konstantin always calls you white rabbit," Ulla explained. "I thought it must be a nickname or something." She shook her head. "I don't know. It's probably stupid."

"No, it's great. Thank you." I dropped the necklace around my neck and smiled at her.

"Anyway, you should probably get going," Ulla said.

I nodded, and she hugged me gruffly. It was a case of her not knowing her own strength, and she nearly cracked my ribs when she squeezed me. When she let go, she started backing away.

"Tavvaujutit," she said, saying good-bye in Inuktitut— *tah-vow-voo-teet.*

"Tavvaujutit," I said, and she turned and jogged back to Mia and Finn's house.

I continued up the slope to the SUV. Tilda and Konstantin had gotten in the backseat, but Ridley waited outside, leaning against the driver's side. He didn't say anything when I reached him, choosing to just get into the vehicle instead.

Ridley started the SUV and headed down the narrow, winding roads of Förening toward the gate, and I leaned back in my seat.

"Just because I'm pregnant doesn't mean I won't hurt you

if you try anything," Tilda warned Konstantin, and I knew that she meant it.

Despite my assurances that Konstantin was on our side, Tilda was reluctant to trust him. I suppose having her husband killed by someone I'd trusted made her question my judgment, and I couldn't really blame her for that.

"I already told you, I'm not going to try anything," Konstantin said, exasperated. "I should've taken the Mustang."

"It's better if we ride together," Ridley explained to him again. "We'll draw less attention, and the last thing any of us want is to garner attention from either the Kanin or Viktor's men."

Konstantin let out a heavy sigh, and I looked up in the rearview mirror to watch him sulking in the backseat. "This is gonna be a long ride to Storvatten."

Yesterday, after we'd gotten back from the meeting with Wendy and Bain where they explained that the Kanin had declared war on the Skojare, we all sat down and talked about what we were going to do. I had already made up my mind that I was going to Storvatten, and Konstantin quickly volunteered to go with me.

Ridley had slowly warmed to the idea. Even though he wanted to do everything he could to avoid getting captured by the Kanin, he knew that the Skojare needed us, and despite his misgivings, he wasn't about to stand by and do nothing.

I'd wanted Tilda to stay behind in Förening, where she'd be safer, but she insisted on coming with us. She wanted to do something to help stop the people who were indirectly responsible for Kasper's death. And as of late, she'd been working as a captain in the Kanin army, helping train the soldiers. She would be an excellent asset for the Skojare in helping them get their troops in shape.

So we'd headed out to Storvatten that morning with a light drizzle following us everywhere we went. It soon became apparent that the eight-hour drive from Förening to Storvatten was going to be even longer than normal, thanks to the frequent pit stops needed by Tilda.

We weren't even halfway through the trip, and we were on our third break. We were on a relatively empty stretch of highway, so Ridley pulled over and Tilda ran out into the thick brush of the ditch.

I got out with Tilda every time, just in case she might need me. I doubted that she would, but I didn't like the idea of leaving a pregnant woman alone like that. While she ran through the ditch, I got out and waited next to the car.

"I told you this would be a long drive," Konstantin said, climbing out of the backseat.

"Why are you getting out?" I asked.

"I need to stretch my legs." He paced alongside the SUV, unmindful of the fact that the drizzle was getting heavier.

Beyond the ditch was a cold gray fog. We'd been taking back roads to avoid suspicion, and it had been a while since we'd crossed paths with another car. It felt still and eerie on the side of the road, and I was looking forward to getting to our destination.

I shivered and pulled my hooded sweatshirt more tightly around me.

Suddenly Konstantin tensed up, looking around like a hunting dog that's found its prey. I was about to ask him what was wrong when he said, "We're not alone."

And then Tilda screamed.

FORTY-ONE

strike

Tilda stood on the other side of the ditch, with brush between us, and her eyes were wide and frantic as she
pointed toward us. "Behind you!"

Before I had a chance to look, Konstantin pushed me out
of the way, knocking me to the ground, and he lunged at
what appeared to be nothing—just empty space. But when
Konstantin's fist collided loudly with his opponent's bare
flesh, I saw the mirage-like shimmer of his skin. The chame-
leon coloring of the stark landscape around us changing to
the tanned tones of Kanin skin.

"Get my daggers out of my bag!" Konstantin commanded.

As I scrambled from the ground, the guy Konstantin was
fighting had finally shifted back to normal, and I realized
that it was Drake Vagn. He'd once been a tracker in Doldastam, but he was more than ten years older than me, so I didn't
really know him.

But I do remember the big fit he'd thrown when he'd been forced to retire six years ago. He'd eventually left Doldastam and the entire Kanin kingdom over it, and it had not been on good terms.

"You thought you could switch teams, eh?" Drake asked Konstantin, smirking as he punched him in the face.

Then came the loud sound of crunching metal, and the SUV lurched to the side, slamming into me and knocking me down. I lay perpendicular with the vehicle, squishing down in the mud as much as I could. For a brief second, the vehicle was actually over me—the metal entrails of it mere inches above my face. I'd turned my head to the side, watching as the tires skidded to a stop in the ditch beside me.

As quickly as I could, I crawled out from underneath toward the back of the SUV, and I got to my feet. Peering around, I discovered why it had suddenly lurched to the side.

A massive beast of a man was standing next to the driver's door, which had been severely dented in, causing the window to crack into a million pieces. That explained why Ridley hadn't gotten out yet—the angry hulk had punched in the door, momentarily trapping him inside.

Based on the hulk's size alone, I guessed he was Omte. He could easily push in the shattered window and grab Ridley, but he seemed to prefer glaring down at him, smiling like a shark. His dark hair went down his back in a thick ponytail, and he was shirtless, displaying a series of thick tribal tattoos that covered his torso.

Konstantin and Drake had moved their fight to the road,

matching each other blow-for-blow, and I registered the insults they were hurling at each other just enough to put together that they'd both been working together for Viktor before Konstantin had defected.

I opened the hatchback and saw that Ridley was crawling across the seats with the aim of getting out of the back passenger door. I grabbed Konstantin's worn leather satchel and hurriedly started digging through it.

Everywhere he went, Konstantin carried two long, sharp daggers. They had been his gift when he'd become the Queen's personal guard, and they were made with the highest-quality metal with ornate ivory carvings in the handle. They were beautiful, but most importantly, they were deadly.

I just caught sight of one of the blades in the bag when I felt a huge hand crushing me around my waist. I tried to hang on to the bag, but suddenly I was sailing backward, and I lost my grip. The bag tumbled to the ground, and I heard the daggers clattering against the pavement.

It all happened so quickly, and I was flying through the air before landing painfully against the damp asphalt of the highway. It took me a second to catch my breath, then I pushed myself up onto my elbows to see the giant stomping toward me with that awful toothy grin on his face.

Across his chest, he had the word MÅNE tattooed in huge black letters, and as he rapidly approached—he walked slow and deliberately, but he took giant steps—all I could think about was Ulla. She was a fourteen-year-old half-Omte and she'd pushed the two-ton SUV out of the snow. And this guy was at least a foot taller than Ulla, with hands the size of her head and arms thicker than her waist.

He was going to crush me with his bare hands.

As I jumped to my feet, my mind raced, trying to figure out how I could possibly fight someone as strong as this Måne guy. Behind him, I saw Ridley running toward him, wielding a huge chain. Based on the size of it and the hooks on either end, I guessed it was a towing chain that had been in the back of the SUV.

Ridley swung it hard, whipping Måne in the back. That would've been enough to knock a normal man down, but it barely fazed him. He stopped walking and turned to face Ridley, and he growled. Actually growled, like a wolf guarding a bone.

But Ridley didn't back down. He swung the chain again, harder, and this time the hook managed to take hold in the tough flesh of Måne's shoulder. I think Ridley's plan was to pull Måne down and tie him up with the chain.

But that's not what happened. Måne yanked the chain and pulled Ridley toward him, and I knew that I would have to act fast if I didn't want Måne to crush both of us.

I raced past Måne back toward the SUV and grabbed a dagger off the highway. Behind me, I heard Ridley let out a guttural moan that made my blood run cold.

When I turned back I saw that Måne had gotten the chain around Ridley's neck. He stood behind him, pulling the chain taut with his enormous hands, and as Ridley clawed futilely at the chain, his face had begun to turn purple.

I charged at Måne, and holding the dagger with both hands, I drove it into his back. I did it again and again, each time causing more blood to splatter back on me. It took five thrusts of the blade between his shoulders before he finally dropped to his knees. That brought him low enough so I could jab it into his spine, severing his brain stem, and he fell forward onto the road.

Ridley crawled out from underneath him, gasping for breath. His neck was red and raw and bleeding in a few places, but otherwise he looked like he would survive.

"Thank you," he said between breaths.

"Anytime," I said, then turned my attention to the fight between Konstantin and Drake.

It was still going strong, but Konstantin's face was looking more bloodied than Drake's. He was taking a beating.

I moved down the highway toward them. Drake had his back to me, and as soon as Konstantin looked at me, I tossed the dagger to him. He caught it easily just as Drake tried to come at him again. With one quick move, Konstantin sliced Drake's throat, and he collapsed to the ground.

Konstantin wiped the blood from his face, then stepped over Drake's body to walk to where Ridley and I were standing in the middle of the road.

"That's it, then," Ridley said, surveying the carnage around us.

Someone whistled loudly from the ditch, and I realized too late that we'd forgotten about Tilda. I couldn't see anything from where I stood, so I ran closer to the SUV, and then I saw them, standing in the brush just on the other side of the vehicle.

Bayle Lundeen—the former Skojare head guard—had one arm wrapped around Tilda, pressing her to him, while the other one held a knife to her throat. She had her hands on his arm, trying to pull it away, but he didn't seem to be budging.

"It's not quite over yet," Bayle warned me.

avenge

K onstantin rushed behind me but I put my arm out to stop him, so he didn't go charging toward them. Bayle's knife was poised to slice right through Tilda's throat, and he raised his arm higher, making Tilda squirm.

Ridley came up beside me, and we stood frozen on the embankment, unsure of what the next move should be.

"You don't have to do this," I said, trying to remain calm, and I was acutely aware of the bloodied blade clenched in Konstantin's fist.

"I really didn't want it to come to this," Bayle admitted, but he didn't relax his stance.

When I'd been at Storvatten before, it had been hard for me to get a clear read on Bayle. He'd been standoffish but professional when Kasper and I interacted with him. We were never able to entirely discern what Bayle's role was in everything that had transpired in Storvatten, but as the head guard, he'd definitely had his hand in things.

It had been his guard, Cyrano, who attempted to murder King Mikko, and it had almost certainly been Bayle who falsified the safe records that got Mikko arrested. From the best I could gather, he'd been working with Kennet from the start of the fallen Prince's plan to dethrone Mikko.

If it hadn't been for Bayle, I wasn't sure how much Kennet would've been capable of on his own. But I doubt Mikko would've been arrested, which meant that Kennet wouldn't have come to Doldastam to pay Mina for her help, and then Kasper wouldn't have been killed.

"I worked my ass off for that *kingdom,* if you can even call it that," he said, his words dripping with venom. "For years. All I wanted was to be paid my dues! And Kennet came up with this plan, and it would all be so simple."

"It can still be simple," I said. "Killing an innocent will only complicate things."

Bayle snorted. "Since Kennet turned against me and deposed me, I've been sentenced to doing Viktor's dirty work. I'm up to my neck in blood! What's one more bitch?"

"Viktor will turn on you too," Konstantin warned him. "The same way he's turned on me."

"I'm not an idiot like you. I just wanna get *paid,*" Bayle sneered. "And right now, Viktor is offering a massive reward for delivering the three of you." He nodded toward Ridley, myself, and Konstantin. Then he looked down at Tilda, almost speaking in her ear. "What's one more body to add to the pile?"

"If you hurt her, you will not leave here alive," I growled at him. "I will kill you with my bare fucking hands, Bayle."

Bayle started to laugh. "Oh, you really think so?"

Something flashed in Tilda's eyes, and her body tensed up. Her expression hardened, and there was a resolve in her that I knew all too well from training with her. Tilda was a master of restraint, but she could destroy someone if she wanted to.

"Wait," Tilda said in a stilted voice. "This is Bayle Lundeen? Bayle, who conspired with Kennet? Bayle, who's one of the reasons my husband is dead?"

I nodded once. "Yeah. That's him."

For the first time, Bayle seemed to realize he might have bitten off more than he could chew, and he looked down at Tilda with new appreciation. Tilda may be pregnant, but she was still tall and strong, with muscular arms and powerful legs.

I was sure that when Bayle had first captured her, she'd been more docile so as not to risk him hurting the baby. But now she was pissed.

With one sudden jerk, she flung her head backward, smashing into Bayle's face. From where I stood several feet away from her, I heard the sound of his nose crunching. Before he could tilt the knife toward her, she grabbed his wrist, bent it backward, and, using her other arm as leverage, she broke his arm with a loud snap.

It all happened within a few seconds, and Bayle screamed in pain and stumbled back. His arm hung at a weird angle, and blood streamed down his face. But Tilda wasn't done yet.

With a swipe of her leg, she kicked his legs out from under him. He fell back into the mud, and Tilda kicked him hard in the groin, causing Konstantin to wince beside me. Then she jumped on top of him, punching him repeatedly in the face with both fists.

His body had gone limp, but I wasn't sure if that was because he was unconscious or dead. Either way, Tilda apparently decided that she wanted to be certain. She grabbed the knife that he'd dropped on the ground beside them, and she stabbed him straight through the heart.

And then she just sat there, kneeling on his dead body and breathing hard. None of us said anything or moved. It felt like she needed the moment to herself.

When she finally stood up, she shook her arms out, probably both because her fists hurt from hitting Bayle so hard and also to get rid of some of the blood.

"Do you feel better?" I asked her.

She nodded, still catching her breath as she walked over to me. "Yeah. We have to do something about these bodies, though. The humans will get suspicious."

"That girl is a fucking beast," Konstantin whispered as she walked by, and he looked at her with newfound admiration.

"You should see her when she's not pregnant," I said.

Tilda went into the SUV and used a bottle of water and a shirt from her bag to clean off the blood. Eventually, the rest of us would probably want to do the same, but right now we needed to focus on getting the bodies out of here before another car came by.

While Ridley and I went to grab Bayle's body, Tilda moved all our bags into the backseat so we wouldn't bloody all our things. Konstantin grabbed Drake's body, throwing it over his shoulder, and then dropping him unceremoniously in the back.

The challenge was not only moving Måne's massive body—which took all three of us—but also loading it into the back of the SUV. We had to fold him into a very strange position to get him to fit.

"There's still one big problem," Tilda said. While we stood at the back of the vehicle, beside the open tailgate, she was still sitting in the backseat and turned to look at us over the pile of bodies. "These guys were clearly Viktor's men, and they found us. How?"

Ridley shook his head. "When we left Doldastam, we threw out our phones, and we ditched the Range Rover and rented a car. I don't know how they could possibly track us." Then he looked over at Konstantin. "Unless someone told them where we'd be."

"They tried to kill me too, remember?" Konstantin snapped. "And how would I know that we'd be at this exact spot on this exact shitty road at this time while Tilda was taking a piss?"

"Then how did they find us?" Ridley asked defensively.

"Probably the same way I found Bryn." He turned back to the bodies and pushed Måne out of the way so he could dig in Drake's pocket. Then he pulled out a lock of dark curly hair and held it up to Ridley. "He was tracking you."

Ridley's face fell, and he ran a hand through his hair, as if he'd be able to feel a missing lock of hair. "Shit."

"Shit indeed." Konstantin gave him a hard look, then he slammed the hatchback shut. He walked around the car and got inside, leaving Ridley and me alone.

"I'm sorry," Ridley said, staring off at the empty field beside us. "I shouldn't have come. Mina knew I would lead her right to you. It's my fault."

"She tricked you," I said. "She's tricked all of us. It's what she's good at."

He set his jaw. "I should've known better."

"It's okay. We're all okay. You're the one that got hurt the worst."

His skin had been red and raw, but it was starting to darken as bruises began to form. He just shook his head. "You guys need to leave me here and go on without me. They could have more people tracking me. You won't be safe with me."

"Ridley, I'm not going to leave you on the side of the road. And even if they do track us, they'd follow us straight to Storvatten, where they plan on attacking anyway. We'll be fine."

He lowered his eyes, swallowing hard. "I'm sorry, Bryn. I shouldn't have come. I just . . ."

"You just what?" I stepped closer to him, and he lifted his eyes to meet mine.

"I just had to see you. I needed to know that you were all right."

I wanted to ask, *Then why are you pushing me away? If you just wanted to be with me, why are you being so distant?*

But I didn't think he would answer, so I just looked up at him, wishing I understood the pain in his eyes.

A car door opened and Konstantin leaned out. "We should probably leave before backup gets here."

FORTY-THREE

crusade

This was the first time Tilda had been to Storvatten, and her eyes widened as she took in the palace. With luminous walls tinged in aqua, curving to mimic waves, it rose from the still waters of the great lake like an enchanted sapphire.

Thick fog had left the palace hidden from the shore, since it sat several miles out in the water. Ridley, Konstantin, Tilda, and I walked almost halfway out on the dock that connected the palace to the land before it started to take shape, a shadow looming behind the gray.

And then there it was, in all its glory. Tilda—who wasn't easily impressed—actually gasped when she saw it. While I still found it magnificent, all the events of the past few weeks seemed to have left me somewhat numb to its magic.

As we approached the large wooden doors of the palace,

they opened before we'd even reached them. The entrance glowed pale white as we walked toward it, and an imposing man stepped forward, reminding me of an alien overlord descending from the mothership.

He was tall and broad-shouldered, especially for a Skojare. They tended to be more petite in frame—Mikko and Kennet Biâelse aside. His blond hair was cropped short, and he was clean-shaven.

The uniform he wore was that of the Skojare guard—a frosty blue, embellished with the insignia of a fish on his lapel. Even without the uniform, there was something very military about him. He stood at attention, with his head high and his blue eyes locked on us.

"I'm Baltsar Thorne." He greeted us formally but politely. He bowed his head slightly, and I noticed the thick black outline of a fish tattooed on the back of his neck. "I'm the new head guard for the Skojare."

Already he looked like a vast improvement from their last head guard, and I'd only just met him.

"It's really you!" Linnea squealed, and I heard her voice echoing through the main hall before I saw her. She dashed across the glass floor, her blue gown billowing around her, and she practically dove at me, hugging me.

When she let go, she stepped back to appraise me. Smiling broadly, she said, "It's really you. The guards at the shack at the end of the dock called up and said you were coming, but I didn't believe them."

"Your Highness," Baltsar said, carefully trying to wedge himself between us. "She has been accused of killing our Prince. It seems prudent to—"

"Oh, she didn't do it." Linnea waved him off, then she took my hand. "Let's go inside and get out of the cold, so we can talk. And you bring your friends—"

It was the first time she'd stopped to look at who was with me, but as soon as she saw Konstantin, her jaw dropped and her already large eyes widened.

"It's you," she gasped and let go of my hand. "You saved my life."

Konstantin lowered his eyes and shifted his weight from one foot to the other, already uncomfortable with her praise. Then she ran over to him and threw her arms around his waist, embracing him tightly.

For his part, Konstantin stood frozen in place with his eyes nervously flitting around. His arms were stiff at his sides, like he was afraid to even touch her.

"My Queen, it's not advised to . . . *hug* guests before we have a chance to vet them," Baltsar tried unsuccessfully to reason with her.

Incensed, she stepped away from Konstantin and glared at the guard. "This man saved my life! He's a hero! He doesn't need to be vetted! They're all guests of the kingdom, and they're all welcome inside."

Baltsar sighed, apparently realizing the futility of arguing with her. "If it's as you wish, Your Majesty."

"Come in, come in, everyone!" Linnea motioned for us to

follow her as she walked inside the palace, her platinum curls bobbing as she walked. Her dress was cut very low in the back, to just above her waist, and it compensated for that by having a long satin train that flowed out behind her.

Baltsar bowed slightly again and gestured for us to enter, so I smiled politely and followed Linnea inside.

"Just to let you know, there's a couple bodies in the back of the SUV you probably want to take care of," Ridley told Baltsar as he walked by.

"We already killed them for you, so it shouldn't be that much of a problem," Konstantin added.

"Pardon?" Baltsar asked, looking startled. "Who did you kill?"

"Don't worry," Konstantin said over his shoulder as we entered the grand main hall. "They were Viktor Dålig's men." When Baltsar still appeared puzzled, Konstantin elaborated. "The men that declared war on you."

Linnea had been walking ahead, intent on showing us all in and seeming to ignore the exchange between Konstantin, Ridley, and Baltsar, but as soon as the word *war* was uttered, she'd stopped cold.

In the rotunda, sandblasted glass shaped like waves surrounded us—opaque, with a hint of light turquoise showing through. Below us, the floors were glass, windows to the pool. Chandeliers sparkled with diamonds and sapphires, casting light all around us. It gave the effect of standing in a whirlpool, and right now Linnea was in the dead center of it.

"Well, the Kanin actually declared war," Ridley said,

correcting Konstantin in a conversational tone. "If you want to get technical."

"He seems like the kind of guy who'd want to get technical." Konstantin pointed toward Baltsar.

"That's true," Ridley agreed. "But either way, Viktor Dålig's men will attack the Skojare. They're probably helping the Kanin, so it's all the same difference."

"Yeah." Konstantin looked over at Baltsar. "The point is that we helped you by killing those men."

Linnea still had her back to us, and she turned around slowly to face everyone. All the lightness and playfulness that usually enveloped her had fallen away. Her skin had paled even more than normal, and the translucent gills on her neck weren't moving.

"Did you say war?" Linnea asked in a voice so soft I wasn't sure that Ridley or Konstantin had heard her from where they stood several feet back. Tilda and I were right behind Linnea, and even I barely heard it.

"Didn't you . . ." Ridley glanced over to me, looking for help, but I had none to give. "Didn't you get the proclamation? From the Kanin?"

Linnea shook her head once. "No. We've received no correspondence from the Kanin since they told us of Kennet's death."

"I saw it yesterday." Ridley motioned to me. "We both did. At the Trylle palace. Mina—um, excuse me, Queen Mina sent the scroll to the Trylle Queen declaring war on the Skojare."

"That's why we came here," I explained. "We wanted to see if you needed help preparing for it."

"Of course we need help," Linnea replied emptily, and then she looked past me at Baltsar. "Our worst fears have come true. They're going to kill us all."

FORTY-FOUR

defensive

Marksinna Lisbet Ahlstrom—the acting ruler of the Skojare and Linnea's grandmother—stood with her back toward the meeting room as she stared out at the dark water that surrounded us. Her golden hair was up, and her sapphire chandelier earrings hung past the high collar of her jacket. Wavelike designs were embroidered in the cerulean fabric, and the hem of her jacket just hit the floor.

We were in the meeting room underwater, where half of the room stuck out from the palace with a domed wall of glass, creating a fishbowl effect. The last time I had been here, King Mikko had been arrested. And now we were discussing war.

Baltsar, Ridley, Konstantin, and I sat at the end of the very long table. Linnea had been too shell-shocked to be of much assistance, and Tilda had feigned needing help to keep her preoccupied. For the past hour we'd been in the meeting room, explaining to Lisbet and Baltsar everything we knew.

While we spoke, Lisbet had paced the room, listening to us tell them about Mina's relation to Viktor, her involvement in Kennet's scheme, and her plot to steal the jewels now that Kennet and Bayle were out of the picture.

When we'd finished, she stopped and stared out at the lake. Night had fallen upon us, making the water too dark to see anything, but Lisbet kept staring out, as if an answer to all their problems would come swimming up to the glass.

"After he was killed, I realized that Kennet had to be involved in Mikko's imprisonment somehow," Lisbet said finally. "I wore black for three days until Kennet's funeral, as is customary, but I haven't worn it since. I mourned publicly because I had to, but I won't shed a tear for anyone that tries to hurt my granddaughter."

Then she turned to face us. In her sixties, she'd begun to show the signs of her advancing years, but she still carried the grace and beauty of her youth. She commanded the room like a Queen, even though she'd never really been one.

"What would you have us do?" Lisbet asked. "How do we stop this?"

Konstantin sat with his elbows on the table and his hands together in front of his face, almost like he was praying except that his hands were clenched too tightly. "You can't stop this. Once Mina has her mind set, there's nothing you can do to talk her out of it."

"What if we offered her our jewels?" Lisbet suggested, almost pleading. "We have so many, we must be able to spare a great deal."

"She wants them all." Konstantin lowered his hands. "And even that won't be enough. Since she's had to wait for them, she's annoyed. And she'll want you to suffer for that."

Lisbet rubbed her temple. "Then what do we do?"

"I've been working as the Överste for the Kanin," Ridley said. "And Tilda's been acting captain. We can work with your soldiers and get them ready. We know exactly how the Kanin fight and what they're skilled at."

Lisbet laughed darkly. "You say that as if we have soldiers."

"If Mina hasn't declared war yet, that means you might have some time," I said. "Time to gather people and get them ready."

"Unless, of course, she's planning a surprise attack," Konstantin corrected me, and I shot him a look. "Well, it's true."

"You have one huge advantage, and that's this palace." Ridley motioned around us. "It's an island fortress."

"And we have the spires," Baltsar said, referring to the five towers that rose from the palace. "I've been doing bow training with the guards, so they can man them and shoot at possible intruders."

"It's not a lost cause," Ridley said, trying to sound optimistic.

"There's something else I think you should do," I said. "You should release Mikko."

"Talk to that one." Lisbet pointed at Baltsar. "I want to let him go. I've known he was innocent for a while, but it's Baltsar and the Chancellor and some of the other royals that don't want him out."

Baltsar shook his head. "It's not that I don't want him released. There's not enough evidence to set him free. I was a Markis and I stepped down—I gave up my title and my inheritance because it was more important to me that Storvatten be kept safe. I took this job to make sure it was done right."

"You're going to war. You need him," I persisted.

"I'm the acting monarch. I have all the same power he has," Lisbet said.

"But you're not *King*," I told her emphatically. "Linnea may be Queen, but she's not strong enough yet to lead anyone into war. Mikko has power and presence. And he has a brother he needs to avenge. If it wasn't for Mina, I don't think Kennet would've ever done any of this. Mikko needs to be on the forefront, fighting for your kingdom."

Lisbet seemed to consider this, then she looked past me to Baltsar. "Do it. Let him go."

"Marksinna!" Baltsar protested. "I'm trying to bring order to this kingdom."

"And there won't be a kingdom to bring order to if we don't do everything we need to do!" Lisbet shot back. "Let Mikko go. He needs to be the one to end this."

valedictory

Dear Bryn—   *May 25, 2014*

Everyone's gone and left, and it's lonely without you all. Not that I blame Tilda and Ridley for getting out of here, especially not after what happened to Ridley. But with all of you gone again, the isolation feels so much more intense.

   Thankfully, Delilah is still here. (She has become my rock, my light, my only salvation in this claustrophobic cage. Last night, I snuck into her room, carefully and quietly so none of the guards keeping watch would catch me. We went under the covers in her bed, hiding away from everything around us, and by the dim glow of the flashlight, we read poems by Gustaf Fröding, Karin Boye, and Pär Lagerkvist, and her Swedish is so beautiful to hear. Forgive me if I'm a little verbose today.)

   I'm sorry for rambling on so much about Delilah. I could go on for pages and pages about the beauty of her eyes and the scent of her hair and the strength of her spirit and the warmth of her arms and the taste of her lips . . . But I'm not writing you to go on about her forever (though I could). It's just the only time I feel even close to free anymore is when I'm with her.

It is so contradictory that life can be the worst it's ever been and the best it's ever been all at once. It's strange how love can blossom even in the darkest places.

And it certainly is dark here in Doldastam, and not just because you and Tilda are gone. I know I could've gone with Ridley the way Tilda did, and maybe I should've. My mom would've preferred it if I had.

Four years ago, we left Förening to escape all the turmoil there. We chose Doldastam because my mom's sister lived here with her husband, and it seemed like a quiet, safe place to live. My mom is starting to believe that there isn't a quiet, safe place in the entire troll kingdom, and at night, when she thinks I can't hear, she whispers to my dad about fleeing to live among the humans.

I wonder how you're finding Förening. It's been so long since I've been there. Are you sleeping in my old room? Finn says he hasn't repainted my room yet, so I hope you're enjoying the blotchy clouds I painted years ago.

Maybe I should have left with Delilah, gone back to my old room, gotten away from here. I'd certainly love to see Finn and Mia and the kids. But I couldn't go.

Not just because of Delilah, or even Linus Berling. I've been training with him as often as I can, and while he tries harder than anyone I've ever met, I still feel like he can't protect himself. And I know there's other people like him here.

For every Astrid Eckwell (who is a star pupil under the Queen's new paranoia campaign), there is a Linus Berling. And for every townsperson that screams about stringing up traitors like you, there is a Juni Sköld, disobeying the wishes of the town by still serving your parents in her bakery.(They have, unfortunately, been blacklisted from most of the shops here.)

There are still good people here, and they need someone like me to help them when it comes time to fight. I don't know when that will happen, but I feel it's gotta happen soon. I don't know how much more we can take of this.

Every day things get worse. Yesterday, Omte guards started appearing around town. You know how huge the Omte can get—all of them are over six foot, some over seven, with big heads and muscles bulging out everywhere. Apparently, where they're from is incredibly warm, and they're having a hard time handling the cold, so they're all bulked in winter jackets and hats and scarves even though it reached the forties.

Even with their ridiculous gear, it doesn't make them any less intimidating. They stomp around the cobblestones like they own the damn place. I've actually seen children cry at the sight of them.

Queen Mina held another meeting in the town square after they'd arrived. She stood on the balcony of the clock tower, still wearing all black, including this odd birdcage veil over her eyes. The Omte had arrived unannounced, and by the time she called the meeting, everyone was on edge and scared.

In her grandiose way, with lots of arm gestures and her fake British accent that annoys you so much, Mina explained that the Omte had come here to help protect us. We have so many enemies we needed a stronger guard.

(Though she didn't specify who any of these enemies were, and she hasn't mentioned the name Viktor Dålig in quite some time—apparently he's no longer a threat? Just you and Konstantin Black. And now the Skojare, apparently, but I'm getting ahead of myself.)

She assured everyone that the Omte are here for our protection. Your mom and dad were at the back of the crowd, and I saw the nervous glances they exchanged with each other. I wanted to look as uncomfortable as they did, but since I'm part of the army, I had to put on my best smile and pretend like I thought this was totally brilliant and not complete insanity.

When the King died, Mina wouldn't even allow Kanins from other towns to come and mourn him. But now she'll open the gates to complete strangers from another tribe, a tribe we've had very little contact with over the past century?

Obviously something bad is going on, but I haven't been able to figure out what yet. It's hard when there's so few people I can talk to about this anymore. If I'm being honest, part of the reason I'm writing you this letter is just so I can sort it all out for myself. In your absence, you've become my sounding board.

After explaining the presence of the Omte, Queen Mina went on to announce that she discovered the culprit behind King Evert's murder—Kennet Biâelse. When the crowd cheered, I actually cheered along with them, because I thought finally you'd be cleared.

But, no. She actually raised the accusations, claiming that you were a coconspirator with Kennet. You actually helped him with the poison or some nonsense like that.

Then she concluded that the Skojare could no longer be trusted. You'd betrayed us because of your Skojare blood, and all Skojare are inherently evil.

It was at that point that your parents quickly and quietly made their exit. Unfortunately, they don't live that far from the town square, so I'm sure they could still hear all the vile things Mina was saying about the Skojare.

Later, after everything had died down, I brought a casserole over to them. My mom had made it for them with root vegetables, since she knows that the market has been refusing service to them. Your parents have mostly been subsisting on treats from Juni's bakery and the kindness of strangers.

Your mom was in the bath when I arrived, and your dad answered the door. He says that your mom spends most of the time soaking now. His temples looked grayer than they were the last time I saw him, but otherwise he *looked okay. He says he's just been reading and trying to keep his head down.*

They rarely leave the house, and they keep their thick drapes pulled at all hours since they caught some kids trying to peek in a few days ago.

When your mom came out of the bath, she hugged me and told me how happy she was to see me. I told them that you're safe, hiding in Förening, and she started to cry. Your dad teared up too, and he spent the next five minutes thanking me for helping you. I don't think I've ever seen two people look as relieved as they did then.

They'll need to escape soon, but with the Omte guard around now, it will be even harder than before. Fortunately, the Queen doesn't seem to have noticed that Tilda has escaped yet. Tilda's parents are covering for her, saying she's on bed rest with the baby, anytime anybody asks about her. I think her parents and I are the only ones that really know where she is.

As soon as I see a break in the defenses, I think I'll get my parents and your parents out of here. It's getting too dangerous. The Queen already turned on the Skojare. It won't be much longer before she singles my family out for being Trylle. We've always had the advantage of blending in better than you and your mom did, but nobody really blends in in Doldastam anymore.

Everyone is suspect.

I shouldn't even be writing these letters to you. If the wrong person reads this, I could end up in the dungeon, just for telling the truth about what's going on around here. To be safe, I'm even writing this in the wee hours of the morning, before the sun comes up. But you can never be too safe in Doldastam anymore.

I think this will be the last letter I write you. I have too much to do here. I can't risk getting caught over something silly like this. Besides, I'm not even sure if you'll ever be able to read these.

Until I see you again—
Ember

FORTY-SIX

torment

The meeting with Lisbet, Baltsar, Konstantin, Ridley, and I had gone on rather late into the night, and I'd been very relieved when I was finally able to go to my room. I had fantasies about falling asleep the second my head hit the pillow.

But, even as exhausted as I was, sleep could be a cruel mistress, and it eluded me. I tossed and turned, and spent most of the night staring up at the water spot on the ceiling above my bed.

The grandeur of the exterior of the Skojare palace was misleading. Even though the guest rooms had an air of luxury to them—fine linens, elegant furnishings, even the exterior glass wall that bowed out in the lake—the reality inside was quite different.

A bedroom underwater was cold and smelled musty. The

wallpaper in the halls was peeling, the tiles were warped, and I spotted a tuft of mold growing in the corner.

The dark water of the lake kept out most of the sunlight during the day, but somehow, even with the waning moon in the night sky, it managed to create an odd glowing sensation in the room. Like being in an aquarium, with the shadows of the moving water dancing across the ceiling.

Eventually I decided that I couldn't be the only one having trouble sleeping. I slid out of bed, and the tiles felt like ice on my bare feet.

Since I was still traveling with my thrift shop clothing, I didn't have much in the way of pajamas. I'd gone to bed in an oversized T-shirt with a kraken attacking a ship on it. The neck hole had been stretched out, so it kept slipping off my shoulder, exposing more of my skin to the cold.

I stuck my head out into the hall, and when I saw no guards in the vicinity, I crept out. Tilda's room was directly on the other side of mine, but I figured that between the pregnancy and brutally attacking a guy today, she probably needed her rest.

Instead, I made a beeline for Ridley's room farther down the hall. We'd hardly had a moment alone together since he'd arrived in Förening, and we needed to talk. There was something strange going on with him, and I had to find out what it was.

Slowly, I opened the door and peered around it. Ridley's room was a mirror image of mine, with the glass wall casting that bluish glow through it. Even though it was dim, I could easily see that the bed was messy, like it had been slept in, but it was empty.

I stepped farther into the room, scanning for Ridley, when suddenly someone grabbed me and threw me roughly against the wall, slamming my back into it. Within a second of me entering his room, Ridley had jumped out from behind the door, thrown me into the wall, and pinned me there with his body and his hand around my throat.

"Dammit, Bryn," he whispered when he realized it was me, and let go. "You scared the hell out of me."

"You're the one that attacked me," I said in a hushed voice.

"Sorry." He stepped back from me. "I heard someone sneaking around outside, and I thought it might be one of Viktor's men tracking me or something. I'm just jumpy."

"Viktor's men usually sneak into your room wearing oversized T-shirts?" I asked, attempting to lighten the mood.

"I don't know how they'll come for me." Ridley's voice was low and somber, and his expression was a dark mask, hiding his normally handsome, playful face.

He stood shirtless across from me, wearing loose black pajama pants. They hung low on his waist, revealing the sharp ridges of muscles just above his hips and a thin trail of hair that started just above his pelvis and ran downward.

Part of me was aware of how sexy Ridley looked and how badly I wanted to pull him close to me. But the other part was all too aware of the gulf between us, and how it only seemed to grow wider and darker with each passing moment.

Amanda Hocking

I rubbed my neck where he'd grabbed me and looked away from him.

"Did I hurt you?" he asked and moved closer to me. His hand was on my wrist, angling my arm back so he could get a better look at my throat. And his face tilted down, so close to mine, as he studied me.

I watched him—the way his hair fell over his forehead, his heavy lashes, his wonderful lips, the stubble on his cheek—as he touched me gingerly, and all I wanted was to be with him. To kiss him and feel him close to me again.

Instead, I whispered, "I'm fine."

He lifted his eyes to meet mine. "You sure?"

I nodded, and that was when I realized his neck had fully healed. The skin had been torn raw by the chain, and he'd been left with awful, thick bruises. But now it all looked normal.

"Your neck is better," I said in surprise.

"Lisbet had a healer fix it up. She wants me in top condition for the impending war."

He hadn't moved back from me, and his hand lingered on my wrist. His fingers were strong and warm on my skin, and I loved the way it felt when he touched me.

A heat burned in the pit of my stomach, a longing so intense it made my heart ache. Being so close to him, being able to touch him, but not really, not really hold him close to me, was killing me.

I looked down, really looking at him up close for the first time, and I noticed ridges on his chest and arms. They were perfectly straight raised bumps, half an inch thick and several inches long.

Without thinking, I reached out to touch one, and Ridley flinched and pulled back from me.

"I'm sorry. I didn't mean to hurt you."

He turned his back to me and shook his head. "It didn't hurt. When the healer fixed my neck, she healed those up too."

"What are they? What happened?"

"I just don't want to talk about it."

"Ridley." I moved closer to him. I lifted my hand, meaning to put it on his back, but I was afraid he'd flinch again, so I let it fall to my side. "Please stop shutting me out. What happened in Doldastam after I left?"

He looked at me over his shoulder. "Can you pretend like nothing happened in Doldastam? Can we just forget about it? At least for tonight?"

"If that's what you want."

"I do."

Ridley turned to face me, and held out his hand to me. I hesitated for a moment, but then I took it and let him pull me into his arms. For a moment, when I lay my head against his bare chest, with his arms strong and sure around me, I closed my eyes and tried to pretend that it was the way things were before.

But there was a stiffness in his muscles, a resistance that hadn't been there before.

"Even though you're right here, in my arms, you still feel so far away," I murmured, and saying it aloud hurt so much I could barely speak. "I can't do this."

"What?" Ridley asked, sounding startled as I pulled away from him and stepped back.

"I can't do this. I want to be with you, but only if you're actually here with me. I don't know what's going on with you or with *us*." I swallowed hard. "I can't keep doing this if you won't let me in."

He lowered his eyes and didn't say anything. I waited, hoping that he would finally say *something* real to me. But he didn't, so I turned and started walking away.

"Mina captured me as soon as I came back in the gates," Ridley said when I reached the door, his voice strong but flat. "The guards hauled me off in front of everyone with my arms in shackles."

I faced him, with my hand still on the door. His mouth twisted up as he spoke, and he kept his eyes locked on the floor.

"She tied me to a rack," he said thickly. "That's a medieval torture device. They tie you up by each one of your limbs, and then they pull. Slowly. *Agonizingly* slow." He motioned to his arms. "But that wasn't enough. Mina burned me—holding hot pokers to my flesh."

That explained the ridges on his arms, the ones I'd touched earlier.

"The worst part about it all," he said, shaking his head, "she never asked me anything. I wouldn't have told her, but she didn't even ask. She wasn't torturing me to find anything out—she was doing it because she *could*."

"Ridley," I breathed. I went over to him and reached out to touch his face. He leaned into my palm and closed his eyes. "I'm so sorry."

"No, Bryn, don't be sorry." He put his hand over mine. "Don't ever be sorry. Not about this."

"I don't know what else to say."

"You don't need to say anything." He lowered his hand, then stepped back, away from me, so I let my arm drop to my side. "It's late, and we have a long day tomorrow. You should probably head back to your room and get some sleep."

Startled by the abruptness, I didn't say anything at first. Then I nodded slowly and turned to leave Ridley standing alone in his room, wondering if I had failed him so much that we would never be able to reconcile again.

offense

T hat's not good enough!" Tilda barked, standing over a sweaty Skojare guard.

I'd been sparring with a different guard, but I stopped what I was doing to look over at her. For training today, she'd done her best to look every bit the part of a captain. Her hair was pulled back in a smooth ponytail, and she'd even gotten her hands on a frosty blue Skojare uniform. It fit her well, except that the jacket had to be left open to compensate for her growing belly.

Baltsar had set us up in the ballroom of the palace, since it had the most space. It was an opulent round room with white marble floors. Above us, the ceiling was domed glass, making this one of the few places I'd seen in the Storvatten palace that let in natural light.

The wallpaper had this magical quality, with a pale bluish sheen and a silver design etched into it, but when you looked at it, it seemed to move, like waves on the water. It was unlike anything I'd ever seen before. Every twenty feet or so, the wallpaper was broken up with a marble half pillar.

Baltsar and Ridley had organized the training today, separating the guards into groups based on their experience. Since taking his position a few weeks ago, Baltsar had already begun to rework the guard and hired thirty new recruits. On top of that, with the threat of war, many commoners and even a few of the royals had volunteered to join the makeshift army being built.

Tilda had been tasked with commanding the group of new recruits and volunteers, and she was running them through their paces like a drill sergeant. When they'd first been assigned to her, I'd heard the recruits snickering about how easy they'd gotten it because she was pregnant and a girl. None of them were snickering now.

At the back of the room, Baltsar was commanding his troop. While Tilda focused on more basic endurance and strength training, just trying to get them into proper physical condition, Baltsar was working on sword skills, while Ridley focused on hand-to-hand fighting.

For the most part, Konstantin and I just floated around, sparring with people and helping to show them proper form as needed. Right now Konstantin was standing with Ridley, discussing what to work on next, while Ridley's group ran laps around the ballroom.

Ridley had asked for Konstantin's opinion on several things today in regard to training, and that made sense since

Konstantin had a lot of experience as a tracker, a guard, and practical application in real life. Since Förening, the two had seemed to get along well, and Ridley appeared to trust Konstantin's judgment.

I'd had no input on what was happening today. Konstantin, Ridley, and Tilda actually all outranked me (discounting the fact that Konstantin and I had been exiled, of course). But that meant that while Ridley, Tilda, and Baltsar had to dress in uniforms like commanding officers, and the four of them had to worry and decide what everyone needed to focus on, I just got to get down and dirty.

I was in my tank top and yoga pants, sweating and fighting with whomever I could. And honestly, it felt amazing. In the chaos of everything around me, training in the gym was the one area I could always count on. This was the first time in a long time I'd had a chance to really work off all the aggression I had about feeling so powerless against Mina and Viktor Dålig.

So today, as I punched another one of Tilda's recruits in the jaw, I couldn't help but smile. It felt great to be back.

"Bryn!" Tilda shouted. "You're not supposed to be making contact, remember? This is just training. You don't want to break all the soldiers before they go to battle."

"Right. Sorry. I got a little overzealous." I waved at her, but by the look in her eyes, I knew that wasn't good enough.

She walked over to me, the trainees parting around her. "That's the fourth time I've called you out on it. We've been going at this all day. Why don't you take five?"

"No, I'm good. I don't need it."

"Bryn." She looked at me severely, and I realized it wasn't a suggestion. "Take a break."

"Fine," I said because there was no point in arguing with her.

I apologized to the guy I'd hit, then I turned and walked away. I tried not to storm off, despite my irritation. But both Konstantin and Ridley turned to look back at me, their eyes questioning. I just forced a smile and hurried on my way.

At the end of the ballroom were two large doors, and I pushed them both with my hands as hard as I could, blowing off a bit of steam. They flew open, and I heard a deep voice rumble in pain.

As the doors swung closed, I looked over to see that I had hit someone with the door. He straightened up, looking down at me with dazzling blue eyes, the thin gills under his jawline flaring when he exhaled. The chandelier directly above us was out, and his broad shoulders cast an ominous shadow over me from the light at the end of the hall.

It was the newly reappointed King, Mikko Biâelse. This was the first time I'd seen him since I'd been implicated in his younger brother's death, and he did not look happy to see me.

FORTY-EIGHT

confrontation

Bryn Aven," Mikko said in a voice that rumbled like thunder. Linnea had once told me that Mikko was painfully shy, and I found that so strange. With his striking good looks, rather imposing size, and a voice like Odin, I'd never met anybody else who had a presence like his. He looked like he'd been created to be King.

I swallowed hard before replying with, "Your Highness," and bowing.

"There's no need for that." He looked uncomfortable for a moment, then folded his arms over his chest. "I heard that I have you to thank for my freedom."

"I . . . I, uh, that was more Marksinna Lisbet," I stammered in surprise. His words sounded kind, but he looked like he wouldn't mind snacking on my bones for breakfast.

"She said that you swayed Baltsar into action," he said. "While I was incarcerated, Linnea told me that you never stopped believing in me and fighting for my innocence. She insisted that you were our greatest ally."

"I . . ." I didn't know how to reply to that. It was an exaggeration, but there was some truth to it, so I said simply, "I just did what I thought was right, sire."

"It's unfortunate how rare it is to find someone who will do what's right."

He turned his attention toward the ballroom doors. A sliver of bright light spilled through the thin gap between the doors into the darkness of the hall, making a line across Mikko's face as he peered inside. Even out in the hall, Tilda could easily be heard, shouting her commands.

The King had apparently come to watch his new army training, and with his attention back on that and off me, now would be a perfect time for me to slip away. I could go down the hall, get a drink of water, and cool off.

But I hesitated, and it caused him to look back at me. "Is there something I can do for you, Bryn?"

"I wanted to say that I'm sorry about your brother," I said finally.

He sighed heavily. "So am I." His normally hard expression softened, disillusionment and sadness wearing down on his features. "And I'm sorry that you got pulled into that mess. Linnea filled me in on what happened, and I appreciate you acting as honorably as you did."

"Thank you," I said, stunned to hear Mikko actually thanking me for my involvement in his brother's death.

"I do wish that Kennet had been able to come to me with

his concerns instead of taking matters to into his own hands."
He turned his eyes to the ceiling, and his exasperation gave
way to anger. "But that's my father's doing. He always said
that a real man would take what he wanted. Kennet was
kinder than that, or at least he would've been without Father's
influence."

From what I understood, Mikko and Kennet's father, the
late King Rune, was not a good man. My mom had bor-
dered on calling him a sadist. He had hoarded sapphires and
let the palace and the kingdom fall into disrepair. He'd been
more focused on maintaining his wealth than the welfare of
anyone, including his own children.

Even after his father's death, Mikko had seemed afraid to
undo his proclamations. The continuing policies of Rune
had led to an inept guard and rifts in the kingdom. It was also
one of the motivations for Kennet's attempt at overthrowing
Mikko.

"Despite everything Kennet did, I do believe that he loved
you," I said.

Mikko lowered his eyes. "I know he did. That's what makes
it harder."

"I'm sorry. I didn't mean to upset you."

"No. In an awful way, this has all been good for me." He
looked up at me, making eye contact for one of the first times
since I'd met him. "I've realized that I need to step out of my
father's shadow and lead in my own right."

"Queen Linnea has talked about the greatness she sees in

you," I said. "They need a strong leader, and I think you're the one to do it."

"The Skojare are good people, and they deserve a strong King." Mikko stood up straighter. "I must become that King for them."

I smiled. "I'm looking forward to seeing you in action."

"You can stay for as long as you want," he said. "I know things with your kingdom have become a terrible mess, but I want you to know that you are always welcome here. As far as I'm concerned, you have a home here in Storvatten."

A footman came running around the corner, going so fast he skidded on the floor. He caught himself, then ruced toward us. As soon as he saw the King, he started yelling, "Sire! Sire!"

"What?" Mikko turned back to face him. "What's the matter?"

The footman reached us, gasping for breath. "The . . . they sent me to get you." He paused, gulping down air. "There's an army waiting at the door for you."

FORTY-NINE

unannounced

Mikko was about to go to the door by himself, but I ran back into the ballroom and grabbed Baltsar and Ridley. I wasn't about to let the King get himself killed when the Skojare had just gotten him back.

Konstantin and Tilda stayed back with the troops, preparing to command them if they needed to. The hope was that since the army had come to the door, they wanted to have some kind of sit-down with Mikko. Maybe he'd even be able to sway them away from battle and come to some sort of compromise.

That seemed unlikely, but at this point it appeared to be our only hope to avoid massive bloodshed.

Before I left, following Ridley and Baltsar behind the King, Konstantin grabbed my arm.

"Do not leave the King alone with her," he warned in a low

voice, referring to Mina. "She'll kill him the second she has the chance."

"I won't." I started to turn away, but Konstantin still hung on to my arm, so I looked back at him.

"Be careful," he said and finally released me.

I ran out after the King. He, Ridley, and Baltsar were walking quickly and purposefully toward the front door. Baltsar was talking to Mikko, telling him everything that he should do and say, and what response he advised based on what the leader of the army might say to him.

"What should we do?" I asked Ridley in a hushed voice as I fell in step beside him.

"Try not to let the King get killed, and try not to get killed ourselves." He glanced down at me. "That's the best I've got."

We reached the front hall, and I was doing my best to slow the racing of my heart. Seven guards—veteran ones who had been working around the palace and not training—stood at attention around the hall. Their hands were on their swords, ready to act if they needed to.

If Mina and Viktor had sent their full army, it didn't matter if the entire Skojare force were in the hall. They weren't ready, and they'd be slaughtered.

Ridley and I flanked the King on either side, while Baltsar went to open the large front door. Mikko stood tall with his head high, and it was definitely a good choice to release him from the dungeon. He was far more intimidating than Marksinna Lisbet.

Baltsar looked back at us, making sure we were ready, and the King nodded. So Baltsar opened the door.

Standing right outside on the dock was a small hobgoblin, maybe three feet tall. In some ways, hobgoblins were like miniature ogres, except that they were far more symmetrical in appearance. His features were humanoid, but his skin appeared slimy, with thick grayish brown hair sticking up wildly on his head. Like ogres, hobgoblins were insanely strong.

I'd met hobgoblins before, and I realized that I'd actually met this one in particular. He was Ludlow Svartalf, the right-hand man of Sara Elsing, the Queen of the Vittra. He'd accompanied her on trips to the palace in Doldastam before.

Just to the right and slightly behind him stood Finn Holmes, offering us an uneasy smile.

Standing behind both Finn and Ludlow were rows of troops, lined up down the dock. Most of them wore the dark emerald uniforms of the Trylle, but a fair amount had the deep burgundy uniforms of the Vittra, worn by both hobgoblin and troll alike.

"Queen Wendy Staad of the Trylle heard about the plight of Skojare, and after considering it, she decided to send half of her army to aid you in your fight against the Kanin," Finn explained.

"In addition, Queen Wendy and King Loki persuaded Queen Sara Elsing of the Vittra to join in the fight," Ludlow added in his low, craggy voice. "Queen Sara has sent a third of her army to join your fight."

Mikko appeared too stunned to speak for a moment, but

finally he managed to say, "I am forever grateful for your of-
fers, but I am not sure that I can ever repay your kingdoms.
We are not in a position to indebt ourselves so greatly to
such powerful kingdoms."

"We are not asking for anything in return," Finn told him.
"We are simply here to help you as you may need us."

"We are here to serve, King Mikko," Ludlow said, and he
bowed before him. Finn followed suit, as did the troops on
the dock—all of them bowing before the Skojare King.

masquerade

W e need to celebrate!" Linnea declared. "We're not all going to die, and if that doesn't call for a celebration, then I don't know what does!"

It was hard to argue with that logic, so I didn't even try, and neither did Mikko.

Since the Trylle and the Vittra had pledged their allegiance and a chunk of their soldiers to us yesterday, we had spent the entire time trying to combine our armies. It required more effort because each of the tribes had such different strengths.

Many of the Trylle had powers of psychokinesis, meaning they could move things with their minds or even start fires. Since the soldiers present were all lower-ranking trackers and civilians (and stronger abilities went along with the more powerful bloodlines of the royals), they weren't very powerful, but they had did have some psychokinesis.

The Vittra were physically stronger than almost any other

tribe, possibly barring the Omte. Despite their smaller stature, hobgoblins were easily as strong as ogres, if not stronger. And while Vittra trolls were generally more attractive and smarter than the Omte, they could be just as quick-tempered and aggressive.

The Skojare could breathe underwater, which wasn't very useful for this fight. They were also the least skilled in combat, and the other two tribes were often frustrated by their inability to properly defend themselves.

More than once during training I saw a Vittra soldier throw a Skojare guard across the room in irritation. Ridley, Finn, and Ludlow were doing their best to keep order and get everyone working together, but it was no easy task.

It was during our training in the afternoon that Linnea came into the ballroom, excited about the cause for celebration. She insisted that everyone needed a morale-booster and a fun way to bond, and the way to do that was with a party in the ballroom.

With that, she tossed everyone out, telling us to go practice outside where the Trylle and the Vittra had set up camp in Storvatten. I spent the rest of the day out in the warm spring rain, teaching Skojare new maneuvers and fighting in the mud.

After a hard day of training, I walked down to my guestroom to wash off all the dirt in a warm shower. I'd almost made it to my room when Linnea came rushing down the hall toward me, carrying three garment bags in her arms.

"Bryn!" she called to me, nearly tripping on her long satin

dressing gown in her hurry. When I turned to face her, she realized how filthy I was, and she slowed down. "I was going to hand these off to you, but you'll get muck all over the bags. I'll just put them on your bed while you go shower."

"Why are you bringing me garment bags?" I asked.

"For the party." Linnea gave me a look like I was an idiot and brushed past me as she went into my room. "I know you weren't able to pack your finer clothes with you, so I grabbed a few gowns that I thought you might like and would fit you."

"That's very kind of you, but I hadn't planned on going to the party," I said as I walked more slowly into my room.

"Don't be ridiculous, of course you are." Linnea kept her back to me as she carefully laid out the bags on the bed. "You're integral to everything that's happening here, and you need to be here to mingle and get people to trust each other."

She unzipped each of the bags, pulling out the gowns a bit so I could see them. I'd owned some nice dresses in my life, but none as fabulous as these.

One was a rich navy-blue fabric that looked like liquid when it moved, and with a slit so high, I would be worried that my panties would show. Another was snow-white satin with diamond and lace embellishments creating an ornate illusion neckline. And the last was pale aquamarine, embroidered with flowing designs and sapphires, and a bit of tulle under the length filled out the skirt.

"And besides," Linnea went on as I stood, transfixed by the lavishness of the gowns, "you've earned it. You've been working so hard lately. You deserve a night to let your hair down."

I nodded slowly. "Okay. I'll go to the party."

She clapped her hands together. "I would hug you, but I don't want to get covered in mud. Now hurry and get ready."

In the end, it wasn't the logic of her arguments that won me over—although she had been right. It was simply the sight of the dresses. Something in the troll blood made it hard to deny luxury, which was why we all had such a penchant for gems and jewelry.

But also, a part of me just really wanted to wear a gown that was made for a Queen.

I showered quickly but thoroughly—there was no way I was ruining one of Linnea's dresses. Then I hurried back to try them all on and pick one.

While I'd been showering, Linnea had sent down a masquerade mask and a pair of pale sapphire earrings. The silver mask was gorgeous and delicate, its ornate flourishes encrusted with diamonds. Attached was a note that read, "Wear me."

The difficulty of the choice was made easier by the fact that the aquamarine one was snug in the chest, squishing my breasts in a very unflattering and uncomfortable fashion. While the darker navy dress felt like heaven on my skin, the slit felt too high, and it also had a plunging neckline, a combination that felt slightly improper for this party.

The white one fit perfectly, almost like it had been made for me. The illusion neckline allowed a hint of cleavage, and it was open in the back, showing off a bit of skin. While the length was longer than I normally liked, it was light and flowed away from me, so I didn't think it would be a problem to run or kick in if I needed to.

Once I'd finished with my hair and makeup, I went down the hall to admire myself in the full-length mirror of the bathroom.

Since I wasn't doing anything other than looking at my reflection, I'd left the door open, which allowed Konstantin to pause and whistle at me.

"Well done, white rabbit." He smiled crookedly at me, but his eyes were serious as they assessed me.

Something about the way he looked at me made my skin flush a little, and I turned to face him. "Thanks."

"It's kind of a shame I'm missing the party tonight," he said.

"Why aren't you going?" I asked in surprise.

Based on the way he was dressed, I assumed he planned to attend. He had on a simple black uniform, similar to the one that Ridley had worn as Kanin Överste, with epaulets on the shoulders, and a sword in a scabbard that hung from a belt around his waist.

While Ridley and Tilda had taken to wearing the shimmery blue uniforms of the Skojare, Konstantin had managed to dig up one that showed no allegiance. No color, no insignia, nothing to tie him to any kingdom.

"I'm walking the perimeter of Storvatten, along with some of the other guards," Konstantin explained. "Since we don't know when Mina and Viktor are going to strike, we're keeping a lookout."

"Damn." I looked down at my gown, suddenly feeling very silly. "I should change and go with you."

"No, no." He shook his head. "We've got enough guys going out. You should go. You should be happy."

I started to tell him that he should still come to the party if he got a chance, but he turned and walked away, leaving me standing there in my beautiful dress feeling flustered and alone.

dalliance

Given the short amount of time Linnea had had to put it all together, the ballroom looked especially impressive.

Under the dark canopy of night displayed in the glass dome, twinkling lights had been strung around the room. Along the walls, tables had been adorned with shimmering linens, crystal centerpieces, and mood-enhancing candles. A buffet of savory and sweet ran along the wall at the end of the ballroom, with an ice sculpture of a fish.

In the far corner of the room, a small chamber orchestra had been set up. When I entered the room, they were just finishing an old Skojare song I remembered my mom singing, then they switched to an ethereal orchestral cover of "Bulletproof" by LaRoux.

I'd arrived late, so the dance floor was already crowded, all the guests wearing masks equally as beautiful as mine. It was a veritable rainbow in the ballroom, and not just because of all the beautiful dresses. All the highest royals were in attendance, along with the Skojare guards dressed in their frosty uniforms.

Most of the allies that had come to the party from the Trylle and the Vittra were men, dressed crisply in their dark uniforms of emerald and claret, but the Skojare women were more than happy to dance with them. After years of living in the rather isolated Storvatten, new faces were exotic and exciting, especially when they had come to save the kingdom.

I stood in the doorway for a moment, content enough to watch so many trolls coming together like this. Talking, laughing, twirling around on the dance floor together. Even at parties, like at King Evert and Queen Mina's anniversary party, everyone was still so segregated. Trylle danced with Trylle, and so on.

This was the first time I'd ever seen the kingdoms so commingled before. It was kind of amazing, and I wondered if Linnea's masquerade theme had helped this happen.

"I wasn't sure if you were coming," a voice said at my side, and I turned to see that Ridley had somehow snuck beside me.

He'd forgone the Skojare uniform, unlike many of the other attendees, and instead wore a simple, surprisingly well-tailored suit. It was pure white, with a satin and diamond finish, and he wore it with a black dress shirt. Based on the exquisiteness of it, I realized that Linnea had procured it for him the same way she had gotten my gown for me.

Since we'd been in Storvatten, Ridley hadn't shaved, leaving him with a light beard along his jawline and above his lip.

His hair was only slightly disheveled, like he'd styled it perfectly but couldn't help himself and ran his hand through it.

His mask was black and thicker than mine, more masculine, but just as gorgeous.

"I wasn't sure you were coming either," I admitted. Since we'd just been focusing on training and hadn't had a chance to talk since our late-night rendezvous, I had no idea where we stood.

"I'd never miss a chance to dance with you." He stepped back and extended his hand to me. He said nothing, but he didn't have to. The question was in his eyes.

Tentatively, I took his hand and let him lead me out onto the dance floor. I wasn't sure if the crowed actually parted for us, or if it just felt that way. Whenever I was with Ridley like this—when he was touching me, and his eyes were focused on me, and my heart was pounding so fast I felt dizzy and drunk—the whole world always seemed to fall away. Like we had become the center of the universe, and everything spun around us.

Ridley pulled me close to him and put his hand on my back—his hand warm and rough on my bare skin, thanks to the plunging back. We stayed that way for a split second—my hand in his, my body pressed against him, and him staring down at me.

I loved the darkness of his eyes. It seemed to overtake me.

And then we were moving. I let him lead me along, following his quick moves step for step. He extended his arm, twirling me out away from him and making my gown whirl out around me, before pulling me back to him again.

The crowd had definitely moved for us by then, creating a space in the center of the room where Ridley and I could show off the dancing we'd learned in school. All trackers learned it, but I had to admit that he was more proficient than most.

When he dipped me back, so low my hair brushed the floor, he smiled, and there was a glint in his eye. With one quick move, he pulled me back into his arms, holding me to him.

The song had changed, shifting to "Love Me Again" by John Newman, so we slowed. He kept his hands on my waist, and I let my hands relax on his shoulders. We were flirting, playing the way we had before, and it made my heart ache.

Because things weren't the way they were before anymore. Not even close.

My smile must've fallen away, because Ridley looked concerned—his eyes darkening beneath the mask, and his steps slowing as his arms tightened around me.

"Why did you come back for me?" I asked him finally, referring to what he'd said when he first arrived in Förening. "*Did* you even come back for me?"

"*Yes,*" he said emphatically. "Of course I came back for you."

"But why? Why, if you're not even really here with me?"

"I am here. I can't be with you more than I am right now."

His gazed shifted out to everyone else dancing around us. "This probably isn't the best place to get into it."

"There's never a good time to talk, not with everything going on here. I just want to know what's going on with us." I looked up into his dark eyes. "Is there even an *us?*"

He took a fortifying breath. "I came back for you because you're my first thought in the morning. Because you push yourself to be better, and in the process, you push everyone else around you to be better. You *make* everything better.

"You are far more courageous and stronger than anyone I've ever known," he continued. "And I never thought you'd ever want anything to do with me. I was certain I'd never be good enough for you.

"But when we kissed for the first time, under the lights of the aurora borealis, everything I'd ever felt about you was proven true," Ridley finished. "I came back for you because you're all I've ever wanted or needed, because I want to be with you always."

For a moment I was too stunned to say anything. I just stared up at him, my mouth hanging open and my heart pounding in my chest.

"You have me," I said simply. "You'll always have me."

His lips turned up slowly into a smile, looking both relieved and amazed. Then he leaned in, and I wrapped my arms more tightly around him. His lips had just brushed up against mine when I heard shouting over the music.

The orchestra finally stopped, and I heard Baltsar shouting, "Ridley! King Mikko!"

"What's going on?" Ridley pulled away from me, but kept his hand around mine. His eyes scanned the crowd, until it parted enough for us to see Mikko standing a few feet away with Linnea at his side.

Baltsar burst through the crowd, standing in the clearing between Ridley and Mikko. "There's been an attack on our men walking the perimeter. Two were seriously injured, and one was killed. We need a medic, and we need to make sure the area's secure."

"Mikko, you go with Ridley and get the men together to make sure we're safe," Linnea said. "I'll get the medic."

Ridley let go of my hand and started hurrying toward Baltsar.

"Who was hurt?" I asked, and it was hard to be heard over the distraught murmurings of the ballroom. I took off my mask and started pushing my way through the crowd, but they didn't part for me the way they had before. "Baltsar, what men were attacked?"

"A couple new recruits." He paused long enough to look back at me. "And Konstantin Black."

FIFTY-TWO

expiry

I n the chaos that followed, I had to remind myself to breathe. Baltsar had said Konstantin's name, then had run off, and I stayed where I was as everyone rushed around me. I didn't know what to do, where I should be, and I looked around, hoping for direction.

Tilda had started commanding the Skojare guards, sending them to various posts around the palace so that any possible entrance would be protected. Marksinna Lisbet took control of the civilians who remained in the ballroom, assuring them that everything would be all right.

"Bryn." Tilda put her hand on my shoulder, momentarily pausing from giving orders. I turned to her, and she had a knowing look in her smoky eyes. She could always see through me, even when everything had gone mad.

"We've got this," she said simply. "Go."

I dropped my mask, letting it fall to the floor, and then I

was running, grabbing up the length of the gown and grateful that the fabric flowed enough to allow me to move as fast as I wanted to. I didn't know where I was going, not at first, but I couldn't slow down. I raced through the soldiers that crowded the halls.

Finally I spotted Linnea, dragging a medic by the hand as she ran in her own sparkly blue gown. She was way at the other end of the hall from me, rushing toward the south wing of the palace, but I could just see her platinum curls bouncing, so I followed them.

I managed to get to the room just after Linnea and the medic had arrived, and I stood in the doorway. It was a small room on the main floor, with a window that showed the stars reflecting on the lake outside. Two twin beds were in the room, but Linnea and the medic were blocking my view so I could only see the legs of the occupants.

And blood. Blood stained the white sheets and left a mess on the floor.

Ridley was already at work caring for the men before Linnea arrived. He'd taken off his white jacket and rolled up the sleeves of his shirt, and his forearms were stained red.

The medic started to take over, and Linnea tried to tell the wounded that everything would be alright.

"Dammit!" Konstantin growled, and I breathed in deeply for the first time.

"I know it hurts, but you need to let him do this if you want him to fix you," Linnea told him, her voice verging between comforting and scolding.

"I don't want him to fix me!" Konstantin shouted back.

"You saved my life," Linnea persisted. "I won't just let you die."

Ridley had been helping the medic tear back Konstantin's shirt so he could get to the worst of it—a horrible gaping wound in his abdomen. He'd assisted enough so that the medic could get his hands on Konstantin, pressing painfully against the gash in order to heal it with psychokinesis.

As soon as the medic got his hands on him, Konstantin started fighting it, trying to push them off. Linnea screamed when he threw his hand out, and she jumped back from him.

"Leave it be!" Konstantin commanded. "Just let me die."

"We need you," Ridley said, trying to hold Konstantin's arms down before he hurt himself or someone else. "Just let us help you."

I pushed past Linnea to get to his side, and when Konstantin saw me, out of surprise he stopped fighting. His eyes widened, and he grimaced. His hair was damp with sweat, and blood was splattered on his cheeks.

Since he'd relaxed some, I leaned on the bed beside him, taking his bloodstained hand in mine.

"Let them help," I said softly, imploring him.

He looked away from me, staring up at the ceiling. He gritted his teeth and breathed in angrily through his nose. That was as close to consent as we would get, so I looked to the medic and nodded.

The medic put his hands back on Konstantin, and he groaned loudly through his teeth. His hand squeezed mine to the point of being painful, but I just let him. It took a few moments, but eventually he began to relax.

I looked down, and the medic was panting as he took his hands off Konstantin. The wound was healed, and other than a fresh scar under the thick layer of drying blood, his abdomen looked completely normal.

The medic began to tell Konstantin to take it easy, and if there were other minor injuries in different areas, they would take more time to heal because he'd focused all his energy on the abdominal wound.

Linnea thanked the medic for his help and took him out to the hallway. Konstantin let go of my hand, so I straightened back up. In the bed across from Konstantin, a white sheet stained red had been pulled up over the man's head. The other guy who had come in with Konstantin hadn't made it.

"I hate to do it at a time like this," Ridley said. He stood on the opposite side of the bed, looking down at Konstantin. "But I have to find out about the attack. We need to so we can prepare ourselves."

"It was just a couple scouts," Konstantin said. "There were only two of them. We killed one pretty quickly, after he took out one of the guys I was walking with, but the second guy— he put up quite a fight." He grimaced at the memory.

"Did they say anything?" Ridley asked.

Konstantin nodded. "Yeah. I finally got my sword to his throat, and then he was quite chatty because he thought I'd spare his life. He said that Viktor sent them down to see how well armed the Skojare were. He said that Viktor is waiting to hear back from the scouts before sending troops."

Ridley folded his arms over his chest. "With them being dead, it ought to buy us a few days."

"That's the good news," Konstantin said. "The bad news is that both of the scouts were Omte, and not just any Omte. These were trained soldiers, which is why they did such a number on us."

"That doesn't make any sense." I shook my head. "I thought Viktor had just been picking up random trolls that had defected from other tribes, like Bent Stum."

"So did I," Konstantin replied wearily. "But we were wrong. The scout told me as much. Viktor and Mina have the Omte working for them now."

"Shit," Ridley whispered. "I need to go find the King and Baltsar to tell them this. It changes everything."

He walked around the bed, heading toward the door, but he paused and reached out, touching my arm gently. "You okay?"

"Yeah." I nodded. "I'm fine."

Ridley lingered like he wanted to say more, or maybe even finish that kiss we'd barely started in the ballroom. But now wasn't the time or place, and he knew it. He glanced back at Konstantin, then let go of my arm and left.

Konstantin closed his eyes and groaned. "You should've just let me die. They shouldn't have wasted their resources and the medic's energy on me, not when there's going to be many other soldiers that deserve it more."

"I'm not gonna let you die." I sat on the edge of the bed beside him.

He laughed darkly. "Death is something that's beyond even your control, white rabbit."

retaliate

Once Konstantin was asleep, Linnea had a footman move the body of the recruit and begin preparing it for a proper burial. She stood out in the hall, watching them carefully and reverently carry the fallen guard away.

I left Konstantin's side to join her in the hall. Her mask rested in her hair, pushing back her ringlets so they stuck out haphazardly. She wrung her hands together absently, her eyes fixed on the retreating footmen.

"How are you doing?" I asked her.

"I haven't even been Queen for a year." She sounded as if she was speaking more to herself than me. "I turn seventeen on the sixteenth of June, and a week after that, it will be my one-year wedding anniversary. That will mark one year as Queen."

"It's been a very busy first year," I commented.

"At first, I think I was only playing at Queen, and if I'm

being honest, Mikko was only playing at King." She turned back to face me, her eyes moist. "We'd never really been challenged, so we were only going through the motions and having parties and putting on these silly costumes."

She lifted up the length of her gown and let it fall back down. "And now we must be the things that we were pretending to be. People are dying, and we must be the ones that protect them."

A solitary tear slid down her porcelain skin. "I feel like I've already failed."

"No, you haven't failed." I shook my head. "Despite how everything turned out tonight, the ball was a good idea. You need to create unity and order and a sense of happiness within Storvatten. While others are out fighting, you need to hold things down here, and when they come back, you take care of them. That's your job as the Queen."

"You really think I did the right thing tonight?" Linnea wiped away her tear.

"Yes, you did everything exactly right," I told her. "But you need to be strong. A Queen must never be seen crying."

She straightened up, pulling her shoulders back and raising her chin higher, and took a deep breath. "You're right. I need to be a leader."

I smiled at her. "You'll be a fine leader."

"I would hug you, but you're covered in blood." She motioned to the bright red splotches that covered the bodice of my dress, staining the lace and satin, from when I'd been attempting to comfort Konstantin.

"I'm sorry. I wasn't even thinking about it."

"Bryn." She gave me a hard look. "There are far greater things to worry about than my silly gown. I couldn't care a fig about what happened to that dress while in service to this kingdom."

I thanked her again, and she excused herself to sit with Konstantin. She didn't want him to be alone, at least not until she was absolutely certain he was better. I looked in on her before I left, sitting at the bedside of an injured outcast without a kingdom, and I wondered how many other Queens would do that.

With Konstantin in her hands, I felt safe heading down to the meeting room. The palace had settled down while I'd been in with Konstantin, now that the imminent threat of attack had been called off. Guards were still stationed around more than normal, but people weren't running around like madmen.

When I walked downstairs, I could even hear the orchestra from the ballroom playing. The ball was under way again, probably under the advisement of Lisbet. If we had been attacked, I imagined her still dancing to the music, like the orchestra that had played on as the *Titanic* sank.

I stopped only to wash the blood from my hands, and then I headed into the meeting room. Finn and Ludlow were seated at the long table, while Baltsar paced alongside it. Mikko stood at the head, his expression grave, and Ridley stared at the dark water outside, his back to the door. He glanced over at me when I came in the room but didn't turn around.

"It all depends on how many Omte they have with them," Finn was saying as I closed the door behind me.

"We're strong," Ludlow added. "But the Omte already outnumber the Vittra, and if they bring their whole army, I'm not sure how well we can hold against them."

"They'll break down the walls," Baltsar grumbled as he paced. "You get those ogres charging, and the walls will shatter underneath their fists. They'll destroy the palace."

"We have to stop them before they get to the palace," Finn said. "The battle needs to happen on land, far from the shore."

"And what if they beat us down and charge past us?" Baltsar argued. "You get the Kanin army and the Omte army and who knows how many others Viktor Dålig's collected, and they come charging at us? They'll trample our army."

"Once they get to the palace, it's all over," Finn said. "They'll break the walls, take the sapphires, and kill anyone who is left."

"I know!" Baltsar shouted. "That's my point. How do we stop them from taking the palace?"

"We go to them," Finn replied with a heavy sigh.

"We can't do that," I said, speaking for the first time since I'd entered the room, and everyone turned to look at me. "The people in Doldastam are innocent. They don't need to end up casualties of our war against their Queen. They shouldn't be punished for her sins."

"My family is there too," Finn reminded me, his eyes pained. "I know how great the risk is. But it's our only chance to stop the Queen and her armies before she destroys another kingdom. And once she's done with the Skojare, there's no telling who she'll go after next."

"We go to them," Baltsar agreed, sounding resigned to the idea. "We take the fight to Doldastam. We still might not win. They still outnumber us, and they're still much stronger. But if we lose, we give everyone in Storvatten a chance to escape. It's our best plan to avoid innocent casualties."

"You're suggesting we abandon the palace?" Mikko asked in his low rumble.

"I am suggesting that if we lose, yes, everyone behind in Storvatten fills their pockets with sapphires and disappears into the lake," Baltsar said. "It's the only advantage we have, that the other tribes can't follow us into the water."

"Konstantin and I know Doldastam and the palace inside out," Ridley said, referring to the fact that as a member of the Högdragen and Överste respectively they had been privy to all the plans and designs of the city. They knew it better than even Tilda and me.

He turned around to face the room. "Do we really have a chance of beating them? I don't know. But if we do, Finn is right. Our best shot is taking Doldastam before they come for Storvatten."

Mikko surveyed the room, waiting for dissenting opinions, but even I just lowered my eyes. It wasn't a perfect plan, and I wasn't sure that we wouldn't all end up dead anyway.

But it was still our best chance at defeating Mina, even if it meant risking the lives of the people I cared about most. The greater good of peace within the five kingdoms outweighed my own personal feelings.

"That settles it, then," Mikko said. "Since they'll be coming for us soon, we don't have time to waste. We leave at dawn for Doldastam."

FIFTY-FOUR

älskade

With my bag slung over my shoulder, I closed the door to my guestroom in the Storvatten palace for the last time. It had a strange finality to it. I didn't know if I'd ever come here again or if the palace would even be standing in a couple weeks.

I started walking down the hall and paused when I reached Tilda's room. She sat on her bed, her legs crossed underneath her, and stared down at her belly as she rubbed it. Her wavy chestnut hair hung around her like a curtain.

I knocked on the open door, and she looked up at me with a sad smile.

"You're leaving already?"

I nodded. "It's time. Ridley's already upstairs."

Her smile became more pained, her full lips pressing into thin lines. I sat my bag on the floor and went over to sit on the bed beside her.

"I wish I was going with you," she said, almost desperately.

"I know. But the battlefield is no place for a pregnant woman, even one as badass as you."

"I know it's the right thing. I know that for the baby, this is where I need to be." She nodded, as if to convince herself. "But this is my war too. I should be with you, fighting alongside you."

"You've already helped so much. Everything you've done with the Skojare army, they're better because of *you*."

"It's just hard." She rubbed her stomach. "I think the baby wants to go too. He's been kicking a lot." Then she looked over at me. "Wanna feel?"

I wasn't sure that I wanted to, but I let Tilda take my hand and place it on her stomach. At first I didn't feel anything, then there was a sudden, soft pushing sensation on the palm of my hand.

"Did you feel that?" Tilda asked, sounding excited.

"Yeah, that's crazy." I let my hand linger for a moment, feeling another, stronger kick, and then I took my hand back.

"Did I tell you that I found out that it's a boy?" she asked, smiling wider now.

"No, you didn't. A boy?" I smiled. "That'll be great."

"I didn't find out the gender until after Kasper . . ." Her smile remained but her eyes were misty. "I mean, we could've. But we were waiting until after we were married. It's silly, but we wanted it to be like a wedding gift to ourselves."

She shook her head. "I don't know. It seemed like a fun idea at the time, but since we didn't know if it would be a boy or a girl, we didn't really talk about names yet. Not in earnest."

"Have you been thinking about anything now?" I asked.

"Älskade Kasper Abbott," Tilda said. "*Älskade* means 'loved,' and I want this baby to know that he's loved more than anything."

I smiled. "It sounds perfect."

"Thanks." She smiled and blinked back tears. "Anyway, I've probably held you up long enough. You should get going before they leave without you."

I leaned over and hugged her tightly. The two of us had never been much for hugging, but we both lingered in this one. Eventually I pulled away and stood up. I grabbed my bag off the floor and offered her a small wave before heading out.

"Bryn," she said, stopping me at the door. "In case I don't see you again, I just wanted you to know that you've been a really great friend, and I love you."

"I love you too," I said, rather awkwardly, since neither of us was usually very sentimental. "And take care of yourself."

Leaving Tilda alone in her room made me feel bad, but I knew that Linnea would be calling on her for help in the very near future. Linnea was going to be running the kingdom in her husband's absence, and Tilda knew quite a bit about keeping things in order.

I went up the winding staircase away from the bedrooms and up to the main floor. As I walked toward the main hall,

I was surprised to see Konstantin hobbling from the other direction, with his own bag over his shoulder.

He'd showered and cleaned up, looking better than he had in a while. Last night, when he'd been brought in, he'd been pale and clammy, on the verge of death, and now he appeared as he always did. Except with a slight limp in his left leg.

"What are you doing?" I asked. He'd stopped, waiting for me to join him.

"I'm going to Doldastam."

"But you need to rest," I reminded him. "The medic told you to, and you've got a limp."

He shrugged it off. "My leg is finishing healing. The limp will be gone in a day."

"Konstantin." I stopped walking, so he did too, and looked back at me.

"Do you really think I'm going to let anything prevent me from missing this fight?" he asked honestly.

"Fine." I sighed. "At least promise me you'll take it easy."

He shook his head and started walking again. "Nope."

FIFTY-FIVE

terrain

With so many of us in our motley of shapes and sizes, we had to avoid main modes of travel, including the train, which was how we usually crossed the vast Canadian territory to get to Doldastam.

Fortunately, winter had come to an end for most of Manitoba, and that made it easier for us to go off-road. To get where we were going, in many places there were literally no roads. We'd be relying on Skojare maps, GPS, and four-wheel drive to get us through.

The Trylle had been kind enough to bring their transports to us, which were modified all-terrain army vehicles. The majority of us managed to fit in the backs of those, underneath the tarp covers, while the rest crammed into the Skojare's small fleet of Jeep Wranglers.

In order for the humans not to spy us, we'd have to stay as far from their civilization and populated roads as we could.

We'd brought along a few of the Skojare tower guards to help cloak us. And if humans did actually see us, like when we needed a pit stop to gas up, several of the Trylle with us could use persuasion, and make them forget that they'd seen anything at all.

Once we got close enough to Doldastam, we'd leave the convoy and march the rest of the way on foot, since all our vehicles would be loud and obvious. That way we could have an element of surprise. The tower guards' cloaking ability worked well on humans, but it was much less effective on other trolls, especially when they were trying to hide such a large moving target.

I sat in the back of one of the transports, between Ridley and the back gate. The bench that ran on either side of the back was full of senior Skojare guards, and though they did their best to look confident, I could see their nerves showing through.

Konstantin had also chosen this transport, but instead of sitting on a bench, he lay on the floor, using his bag as a pillow. Some of the guards had complained, but Konstantin said he needed to stretch out his leg so it would heal faster, so they let it go.

Despite the bumps and jolts of the journey, Konstantin seemed to sleep through it, bouncing around undisturbed. It was a rough ride over rocky terrain, one that left me aching and sore whenever we stopped to stretch and take a bathroom break.

Through most of the ride, none of us really said anything.

It was hard to hear over the sound of the vehicle, and there wasn't much to say. *Are you scared that the Omte will literally crush you? Oh, me too!*

Ridley only spoke to me once, asking me if I wanted part of his lunch. Since his confession last night during the dance, we hadn't really talked, other than discussions of war and what we needed to do. But I didn't mind. There wasn't time for anything else.

When we got back into the transport together after one of our stops, he put his hand on my leg, gently squeezing when we hit a large bump, and there was something more comforting in that than anything he could've said.

By nightfall, we'd made it about two-thirds of the way through our journey, and we stopped to camp out. Driving off-road during the day was difficult enough as it was, and we all needed a chance to rest before we arrived at Doldastam. We'd known that we'd have to camp out, so we'd packed well for it.

It was in the low twenties, which made for a very chilly campout, so we hurried to set up our tents. A girl from the Trylle had asked to share a tent with me, and I'd obliged. Other soldiers had gotten fires going, but we set up our tent near the outskirt of the campsite, since I'd rather get sleep than stay up all night talking around a fire.

While she finished setting up the tent—a small white one, made of thick canvas that helped to keep the cold out and the heat in—I went back to the trucks to get thick animals hides to keep out the iciness of the ground.

When I went over to the truck, Ridley was already there, working beside Finn, helping to pass out hides and sleeping bags. Five others were already in line, waiting for their sleeping gear, and as I joined them, Ridley looked up at me, the dim lights from a nearby fire playing off the darkness in his eyes.

"We already have sleeping bags," I said as I reached the front.

"Hey, Finn, can you handle this?" Ridley asked, glancing back at the two people waiting behind me. "I wanted to talk to Bryn for a minute."

"Yeah, sure." Finn shrugged. "I think most everyone has got their stuff already."

"Great. Thanks." Ridley smiled briefly at him, then turned his attention to me.

"What did you want to talk about?" I asked.

He shook his head. "Not here." He turned, walking back between the covered trucks, so I followed him.

The majority of the vehicles were parked together at the edge of the campsite, creating an area that felt private and quiet, with large trucks blocking out the sound and most of the firelight.

"What's going on?" I asked Ridley when I felt like we'd gone far enough. I stopped first, and he turned back to face me. The moon above us illuminated his face, and he looked around me, as if expecting a spy to be following at my heels.

"Ridley, what is it?" I demanded, starting to feel nervous, since he wasn't saying anything.

He chewed his lip for a moment, staring down at me, and then, without warning, he rushed at me. His mouth pressed roughly against mine, cold and exhilarating against my warm flesh.

He pushed me back, and I began to stumble over my feet, but his arms were there, holding me up, carrying me until I felt my back pressing against the icy metal of the truck. His kisses were fierce and hungry, his teeth just barely scraping against my skin, sending delicious heat surging through my body.

But I matched his ferocity, wrapping my legs around him, burying my fingers in the tangles of his hair.

Almost instinctually, I began pulling off his jacket, desperate to get to the hot, hard contours of his body. Ridley moved his hands underneath my butt and thighs, gripping them firmly, as he carried me around the corner to the back of the truck.

Once he'd set me down, I started to scoot back, and he climbed up on top of me, his eager lips on mine. With quick desperation, his hands found their way under my layers of shirts, cold against my bare skin.

Ridley sat up, pulling away from me so he could hurriedly tear off his shirt. I don't think I'd ever undressed so quickly, and when my sweatshirt got stuck going up over my head, Ridley was more than happy to help.

He pushed it back over my head, but in his haste to kiss me again, he'd left my arms tangled in it, trapped behind my back. His mouth traveled lower, trailing down my neck.

His lips and the gentle scrape of his beard sent tingles all through me.

With one arm, he supported himself, and with the other, he unhooked the front clasp of my bra. My arms were still trapped behind me, but I'd stopped wiggling and trying to get free. I didn't want to stop Ridley from touching me.

He wrapped an arm around me, lifting me up so my back arched slightly, and then his mouth was cold on my breast. I moaned desperately, wanting more of him.

With that, he released me, so he could pull off his jeans. I finally got my arms free from the sweatshirt and tossed aside my bra. Ridley had turned his attention to my pants, pulling them off in one rough, fast move.

He crawled over me, his body above mine, and I stared up into his eyes. I put my hand on his cheek, and he tilted his head, gently kissing my wrist. He lips moved down my arm, until they found their way to my mouth again, kissing me deeply.

Despite the cold, his body felt like fire against me. He felt strong and sure, holding me, completing me.

And then I pulled him to me, unable to wait any longer. I raised my pelvis up, pushing against him, and with a shaky breath, he finally slid inside me. I moaned again, unable to help it, and he silenced me with his mouth on mine.

Soon I was breathing into his shoulder, digging my fingers into his back to keep from screaming, and he moved deeper inside me until he exhaled deeply and relaxed on top of me.

FIFTY-SIX

covet

We stayed that way for a moment, neither of us wanting to untangle ourselves from each other. But eventually we had to deal with the cold.

The covered canvas kept some of the frigid air at bay, but not enough for us to lie comfortably naked for long. Ridley sat up and lay his jacket over me as a temporary blanket as he searched around for something to cover up with.

Underneath one of the benches, he found a silver Mylar blanket from an opened emergency kit, and he spread it over us. He lay down beside me and pulled me into his arms.

"Well, that was a nice talk," I murmured, resting my head against his chest and pressing myself closer to him.

"I actually did want to talk to you," he said, his words muffled in my hair.

"Yeah?" I pulled back a little and titled my head so I could look up at him. "What about?"

"I don't know when we'll be able to talk again," he said finally. "And I just wanted to be sure that you knew everything and understood how I really feel."

My heart skipped a beat. "Everything about what?"

"About why I've been so cold and distant." He stared at the canvas above us. "I never wanted to hurt you or push you away. It's just . . . when I was in Doldastam, while we were apart, and Mina had me locked up in the dungeon, she never asked me anything about you. Not once. The entire time I was there."

"You mentioned that," I said softly.

"I know." He nodded. "But I didn't say that she never talked about you. Because she talked about you a lot. Constantly, actually."

"What do you mean? What did she say?" I asked, tensing up.

"She talked about how strong and capable you were, and how you'd never had any trouble until you started getting involved with me." He looked down at me. "I don't know how she knew that we'd kissed or slept together, but she'd found out somehow."

I shivered, and not from the cold. I'd never told anybody about the night that Ridley and I had spent together. And all of the ways I could imagine she'd discovered that secret were creepy and disturbing.

He lowered his eyes, his voice growing thicker as he spoke. "Then she started telling me how I'd brought you down and destroyed your chances of being on the Högdragen, how all I did was ruin everything I touch."

"Ridley, that's not true." I shook my head. "You didn't do anything to me. I made choices on my own, and most of the ones that have gotten me in trouble have had nothing to do with you."

"I know. I mean, part of me knew that." He sighed. "But after you hear it, over and over . . . Eventually, her words just took hold somewhere inside me, and she had me convinced that I would be the death of you."

I put my hand on his face, forcing him to look at me. "It's not true. Nothing Mina said was true."

He swallowed hard. "When I was there, all I could think about was how I could get back to you, and how I was terrified of what would happen to you if I did. I couldn't live with myself if I hurt you."

"I know you'd never hurt me," I whispered.

He kissed me again, softer this time and less insistent. "I love you, Bryn," he breathed deeply. "And I want to spend all night with you like this, but we should get back and get some sleep."

"Tomorrow we'll arrive in Doldastam," I said with a heavy sigh. His arm tightened around me. "Are you scared?"

"Yes," he admitted. "But I'm mostly afraid that I'll lose you again." He rolled onto his side, so he could face me fully. He reached out and touched my face. "You have to promise that you won't do anything too risky, Bryn. I know that you'll fight, and that you won't shy away from trouble. But I can't lose you again."

"I promise," I said, but even then, I wasn't sure if it was a promise I could keep.

home

At the top of the hill, I lay down on my stomach. The ground beneath me was a cold mixture of snow and mud, and it soaked through my clothes, but I barely noticed. The sun had just begun to set, casting everything in a beautiful bluish glow as the sky darkened from pink to purple along the horizon.

From the hill, we could see beyond the thick pine trees that rolled down the valley going toward the Hudson Bay. And there, on the flat land, was Doldastam in a way that I rarely saw it.

I could see the four stone walls that surrounded it. Over twenty feet tall, the stones kept out most of the invaders of the past two centuries. The palace loomed along the south side of town, with its back to us. The sheer size made it appear like a castle, and the outside adornments and stained-glass windows definitely added to the effect.

The west side of town held the large brick mansions of the Markis and Marksinna, but most of the town consisted of smaller cottages, looking like a quaint village from another time.

Not too far from the palace was the stable, where my loft apartment had been. The huge Tralla horses were out in the yard beside it, and though I was too far away to see for sure, I imagined that I saw Bloom running out with them, with his silver fur and lush white mane flowing behind him.

In the town square, the clock tower soared above everything, and it began to toll for the last time of the night. Between ten p.m. and six a.m., the clock went silent.

My parents lived right off the town square, and I tried to pick out their place. But the houses were packed in tightly, like town homes, and they all had matching roofs. There was no way to know for sure, but I strained my eyes, as if I would somehow be able to see my parents through the walls.

On the far east side of town along the wall was the house Ember shared with her parents. It was easier to pick out, because the houses were a bit more spread out in that area to make room for "farming." Ember's mother raised angora goats and Gotland rabbits, but I couldn't really see them.

I could see people walking around town, and though I wanted desperately to see a familiar face, they were all too far away to discern. Occasionally, I caught a flash of light from the epaulets of the Högdragen uniform, so I knew there were many guards out patrolling Doldastam.

Mixed in with them, I saw much larger figures bundled up

in brown coats. The Omte were inside, working with the guards.

Just outside the walls, a huge campsite had been set up in the valley. Personal tents were set up, along with larger rectangular marquee tents, where meetings could be held or meals could be served. Several fires were burning, casting plumes of smoke over the site.

Flying above the camp, bearded vultures circled. The Omte had brought along their birds. Legend had it that the Omte had chosen the vultures because of how much the Omte liked killing others. Since the vultures subsided mostly on bones, they would clean up the mess the Omte left behind.

"What do you see?" Finn asked. He stood back behind us, with Ludlow and Konstantin.

Baltsar, Ridley, and I lay at the top of the hill, scoping out Doldastam. Baltsar had a pair of binoculars, while Ridley and I were left gauging it with our eyes.

"It's definitely not good." Baltsar lowered his binoculars, so I held out my hand for them, and he passed them to me.

"What do you mean?" Finn asked. "Is it worse than we thought?"

I adjusted the binoculars, fixing them on the campsite outside the walls, and I immediately saw what the problem was. Not only were there a great deal of Omte soldiers, but members of the Högdragen and Kanin soldiers were mixed among them. It appeared that Viktor's army had fully acclimated with the Kanin and the Omte, and they were all blended together.

Konstantin had said that Viktor's army had been camping outside of Doldastam, and we were hoping that we could take care of them before moving on to deal with the Omte. Doldastam was too big to house the entire Omte army, so we'd assumed they'd also be camping outside the city walls.

Our plan had been to take out Viktor's men and the Omte without ever having to touch a Kanin. If we eliminated the first two threats, there was a good chance that Mina and her army would surrender, because at that point they would be outnumbered. Assuming we could take out Viktor and the Omte first.

But I wanted to avoid Kanin bloodshed as much as possible. These were people I had grown up with and trained with. They were good people, and they were going to end up dead.

fortified

S hit," I swore as I lowered the binoculars.

Baltsar stood up, wiping the mud from his clothes, and turned back toward Finn and Konstantin. "We're going to have to take on everyone all at once."

"We can't do that," I protested. As I got up, Ridley reached out and took the binoculars from me. "Innocent people will get hurt."

"You act like all the Kanin are saints and everybody else is a sinner," Konstantin said harshly. "Those Omte soldiers down there are just following orders, the same as the Kanin. And you don't have any qualms about killing them."

I shook my head. "It's different."

"It's different how? Because they're not like you? Because you didn't grow up with them?" Konstantin shot back. "Proximity doesn't make some people more worthwhile than others, Bryn."

"That's not what I'm saying. I don't want to kill anyone, but the Omte volunteered for this fight," I argued. "The Kanin were manipulated into it."

"You don't think the Omte were manipulated at all?" Konstantin arched an eyebrow. "You said yourself that weird things were going down in Fulaträsk."

And I had. I remembered how the Omte Queen Bodil had seemed eager to help Konstantin and me stop those who had gotten her nephew Bent Stum tangled up in the mess. She'd agreed to aid us in our quest to stop Viktor Dålig.

But later that night, her right-hand man Helge had done a total about-face. Not only had he refused to help us, he'd banished us from Fulaträsk in the middle of the night.

It all seemed very odd, and now it seemed even more suspicious that the Omte had aligned themselves with Viktor and the Kanin. Bodil had wanted revenge on Viktor one moment, and then she was apparently helping him the next.

The Omte were known for being finicky thanks to their short tempers, but this was ridiculous even by their standards.

"Fulaträsk?" Baltsar asked, looking from Konstantin to me with a quizzical expression. "When were you in Fulaträsk?"

Both Konstantin and I had failed to mention our excursion to the Omte capital city, since it hadn't been relevant before. But now, with the Omte so involved, it definitely wouldn't hurt for everyone to know.

"Finn." Ridley stood up, extending the binoculars toward Finn. "You should come see this."

"What?" Finn rushed up the hill, nearly knocking me over, and he snatched the binoculars from Ridley. "Oh, hell."

"What?" I demanded.

"My sister is with them." His shoulders slumped. "I just saw her go into a tent with Viktor Dålig."

"But she's not *with* with him," I said, almost insisting it when I looked at Baltsar and Ludlow, so they wouldn't think less of her. "Ember would only work with him to bide time. And this is what I'm talking about. We can't just storm Doldastam and hurt innocent people like her. We need to get them out."

"Most of the 'innocent' people down there would kill us on sight." Konstantin motioned toward the town. "They think *we're* the villains. So how do we decide who is safe and who dies?"

"Let's stop this before it gets too heated." Baltsar stepped in between us, raising his hands palms-out toward us. "It has been very a long day, and pressure is high. It's getting dark, so we should camp out tonight, and we'll come up with a plan of attack in the morning."

Below us, most of the troops were already setting up camp. We'd driven most of the day, and then spent the last four hours making the arduous walk toward Doldastam, through crowded forests and rough terrain. Everyone was exhausted, myself included, but that didn't stop the adrenaline from surging through me.

Baltsar managed to calm us down, and Finn agreed to a meeting at dawn with Mikko and all the captains. While everyone made their way back down the hill, I lingered behind to walk with Konstantin, who still moved more slowly because of his leg.

Ridley paused, looking back up at me with concern in his eyes. I nodded my head, motioning for him to go on ahead without me. He let out a heavy sigh, but he left me to argue with Konstantin on the side of the hill

"Why are you fighting with me so hard?" I asked him in a hushed voice.

"Because you've got to get the fantasy out of your head that you can ride in on a horse like some white knight and vanquish the dragon and save the kingdom," he replied wearily.

I stopped. "I don't have that fantasy."

"You do," he insisted, and he stopped so he could look at me.

It had started to rain, and it was just above freezing, so the rain felt like ice. We stood on the side of the hill, among the trees that smelled of damp pine. The light was fading, thanks to the expanding cloud cover blotting out the setting sun, but I could still see the steel in his eyes.

"There is no such thing as a good war, Bryn," Konstantin said. "Good people will die. Innocent lives will be destroyed. And in the end, one unfit person will still hold the crown."

"But Mina is evil, and she needs to be stopped," I argued. "How do you propose we do that without war?"

"She does need to be stopped, and you're correct that this is probably the only way to do it," he agreed. "But that still doesn't make it good or easy or bloodless."

kingdom of ice

The flaps to the tent were frozen shut when we awoke, and when I kicked them open with my foot, ice shattered to the ground like broken glass.

My tentmate had found herself another place to sleep, and Ridley had taken residence in my tent. Despite our exhaustion, we had stayed up for a while, trying to concoct a plan to save our families from the worst of this war, but eventually we succumbed to sleep, our bodies pressed together for warmth, as the rain beat down on the canvas.

While we were sleeping the temperature had finally dropped enough to freeze, but the rain must've kept on for some time. When we emerged from the tent, the sky was beginning to lighten, casting us in an ethereal blue glow, and everything around was covered in a thick layer of ice.

Overnight, the world had turned into a frozen wonderland. Branches were encased in ice, their early buds trapped in crystal tombs. As difficult as it was getting around on the ice, there was something oddly magical about it. The way it changed the landscape completely.

Mikko held court in a large round tent, the sides of which now looked like panes of glass. He stood inside, hunched over a table with a map of Doldastam spread out on it, wearing a dark gray fur coat. Someone had made a pot of tea over a fire, and he sipped from a chalice as he studied the map.

The large hill kept our armies and the fires mostly hidden from Doldastam, but the Skojare tower guard cloaked any smoke or light that might be visible. Still, the guards' powers weren't very strong, so we kept the fires to a minimum.

Ludlow, Finn, and Baltsar were already in with him when Ridley and I arrived. None of them were speaking, so it didn't seem like we'd missed much.

"It's damn early for all this," Ludlow muttered, pouring himself a cup of tea.

Darkness only lasted for roughly six hours this time of year, and the plan before we'd gone to bed was that we wanted to hit Doldastam as close to daybreak as possible. Well, that was the old plan, at least. I was hoping to change it.

"If we go around—" Finn began to say, but I cut him off and stepped closer to the table.

"Sire, I would like to make a request," I said, and Mikko slowly lifted his head to look at me. "I would like it if you waited to launch the assault against Doldastam and allowed myself and a few others to sneak in past the walls so we can get people out before the bloodshed starts."

Mikko straightened up, resting his solemn gaze on me. "I know that you've grown up here, so you have friends and family to consider. But you can't evacuate half the town, at least not without everybody noticing."

"I'm not asking for half the town," I persisted. "I'm asking to get my parents out, and Ridley wants to get his mother." I motioned to Finn. "Finn's parents and sister are there."

Mikko's gaze hardened, and though I wanted to go on and on listing people I'd like to get out of there—like Tilda's parents, her sister and brother-in-law, and her three-year-old niece, or Kasper's family, which had already had enough loss. Even Linus Berling and his parents, who had been nothing but kind, a rarity among royals.

I knew Mikko's fear. I would evacuate the whole town if I could, but that wasn't an option. But I'd be damned if I left my parents trapped behind those walls. Tilda had told me that the town was already turning against them, and I wouldn't let them die there.

"Do you know a way that you can get in without being seen?" Baltsar asked, his curiosity clearly piqued.

"Yes, we think so." Ridley moved to the map and tapped on the east side of the wall. "There's a narrow pipe that drains out to the Hudson Bay. It wouldn't be large enough to sneak an army in, but a few of us should be able to go in undetected."

"I would like to get my family out of there," Finn said. "They have no part in this."

"I'd like to go too, my lord," Konstantin said, appearing behind us in the tent, and I turned to look at him. "I've already had to escape Doldastam once by going out through the sewers. I can get back through them."

Baltsar rubbed his chin, staring down at the spot on the map. "I would like to see the interior of Doldastam so I can plan my attacks better, but I don't think it's worth the risk."

"You've been looking for a weak spot in the wall," Konstantin pointed out, walking over to him. "And it's hard to detect from this distance. If we were inside, I could show you the weakest points, and you can decide where you want to attack."

Baltsar arched an eyebrow. "That would be invaluable information. Our only way into Doldastam will be by taking down that wall."

"It will only take us an hour, maybe two," I persisted. "Baltsar could gather information that would give us a great advantage in the war, and then we'll return. We can go to war without anything lost."

"Go, then," Mikko said, his thunderous voice rumbling with irritation. "Leave before anybody else decides to join you."

There wasn't time to waste. If we wanted to rescue our families, it would be best to use what little time we had before the sun rose.

Just before we left, Konstantin stopped me at the bottom of the hill. He held one of his prized daggers, the handle pointed toward me. "Take it, white rabbit. It'll come in handy if we run into trouble."

I'd planned to grab one of the swords from the arsenal, but

a dagger would be easier to carry. Not to mention that none of the weapons here would be as nice or as strong as Konstantin's.

"Thank you," I started to say as I tucked it in the back of my waistband, but he'd already turned and started walking up the hill.

Climbing back up the hill outside of Doldastam was much harder work than it had been last night, thanks to the ice. Once we reached the peak and looked down below, I had to pause to marvel at the beauty of it.

Even in the dim light, the ice made it all sparkle. Every inch of it was frozen. It looked like a kingdom made of crystal.

Ridley soundlessly came up beside me, and I didn't even know he was there until he started to speak.

"It's so strange to see the town this way." He exhaled deeply, his breath coming out in a plume of white fog. "I don't just mean the way the ice makes it look like diamonds. From up here, so far away, it looks like a quiet, peaceful little village. You'd have no idea about the lives it holds, or all the dark secrets it's hiding."

"I know," I agreed. "But it really is beautiful."

I looked over at Ridley. A strange expression was on his face, somewhere between wistful and pained. But I understood exactly, because Doldastam made me feel the same way. Homesick and angry and scared and happy and terrified.

Doldastam was the only home we'd ever really known, and it was home to everyone we'd ever really loved. And we were trying to save it, assuming that it didn't kill us or that we didn't destroy it in the process.

I reached out, taking Ridley's cold hand in mine. He squeezed it, the intensity of his grip promising me that somehow we would be strong enough to take this on.

"Ready to go back home?" he asked with a crooked smile.

"Are we going, or are you gonna stand up there all day having a chat?" Konstantin called up at us, and he was already a quarter of the way down the hill.

I tried to give Ridley a reassuring smile. "Let's go."

Then we were moving again, skidding down the hill, and sneaking around the camp. We stuck close to the bay, which put about four miles between us and Doldastam. There weren't any trees along the shoreline, but the distance from where the Omte and Viktor's men were camped made it nearly impossible for them to see us.

Eventually we reached the frozen stream that let water waste flow out from the town. It was in a trough dug eight feet down, so we were able to walk along it without fear of being seen. Assuming, of course, that no one came over and looked in.

Underneath the stone wall there was an iron grate to keep people or bears from getting in. Icicles hung from the bars, and Konstantin knocked them off. At the ends, where the grate met the wall, he used the handle of his dagger to hammer on the grate until it started to come free. Then, with Ridley's help, he pulled the grate back, creating a gap large enough for someone to slide through.

He stepped aside, looking at me, and then motioned to the gap. "Ladies first."

I smiled at him, then squeezed in through the gap, and entered Doldastam for the first time in almost a month.

burial

We came up in the cemetery. There were other access points, Konstantin explained, but most of them led into highly visible areas. This would be the least conspicuous place to climb up out of a sewer grate.

The cemetery was a narrow rectangle a few blocks from the center of town. Evergreen hedges created a living fence around the outside of it, providing us with some much-needed cover.

Thick, dark deciduous trees surrounded us, and their branches came together overhead, creating a canopy. In the summer, they bloomed brightly with flowers, but now icicles hung down from them, like diamond ornaments.

Almost hidden in the dim light, I saw a bearded vulture perched on one of the branches. It cocked its head, its sharp eyes locked on me. I held my breath, waiting for it to cackle and give away our position, but it only watched us before taking flight.

Four large mausoleums sat in the center of the cemetery, pointing to each of the four directions, and the royal family and high-ranking Markis and Marksinna were buried within them. Since plots were scarce, most people had burials at the bay. What few spaces were left were usually reserved for dödsfall—or a hero's death, someone who died in service to the kingdom.

We crept along, keeping our heads low in case guards were patrolling nearby, then Ridley stopped short, causing me to run into him. Konstantin was leading the way, weaving through headstones, with Baltsar and Finn following close behind.

I was about to ask Ridley why he'd stopped, but then I looked to see what he was staring it. It was a headstone, broken in half. The bloody carcass of a fish with its guts hanging out had been left on the stone, the blood and entrails frozen to the granite.

Even though it was broken, I could still make out most of the words, and I filled in the rest:

REINHARD MIKAEL DRESDEN
1963–1999
HERO TO THE KING
BELOVED FATHER AND HUSBAND

Ridley's father had been killed protecting the King during Viktor Dålig's revolt. He'd been revered as a hero . . . until Ridley had defected from Doldastam, and now, based on the dead fish, they were punishing Reinhard for Ridley's assumed loyalties to the Skojare. To me.

I put my hand on his arm and whispered, "I'm so sorry." His jaw was set, and his eyes were hard. Then he shook his head once. "We just need to get out of here."

He turned and walked away. I wanted to right the stone and clean off the frozen blood, but we really didn't have time. And what would it matter if we did? The damage had already been done.

When we reached the edge of the cemetery, Konstantin, Baltsar, and Finn were long gone. I knew that Finn would go after his family, but I had no idea what Konstantin and Baltsar might be up to. Crouching beside the hedges, Ridley whispered that we should split up—he'd go get his mom, while I got my parents.

It seemed like the safest bet to get us out of here the fastest, so he kissed me briefly on the lips, then turned and darted in the opposite direction, while I dashed across the icy cobblestone streets toward the town square.

I was just thinking about how nice it was that I had yet to see a guard when I caught sight of two massive Omte soldiers marching right in my direction. I ducked into a narrow gap between two houses, just barely big enough to fit my body in sideways, and I started sliding through. In the middle, it started feeling very tight on my ribs, and I had to hold my breath so I could squeeze by.

When I poked my head out on the other side, I saw a member of the Högdragen patrolling at the end of the block, only three doors down from my parents' house. He kept going back and forth, walking the same beat. He'd disappear for about ten seconds, then he'd return.

I was not his commanding officer, but I knew for certain that he was supposed to be patrolling a larger area. But thanks to him being a lazy idiot, he was making it much harder for me to get to my parents' house.

By my count, I had twenty seconds to run down to my parents'. Since I had no choice, I made a break for it, running on the ice much faster than I should. When I tried to stop, I almost slid past their cottage, and I actually had to grab on to the side of it. Just in the nick of time, I jumped into the gap between my parents' house and their neighbor's.

Above the kitchen sink was a useless window. Well, my mom had always called it useless because it only gave her a view of the neighbor's wall. But today it was going to prove itself not useless as I jimmied it open and climbed inside.

I managed to squeeze in by grabbing on to the kitchen sink and pulling myself through. I'd been hoping for a more elegant landing, but I ended up tumbling headfirst onto the floor, knocking a few glasses down with me.

It was enough commotion to wake my parents, and the upstairs light clicked on. I'd just gotten to my feet by the time my dad came rushing down the stairs in his pajamas with his hair sticking up all over the place. He'd never been much for weapons, so he was wielding an antique Scandinavian sword that he'd gotten because of its historical value.

"I'm not afraid to kill you little punks," Dad growled and flicked on the kitchen light.

"Dad, it's me." I pushed back my hood so he could actually get a look at me, and he nearly dropped his sword in shock.

"Oh, my, Bryn." He just stood there staring at me for a moment, then he finally did drop the sword and ran over to me.

"Iver?" Mom called from upstairs. "Iver? Is everything okay?"

"Runa, get down here," Dad said, while giving me such a bear hug, I thought he might actually break me. But I hugged him back just as tight.

"Iver?" Mom asked cautiously, but then she must've seen me, because I heard her gasp.

By the time she'd reached me, she was already crying, and I let go of my dad with one arm so I could pull her into the hug.

"Oh, Bryn, we weren't sure if we'd ever see you again," she said between sobs.

"I know, I know." I finally pulled away from them. "I love you, and I missed you guys too. But we can talk about all that later. Right now we have to get out of here."

Mom nodded, wiping at her eyes. "I've got my bag ready. We've been waiting for our chance to escape. Just let me put on real clothes."

liberate

Getting out of my parents' house had been much easier than getting in. I didn't have a key, so I'd had to break in, but now we were safe to sneak out the back door.

Behind their house was a very small yard—a tiny strip of frozen grass separated by worn wooden fences. In the summer, my mom kept a garden there, and several of their neighbors kept chickens.

Most of the fences weren't very high, which was fortunate, since my dad had trouble jumping them as it was. Dad had always been more of an intellectual, and Mom fared much better at athletics than him, so she had no problem leaping over the fences.

We went down through the yards until we found two houses that appeared to be the farthest apart. Some of the spaces between houses were mere inches, but this gap was several feet. It was still tight to get through, especially with my parents' overstuffed rucksack, but it was much easier than the gap I'd used earlier.

From there, it was just a few mad dashes across the streets when guards weren't looking and hiding behind whatever was available. I led my mom and dad through the cemetery, around all the headstones, and as we got closer to our exit, I could see that Finn had beaten us there.

He was helping ease his mother down through the open hole. There wasn't a ladder down into the tunnel, so it was just a straight eight-foot drop to the bottom. He held Anna-li's hands, slowly lowering her down to his father, who put his hands on her waist and set her carefully on the ground.

I peered down into the hole, excited to see Ember after all this time, but she was conspicuously absent. Only Finn's parents waited in the tunnel.

"Where's Ember?" I whispered.

"She didn't come," he said in a low grunt.

"What do you mean, she didn't come?" I pressed.

Finn gave me a hard look. "I'm not going over this again. I barely managed to convince my parents to leave without her by telling them that their grandkids needed them. Ember refused to leave, and that's all there is to it."

That was apparently all he would say on the matter, because then he crouched, grabbing on to the edges of the hole, and dropped down into the sewer.

I motioned for my dad to go next, and Finn and his father

helped him. He landed with a bit of a clunk, but he wasn't any worse for the wear. Once he was standing, I helped lower my mom down.

I waited until she was safely on the tunnel floor. Above me, the sky was starting to lighten even more, and though I couldn't see it from where I sat crouched in the cemetery, I knew the sun had started its ascent above the horizon.

My parents had taken longer to get ready and get their things than I would've liked, but they were running away from the life they'd spent the past twenty years building. I couldn't blame them.

"Bryn, come on," my mom said, staring up at me. "Your dad and I will help you down."

"I have to go back and get Ember," I told her. "You go on with Finn and his parents. He'll take you back to camp."

"*Bryn!*" Mom nearly shouted, her voice cracking in desperation. "I'm not leaving without you."

"Mom, *go*," I told her. "I'll be fine. I have to do this. You and Dad need to get to safety."

"Bryn," Dad said, pleading with me to go with them. But I couldn't be persuaded.

"I gotta go. I love you guys. Stay safe." I placed the grate back over the hole, and my mom said my name again, but I didn't stay to hear more.

Since Ember had moved to Doldastam over four years ago, she'd instantly become one of my closest friends. She'd always had my back, even sometimes when no one else did. Because she was a couple years younger than me, I'd always kind of thought of her as a little sister. I was an only child, and her brother lived so far away, so we'd made each other family.

I wouldn't leave her here to die. I didn't know what Finn had done to try to convince her, but I would drag Ember out of here kicking and screaming if I had to.

The good thing was that Ember lived on the far east side of town where the poorer people lived, and that meant that guards weren't patrolling it so hard. The east also faced the bay, and the guards probably weren't counting on an attack from the water.

On the last half of my dash across town to Ember's farm, I didn't see a single guard. That made getting there much easier. I hopped the fence into the goat yard and ran over to her house.

The exterior had dark wood beams that ran along the outside, both for decoration and for support. Using the beams, I managed to climb up until I could reach the balcony that extended from her second story. That was far harder than it sounded, since everything had that nice layer of ice on it.

I grabbed the metal railing and hoisted myself up. For a moment I just lay on the balcony on my back, catching my breath and staring up at the fading stars. But then I was up, jamming open the French doors, and pushing my way inside Ember's house.

I'd just stepped through the doors and was about to say her name when I felt a hard punch slamming into my jaw, knocking me to the floor.

SIXTY-TWO

reunion

O h, Bryn, oh, my gosh, I'm so sorry!" Ember pounced on me, hugging me while I was lying stunned on the floor. "I thought you were a guard that caught my parents leaving."

"No, it's just me."

She sat back on her knees so I could sit up, and I rubbed my jaw where she'd hit me. Then I just stared at her. It seemed so unreal to be seeing her again.

Her wide eyes were so dark they were nearly black, and her bangs landed just above them. Her long chestnut hair hung over her shoulder in a thick braid. She wore shabby leggings and a patterned long-sleeve thermal shirt, and I felt a tad envious knowing that she'd slept in a nice bed in a warm house while I was out sleeping in the storm.

Her mouth spread into a toothy grin. "I can't believe it's really *you*."

"I know. It's crazy."

We'd been apart for long periods of time before. I'd gone on missions tracking changelings, and so had she. But this time it felt different. So much had happened, and neither of us was sure that we'd ever see each other again.

And then, since she couldn't contain herself, Ember hugged me again, and this time I was able to hug her back.

"I'm not going with you," she said softly, still hugging me.

I let go and pulled back. "What? Why the hell not?"

"I can't." She shook her head. "I don't have time to explain it all, but I can't. I have to stay here and help the people that are left behind."

"Ember, you're being ridiculous. Did Finn tell you about all the soldiers we have stationed out beyond the hill?" I asked. "It's going to be brutal here. You could die."

"I know, I do, but that's exactly why I have to stay," she said with a sad smile. "I can't leave everyone defenseless. Tilda and Kasper's families are still here, not to mention Juni Sköld, Simon Bohlin, and Linus Berling, and so many other of our friends." She paused. "I won't leave Delilah."

"Delilah?" I asked, and then I remembered.

The Marksinna whom Ember had been training with before. When I'd still been here, it had only seemed like a flirtation, but by the conviction I heard in Ember's voice, I guessed that their relationship had turned into something more.

"Ember, you can't risk your life for someone like this. You

need to do what you must to survive. That's what Delilah would want, if she really cares about you."

"Of course I can, and I will," Ember replied simply. "I love her."

"That's great, but—"

"I don't expect you to understand. I know that you'd never sacrifice anything for love," she said, sounding almost as if she pitied me. "For honor, for loyalty, for the kingdom, you'd give up anything. But love . . . you never had time for that."

Her words stung, probably harder than she'd meant them to, like a knife cutting straight through my heart. I wanted to argue with her, to tell her that I loved, that I loved very deeply. And not just her and Tilda and my parents, but Ridley and Konstantin.

It wasn't that I didn't have time for love, or that I wouldn't sacrifice for it. I had just been so afraid that I would lose myself and my place in the world, the way my mom had, the way Ember's mom had, and the way I had seen so many other women do before her. I refused to be sidelined by romance.

But when it came down to it, I would give anything for love. I would lay my life down for Ridley, if it meant I could spare him pain.

That's when I realized there was no point in arguing with Ember. Just as no one would be able to change my mind when it came to protecting those that I cared about, I wouldn't be able to change hers. Besides, Ember was nothing if not stubborn and loyal.

"You have to be careful," I told her finally. "All hell is going to break loose here."

"I know. You should go, before they start noticing that people are missing," Ember said. Then she suddenly exclaimed and jumped to her feet. "You're here!"

"Yeah?" I stared up uncertainly. "I've been here for a couple minutes."

"No, I mean—just wait." She turned and dashed back into her bedroom. A few seconds later, she came back carrying a handful of envelopes. "You can read these."

I took them from her, and as I flipped through them, I saw that *Bryn* had been handwritten on each one. "What are these?"

"I wrote to you while you were gone, but I didn't mail them because I had no idea where to send them." She stood with her arms folded over her chest. "Also, the Högdragen are checking all the mail going in and out, so that wouldn't have gone over well."

"Thanks, Ember." I stood up. "That was really nice of you."

She shrugged. "I missed you, and it was the only way I could talk to you."

"I missed you too." I smiled at her, and I tucked the letters in the back of my pants, next to the dagger, safely protected from the elements. "But I should go now."

"I don't know when I'll see you again," Ember said, and there was a hesitation on the word *when*, since it really should've been *if*. "Take care."

"You too."

I walked out of her house onto the balcony. I hung over the edge, and then dropped down carefully into the yard. I took a step backward and looked up to watch Ember closing the French doors.

Then I turned around and ran right smack into Ridley, who smartly put his hand over my mouth to prevent me from screaming.

"What are you doing here?" I hissed when he removed his hand.

"Looking for you. Finn told me you went back to get Ember, and I didn't want to leave you behind."

"What about your mom?" I asked.

"Finn is taking her out with the rest of the parents," he explained. "Where's Ember?"

I shook my head. "She's not coming." He didn't press any further, and it was for the best. "Do you have any idea where Konstantin and Baltsar went?"

"All I know is that Konstantin was trying to show Baltsar weak points in the town."

We hopped the fence out of the yard and started the trek back to the cemetery. We cut through alleys and backyards, taking much the same route I had on the way to Ember's house. But it was starting to get brighter out, and we no longer had darkness to help cloak us.

It had begun to snow, heavy wet flakes, and while it was only a flurry now, it felt like it could take a harder turn.

Two blocks from the cemetery, we paused, waiting in an

alley. An Omte soldier was patrolling the street, and Ridley stood with his back pressed against the nearest house, craning his neck around to watch the soldier. I crouched down beside him, trying to get a better look.

Both of us were so focused on the Omte soldier in front of us that we didn't notice anyone creeping up behind us, until I heard Helge Otäck's gravelly voice say, "Well, isn't this a nice surprise?"

SIXTY-THREE

overtaken

Helge Otäck was the Viceroy to the Omte Queen, and while that sounded like a cushy job, Helge looked more like an old biker than a politician. His leathery skin showed signs of a hundred bar fights, and his scraggly hair hung past his shoulders.

Even under the thick brown winter coat he wore, it was still obvious that Helge himself was a large man. He easily towered over us, making him appear strong by human standards, and he had the Omte strength to boot.

When he grinned down at us, I realized that two of his front teeth had been replaced with gold caps, but that was really all I had time to notice, because then Helge was moving.

Before either of us could act, Helge grabbed Ridley. Ridley tried to fight him off, hitting and kicking him any way he could, but it was futile. Helge wrapped one arm across Ridley's throat, and grabbed his hair with the other hand. Ridley clung on to his arm as Helge lifted him from the ground.

I pulled the dagger from the back of my pants and held it out toward him, not that I knew what to do to stop him.

Helge clicked his tongue at me. "Think carefully before you move with that knife, little girl. How long do you think it will take you to reach me? One second? Two? Because I can have your friend's neck snapped in half that."

"Just let him go," I said, watching Ridley struggle against Helge. "You don't want him. You want me. I'm the one that made the Queen's most-wanted list."

"Maybe so. But who says I can't have you both?" Helge grinned, and I heard a growl behind me.

I glanced over my shoulder to see a giant Omte soldier standing a few feet back at the opening of the alley. I turned again to Helge and kept my eyes on Ridley as my mind raced, trying to decide what to do. I could hear heavy footfalls as the Omte stepped closer behind me, and I waited, gauging his movements until I thought he was right behind me.

Then, in one fell swoop, I crouched and whirled around. I raised the dagger up quickly, jabbing underneath the jaw and straight up through the head of the Omte. His blood ran warm over my hand, and when I yanked the blade out, it made a sickening wet sound.

The body collapsed to the ground, and that should've been a relief, except there was another Omte guard standing right behind him. He saw what I'd just done to his friend, and he did not look happy about it.

He growled and lowered his head like he meant to charge at me, but just before he did, I saw movement to his left. An arm cloaked in a black jacket was wielding a long sword, and with the guard's eyes still locked on me, the sword sliced through his neck, decapitating him.

Baltsar stepped into the alleyway, holding his bloodied sword, and Konstantin pushed past him. He grabbed my arm, yanking me away. I looked back over my shoulder, at a grinning Helge holding Ridley hostage.

"Helge has Ridley," I said, trying to pull away from Konstantin.

"Helge also has guards coming. We can't fight them all, and we need to go before they get here," Konstantin said, still dragging me. I tried to dig my feet in, but the ice kept making them slip.

"They'll kill him," I insisted, barely able to keep myself from shouting, but I couldn't draw further attention to us.

Konstantin stopped long enough to turn on me. "No, they won't. Not yet. Mina will use him as bait. Let her."

I wanted to protest further, because it killed me to leave Ridley. And even though I knew Konstantin had a point, it felt like too great a risk.

Still hanging on to my arm, he broke the door in to a public outhouse. He went inside and kicked out the wooden base for the toilet. We couldn't risk being seen, which meant that we couldn't go back to the cemetery, so this would have to do.

Baltsar jumped in first, but I waited a moment longer.

Konstantin put his hands on my face, forcing me to look up at him.

"You can't save him if you're dead," he said roughly. "But I won't make you come with me. This is your choice."

He jumped down through the hole, and I looked back, as if I could somehow still see Ridley. I realized painfully that if Helge was going to kill Ridley, he would already be dead. Helge would've snapped his neck the second we walked away so he could go round up more of his guards.

It was either already too late, or I needed to get out of here if I wanted to come back with a rescue team. I closed the outhouse door, making it a bit more difficult for the guards to figure out where we'd gone, and I jumped down after Konstantin and ran after him through the sewers.

SIXTY-FOUR

tempest

By the time we made it back to our camp, the snow was coming fast and heavy, creating whiteout conditions. The wind had picked up, officially turning it into a late-spring blizzard. They were rare for Doldastam, but not unheard-of, and it started to feel like even the weather was against us.

My mom was waiting at the bottom of the hill for us to return. Finn and the families had arrived at camp before Konstantin, Baltsar, and I, even though we'd run most of the way back. I didn't know if Konstantin's leg was still bothering him, but he pushed himself on it just as fast as Baltsar and I.

Mom hugged me as soon as she saw me. But I just stood stiffly and didn't embrace her in return. Through the thick snowflakes, I saw Konstantin and Baltsar heading toward the King's tent, so I untangled myself from my mom and ran after them.

"If it keeps up like this, the men won't be able to see any of us commanding them," Ludlow was telling Mikko when I pushed my way into his tent. Snow came up behind me, forming a drift in his doorway.

Mikko stood on the opposite side of the table while his advisers, Finn and Ludlow, stood across from him. Baltsar moved up to take his place beside Ludlow, while Konstantin lingered by the entrance.

"As much as it pains me to say so, I agree," Finn said. "We should wait until the storm dies to make our move. We can't properly give orders or create a formation if we can't see anything."

"We can't wait. We need to go in and get Ridley." I stepped forward, but Konstantin put his arm out, blocking me and holding me back.

Mikko cast his severe gaze on me. "What's become of Ridley Dresden?"

"Give me a minute with Bryn," Konstantin said. "Baltsar, fill the King in."

Baltsar cleared his throat. "The Omte surprised Ridley and Bryn as they were retreating . . ."

I didn't hear anything he said beyond that because Konstantin had started pushing me out of the tent. When I tried to resist, he put his arm around my waist and carried me away.

"Put me down! What are you doing?" I demanded, but I didn't really fight him. After everything that had happened that morning, I didn't have the strength to defy him on things that weren't life-or-death.

He set me down once we'd gotten far enough from the

King's tent and the campsite that we could have some privacy. Bright white snow swirled around us, getting caught in his raven curls and eyelashes.

"I'm saving your ass," Konstantin said finally.

"How was that saving me?" I shot back.

"You were about to go in there and demand the King send a rescue mission after Ridley, even though you know that's suicide. Look around!" He gestured to the growing snowstorm. "We can't conduct our men in this, not if we want to win the war. And a rescue mission would only get us caught.

"Right now Mina only knows about me, you, Ridley, and Baltsar," he explained. "She already knew you, me, and Ridley were working together, and she'll likely assume that Baltsar is just someone else we picked up along the way. Even capturing Ridley, she hasn't found out anything new.

"But this army—" He pointed back to the campsite. "*That's* news to her. And if we go in with the kind of team we'd need to rescue Ridley, she'll figure out that we have a lot more muscle behind us."

He stepped closer to me, his gray eyes locked on mine. "Right now she has no clue what we're really up to, and we can't let her find out until it's too late."

I wanted to argue with him. I wanted to grab bigger weapons and gather all the men I could and storm the palace, tearing it apart until I found Ridley. But no matter how much the truth hurt, I knew Konstantin was right.

"I know it's hard setting your feelings aside to do the right thing." He smiled bitterly. "Believe me, I know better than anyone. But you can't let your feelings for Ridley—or for anyone—cloud your judgment right now." He paused, still looking down at me. "We need you, Bryn."

I breathed in deeply, relishing the way the cold air stung my throat and lungs, as snowflakes melted on my cheeks.

"I can't leave him there for very long," I said thickly.

"She won't kill him," Konstantin assured me, and with a gloved hand he gingerly wiped away the melting snowflakes from my face. "Not yet. She'll want to find out everything she can from him, and then she wants us to fall into a trap trying to rescue him. Ridley is strong and smart, and he's still alive. I promise you that."

I lowered my eyes. "He came back for me. It's all my fault."

"It is not your fault," Konstantin growled in anger, startling me into looking up at him. "Ridley chose to go back, and he wasn't paying attention in that alley either. You can't always take the blame for everything, Bryn. Sometimes bad things happen for no reason and sometimes they happen because other people fucked up. It's not always on you."

He sighed. "I'm sorry. I didn't mean to yell at you."

"No, it's okay. I think I needed to hear it." I brushed my hair back from my face. "So what do we do now?"

"You should go get your parents settled in. The snow will have us hunkered down for a while." He squinted into the oncoming storm. "Things are only going to get worse before they get better."

I wasn't sure if he was talking about the storm or the war, but it was true either way.

disturbance

The tent was sagging low on me again, and I knew I would have to go out and scrape off the snow soon before it collapsed on me entirely. The batteries were going out in the little electric lamp, making it flicker dimly, but I tried to ignore that.

I lay on my back with one arm underneath my head, buried under my sleeping bag, with Ember's letters spread out around me. The snow hadn't let up yet, so the rest of the camp had gone to bed.

Everyone else around me was probably sleeping, but every time I tried to close my eyes, all I could think about was how last night Ridley and I slept curled up against each other, and tonight he was being held in Mina's torture chamber. The very last place on earth he wanted to be.

So I lay awake, reading through Ember's letters over and over again. It was my fifth time through reading her final letter, and it still made my stomach twist in knots. To read about how Doldastam had slowly collapsed, becoming a twisted dictatorship under the harsh rule of a paranoid madwoman.

It also made me realize how much I'd missed out on in Ember's life, and Tilda's, my parents', and Ridley's. So much had befallen them, and I hadn't been able to help them with any of it.

I also missed Ember terribly. She had been shouldering such a huge burden these past few weeks, with Tilda reeling from Kasper's death, and Ridley dealing with the trauma of Mina's torture. Not to mention that Ember had taken time out to check on my parents when nobody else would. And all the other trackers and royals she was trying to train so they could protect themselves.

I wished I'd been able to talk to her more, and I couldn't wait for the day when this was all over so I could thank her for everything she'd done and tell her how proud of her I was.

Putting her letter down, I let myself indulge in a fantasy for a moment. One where there would be peace again, and Tilda, Ember, and I could go out together for a few glasses of wine the way we had before. And when I'd finished, I could go home and curl up with Ridley. Even though it hurt to think of Ridley, I couldn't help myself. I closed my eyes, remembering the feel of his skin against mine and the safety of his arms.

But it hurt too much, so I moved the thoughts along, trying to think of all the other things I would do when this was over. Like taking Bloom for a very long ride. And having dinner with my parents and asking my mom to make her gooseberry pie for me. And Konstantin would—

The thought of Konstantin jarred me out of the daydream. We had grown close, and he'd definitely become someone I could rely on. When this was all over, I did want him to be a part of my life still, but I realized painfully that I had no idea where he would fit in it.

A scuffle outside brought me from my thoughts, and I grabbed the dagger from where it sat beside me. I opened the flap, pushing back the foot of snow that had built up around the tent since the last time I'd cleared it away.

Next to the King's tent a campfire burned, and it cast enough light that I could see two guards dragging someone toward the large tent.

"Let me go," a woman insisted. "You've got it all wrong."

The guards didn't listen, so she broke free. With a few well-placed punches, she had knocked them both to the ground, and the ease of her fighting immediately made me think Omte.

I jumped out of the tent, wielding my dagger, ready to stop any Omte who dared come into our camp. She stood over the guards with her back to me, snow clinging to her dark hair and fur-lined jacket. When she turned around, I got a good look at her for the first time, and I recognized her.

In her late twenties and beautiful, especially for an Omte, she had the face of a warrior, with determined dark eyes and smooth olive skin.

"Bekk Vallin," I said, but I didn't lower my dagger.

When Konstantin and I had been to Fulaträsk, she had been kind to us, and even helped save us from the wrath of an ogre. But she had been a Queen's guard, and now she was sneaking into our base camp. So things didn't look good.

"Bryn Aven." Bekk sounded just as surprised to see me as I was to see her, but relief washed over her face. "I was trying to tell the guards but they wouldn't listen to me. I came here to help you."

I narrowed my eyes. "Why should I believe you?"

"Helge Otäck betrayed our Queen and our kingdom. He's dragged us into a war that we have no place in, all for a few gemstones." She wrinkled her nose in disgust. "He sold out our entire tribe. Queen Bodil doesn't see it yet, but I do, and I won't continue to do their bidding."

"So you're saying that you want to fight on our side?" I lowered my dagger a bit, and she nodded.

"I want to fight with whoever is going to kill Helge," she replied coolly. "And I'll help you however I can."

"I think I should take you to see King Mikko, and I'll let him decide what to do with you."

She nodded. "That only sounds fair."

dialogue

Mikko pushed in the canvas door to the round tent that had been used for planning our strategy, his long silver fur robe dragging on the ground behind him. Baltsar and Finn followed.

I'd gotten his footman to wake him, and he'd apparently decided to wake Baltsar and Finn too, but that was just as well. Bekk and I had been standing by his table, warming ourselves by the thick pillar candles that covered it.

As soon as he came and eyed up Bekk, his mouth turned down into a deep scowl. "I thought we'd decided we're taking no prisoners."

"I'm not a prisoner," Bekk said fiercely and stepped back from the table.

I put my hand on her arm in an attempt to calm her, and even through the thick leather of her jacket I could feel her thick muscles coiled. She could take us all out if she wanted to.

"She came here voluntarily to talk," I interjected hurriedly.

"What does she have to talk about?" Baltsar asked, eyeing her with the same suspicion as Mikko.

"Why don't you ask me yourself?" Bekk shot back, and I was beginning to wonder if bringing her had been a bad idea.

"All right." Mikko took a deep breath, and his broad shoulders relaxed a bit, as he attempted to start over from a less offensive position. "If you came into our camp tonight, risking a great deal, you must have something valuable to tell us."

Bekk responded by relaxing herself. "I do. I came to tell you about Helge Otäck. He duped Queen Bodil, and he's been working with Viktor Dålig. He's helped orchestrate the whole thing."

Mikko's brow furrowed. "Helge Otäck? I don't think I'm familiar with him."

"He's the Viceroy to the Omte," I said, and I bit my tongue to keep from adding that he was the bastard who was holding Ridley hostage.

"The Omte are working for the Kanin and Viktor Dålig. We all know that." Baltsar shrugged. "How is this exciting news to us?"

Bekk glared at him, her amber eyes seeming to blaze in the candlelight. "Helge helped orchestrate this whole thing. For over a year, Helge has been getting the strongest members of the Omte tribe exiled on the tiniest infractions, then passing them along to Viktor for his army."

"Why would Helge do that?" Finn asked.

"Viktor traded our men for a few sapphires. Helge has been selling off our tribe bit by bit for a few lousy blue rocks." Bekk shook her head in disbelief. "He even sent off the Queen's own nephew, and he got killed running errands for Viktor!"

The Queen's nephew was Bent Stum. From what I'd gathered from Konstantin, shortly after Bent had been exiled, he'd joined up with Viktor and was immediately paired with Konstantin to track down changelings. Viktor had brought Bent to help ensure that Konstantin would do his job.

"How do you know all this?" Mikko asked. "I'm not saying I doubt your story, but I can't imagine that Helge just confessed this all to you himself."

"I've never trusted Helge, but I started putting it together when we arrived in Doldastam and I met Viktor Dålig," Bekk explained. "I realized it wasn't the first time I'd seen him. He'd been sneaking around Fulaträsk before, whispering with Helge in the hallways of the palace.

"But last night I overheard Helge and Viktor talking and laughing about how their plans were coming together." Her lip curled in disgust. "They didn't even care if anybody overheard anymore. They think they've won already, that Viktor will be King of the Kanin and Helge will be King of the Omte, and then they will take out the rest of you, until the tribes and all your jewels are theirs.

"That's why I came here," she finished. "I can't let that happen. I'd rather see the entire Omte kingdom destroyed than those two bastards win."

Mikko stared at the floor, his hands on his hips as he

breathed in deeply through his nose. Baltsar and Finn exchanged a look, one that appeared as if they'd just realized they were in deeper shit than they'd originally thought.

"Thank you for coming here with this," Mikko said finally, and he lifted his head to look at Bekk. "What you have said is interesting, perhaps even valuable information, but it won't help us win this war or defeat Helge Otäck or Viktor Dålig."

"How about this, then?" Bekk challenged him. "The Högdragen and Kanin soldiers are inside the walls at night. If you want to avoid fighting the Kanin, attack at first light. It will only be Omte and Viktor's men on the outside."

Mikko nodded once. "Now, that might actually help."

Mikko, Baltsar, and Finn began talking among themselves, coming up with a revised battle plan. When it became apparent that Bekk and I were no longer needed, Baltsar told us that we should go rest as much as we could.

"Thank you bringing me to them," Bekk said as we walked back to my tent. I didn't know where else to put her, and it would be good if we could get some sleep tonight.

"Well, thank you for helping us," I said, then I stopped to look at her. "I do just have one favor that I'd like to ask you."

She cocked her head, appraising me. "You've got balls so big they'd make an ogre jealous. Whatever you want, I'm game."

SIXTY-SEVEN

battle cry

The snow came up past our knees, but we marched on down the hill toward Doldastam. Mikko led the way, with each of the captains leading their respective armies—Baltsar headed the Skojare, Finn the Trylle, and Ludlow the Vittra.

Konstantin, Bekk, and I had no real allegiance, so we simply walked near the front, following Mikko's long strides through the drifts. This time, since I wasn't sneaking around the town, I'd gone for a Skojare sword made of Damascus steel.

Before dawn even broke, we had started our descent down the hill. Most of the Omte were sleeping, and we'd nearly reached them before one of them caught sight of us and sounded the alarm.

Within moments the Omte were in formation. Mikko yelled his battle cry, and the war officially began.

I had a very singular plan—to get to the wall. I didn't want to be slowed down by fighting, but I would plow through anyone who stood in my way. Bekk had agreed to help me, and she quickly proved herself to be an amazing ally, knocking a giant ogre out of my way.

I'd drawn my sword, and I sliced through anyone who came at me. An Omte wielding an ax—I cut off his head. A scraggly ex-Kanin-looking guy with two swords—I cut off one hand, and then stabbed him through the chest.

I didn't think about what I was doing. I just moved on instinct, jumping over bodies and broken tents. The Omte had been living here for days, and bones littered the ground. It was a mess of garbage, rotting food, and expired campfires. It was like an obstacle course, but with murderous maniacs charging at me.

Bearded vultures circled above us, squawking their rage. All around me, I heard people crying out in pain. I saw a Skojare soldier fall to the ground, bleeding profusely from his neck.

But my mission was clear, and I couldn't save him. So I charged on.

Bekk stayed near me the entire way, stabbing or punching anyone who got too close. By the time we'd reached the wall, both of us were covered in blood. So far, none of it was our own, but that was bound to change.

I sheathed my sword and stared up the wall. It was still slippery from the ice and snow, and with all the fighting going on around us, it would be an impossible climb.

"Ready?" Bekk asked, right after stabbing a man through the head who had come running at us.

"Yeah, I'd better be," I said.

She grabbed me by the back of my jacket and the waistband of my pants, and with a grunt, she swung me back and then tossed me up. I flew into the top of the wall, with it hitting me right at the waist. I started to slip down, so I hurried to get a foothold. With my arms I brushed the snow out of my way and finally managed to get a grip on the wall and hoist myself up onto it.

I looked back down at Bekk and gave her a thumbs-up. She smiled and proceeded to punch someone so hard that his face actually caved in. I'd never seen anything like it, and I hoped I never would again. We were incredibly fortunate that she was on our side.

Then I stood up and turned my attention toward Doldastam. Since the Omte had sounded the alarm, the Högdragen and Kanin soldiers were filling the streets. I was near the palace, which was where most of them were running to—to protect the Queen.

"People of Kanin!" I shouted as loud as I could. The sounds of the battle were raging on behind me, but thankfully, the walls had a somewhat dampening effect. "Listen to me!"

Some of the people were still running around, but many looked up at me. I wasn't wearing a hood. I made no attempt to hide who I was, because I wanted them to know.

"Mina is not your true Queen!" I yelled. "You have been deceived! She killed your King! She's lying to you because she is Viktor Dålig's daughter!"

Some of the soldiers and even the panicked townspeople

gasped. Others were skeptical, but I knew they would be. I knew I couldn't reach all of them, but I hoped I could reach some.

Beneath me, the wall began to shake, and I glanced behind me to see that the Vittra hobgoblins had started going at it with an iron battering ram. They were knocking down the wall to make an entrance for our army.

The fight was still raging behind them, with the Skojare and their allies trying to take out as many of Viktor's men and the Omte as they could. Bodies littered the ground, blood staining the fresh snow, but it was hard to tell for certain if the fallen were allies or enemies.

Either way, the hobgoblins had decided it was time to move in past the wall, to get to the Kanin before they organized themselves.

"Do not let her deceive you any longer!" I shouted at the ever-gathering crowd. More and more were coming closer to hear what I had to say. "You have no allegiance to her, because she is a liar, a traitor, and a murderer! Rip off your uniforms and fight with us today! Fight against the oppression! Fight against the Queen! Fight for your freedom!"

In the crowd, I saw Ember standing with Linus Berling, both of them smiling at me.

Then a dozen Högdragen made their way to the front of the crowd, took a knee, and pointed their bows and arrows at me. The wall beneath my feet felt very unstable, and I knew I had overstayed my welcome.

Just as they began to fire, I threw my sword to the ground

on the village side and jumped down off the wall after it. The big drifts of snow helped cushion my fall, and I immediately rolled, attempting to limit the force on my legs and ankles. I grabbed my sword and scrambled out of the way to avoid getting hit by the stones that were tumbling down.

The hobgoblins had broken through, so the Högdragen turned their attention on them as the army began spilling in over the rubble. I ran back behind the buildings alongside the crumbling wall, toward the palace. Toward Ridley.

SIXTY-EIGHT

absolution

The sound of a little girl crying stopped me in my tracks. From where I stood, with snow coming up to my knees, I could see a back door to the palace half a mile away. It wouldn't be easy to break in, but that was all the more reason that I should get moving.

Just to my left was the wall, and to my right was the small dormitory where unmarried Högdragen lived. That meant this wasn't the safest place for me to stop.

All around me I could hear men and women screaming, the clash of swords, and stones crashing against each other as the wall continued to crumble. The sounds echoed off the remaining walls and outlying buildings, and became the continuous growl of battle. But over all that, I could hear the little girl crying, which meant she had to be close. Which meant that I might be able to help her.

I took a few steps forward, following the sound of the

crying, and I peered around the dorm. There in the corner, where the dorm met the Högdragen gym and the snow had drifted away, leaving a quiet spot, a little girl sat on the ground with her head buried in her arms.

I looked around, making sure there wasn't anyone lying in wait, and I crouched down and made my way toward her.

"Hey," I said softly when I got close, and she lifted her head. When I finally saw her, I almost stumbled back in surprise. She looked so much like Kasper, it was like seeing a ghost. Since she was only ten, she had the chubbier cheeks of a child and her features were softer, more feminine, but she had his dark eyes beneath her black corkscrew curls, and his nose, and even his thick eyebrows.

It was Naima Abbott, Kasper's little sister, and I knew that I couldn't leave her.

"When the fighting started, I came here to get Kasper's sword," she explained with tears streaming down her cheeks, and I couldn't tell if she recognized me or not. "But I couldn't get in. I just wanted to protect my family the way Kasper would've."

"That's very noble, but Kasper would just want you to be safe." I held out my hand to her, the one that wasn't holding my sword. "We need to get you back to your family."

She looked at me uncertainly, then she sniffled and took my hand, and I tried to figure out what I would do with her.

I knew I couldn't take her into the palace with me, since that would be full of guards who wanted me dead, and there was a good chance she could end up as collateral damage.

The safest bet would be getting her back to her family, since her father was a former Högdragen and her other brother was going to tracker school. They could protect her, and if she stayed inside her home, odds were that nobody would attack her.

Neither side of the war wanted to hurt innocent children. But with her out on the street, and ogres throwing people around, and people killing each other, it would be far too easy for her to be hurt in the chaos of it all.

Fortunately, the Abbotts didn't live very far away from the palace. Unfortunately, that meant we wouldn't be able to avoid the fighting on our way to her home.

"I'm gonna take you home," I promised her. "But if I tell you to get down, you need to find the best hiding spot you can and hide, okay?"

She nodded, so I led her around the dorm, down the alleyway between the Högdragen facilities and the palace, and toward the main street. The worst of the fighting was concentrated half a mile down, where the hobgoblins had broken through the wall.

That didn't mean others weren't fighting down here, though. A Trylle soldier and a Högdragen were fighting each other rather brutally right on the street in front of us. The Högdragen was using a sword, but the Trylle had gotten a battle-ax, and they were mercilessly hacking at each other.

I pulled Naima behind me, trying to shield her with my body so she wouldn't see the worst of it, and I pushed up my hood, hiding my blond hair. If they saw someone running across the street with a child, I would attract less attention if it wasn't obvious that I was Skojare.

The Högdragen had knocked the Trylle to the ground, and it looked like he might be about ready to finish him off, so it seemed like a good time to make a break for it.

"Run," I told Naima, and then I bolted across the street, still holding her hand.

I was hoping that we could make it across unnoticed, but behind us I heard the angry growl of an ogre. We turned sharply off the main road, running down the narrow cobblestone street toward the Abbotts' house.

The heavy crunch of the ogre's feet destroying the cobblestones as he ran behind us began to speed up, and I realized that there was no way Naima would be able to outrun him. I wasn't sure if even I would be able to without her.

"Hide!" I shouted, and pulled her to the side, practically tossing her toward the thin gap between a couple houses. It was big enough for a normal adult troll to fit in, but an ogre would be unable to grab her.

With Naima safely out of the way, I drew my sword and turned back around to face the ogre charging toward me.

SIXTY-NINE

ogre

Grinning crookedly with his oversized mouth, the ogre slowed as he reached me, and I realized that it was Torun, who had so badly wanted to squash Konstantin and me when we came across him in the swamps outside Fulaträsk.

He was over eight feet tall, with arms like tree trunks. He was completely lopsided, with everything on his right side larger than that on his left. His right hand was much larger than his left, and he had it balled into a fist.

"Squash you now," Torun grunted with an angry laugh.

"Last time you caught me without my sword," I told him. "I won't go down as easy as you think."

Torun raised his right fist high above his head, and I waited until he started bringing it down toward me, to squash me. Then I lifted my sword and jabbed it straight through his wrist. He howled in pain and when he yanked his arm back, he took me with it.

I wrapped my legs around his arm, so when he tried to shake me off, I had a good grip, and I began twisting the sword, cutting through the tendons and bone. Ogres were bigger and stronger than regular trolls, but their bones broke just as easily as for the rest of us.

Realizing I wouldn't let go, Torun grabbed me with his left hand and threw me aside. I crashed into a house, and fell into a pile of snow. The landing had been hard enough that it left me dazed and out of breath for a moment, but I stumbled to my feet as quickly as I could.

Torun's massive hand was hanging on to his arm by a flap of skin and a few tendons. He cradled it with his good hand, crying out in pain, as blood poured out, soaking the street.

When he saw me getting up, he growled in rage, and I knew I had to finish him off quickly. He charged toward me, and I dove out of the way, so he crashed into the house and knocked himself off balance. The loss of blood seemed to be affecting him, and he stumbled backward.

My sword had fallen to the ground, and I grabbed it in a flash. I went up to his right side and stabbed between his ribs, straight into his enlarged ogre heart. Torun growled once more, and that was it. He slumped over and slid off my sword, onto the street.

I wiped the blood off my hand, then held it out to Naima. She hesitated before coming out, but she finally did, and we started running down the street.

We rounded the corner, Naima's house finally in sight, and a small Omte guard came out of nowhere. He had jumped out from between two houses, and now he was charging at me. I pushed Naima behind me, using my body as a shield.

The Omte raised his sword at me, so I blocked it with my own. Since that move would only leave us at a standstill, with him pushing his blade toward me while I pushed back, I kicked him in the stomach, knocking him back.

Moving quickly, I stabbed him through the chest before he had a chance to block me. I pulled my sword free, and he fell to the ground.

That was when I looked down the street again, and I saw Rutger Abbott standing in the middle of the street. His sword was drawn, and he had the rigid stance of a Högdragen. His face was much harder than Kasper's had ever been, but he had the same eyes as both Kasper and Naima.

I stepped out from in front of Naima and whispered, "Go to your dad."

Rutger had to have seen enough to know that I had just killed an ally of the Kanin kingdom. He walked toward me with cold deliberate steps. When Naima ran to him, he hugged her, but kept his eyes on me.

I was terrified about how this would play out. If Rutger believed the lies that Mina had told him, he would blame me for Kasper's death and believe me to be an evil traitor. With that in mind, he might very well want to kill me, and I did not want to fight Kasper's dad in a battle to the death.

"Go in the house," he told Naima.

She did as she was told, rushing toward the relative safety of her home, and leaving Rutger and me alone in the street.

At least for a moment. Other guards would surely be coming soon.

"Thank you for protecting my daughter," he said finally.

"I'm sorry I couldn't protect your son," I said.

He lowered his eyes. "Go, and finish this for him." That was all he said before he turned and walked back toward his house.

I looked back over the roofs of the cottages around us, toward the palace looming over everyone and everything, and I started running toward it, my legs moving as fast as they could.

conspire

On the way to the palace, I tried to avoid as many main roads and conflicts as I could. Not only because I wanted to get there as quickly as possible, but also because I wanted to avoid killing any Kanin if I could help it. And it was a bonus if I ended up not getting killed myself.

Still, I'd had to kill two more Omte soldiers before I found myself in close proximity to the palace. I crouched down next to Astrid Eckwell's mansion, with the body of Simon Bohlin in the snow beside me.

On my way here, I'd seen Simon, with his head lolled to the side, bleeding from a fatal wound in his stomach.

For a nearly year we'd dated, until I'd broken up with him because I was looking for something more casual. He had been a great tracker, though, which was one of the things that attracted me to him. We'd grown up together, and he'd always been kind to me in a school where a lot of kids hadn't been.

I couldn't leave him in the middle of the street to get crushed under ogres' feet, so I dragged him to the side of the house. I knew I couldn't move all the bodies, that I couldn't save everyone, but I couldn't bear the thought of leaving Simon out like that.

Leaning with my back against the cold bricks of the mansion, I tried to catch my breath and gather myself. I didn't have time to mourn Simon or anyone else who would die today. Not if I wanted to save Ridley and stop Mina.

I looked back out to the street, where the fighting raged on, just in time to see Ember, fighting her way through the crowd. Behind her was Linus Berling, and while he wasn't doing an amazing job, he was holding his own fairly well. He hadn't been killed yet, but he did appear to be bleeding from his arm.

Ember finally managed to break free from the fighting, and Linus chased after her, following the path she'd made. They ran right up to the mansion next door to Astrid's, diving over the fence and running around to the back door.

If I wanted to storm the palace, it wouldn't hurt to have someone like Ember at my side. She was a quick, strong fighter, and there were going to be many more guards left to face.

I decided to go to Ember and see if she would help me free Ridley. I ran around the back of Astrid's house, and then I jumped the neighbor's fence. I wasn't sure if I should knock or not, but since Ember had just gone in through the back door, I decided to try it for myself.

As soon as I pushed it open, Ember was there with her sword in my face.

"Oh, jeez, Bryn." She sighed and lowered her weapon. "You really need to start knocking." She opened the door wider for me, letting me in.

The door opened into the kitchen, where Linus sat shirtless at the kitchen table. A girl stood beside him, her dark hair falling around her, as she tried to clean up a nasty gash on his arm.

"Bryn." Linus tried to smile at me, but his injury caused him to wince instead. "When I saw you on the wall today, I was so happy that you were okay and fighting to get rid of that witch in the palace."

It had been nearly two months since Linus had first arrived in Doldastam, and in that short time he'd already grown and changed so much, even though he was barely eighteen. He'd spent time training with Ember, and his arms and chest had begun to fill out, with muscles bulking up his lanky frame.

Light freckles dotted his face, and he still had an openness to his expression, like he could never completely hide what he was feeling, but his eyes had darkened, taking some of the innocence he'd arrived with.

Around his wound, his skin had begun to change color, shifting to blend into our surroundings. When the girl tending his wounds tried to stitch up the gash on his arm, Linus winced, and the color intensified, making it almost appear as if his arm had disappeared, other than the parts stained red with blood.

"We just came here to fix Linus up, and I wanted to get

Delilah somewhere safe," Ember explained as she closed and locked the door behind me.

Delilah looked back at me, and I hadn't recognized her right away because I'd only met her once before. She was very beautiful, with dark almond-shaped eyes and a soft smile. In her jeans and tunic sweater, she appeared slender and tall.

"We got Linus's parents out of here already," Ember went on. "My brother is helping refugees escape. Since most of the fighting is going on around the back wall, Finn is leading evacuees right out the front gate and to your camp on the other side of the hill."

"I came back to help other people escape," Linus said, and he gritted his teeth when Delilah turned her attention back to fixing him up.

"My parents won't leave." Delilah scowled, and she began wrapping Linus's arm with gauze. "They're in the basement hiding in a panic room, and I'm actually surprised they haven't come back up here to drag me down with them."

"So that's what we've been doing—trying to help people evacuate." Ember looked me over, her eyes lingering on my bloodied sword. "What have you been doing?"

"I've been trying to get to the palace," I said.

I thought about explaining to her about Ridley, and how he'd been captured, and how I had to get him free before they killed him. But it all felt like too much to say aloud, and there was enough going on here. Everyone in this room had more than their share of problems to deal with.

"I saw you, and I wanted to make sure you were okay," I

said instead, my words sounding tight around the lump in my throat.

"I think we can handle it," Ember told me, trying for a reassuring smile. "I know you've got your work cut out for you."

A loud knocking at the front door interrupted our conversation. The kitchen was at the back of the house, so we couldn't see the door from where we stood, but we all turned toward it.

"I locked and bolted the front door," Delilah said softly.

But the knocking just grew louder and more intense, until it changed from knocking to someone trying to break down the front door.

SEVENTY-ONE

adversary

Ember and I both drew our swords and moved closer to the entryway from the kitchen so we could see into the front hall, when the door came crashing in.

"Markis or Marksinna Nylen?" a man asked in the strong, clipped tones of a Högdragen. "Are you safe?"

"I saw her run in here!" a female voice shouted shrilly, and it was like nails on a chalkboard, so I placed it instantly—Astrid Eckwell. "Go inside and get her! She's the one behind it all!"

I grimaced, realizing that Astrid must've seen me coming over here. She had probably been holed up in her mansion with her family and their own personal Högdragen standing guard. But her contempt for me was so strong that she'd left the safety of her home to make sure that I got my punishment.

We'd grown up together, and Astrid had been unrelentingly vicious to me. She had been the first one to ever call me a half-breed, and she had made certain that it caught on as a cruel chant that the other kids would sing to me during recess.

It wasn't until my teenage years that I realized the sheer level of her hatred stemmed from jealousy and feelings of inferiority. Her house and most of her riches came from an inheritance that should've been my dad's, and would have been my own, had my grandparents not disinherited my dad for marrying a Skojare. The Eckwells—as second cousins to my dad—were the closest relatives and next in line.

Astrid only had her status because my dad had given it up. Her life should've been mine, and I think that secretly she was always afraid I would take it from her.

But I had never wanted her life, and now she was trying to get me killed.

"I'm here," Delilah said, stepping out from the kitchen before either Ember or I could stop her. "I'm Marksinna Delilah Nylen, and I'm here and I'm safe."

"Where is she?" Astrid demanded.

I leaned against the kitchen wall and carefully peered around the entryway to watch the scene unfolding. The Högdragen was Janus Mose, a tracker I'd gone to school with who was only a couple years older than me. He didn't appear as confident about their intrusion into the Nylens' home as Astrid did, and she pushed her way around him.

A war was raging on half a mile from her doorstep, and she wore a gown with a fur stole. It was typical of her arrogance and stupidity.

"I saw that Skojare traitor run in here, and if you're housing her, you'll go to prison too," Astrid said, sneering at Delilah. "Or you'll be executed. Janus could do it right on the spot."

"There's no need for that." Ember sheathed her sword and rushed out to the main hall.

Linus pulled on his shirt and stepped out from the kitchen. "You probably just saw us. Ember and I ran in here to get away from the fighting."

"I wanted to keep the Markis safe," Ember explained, standing beside her girlfriend.

"With all due respect, Markis Linus, you look nothing like a little blond half-breed traitor," Astrid told him, doing her best to keep her cool when talking to a royal who outranked her. "Bryn Aven is here, and I know it. And if you all keep covering it up, Janus will have no choice but to execute you all."

I gripped my sword tightly in my hand, but I didn't move. Not yet.

Theoretically, Astrid was right. In times of war, a member of the Högdragen had every right to execute those who were standing in the way of the kingdom or harboring traitors. But while Janus hadn't been the brightest guy I'd gone to school with, he'd gone through enough training to know that he shouldn't act rashly on the word of a spiteful Marksinna.

"Are you housing Bryn Aven?" Janus asked them directly, standing tall in his Högdragen uniform. The light coming in through the open windows caused his epaulets to shimmer, and he kept his expression hard but blank, the way Kasper always had.

"It's just us here," Delilah said, speaking as calmly as she could.

"Then where are your parents?" Astrid demanded, and she looked up at Janus. "They haven't left yet."

"My parents are in the panic room—" Delilah began, but she couldn't even finish her sentence before Astrid let out a delighted gasp.

"They have a panic room! They're hiding Bryn in there!" Astrid shouted, pointing wildly into the house. "Search the house until you find her."

"Is this really necessary?" Linus asked. "This all seems to be getting out of hand, especially with everything that's going on outside. You should take Astrid back to her house so she can be safe."

"As soon as we find the traitor, this will be all over," Janus told him firmly. "And then everyone can be safe."

That was when I knew that this wouldn't end peacefully, and I couldn't let Ember, Delilah, and Linus fight my battle for me. I stepped out from the kitchen. Astrid screamed when she saw me, but her eyes were wide with excitement.

"I told you she was here!" Astrid squealed.

Janus raised his sword, and his eyes were unforgiving and his jaw was clenched. I knew that look—he meant to kill me, with Astrid cheering him on.

"It doesn't need to come to this," Delilah said.

She stepped closer to him, perhaps meaning to reason with

him, but she didn't understand the severity of the situation. With the tension of the war, Mina's fabrications about me, and Astrid screaming in his ear, Janus was like a gun, cocked and loaded, just waiting for something to set him off.

When Delilah stepped toward him, that was it. He drew his arm back—he was going to kill her, the way he would kill anything that stood in his way. Everything unfolded so quickly, but it felt like slow motion—like the world had stopped and I could see it all but I couldn't move fast enough to change anything.

Linus shouted the word *stop*, but Ember was already moving, diving at Delilah and pushing her out of the way. Delilah fell to the floor just as Janus drove his sword straight through Ember, and she hit the floor with a sickening thud.

SEVENTY-TWO

allt är mitt

I ran at Janus, not caring if he was a Högdragen or if he truly believed he was justified in what he'd done. For a moment my anger blocked out any rational thought, and I was just moving.

Janus raised his sword, blocking me, but I was moving faster and faster. So each time he blocked me, I would move away and come at him quicker, until I finally found my opening. I drove my blade through his throat, pushing him back against the wall, until I'd pinned him there like a bug in a glass case. Blood poured from his throat, staining the dark fabric of his uniform.

I left him that way and turned back to survey the scene. Astrid stood with her back pressed against the wall, looking rightfully terrified. Linus stood off to the side of Ember with tears in his eyes, and Delilah was sitting with Ember, holding her in her arms as she slowly bled out.

I walked over to them and fell to my knees.

"Why did you do that?" Delilah asked through tears, and brushed Ember's hair back from her face. "You shouldn't have done that."

"Of course I should have," Ember said, her voice soft as she stared up into Delilah's eyes. "You're alive, and you're safe, and I love you. There is no greater thing I could do than die to save my true love."

"Ember, I love you," she sobbed. "What will I do without you?"

"Fight." Ember closed her eyes, but her chest was still rising and falling with shallow breaths. "And live. My love will go on with you, so live as long as you can."

"*Allt är mitt, och allt skall tagas från mig,*" Delilah said, reciting a Pär Lagerkvist poem in Swedish, sounding lyrical and beautiful. "*Inom kort skall allting tagas från mig.*"

While my Swedish wasn't as good as it should be, I thought what she said translated to, "All is mine, and all shall be taken away from me, / within moments all shall be taken away from me."

Then Ember took her last breath. Delilah leaned over and gently kissed her on the lips, and then she laid her head on Ember's chest and wailed like her heart had just been ripped out of her.

One of my best friends had just died, and I wanted to fall apart the way Delilah was doing, but I knew there wasn't time. Later, I would mourn for Ember the way she deserved.

But now I had to finish things so that she wouldn't die in vain. I needed to get Delilah safe.

I stood up and pulled gently on her arm. "Delilah. You need to let Linus get you to safety." I looked back at him. "You do know how to get the refugees out of here, right?"

He nodded, wiping at the tears in his eyes. "Yes. Ember showed me. I know what I need to do."

"Good. I need you to take Delilah out of here and keep her safe." I turned back to Delilah, since she still hadn't gotten up, and I pulled her to her feet. I put my hands on her face, forcing her to look at me. "Listen to me, Delilah. I know this is hard, but Ember died so that you could live. So you *need* to live. You have to pull yourself together, and follow Linus out of here. Do you understand me?"

She tried to stop her tears and nodded. "Yes."

"Good." I took Ember's sword and handed it to Delilah, since Linus already had his own. "Move quickly and stay safe." I looked from one of them to the other. "Both of you."

"I will," Linus assured me. "I'll finish what Ember and I started."

He stood up tall, looking more confident than I had ever seen him before, and I hoped I was doing the right thing, leaving him to protect the thing that meant the most in the world to Ember. But I had trust that she'd trained him right and he could do this.

Linus took Delilah's hand and led her out the front door, looking for the quickest escape route to the front gate, where

Finn could lead them to. And that meant I was alone with Astrid.

I turned back to face her, and she flinched. She hadn't moved from where she'd been before, with her back pressed against the wall.

"Bryn, I'm sorry. I didn't mean it. I didn't mean any of those things," she said in one hurried sentence, almost as if it were all one word.

I grabbed the sword from Janus's throat, which caused him to fall to the floor, and she cringed. I stalked over to her with slow, deliberate steps and Astrid began to whimper.

"Please, Bryn. I'm sorry. I didn't mean—"

Astrid kept right on talking until I pressed the blade to her throat, still warm from Janus's blood. Then her eyes flew open and her mouth flew shut. I didn't break the skin—I held the blade just hard enough so she could feel exactly how sharp the edge was.

"I could kill you right now," I growled. "And I should. But I'm not going to." I stepped back from her and took the sword from her throat.

"Thank you, Bryn. Thank you so much. I don't know—"

"But I'm not going to save you," I said, cutting her off.

Her hand was on her throat, rubbing where the sword had been. "What are you talking about?"

"There's a war going on, and I just killed your only protection." With my sword, I pointed to the window, where the fight was coming increasingly closer to the doorstep.

I grabbed her wrist and started dragging her outside. She

was pleading with me to stop, but it fell on deaf ears. As I pulled her out to the street, a Tralla horse came racing by, its heavy hooves pounding on the snowy cobblestones. With all the fighting, the fence outside the stables must've been broken down, freeing all the horses.

But that was the least of my concerns. I dragged her toward two hobgoblins who were just finishing taking down an Omte ogre at the edge of the fray. Astrid began to scream as soon as she saw them, since she was unaccustomed to them and frightened by their appearance.

"Bryn! Please! Let me go!" she begged.

"Hey, guys!" I yelled, and the hobgoblins looked over at me, and then I motioned toward Astrid. "She just had a soldier killed that was helping us, and she has close ties to the Kanin Queen."

"Queen Mina will have your head if any of you lay a hand on me!" Astrid shouted, her voice growing shriller.

Since she seemed like she would do just fine digging her own grave, I let go of her and started walking away. The two hobgoblins smiled before they pounced on her. I heard her screaming, but I didn't look back. I didn't need to.

bloodied

At first I'd been trying to avoid hurting any of the Hög-dragen. But after Janus, I would kill anyone who ran at me with a sword. I'd always known that war wouldn't be so black-and-white, but I'd come to realize that there was a darker shade of gray, where right and wrong came second to simply surviving.

I wanted to make a straight line to the palace and find Rid-ley, but the fighting made it hard to move quickly. I could make it a few feet, stepping over bodies, before I'd find my-self in combat with someone else. My hands and clothing were soaked with blood, and there had to be a quicker way to get to the palace.

Then, almost like a guardian angel, I heard Bloom. I looked back and saw the massive Tralla horse running through the streets. His sterling mane flew behind him, and I whistled for him. He reared up on his back legs, braying loudly, and

I saw that the fur around his hooves had been stained dark crimson.

He saw me and raced toward me through the crowd, knocking over anyone who got in his way. When he reached me, I sheathed my sword, and I jumped up to grab on to his mane. I tried to hoist myself up, but Bloom was over seven feet tall at his shoulders, so I couldn't exactly just hop up on him.

Then I felt a hand under my feet, pushing me up, and I finally got high enough so I could swing my leg over. I looked down to see who'd helped me, and Baltsar smiled up at me before taking on a Högdragen guard.

"Go, Bloom," I commanded, but he didn't need more prompting. Even he knew that a war zone was no place to pause.

He charged ahead, his massive size chasing everyone out of the way. People either dove to the side, or he ran them over. I buried my fingers in his mane, leaning into him and urging him to go faster.

After losing Ember, I knew I had to get to Ridley as soon as possible. I couldn't waste any more time killing Omte or helping anyone. I couldn't let him die because I'd been busy somewhere else.

Delilah's last words to Ember, the poetry, pounded in my head like a death knell. I wouldn't let all be taken away from me. Not without a fight to the bloody end.

For so long, I had thought of love as a weakness—as something that would only make you distracted and vulnerable.

But what I'd come to realize was that love had only made Ember braver than she'd ever been before. Love made Tilda find the strength to carry on. Love made my parents willing to sacrifice everything for each other.

And love made me stronger. I would do anything to save Ridley. I would do *everything* I needed to do.

The massive door to the palace had already been knocked down, but after seeing the way the hobgoblins had handled the wall, I wasn't surprised. The door was over twenty feet tall, so Bloom ran through the opening with ease and straight into the grand front hall.

It was a massive stone room with high ceilings that rose several stories high and had iron chandeliers. The only natural light came through stained-glass windows that faced different directions. Right now the sun shone through the window depicting the Long Winter War, which left everything glowing red.

Other than a few dead bodies scattered around, the front hall appeared empty. The rest of the palace wouldn't be so easy for a horse of Bloom's size to maneuver around, and I really didn't want him getting hurt either. I swung my leg over and hopped to the floor.

"Son of a bitch," Konstantin said, and I looked over to see him coming in from a corridor off to the left of the hall. He looked up at Bloom, shaking his head.

"What?" I looked up to make sure Bloom was okay, but the horse seemed fine.

"I told you that you couldn't come in riding on a horse like a white knight, and so you had to go and prove me wrong." He smirked at me.

I stroked Bloom, telling him he'd done a good job, then I smacked him on the side and told him to get out of here. He did as he was told, racing back out through the doors again, and I turned to Konstantin.

"Have you found Ridley or Mina?" I asked.

He shook his head. "Not yet. I checked the dungeons for Ridley, but there was no sign of either of them there. I was heading to the throne room."

"You think Mina will be there?" I asked.

"She's obsessed with the crown, so it would make sense," he said. "And if we find her, I'm sure she can tell us where Ridley is."

I nodded. "Then I'm going with you."

The throne room was rarely used, except for coronations and the occasional ceremony. It was at the south end of the palace, straight at the end of a long, narrow corridor that led out from the main hall.

I let Konstantin lead the way, jogging a few steps ahead of me, but we both slowed when we saw someone standing in front of the doors to the throne room, blocking us.

Wearing only a leather vest to reveal the scars and tattoos that covered his thick biceps was Helge Otäck. His greasy hair hung around his face, and he grinned at us as we approached, showing off his gold teeth.

"Well, well, well. You thought you could just come waltz-
ing up here—"

"I really don't have time for this shit," I muttered, so I took
my sword and threw it at Helge like a spear, right at his stupid grinning mouth with his gold caps.

The blade went through, knocking out one of his teeth, and
going out the back of his skull. His open mouth tore around
the blade, making him look like a mutilated clown, and when
I pulled the sword back, the top half of his head fell to the
floor.

"Well done," Konstantin said. He kicked Helge's body out
of the way, and then he pulled open the door to the throne
room.

It was a small square room, with white velvet drapes hanging over the stone walls, from the ceiling down to where they
pooled on the floor. Two thrones sat at the back of the room,
and Viktor Dålig sat in the larger of the two, looking like he
owned the place. But that wasn't what really caught my attention.

Hanging from the center of the room was a large metal
cage. A black-bearded vulture sat perched on top of it,
squawking at us, and Ridley was inside it, lying on the bottom with his clothes torn, looking badly beaten.

He lifted his head when the door opened, and I could see
dried blood had crusted along his temple. He knelt at the bottom of the cage, looking down at me with fear in his dark
eyes, and he clenched the metal bars.

"Bryn, get out," Ridley warned me frantically. "It's a trap!"

SEVENTY-FOUR

ensnared

The white velvet drapes along the wall began to move, rippling like waves, and men dressed in black stepped out. There had been just enough space between the fabric and the cold stone to conceal them, and a dozen of Viktor's soldiers filled the small room.

Behind Konstantin and me, the doors slammed shut, and that's when Viktor threw back his head and began to laugh. His long, black hair swayed as he did. The dull red of his scar ran from just above his left eye down to his right cheek, a present from Ridley's father before Viktor had killed him.

"The prodigal son returns," Viktor said, grinning broadly at Konstantin.

"I was never your son," Konstantin spat at him.

I had my sword at the ready, waiting for the soldiers to attack, but Konstantin stood with his weapon at his side, his eyes fixed on Viktor.

Viktor's smile finally fell away. "I told you what would happen if you betrayed us. And I knew that eventually you would return to collect your punishment."

"No." Konstantin shook his head and pointed his sword at Viktor. "I told you that I would return to give you *yours*."

"Enough of this," Viktor growled. "Capture them. The Queen wants to torture them herself."

The soldiers started coming toward us, and Konstantin and I moved so we were back to back. Our only advantage was that it was a small space, so we could rely on each other. That, and Konstantin was the best swordsman I'd ever met.

I pushed down my fear, my worry for Ridley, my anger toward Viktor and Mina. I blocked out everything, leaving my mind blank, so when a solider struck out at me, I reacted only on instinct. I let my body move the way it had been trained to, blocking every attack, and lunging when I saw an opening.

From the corner of my eye, I kept trying to look for a way to free Ridley as Konstantin and I pivoted around the room, fighting off the soldiers as quickly as they came at us. The cage hung from the ceiling by a long chain, and I finally saw where it attached to the wall, in a small gap between the drapes.

Viktor sat on the throne in the center of the room, watching it all as if we were putting on a performance solely for his entertainment, and then I realized sourly that we were. He had staged this all with the expectation of trapping Konstantin or me here, and he'd lucked out by getting both of us.

Above, I heard the cage rattle, and I glanced up to see the

bird had taken flight, as Ridley started swinging the cage. He used his body weight to rock it, and I could see the anchor straining in the brick wall.

The cage had been meant to hold doves, which Mina released during special ceremonies. It hadn't been built to withstand the kind of tension Ridley was putting on it.

"Bryn!" Konstantin shouted, trying to direct my attention back to the fight.

I turned to see a soldier charging at me. I kicked him in the stomach, sending him flying back into the wall, and he dropped his sword to the floor. I ran at him and before he could get to his feet, and I stabbed him through.

Looking around the room, I realized that it was full of dead bodies, and Viktor's expression had turned to an angry scowl. We'd killed all but three of his men, and Konstantin was dealing with two of them.

The third ran at me, and I lunged at him, driving my sword through his stomach. Then Ridley shouted a warning, and before I could even think, his cage clattered to the floor mere inches from me.

I ducked out of the way just in time. I narrowly avoided getting crushed by the metal enclosure, but I dropped my sword in the commotion. The cage bounced over the bodies and crashed into the wall.

I ran over to help Ridley open the door, but as I did, his face blanched with horror.

"Bryn, watch out!" he shouted, and I whirled around just in time to see Viktor behind me, carrying a bloody sword.

reprisal

I felt the sharp point of the blade tear my clothes and pierce the tender flesh of the left side of my abdomen, just above my hip. I staggered back, my eyes scanning the floor for a nearby sword. Konstantin was busy on the other side of the room, finishing off the last of the men, so he couldn't toss me a weapon.

Viktor sneered at me, and I spotted my sword—the handle red with blood, lying a few feet to my left, directly beside the birdcage. But before I could make a play for it, Ridley kicked open the door to the cage. He climbed out and stepped toward Viktor, blocking Viktor's access to me.

"Enough games," Viktor growled at him. "It's time to finish this."

He lunged at Ridley, but Ridley dodged to the side and grabbed Viktor's arm. He twisted his wrist back, and even after Viktor dropped the sword, Ridley kept twisting until the bones in his hand and wrist finally made a loud cracking sound.

Viktor was bigger than Ridley, but he was also older and out of practice. And I knew that Ridley wouldn't let him get the best of him again.

Viktor let out a loud pained groan, and Ridley let go of him, allowing Viktor to stand up.

"I thought you were going to finish this, old man," Ridley growled at him as Viktor staggered back away from Ridley.

"There's still time," Viktor assured him with a sick smile.

Ridley moved toward him and kicked his feet out from under him, and Viktor fell back onto the bodies of his fallen men. He lay at an awkward angle, with his back curved up over the bodies and his head on the cold stone floor.

Ridley jumped on top of Viktor and grabbed him by his greasy hair, and he slammed his head into the floor three times. He wasn't dead—not yet anyway—but he wasn't really moving either.

"That was for Bryn," Ridley said as he got to his feet.

The scar that ran along my temple seemed to throb in sympathy, the one that Viktor had given me when he had bashed my head into a stone wall.

Konstantin had killed the last two men, and he stood on the other side of the room, catching his breath. With Viktor incapacitated, Ridley turned his attention to me.

"Are you okay?" he asked, his eyes darting down to where my blood was staining my shirt.

"Yeah, it's just a flesh wound." But it did hurt far worse

than I was willing to let on. Then I motioned to him. His shirt was unbuttoned in the front, revealing dark bruises all over his body. "Are you okay?"

"Hey, hey," Konstantin said, interrupting us.

When we looked over at him, he tossed his sword to Ridley, who caught it easily. I turned back to see that Viktor Dålig had gotten up and was stumbling toward us. Blood streamed down the side of his face, but he'd picked up a sword and managed to wield it with his shaky left hand, the one that Ridley hadn't broken.

Ridley stepped away from me and walked toward Viktor. Viktor tried to lunge at him, and Ridley countered by easily knocking the sword from him. Viktor stood before Ridley, with his head high, and began to laugh.

"What's so funny?" Ridley asked.

"I should've killed you the second Helge brought you in," Viktor said through his laughter. "I could've split you in two, just like I did your idiot father."

And that was the last thing Viktor ever said, because Ridley stabbed him in the stomach. Viktor stumbled back and collapsed onto the throne. He let out a few more raspy breaths before expiring.

"And that was for my dad," Ridley said.

"He would be proud of you," I said, trying to comfort Ridley.

He turned back to face me, and I stood up as straight as I could, with my hand pressed against the wound Viktor had given me. Ridley's eyes were dark, and he put his hand gently on my face.

"You sure you're all right?" he asked.

"Yeah." I smiled up at him. "As long as you're okay, I'm okay."

Konstantin took his sword back from Ridley and wiped the blood off on his shirt, then turned toward Ridley and me. "Shall we move on? There's still plenty more enemies to take down."

SEVENTY-SIX

chambered

The fighting had moved into the main hall of the palace. As Ridley, Konstantin, and I ran down the narrow corridor from the throne room, we could already hear the clash of swords. Baltsar and Bekk were fighting alongside other Skojare and Trylle allies against twenty or so Kanin guards and Omte.

Before we left the throne room, I'd torn off a strip from the white curtains and tied it around my waist, putting pressure on my wound to stop the blood loss. That helped some, but I could still feel myself moving more slowly than I should have. But I pushed myself on, refusing to quit or fail now, not when we were so close to defeating Mina.

Ridley had grabbed a sword, and when we reached the main hall, he joined the fight without missing a beat. Nothing that Viktor or Mina had done to him slowed him down, and I wished I had the time to admire that about him. Or admire anything about him. I wanted to relish the fact that he was safe and alive again, but an Omte soldier was trying to stab me.

I started fighting beside Ridley, but from the corner of my eye, I saw Konstantin running. He raced down the hallway toward the private quarters. I dodged the attack from the Omte soldier, and then I took off after Konstantin, running as fast as I could to catch up to him.

So far, the private wing looked untouched. The pearlescent tile wasn't stained with blood. The ivory drywall covering the stone had no holes or dents. None of the furniture was broken and none of the paintings were torn.

Konstantin had stopped where the hallway T'd, looking in both directions, and that's when I reached him.

"Where are you going?"

"To find Mina." He looked down at me. "I should finish this on my own. You don't need to come with me."

"Of course I'm coming with you," I insisted. "I want her dead just as badly as you do, and you don't know what she's up to."

"Yes, I do. She knows she's losing now, and she's going to make an escape." He turned to the hallway to the left, jogging ahead, and I went after him. "She's in her room, gathering everything she needs to start over."

The Queen's chambers were in the top of the tower on the south side of the palace. On the stairwell just outside the landing were two dead Högdragen soldiers, both with their throats slit. These were the first bodies we'd seen in the private wing so far.

"She killed them," Konstantin whispered. "They served their purpose, and she didn't want them taking her jewels."

He crept quietly across the landing, leading the way, and slowly pushed open the door. I peered in over his shoulder, and the room looked empty. Everything was in order—the satin bedding on the four-post bed was made, the lush white rugs were unruffled, and the sheer curtains were undisturbed over the windows.

I was about to ask if she was still here when I saw a small white rabbit hop across the floor. It was Vita, Mina's pet rabbit, and on every trip she'd ever gone on, she'd taken it with her. As far as I could tell, Vita seemed to be the only thing Mina really cared about. The rabbit scampered under the bed at the sight of Konstantin and me, hiding from us.

Then I heard a sound, reminding me almost of rain on a windshield, coming from the dressing room off the bedroom.

"She keeps her private safe in there," Konstantin whispered and pushed the door open farther. He crept into the room with his sword drawn, watching the half-open door to her dressing room warily.

I followed him inside, and he motioned for me to go toward a large armoire near one of the windows. It been painted white, but it was made out of wood, with an old legend carved into it with pictures—Odin gifting the Kanin people with the Gotland rabbits.

Konstantin came up beside me and quietly opened the armoire doors. From the dressing room, we could hear Mina softly singing an old Kanin war song to herself, and I heard the tinkling glass sound of jewelry and gemstones colliding with each other as she loaded up a bag.

"Get in," Konstantin whispered, his voice so soft it was almost inaudible.

I did as he commanded, stepping up into the armoire, thinking that he meant for us to hide in here until Mina came out of the dressing room. If she was packing up all her riches and planning to make a break from a kingdom at war, she had to have a weapon on her, and clearly she knew how to use a dagger, given that she'd left two guards dead on the steps.

The armoire was large enough that I could stand up in it, and with the lift at the bottom, it made me as tall as Konstantin. He looked at me for a moment, his eyes studying me.

Normally his eyes were cool like steel, even when he was vulnerable, but now there was a strange smokiness to them, masking his thoughts. His hair fell across his forehead, and I wanted to ask him what was going on, but he suddenly grabbed me. He put an arm around my waist, his hand strong and demanding on my back, and pulled me closer to him. Without waiting for my reaction, he kissed me roughly on the mouth.

His mouth was cold, but heat rushed through me anyway. Under his insistent desire, I felt something tender and passionate. I wasn't sure if I should embrace him or push him, and parts of me wanted to do both.

When he stopped kissing me, he kept his arm around my waist, and his eyes were filled with a yearning so strong, it took my breath away. Then he stepped back, and I still felt his touch lingering on my lips.

"I'm sorry, white rabbit," he whispered, and shut the doors. I heard a soft clicking sound, and I realized too late that he'd locked me inside the armoire. "I want you safe this time."

SEVENTY-SEVEN

white rabbit

Konstantin," I hissed but didn't say more. I wanted to break down the doors and jump out, but I couldn't. Not if I didn't want to risk giving away his position.

Through in the gap between the doors of the armoire, I watched Konstantin back away. He'd trapped me, knowing that I wouldn't try to break out because it would mean risking his life.

Then, slowly, as he stepped back, I saw his skin begin to change. Going from its normal deep tan to blend in with the stark white of the Queen's chambers. He slipped off his shirt, kicking it underneath the bed, and stood against the wall beside the four-post bed.

His daggers remained tucked in the back of his pants, and he stood so that from his waist down, he was mostly hidden behind the abundance of linens on the bed. He'd almost disappeared completely.

Mina came out of the dressing room a few moments later, dragging a large suitcase across the floor with great difficulty. All her gemstones must've weighed it down quite a bit. Still in "mourning" over Evert's death, she wore a long black gown.

The satin of the bottom of the gown clung to the curves of her hips before flaring out around her feet. The top of her bodice went up to her throat, but it was made of a thin, open lace so that her breasts were almost entirely visible through the fabric. The sleeves went down over her hands, ending in a long point. Since the openness of the dress could provide no warmth, she wore a black fur stole around her shoulders, and its effect reminded me almost of glamorous, oversized epaulets.

"Vita, darling," Mina said, calling to her pet rabbit, and I noted that her British accent had grown even stronger since the last time I'd heard her speak. She'd completely devolved into the character she'd created for herself. "It's time for us to go."

Leaving her bag, she began looking around for the rabbit. She put one hand on the bed, and I noticed that even her nail polish was black, as she leaned down to look underneath the bed. With her back to him, Konstantin started moving slowly toward her.

"Vita," Mina cooed to the rabbit. "Come here, love."

Konstantin pulled the dagger from his pants, and his skin began to shift back to its normal flesh tone. I held my breath, watching through the crack, as he came up behind her.

"I know you're there," Mina said, her voice sharper than

it had been when she'd been speaking to Vita. "And I know that you're not going to kill me."

She stood up and turned around to face him, a smile playing on her lips. He glared down at her, his expression hardening as he seethed, and she began to laugh.

"You can't kill me, Konstantin. You love me too much."

He grabbed her and whirled her around, pulling her roughly against him so her back was pressed to his chest, and he held the dagger to her throat. The lace of her dress covered her throat, forming a choker-like feature, and his blade sliced through it. He didn't kill her, but he held the dagger hard enough to draw the faintest bit of blood.

"Please, Konstantin," Mina begged, sounding frightened. "You don't need to do this. Not after all we've been through. This is the moment we've been plotting for all these years. I have the riches! We can finally run off and be free together, just like you always wanted."

"*You've* been plotting," he corrected her, speaking into her ear like an angry lover. "I was only ever just doing your bidding."

"Konstantin, please. Don't be like this." She softened, trying to sound as gentle as she had when she'd spoken to her rabbit. "We've shared so much, and I don't know why you've taken such a turn. But I forgive you. I still want to be with you, even after all you've done. I still love you."

"After all *I've* done?" Konstantin growled, and then he threw her to the floor. She sat on the white rug looking up at him, and somehow managed to have tears in her eyes. "You are an evil, ruthless bitch, Mina. Don't act like I'm the one in the wrong here."

"Look, Konstantin, I know we've had our differences, and that you haven't always approved of the way I've taken care of things," Mina said. "But I just did what needed to be done. But that doesn't mean that I didn't love you. That I don't still."

She reached out, meaning to touch his pant leg, and he stepped back from her.

"I should've killed you years ago," he said harshly. "But I was too blinded by my own foolish love, and I hate myself for the parts of it that still linger on. The parts of my heart that I gave to you that I can never get back."

"Konstantin," she pleaded with him.

He inhaled sharply through his nose, and he turned away, trying to hide the emotions on his face. It was just the slightest bit of vulnerability, but that was all Mina needed. His back was half to her, and she could see the dagger holstered in the back of his pants.

With steathy fast reflexes, she moved, grabbing the dagger before I could even shout Konstantin's name. He started to turn toward her, but it was already too late. She stabbed him in the left side, digging the dagger right into his heart.

Konstantin didn't even try to fight back. He let his other dagger fall from his hand and stumbled back until he hit the wall, then slid down and sat slumped on the floor.

gutted

You think you couldn't kill me because you loved me?" Mina sneered at him. "It was because you were *weak*. That's why I *never* loved you. You were always a weak, stupid boy."

I pounded on the armoire doors, and Mina turned back to look at me. She cocked her head, realizing that she wasn't alone, and picked up the dagger Konstantin had dropped on the floor. I hit the doors again, harder this time, and they flew open.

"Oh, I should've known." Mina snickered. "He brought his dumb little bitch with him too."

"You've always underestimated me," I said. "But not today."

I ran at her. She tried to stab me, and I grabbed her wrist, bending it back until she dropped the dagger. Then I punched her as hard as I could. Mina staggered back, her lip already bleeding.

"I know you always wanted to fit in, and you never could," Mina said, giving me a wide berth as we circled each other. "But I've the means for it. I've got the one thing you always needed, to be accepted—money. You let me go, and I'll give you everything you've ever wanted. Respect. Acceptance. A kingdom."

"You know, that's what Konstantin always thought you wanted," I said. "That if you had enough money, and the crown, and the throne, and the kingdom, eventually you'd be happy. But I don't think you really *wanted* any of it. You just wanted to destroy it all."

She smirked. "Greed is always such a great motivator, and I know it's worked for so many of those that have joined my team. But you're right. The truth is that I just wanted to take everything from those that had taken from me. I just wanted to see the Kanin obliterated from this earth."

"The only thing I want is to see you dead," I told her. "And that's something that I'm gonna have to do for myself."

She dove toward me, scratching at me with her nails, fighting the only way she knew how. I punched her again, and then I kicked her in the stomach. Mina doubled over, but she didn't go down.

As I walked over to her, I picked the dagger up from the floor, and I kicked her again. Mina started promising me all the money in the world, and I grabbed her by the hair, yanking her back up.

"Please, anything. I will give you anything and everything," she tried, pleading for her life.

"I would stab you through the heart, but I don't think you have one," I said, and then I slid the dagger across her throat. I let go of her hair, and her body fell lifeless to the floor.

"I wish I had the strength to clap," Konstantin said faintly.

He was slumped low on the wall, barely breathing, and I raced over to him. I knelt beside him, and he was starting to slide to the side, so I put my arms around him and held him up. His body felt cold and heavy, and I didn't know how much time he had left.

"Why did you do that, Konstantin? Why didn't you let me help you?"

"I didn't want you getting hurt anymore. You've already been hurt so much by the things I've done. This time I just wanted to protect you." He reached up, brushing my hair back from my face before letting his hand fall back down.

"You don't need to protect me. You never did."

"I know." He smiled weakly. "Do you remember when I told you that for love, I'd kill myself again?"

I nodded. "Yeah, when you were in the dungeon. You were talking about Mina."

"I would go through every awful moment, every terrible mistake, and even this knife to the heart. I would gladly go through it all again, but not for Mina. But because it brought me here with you."

A tear slid down my cheek. "Konstantin. There were better ways you could've ended up here."

"Maybe," he admitted, and his eyes started to close. "But I just wish I'd been deserving of your love."

"You always were," I told him, and a smile started to form on his lips before his last breath came out. I held him against me, crying onto his chest and wishing more than anything that I would hear his heart beat again. But it never did.

dödsfall

B ryn?" Ridley was calling my name from the stairs. I honestly didn't know how long I had been kneeling there with Konstantin.

I blinked my eyes, feeling as if I'd just woken from a dream, and looked around at the disarray of the Queen's chambers. A few feet away from me, Mina lay dead on the rug, which was now stained red. Her rabbit Vita hopped out from underneath the bed, inspecting the situation.

"Bryn?" Ridley yelled again and pushed open the bedroom door. "Holy shit." He stepped into the room, his eyes fixed on the Queen's body, and repeated, "Holy shit. She's dead."

Then he looked over at me. "Are you okay?"

"Yeah." The tears had dried on my cheeks, and I nodded. "I'm okay. Konstantin is dead."

"Yeah, I figured that." Ridley moved carefully toward me. "Are you ready to let him go?"

I looked down at the body in my arms. His skin had paled so much, and he felt like ice against me. All of the determination and life had drained from him. Everything about that body that made it so wonderfully Konstantin was gone.

I set him gently on the floor, and I held out my hand to Ridley, letting him pull me to my feet. I'd been kneeling for so long, my legs had gone numb and weak, and I had to lean on Ridley to keep from falling.

"Bryn." His arm was around my waist, and he put his other hand on my face, gently encouraging me to look at him. "Are you okay?"

"The kingdom is in chaos. Many of my friends and neighbors are dead. Ember is dead. Konstantin is dead. I killed the Queen." I shrugged my shoulders limply. "I honestly don't know if I'll ever be okay again."

"It will be okay," he promised me, with his fingers in my hair. "You're stronger than this, and you will be okay again."

"How can you be so sure?" I asked, looking up at him. In the darkness of his eyes, I saw the same despair that I felt, but also his perseverance pushing him on.

"Because I know you, and I know how much fight you have in you. You won't let anything keep you down for long." He ran his thumb along my cheek. "That's why I love you so much."

He leaned in, kissing me softly and sweetly on the mouth. We'd kissed more deeply before, more passionately, but this was a much different kind of kiss. This was relief and sadness and simply because we needed to. Because we were still alive, and we needed to remind ourselves that there was still so much left to live for.

"I need to go," he said softly. "I need to go tell King Mikko that the Queen is dead, so we can stop the fighting. With her and Viktor out of the way, there's no reason a truce can't be reached."

"Go," I told him as I stepped back from him. "Go and stop this before more people get hurt."

He nodded. "I'll be back for you."

I smiled weakly at him. "I know."

Ridley hurried out of the room, to put a stop to all the death and carnage. I picked up Vita before she hopped into any blood, and I carried her over to the window. I pushed back the sheer curtains to see what had become of my town, while absently petting the soft white fur of the rabbit.

So much of the snow had gone red with blood. Broken bodies littered the ground. Homes and buildings were smashed up in places, some destroyed entirely. Doldastam was in shambles, exactly as Mina had wanted.

But I couldn't let her win. The Kanin people wouldn't. They were stronger than this. I'd learned to be a fighter growing up here, watching people rise above their places in this world, and together, somehow, we would find the strength to put this back together.

We could not let anyone destroy us.

hope

June 7, 2014

In the days that followed, the ice began to thaw. The snow that had covered the town melted away, and while it wasn't exactly a heat wave, green began sprouting up in the patches of lawn between the cottages. In a few places, pink and purple wildflowers were beginning to blossom.

The sun shone brightly above, warming the chill in the air, as everyone gathered at the town square. Many of the surrounding businesses were still in various states of repair. The sign for the bakery where Juni Sköld worked still hung at a haphazard angle, but the broken panes of glass in the front window had been replaced.

The cleanup was still under way, as it would be for some time, but we were making progress. The people of Doldastam always managed to pull together when they needed to.

After Ridley had told King Mikko that Mina was dead, the King had attempted to end things immediately. The fighting still went on for longer than it needed to, but eventually Mikko was able to talk to the head of the Högdragen, and a cease-fire was declared.

The next few days were spent hammering out a proper truce, but once a new King was decided for the Kanin, everything went smoother. The Omte still seemed reluctant to put aside their resentments, but Queen Bodil called them back to Fulaträsk, so they had no choice.

While Linus Berling had been officially crowned three days ago in a private ceremony in the palace, today was meant to be his public coronation and an official celebration for the end of the war.

Since it was a celebration, the town square had been decorated accordingly. Ribbons of silver and white streamed from one building to the next, helping to disguise the damage, and large bouquets of fragrant white flowers were placed everywhere imaginable.

Folding chairs covered in white satin and accented with ribbons filled the square. Just beneath the clock tower, a large stage had been erected. Linus wanted to distance himself from Mina, who lorded over the town from the balcony, so he wanted to speak at our level.

From where I sat in the back row, I could see everyone, and the entire town had turned out. Juni Sköld sat a few rows in front of me, holding the hand of her new boyfriend, and looking as radiant as ever. Bekk Vallin had decided not to return to Fulaträsk, even after the Omte agreed to the truce, and she sat a few seats down from me, her arms folded over her chest.

Nearer to the front, Delilah Nylen sat with her parents, crying softly. We'd hardly spoken since Ember had died, but whenever I saw her, she looked so lost. I hoped that soon she could find the peace and strength to carry on.

King Mikko and Queen Linnea Biåelse sat in the front row, along with King Loki and Queen Wendy Staad of the Trylle and Queen Sara Elsing of the Vittra, all of them honored guests of the Kanin because of their help in the war. Queen Bodil Elak of the Omte had been invited, as a gesture of peace, but she had declined, saying that it was still too soon.

With the fighting over, Tilda had returned a few days ago, and she seemed to be doing better. Knowing that Kasper had been properly avenged seemed to ease some of her anxiety, but none of this could be easy for her. She sat beside her parents, and her mother kept gently rubbing her back.

Finn sat with Mia and their children, but his parents were noticeably absent. After what had happened here, and how they'd lost Ember, they had finally had enough. They'd left the entire troll world to start a life anew among the humans.

My parents felt much the same way, and they had taken up residence in Storvatten. Marksinna Lisbet Ahlstrom once told me that she'd do anything to thank me for saving her granddaughter, and I'd asked her to repay the debt by welcoming my mom back with open arms.

So she had, and after years of hating Storvatten, my mom seemed to be actually enjoying her return. She said it was all so much different than when she was a girl, more relaxed, and she was happy to reconnect with old friends and family.

Meanwhile, my dad was working with their Chancellor to help get the Skojare where they needed to be. Mikko and Linnea had been working very hard to improve things in Storvatten, and it looked like they might finally be on the right path.

With Linus taking the stage now, the tall platinum crown upon his head, I hoped I could say the same thing about Doldastam. Linus was less experienced than most of the townspeople would've liked, but his bloodline was the closest to Evert Strinne, so he was next in line.

As he walked across the stage, the crowd erupted in applause. No matter what differences had existed before, everyone here was ready for a change, for someone new to lead us to a better place, and their excitement came from the belief that Linus would be that leader.

I was optimistic because of his kindness and genuine empathy for the people. I wondered if growing up outside of the cold walls of Doldastam, unlike Evert and so many of our past Kings, had made him more compassionate, and I believed that with the right advisers and tutelage, he could stay that way.

Behind Linus in lavish chairs on the stage, his parents were seated along with the head of the Högdragen, and nearby was a large rectangle beneath a satin sheet. I had been asked to join him—and to wear onstage, I'd even been given a new crisp white suit with silver embellishments, including the platinum rabbit, our highest military honor. I'd elected to wear the suit, but declined the stage.

As one of his first acts as King, Linus had appointed me as his personal guard, and I'd accepted because I thought I could help steer the kingdom in the right direction and I could protect the King from corruption.

But I no longer craved the honor that went along with it. I didn't need or deserve the accolades. I just wanted to serve my kingdom.

He wanted to pull me onstage today to exalt me as a hero, but that wasn't something I could accept. I wasn't a hero, and in so many ways I still felt like I'd failed. Like I should've done more to protect the people. Nobody should've had to die.

"Thank you all for coming here today," King Linus said, speaking loudly so his voice would carry over the crowd. "We've all been through a great deal, and I know how hard it was for some of you to come out. So many of you have lost so much, and are in no mood to celebrate."

Delilah began to sniffle at that, and her father put his arm around her, pulling her close to him, and throughout the crowd I could hear others sobbing faintly.

"That's why today isn't about honoring me as your King." Linus stepped over to the side toward the sheet-covered rectangle. "It's about honoring those you've lost, everyone who laid down their life defending this kingdom so that we can all be here celebrating our freedom today."

He pulled back the sheet, revealing a white marble stone

ten feet high and five feet wide, in large black letters listing all the names of the people who had been killed. At the top was *Evert Strinne*, since he had been one of Mina's first victims, but there were many names below his.

Kasper Abbott, Ember Holmes, Simon Bohlin, and the names of so many others I had seen nearly every day in this town. So many lives that could never be replaced, voids that would never be filled.

Near the bottom, in letters just as bold and dark as everyone else's, was *Konstantin Black.*

A lump formed painfully in my throat. I'd been so afraid that nobody would know that Konstantin had died to protect the kingdom, or be aware of all the things he'd done to aid in this battle. I had been terrified that I would be the only one who mourned him.

But now everybody would know. For generations, people would see his name, and know that he'd died a true Kanin hero.

Linus continued his speech, telling Doldastam how he planned to honor the dead by giving the kingdom new life, but I'd heard all I needed to. I got up quietly and snuck away from the crowd, walking out of the town square.

I hadn't made it very far when I heard Ridley's footsteps behind me. The cobblestone streets were empty, since everyone was at the celebration, and I turned to face him.

His chestnut hair was slightly disheveled, and he brushed it back from his forehead. He'd left the top buttons of his shirt undone, the way I liked it, but his rabbit amulet was still missing. As soon as the fighting ended, he'd stepped down from his position as Överste and Rektor.

"What's going on?" His dark eyes were filled with concern as he looked down at me.

"I've spent enough time thinking about the dead lately," I said honestly. "I need a break from it. I think I just need some time to think about the future and try to feel optimistic again."

"I get that," Ridley agreed. "The last few weeks have been so dark, you need to start looking for something bright."

I nodded. "Exactly."

"Where you heading now, in search of your something bright?"

I shrugged. "Just back to my loft."

"Let me walk you home."

"You know you can always walk me home." I smiled up at him.

"I know. But I like it when you tell me I can anyway." He put his arm around me as we started walking across town toward my place.

"Have you decided what you're going to do yet?" I asked, looking up at him. "Now that you're not in charge of the trackers?"

"Not yet," he admitted. "But I've got time to figure it out."

"That's true," I agreed. "We've got the rest of our lives to figure it all out."

He kissed my temple. "And I think we've proven that together, we can take on anything."

GLOSSARY

Changeling—a child secretly exchanged for another.

Doldastam—the capital and largest city of the Kanin, located in northeastern Manitoba, Canada near the Hudson Bay.

Eldvatten—literally translates to "firewater." Very strong alcohol made by the Omte.

Förening—the capital and largest city of the Trylle. A compound in the bluffs along the Mississippi River in Minnesota, United States where the palace is located.

Fulaträsk—the capital and largest city of the Omte. It's located in the southern part of Louisiana in the wetlands, with many of the Omte residing in the trees.

Hobgoblin—an ugly, misshapen troll that stands no more than three feet tall known only to the Vittra tribes. They are slow-witted but possess a supernatural strength.

Högdragen—an elite guard that protects the Kanin kingdom.

They must go through a specialized training process after tracker school in order to qualify, and many students are unable to pass because of the difficult requirements in order to graduate. Members of the Högdragen are respected and revered throughout the kingdom, despite the fact that most are born lower-class, because of their skill and their unparalleled ability to protect the royal families and the kingdom at large.

Host family—the family that the changeling is left with. They are chosen based on their ranking in human society, with their wealth being the primary consideration. The higher ranked the member of troll society, the more powerful and affluent the host family their changeling is left with.

Iskyla—small Kanin arctic community in northern Canada.

Kanin—one of the more powerful tribes of trolls left. They are considered quiet and peaceful. They are known for their ability to blend in, and like chameleons, their skin can change color to help them blend into their surroundings. Like the Trylle, they still practice changelings, but not nearly as frequently. Only one in ten of their offspring are left as changelings.

Lysa—a telekinetic ability related to astral projection that allows one troll to psychically enter another troll's thoughts through a vision, usually a dream.

Mänsklig—often shortened to "mänks." The literal translation for the word "mänsklig" is human, but it has come to describe the human child that is taken when the Trylle offspring is left behind.

Markis—a title of male royalty in troll society. Similar to that of a Duke, it's given to trolls with superior abilities. They have a higher ranking than the average troll, but are beneath the King and Queen. The hierarchy of troll society is as follows:

King/Queen

Prince/Princess

Markis/Marksinna

Högdragen

Troll citizens

Trackers

Mänsklig

Host families

Humans (not raised in troll society)

Marksinna—a title of female royalty in troll society. The female equivalent of the Markis.

Ogre—similar to hobgoblins, except they are giant, most standing over seven-feet tall with superior strength. They are dimwitted and aggressive, and they are known only to the Omte tribes.

Omte—only slightly more populous than the Skojare, the Omte tribe of trolls are known to be rude and somewhat ill-tempered. They still practice changelings but pick lower class families than the Trylle and Kanin. Unlike the other tribes, Omte tend to be less attractive in appearance.

Ondarike—the capital city of the Vittra. The Queen, along with the majority of the powerful Vittra, live within the palace there. It is located in northern Colorado.

Överste—in times of war, the Överste is the officer in charge of commanding the soldiers. The Överste does not decide any battle plans, but instead receives orders from the King or the Chancellor.

Persuasion—a mild form of mind control. The ability to cause another person to act a certain way based on thoughts.

Precognition—knowledge of something before its occurrence, especially by extrasensory perception.

Psychokinesis—blanket term for the production or control of motion, especially in inanimate and remote objects, purportedly by the exercise of psychic powers. This can include mind control, precognition, telekinesis, biological healing, teleportation, and transmutation.

Rektor—the Kanin in charge of trackers. The Rektor works with new recruits, helps with placement, and generally works to keep the trackers organized and functioning.

Skojare—an aquatic tribe of trolls that is nearly extinct. They require large amounts of fresh water to survive, and one-third of their population possess gills so they are able to breathe underwater. Once plentiful, only about five thousand Skojare are left on the entire planet.

Storvatten—the capital city and largest city of the Skojare, located in southern Ontario, Canada on Lake Superior.

Tonåren—in the Skojare society, a time when teenagers seek to explore the human world and escape the isolation of Storvatten. Most teens return home within a few weeks.

Tracker—members of troll society who are specifically trained to track down changelings and bring them home. Trackers have no paranormal abilities, other than the affinity to tune into their particular changeling. They are able to sense danger to their charge and can determine the distance between them. The lowest form of troll society, other than mänsklig.

Tralla horse—a powerful draft horse, larger than a Shire horse or a Clydesdale, originating in Scandinavia and only known to be bred amongst the Kanin. Once used as a workhorse because they could handle the cold and snow, now they are usually used for show, such as in parades or during celebrations.

Trylle—beautiful trolls with powers of psychokinesis for whom the practice of changelings is a cornerstone of their society. Like all trolls, they are ill-tempered and cunning, and often selfish. Once plentiful, their numbers and abilities are fading, but they are still one of the largest tribes of trolls. They are considered peaceful.

Vittra—a more violent faction of trolls whose powers lie in physical strength and longevity, although some mild psychokinesis is not unheard of. They also suffer from frequent infertility. While Vittra are generally beautiful in appearance, more than fifty percent of their offspring are born as hobgoblins. They are one of the only troll tribes to have hobgoblins in their population.

Biâelse Family Tree

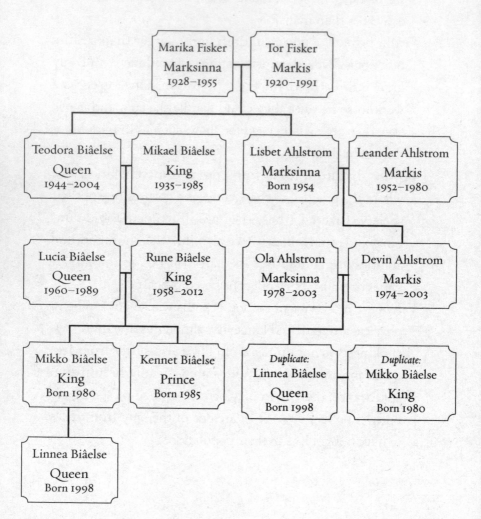

Marika Fisker
Marksinna
1928–1955

Tor Fisker
Markis
1920–1991

Teodora Biâelse
Queen
1944–2004

Mikael Biâelse
King
1935–1985

Lisbet Ahlstrom
Marksinna
Born 1954

Leander Ahlstrom
Markis
1952–1980

Lucia Biâelse
Queen
1960–1989

Rune Biâelse
King
1958–2012

Ola Ahlstrom
Marksinna
1978–2003

Devin Ahlstrom
Markis
1974–2003

Mikko Biâelse
King
Born 1980

Kennet Biâelse
Prince
Born 1985

Duplicate:
Linnea Biâelse
Queen
Born 1998

Duplicate:
Mikko Biâelse
King
Born 1980

Linnea Biâelse
Queen
Born 1998

Strinne Family Tree

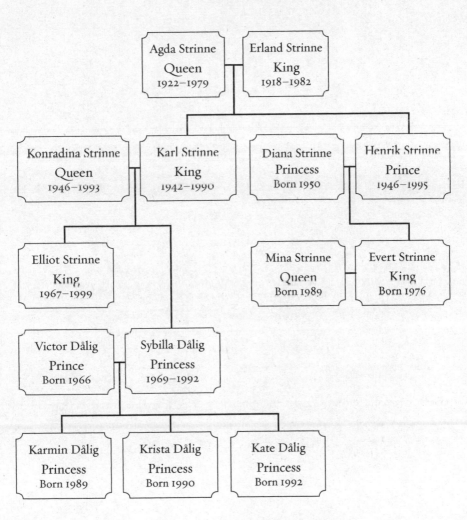

PRONUNCIATION GUIDE

Älskade Abbott—*Al-skah-duh Ab-bot*

Baltsar Thorne—*Bal-tsar Thorn*

Bayle Lundeen—*Bail Lun-deen*

Bodil Elak—*Boh-deel Eee-luck*

Bryn Aven—*Brin A-ven*

Cyrano Moen—*Sear-uh-no Moe-en*

Doldastam *Dole-dah-stam*

Eldvatten—*Elld-vah-ten*

Evert Strinne—*Ever-t Strin*

Förening—*Fure-ning*

Fulaträsk—*Fool-uh-trassk*

Gotland rabbit—*Got-land*

Helge Otäck—*Hel-ga Oo-tech*

Högdragen—*Hug-dragon*

Iskyla—*Iss-key-la*

Iver Aven—*Iv-er A-ven*

Juni Sköld—*Joon-y Sh-weld*

Kanin—*cannon*

Lake Isolera—*Lake Ice-oh-lar-uh*

Linnea Biâelse—*Lin-nay-uh Bee–yellsa*

Lisbet Ahlstrom—*Liz-bet All-strum*

Ludlow Svartalf—*Lud-loe Svare-toff*

lysa—*lie-sa*

Måne—*Moe-nay*

Markis—*marquee*

Marksinna—*mark-iss-eena*

Mikko Biâelse—*Mick-o Bee–yellsa*

Mina Strinne—*Mee-na Strin*

Modi & Magni—*Mow-dee & Mahg-nee*

Naima Abbott—*Na-eema Ab-bot*

Omte—*oo-m-tuh*

Överste—*Ur-ve-sh-ter*

Ridley Dresden—*Rid-lee Drez-den*

Runa Aven—*Rue-na A-ven*

Skojare—*sko-yar-uh*

Storvatten—*Store-vot-en*

Tilda Moller—*Till-duh Maul-er*

tonåren—*toe-no-ren*

Tralla horse—*trahl-uh*

Trylle—*trill*

Ulla Tulin—*Oo-lah Two-lin*

Viktor Dålig—*Victor Dough-leg*

Vita—*Vee-tah*

Vittra—*vit-rah*

Royalty

Kanin
King Evert Henrik Strinne
Reign 1999–
Born 3/8/1976 in Doldastam
Crowned 1/17/1999
Married 4/12/2009
Son of Prince Henrik Strinne and
Princess Diana Strinne, née Berling

Queen Mina Viktoria Strinne, née Arvinge
Born 9/3/1989 in Iskyla
Married 4/12/2009
Orphaned daughter of Alva Arvinge and Viktoria Arvinge

Skojare
King Mikko Rune Biâelse
Reign 2012–
Born 5/7/1982 in Storvatten
Crowned 9/13/2012
Married 6/22/2013
Son of King Rune Biâelse and
Queen Lucia Biâelse, née Ottesen

Queen Linnea Lisbet Biâelse, née Ahlstrom
Born 6/16/1998 in Storvatten
Married 6/22/2013
Daughter of Markis Devin Ahlstrom and
Marksinna Ola Ahlstrom, née Fisk

Prince Kennet Tor Biâelse
Born 12/3/1985 in Storvatten
Son of King Rune Biâelse and
Queen Lucia Biâelse, née Ottesen

Trylle
Queen Wendy Luella Staad, née Dahl
Reign 2010–
Born 1/9/1992 in New York
Crowned 1/14/2014
Married 5/1/2010
Daughter of Trylle Queen Elora Dahl and
Vittra King Oren Elsing

King Loki Niklas Staad
Born 11/17/1987
Married 5/1/2010 in Ondarike
Son of former Trylle Chancellor Alrik Staad and
Vittra Marksinna Olivia Staad, née Härlig

Crown Prince Oliver Matthew Loren Staad
Born 10/6/2010 in Förening
Son of Queen Wendy Staad and Loki Staad

Omte
Queen Regent Bodil Freya Elak, née Fågel
Reign 2011–
Born 3/24/1978 in Fulaträsk
Married 9/1/2006
Widowed 8/13/2011
Crowned Acting Monarch 8/14/2011
Daughter of Markis Boris Fågel and
Marksinna Freya Fågel, née Dam

King Thor Osvald Elak
Reign 1992–2011
Born 4/2/1969 in Fulaträsk
Married 9/1/2006
Died 8/13/2011 in Fulaträsk
Son of King Draugr Elak and Queen Märta Elak, née Asp

Crown Prince Furston Thor Elak
Born 3/4/2010 in Fulaträsk
Son of Queen Bodil Elak and King Thor Elak

Vittra
Queen Sara Adrielle Elsing, née Vinter
Reign 2010–
Born 2/1/1977 in Ondarike
Married 11/2/1996
Crowned Acting Monarch 1/15/2010
Widowed 1/14/2010
Daughter of Markis Luden Vinter and
Marksinna Sarina Vinter, née Dron

King Oren Bodvar Elsing
Reign 1985–2010
Born 7/1/1914 in Ondarike
Crowned 11/23/1985
Married 5/19/1990
Annulled 7/30/1992
Married 11/2/1996
Died 1/14/2010 in Ondarike
Son of King Bodvar Elsing the II and Queen Grendel Elsing

Prepare to be swept away by the magic of the

TRYLLE TRILOGY!

Book 1   Book 2   Book 3

Return to the beloved world of the Trylle with

THE KANIN CHRONICLES

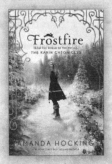  

ON SALE
8.4.15

Book 1   Book 2   Book 3

ST. MARTIN'S GRIFFIN

Step into the spellbinding world of
WATERSONG

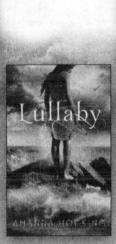

"Hocking knows how to tell a good story and keep readers coming back for more."
—*KIRKUS REVIEWS*

St. Martin's Griffin